MIAMI

A novel

E. TED GLADUE

COMMONWEALTHBOOKS INC.

New York 2020

A Commonwealth Publications Paperback
MIAMI
This edition published 2020
by Commonwealth Books
All rights reserved

Copyright © 2020 by E. Ted Gladue
Published in the United States by Commonwealth Books Inc.,
New York.

Library of Congress Control Number Has Been Applied For

ISBN: 978-1-892986-14-6

No part of this book may be reproduced or utilized in any form or by any means, electronic or mechanical, including photocopying, recording, or by any information storage retrieval system, without permission in writing from the publisher, except by a reviewer who may quote brief passages in a review to be printed in a newspaper, magazine or journal.

This work is a novel and any similarities to actual persons or events is purely coincidental.

First Commonwealth Books Trade Edition: January 2020

PUBLISHED BY COMMONWEALTH BOOKS, INC.,

www.commonwealthbooks@aol.com
www.commonwealthbooksinc.com

Manufactured in the United States of America

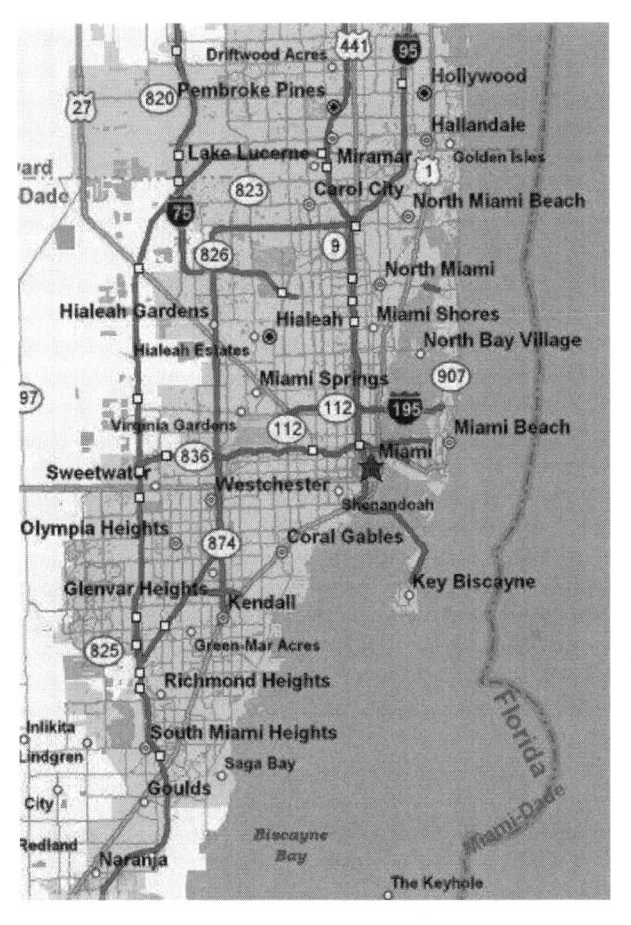

This novel is dedicated to

James Haddad

a writer's writer

Table of Contents

Chapter One: Opening night on the beach
Chapter Two: The mystic sea spits up forbidden treasure
Chapter Three: A Gift or a Curse?
Chapter Four: The Hemp Does Smoke
Chapter Five: The Moral Dilemma
Chapter Six: Driving North and Near Death
Chapter Seven: The Nightmare Night
Chapter Eight: The Drug Bust
Chapter Nine: The Lie Detector
Chapter Ten: Lock-Up
Chapter Eleven: Prison
Chapter Twelve: Freedom in New York City
Chapter Thirteen: The Rockefellers
Chapter Fourteen: Going South
Chapter Fifteen: The "Beach" of Miami
Chapter Sixteen: Like It All Never Happened
Chapter Seventeen: The Foreclosure
Chapter Eighteen: New World/New Book
Chapter Nineteen: Hello Gainesville, Goodbye Gainesville
Chapter Twenty: Love, Chaos, Publishers
Chapter Twenty-One: Happy Birthday in South Florida
Chapter Twenty-Two Hard Work, Hot Sun, Cheap Labor
Chapter Twenty-Three: The Drug Trial
Chapter Twenty-Four: The Lying Irish Publisher
Chapter Twenty-Five: Goodbye Miami, Hello New Zealand

MIAMI… MIAMI

Oh Miami
Miami, I knew you as a virgin green, years when your canals glistened
like clear blue seas
--
A cannon ball could be shot down Miami streets in summer months, for only
The fishermen, divers, and the gold hunters
Remained by the sea.
--
Nature of tropical beauty, overwhelmed with fruits and birds alike,
Sweet oranges, mangos,
And wild pink flamingos.
--
Coral reefs for searching, blue of under, colors upon colors, depths so steep,
As youth does dance with death, in the fathoms and curiosities
Of the deep.

Like cities.
--

Ugly mountains of vertical glass and stone hide
One of the world's greatest wonders,
…Those Miami sunsets.
--

Those amazing coral reefs are dying, the coconut palm tree went first
As police trucks roll over beaches as green military drug planes
Fly overhead.
--

Ah…my Key West, of another time. Fort Myers, unpretentious fishing
Town. So slow…
Key Largo.
--

Oh Miami…Miami….what will happen? Will the sun burn you up? Will
You sink into the earth? Will you be blown away? Will our friends who
Wrestle the alligators have it back, to be in nature's best care, once again,
--

For future millenniums.
A tropical paradise of a long-ago era

Prologue

In the Fell Clutch of Circumstance

He quietly closed the thick oak door behind him. He was tempted to rip the brass knob off in his hand. A war trophy for battling against those who finagled to take his house away. The bank lawyers, his ex-wife's lawyers, and even his own lawyer wanted it not for its beauty, but for its worth.

He left the courthouse for the brightness of a South Florida afternoon. His red convertible flew down the I-95 freeway like a small fighter plane with pistons pounding. He threw open the windows and laughed; otherwise he might've cried. Not only was he losing his home, but the last tangible link with his fun-loving five-year old son.

He parked in the shade of the ancient Ficus trees whose branches touched the ground around his old Spanish style estate. He collapsed into the seat; mentally, physically, spatially drained. He needed to do something to assuage this anguish. He fumbled for pen and paper attempting to relieve his angst in a poem, "Lawyers, Courthouses, Judges."

He entered the house and went directly to the outdoor pool. He read the poem again and crushed it in his hand. He flung it. It landed with a light splash near the pale green Buddha atop the waterfall. He went inside and upstairs to seek solace in his study. He cherished this room where he'd spent those last precious moments with his beloved son, Michael.

The thump of the wooden front door told him Ashley was home. The clacking of her high heels hitting the aged Cuban stone tile floor made him smile from the second story window he saw her sitting by the pool barefooted. Her skirt hiked up; her head dropped to her knees; her long hair falling onto the water. The sun's slanting rays cast her shadow eastward toward the ocean. The hanging plants began dancing to the upbeat tempo of the wind chimes. He searched desperately for answers, but found only questions. Why had this happened? How would this new circumstance change his relationship with Ashley? What forces were conspiring to drive him from his home and across the seas seeking refuge in other worlds.

The struggle of creating and writing an original dissertation had brought him to a different understanding of himself, something new inside of him. The process had made him a writer. A new fire inside him wanted to continue exploring, to search, to question, to see, to smell, to be nothing to see everything. Not to be, but to experience.

That moment's awareness transformed not just dreams and points of view but consciousness. During those years in New York many of his best friends were painters, writers, actors, playwrights, dancers...creative artists whom he admired and loved for their dedication; but to Semineaux their lives in art were a bore compared with his international political experiences and travels. He never expected to be like them for they had given up far too much in pursuit of their artistic dreams. Now, he was one of them. No job, profession, woman, nor comfort, would interfere. Only adventure and more experiences would sidetrack him, but these could be molded into novels and poetry.

It was by no accident that while at the UN Semineaux was most curious about Peacekeeping and worked on various planning operations in the Political and Security Affairs division. But the real drama at the UN for Semineaux stemmed from his investigation of all Chinese behavior and activities in research for the writing. This brought him under the scrutiny of the Russians, which meant he was under KGB surveillance for eight years, in turn attracting the FBI and CIA whose efforts to recruit him were rejected time and time again. Years later it was revealed he had rejected the FBI's most sensitive post on KGB surveillance in the United States. But he simply wanted to be a scholar, not a spy.

He had closed his eyes and dropped his head to block out the intense glare flashing off the water that day, pulled the cool East River winds deeply into his lungs...again and again, with each exhale feeling cathartic. For he knew that acceptance in that moment of truth would change his entire life and future in ways unknown the new horizon, the new dream, was a creative one. This decision to follow his Tao, to be what he was to be, was a decision he would question often after that day of truth.

Trickling water and the smell of the tropics interrupted his remembrances. The slatted windows of the room were opened slightly allowing him to hear the faint sounds of the water-fall, and increased sea winds carried the smells from hundreds of flowering trees and bushes. He could no longer see her shadow on the pool deck for nightfall has come quickly, but thought of how much he loved her more than any other woman in his life remembering their decision five years before to move from their comfortable Manhattan apartment to his small Spanish estate with his two precious daughters from another marriage.

He glanced out the door and into the next room where he could see copies of his first book published the past week and thought of how life should now begin to come together. He loved his woman, his home, his working life style of dividing work with UN contracts, teaching at several south Florida universities, and working as a ship agent in the ports of Miami and Fort Lauderdale. He was beginning work on his second novel and a book of poetry, and all should be well. Except, the judge, a few hours earlier, said the home was no longer his, the only place in the world he felt any spiritual attachment.

The slight noise of squeaking wood from of the next to the top step before the second floor… Ashley was next to him now…as soundless as the shadow on the pool deck… holding a glass of wine.

He could feel the quiet trembling of anxiety within her as she leaned her body against his, for the phone call he made to her during his court house exit had done little to convince her that all was well. Then she backed away from his body and stood several yards from him; for that was her English way, not too close.

What are we going to do Sean?

The words hung in the stillness of the room where they slept and loved but he could not answer as his whole being had resisted any notion of defeat, stubbornness of spirit from his street fighting youth, a rather useless quality at this moment.

Her question shocked him into dealing with the fact that this property was no longer his home, nor the room but four steps away that held the memory of his life's transfiguration.

He could not but notice her lips trembling ever so slightly as she nervously anticipated an answer. He wished to hold her and love her and protect her and tell her all would be well. But his intuition told him all would not be well. He did not speak.

The silence was eerie, present in everything from the animals to the living vegetation of dozens of plants to the non-living things of book filled rooms, lights of lamps and flickering tips of flames from the fireplace, all beneath the towering palm trees outside that hung in wait… overlooking the pool lying in absolute tranquility with the surface of the water reflecting the bright December skies and stars of the night heavens.

She stood in that one spot as he walked slowly from room to

room looking only at his feet, for all around him begged for an answer as seconds became minutes and the minutes pushed to nearly an hour before some relief came from winds that had slipped in from the sea giving movement to the flapping palm leaves and whirling whispers of bamboo trees and the singing of simple chimes made of sea shells and wooden pieces of nature's symphony. And then the winds picked up to storm level.

The sudden storm was unusual for this time of year in the tropics although quite common during unpredictable summer nights long since passed. His pace quickened as the noise of the winds drowned out the sound of his footsteps on the wooden floor of the second story, his mind skipping through ideas on how to save his home faster than he was able to evaluate them; but as he walked the brewing storm kept drifting into his thoughts.

Semineaux knew these tropical seas as well as anyone having come to them in a great deal of pain after four years of military life. Back then he found work in Key West working as a diver for some of the first gold treasure hunters to occupy Key West when it was nothing more than a US navy town, searching for the gold of Spanish wrecks in the keys and the Bahamas, long before college, long before marriage, and long before love.

He could not hear the sea from that second story but knew the ocean would be surging into whitecaps from the winds lifting the Gulf Stream's warm waters and driving everything that floated onto the beach.

He never gambled at any of South Florida's many establishments despite his lifelong risk-taking streak; but he suddenly stopped in his tracks and within split seconds returned to the master bedroom where Ashley was standing in the same spot as before looking thought the blinds into the pool below the bedroom window.

Then he announced his plan:

Baby... I will save it all by finding a large bale of ganja in the sea. His blue eyes now blazing and his body energized and bouncing.

She continued looking down into the pool area but he could see her eyes narrow from the profile and when she finally turned her head, she looked at him as if he had gone mad, without saying a word...he knowing what she was thinking.

And with a big grin on his face, you know I get psychic sometimes. You know I predict things. It gets

powerful.
 Sean... She said quietly, taking a step towards him...
 Please Sean, that's absurd for any chap to say... her tone changing slightly, the word absurd hanging in his ears.
 English... disbeliever. You people didn't think we had the guts to declare independence or whip your asses. His eyes were aglow and his grin a huge smile.
 Shaking her head and ignoring his remark, throwing her nose upward... flicking her long eyelashes, and sarcastically,
 What did you ever predict, Chap...?
 Hearing intonations change and whenever she called him "chap," he knew he was in trouble. She was reverting to her upper-class English accent pronouncing her words with grace and the coldness of a ruling class. She was going to turn this one into a debate. Sometimes these small debates became six-day wars.
 Baby... you ask what did I ever predict?... placing his hand upon his chest and raising his head confidently, his smile disguising his momentary uncertainty as his memory went into emergency mode.
 I hate to pull this one out, the smile leaving his face and eyes taking on a serious, and somewhat terrifying gaze, suddenly looking twenty years older in a faction of a mini-second.
 But... but... stumbling with his words, rare for him in close verbal situations...it is close to my heart right now... and it's true, damn it... I wish it weren't true... then suddenly he seemed more than disturbed, he looked as if he just got hit in the stomach with a huge rock; he dropped his head, not wanting her to see his eyes.
 When she saw his cocky attitude crash into his spirit, she stepped forward immediately and pressed her body up against his and wrapped her long arms around him as she placed her lips on the side of his head kissing him over and over and licking the tears from his cheeks.
 I'm sorry honey... I forgot. It never dawned on me.
 I know. I don't know where that came from myself. I wish I had thought of another example. I asked for it baby.
 His arms now wrapped around her, their ears only hearing the slight breathing from each other, both concentrating on the softness of the other's mouth alongside their ears, trying to ignore nature's furious winds on the other of the glass slats beginning to shake ever so slightly; the silence lonely broken

when he spoke in a muted tone she could barely hear…

Honey, why is it you can always read my mind?

Ashley had remembered a conversation they had over a great deal of wine years ago when in the midst of a strange conversation Semineaux had revealed to her that he once predicted the death of his only son.

They spoke no more. Just listened to the threatening winds outside as they lay upon the bed in each other's embrace, in love, as deep as either had ever been.

Chapter 1

Opening night on the beach

They remained locked in each other's embrace for over an hour. The sound of the winds awakened him to the reality of his dilemma, he carefully slipped her arms from around him and slid from the bed onto the floor until he was standing by the window to get a good look into the dimly lit pool area below. Some plants had been blown over and several small canvas chairs were floating in the pool. They had slept through it all, the tension in their lives eclipsing the disruptions of the small storm.

He knew winds like this in South Florida often blew bales of marijuana abandoned by drug smugglers fleeing from the authorities up onto the beaches. A heave-ho over the side of the ship was better than getting caught with the hand in the grass.

At other times large vessels called "mother" ships would drop off dozens of bales for pickup by smaller boats lying in wait to run into the thousands of bays and inlets in South Florida. At times these floating bales were abandoned when the authorities moved in to surprise them. But no police, no coast guard, not even military aircraft shooting down suspected drug smuggling planes could stop this, at best all they could do was slow it down.

This he knew not from the news but from first hand stories told over a few beers by some of his pirate buddies that hung out at McGowan's pub on the beach. Men he knew for years but never got too close because of their drug dealings. Some were construction workers, fishermen, divers, bartenders, you name it; but at some point, they took a shot for a quick score. Some got lucky and made enough money they never had to work again. Others were able to use the money to save their often-shaky marriages, or to buy that home, boat, or new car.

He had a strange relationship with these guys who felt comfortable with this overly-educated writer they respected for reasons closer to those things very adventurous men share in common: a complete breakdown of walls as trust permeates the space between them. No temperamental egos, one up-manship, or status plays; for their mutual respect is merely the outcome of survival, each of them remained standing in situations when all others dropped around them. Survival leaves one with a humble soul, and at the heart of really tough men is this gem of humility, given birth by hardship and life through survival itself.

At times he felt they thought he was stronger than he was, for their handshakes and bear hugs nearly broke bone on those occasions when he had been traveling and they had not seen him for a while. When he heard, "Sean, where the hell you been," he knew there was a sincere love coming his way, but also perhaps, a little pain from a bear hug or two.

Sometimes they hinted at wanting to help him "get" some money so he could write the books without having to "kiss ass" to teach at the universities, or work those "shit" jobs which also happened to be dangerous.

But Semineaux get involved with drug smuggling...he never, never considered. Money, possessions, comfort, status, or all the normal things that motivate people did not fire passions inside him. He had learned enough about money to live comfortably in Manhattan for six years on income from Florida real estate investments. But had witnessed the obsession for money selling commodities on Wall Street, saw how money and nepotism ruled at the United Nations, remembered the emptiness and heavy drinking of those retired men living on huge sailboats he met when diving for treasure and gold in the islands, or the hundreds of successful men he had known who had no greater desire in life than to play golf. His passion was a long shot, to write something great. Not to be a king or president, but to create something new and original. Something on one else in the entire world could do, only him, within the map of his mind, heart, and soul. There was one slight problem. There were more places to see, more adventures to be had, and a career, any career, would only be undertaken to support his adventures and dreams. Any plan, would be one too many obstacles. Friends would often say Semineaux had experienced everything. But to him, he was only beginning.

Ashley cooked one of her wonderful meals while he slipped into the pool for a swim. With the sun down and only the spot light above the Buddha casting some light over the surface of the pool his head cut through the smooth water as would the bow of a boat, silent without the fluttering of the feet as his strong arms and shoulders pulled his body for fifty laps.

Emerging naked from the very cold water into winter air he was covering himself with a robe when he saw the shape of her head through the closed window, knowing she was preparing another of her tasty creations created by instincts gleamed from dinning in Paris where her English father had maintained an apartment. When he opened the glass door and stepped in, he could smell she was experimenting with a Chinese dish. He never knew her to cook anything that was not exquisite. After sitting and pouring himself a glass of Bordeaux he leaned back, as he often did, and watched her cook admiring her tall body with the curve of her rear end holding up her long skirt which dropped through the separation of her cheeks and covered legs so sensuous they were the envy of most women.

The green lamp above the dining room table cast shadows of ferns and plants against the rough white walls, as music seemed to be coming from old dark wooden beams above. It was a cold enough December night that the gas log fireplace in the main room was set to a low flame. He quickly went upstairs to put on some clothes.

Time seemed to stop at moments like this. A good swim in cold water, the table filled with delicious food and several bottles of chilled white Greek wine. They would eat, drink, and banter for hours on most evenings. She was the most brilliant woman he had ever met. As their discussions increased in tempo, she would forget her shyness, and in attempting to prove a point became less self-conscious and often threw one lovely leg over the other as she spoke, exposing her long thighs and ever so little of her knickers.

Night after night they would enjoy each other like this. They would discuss art, politics, writing, life, her Europe, his travels; feeling like soul mates. But after a while she would be trying to keep the conversation going; while he tried to seduce her. He could never get enough of her.

But this night his mind was set on something else and after

winter ski jacket surprising her somewhat.

Where are you going?

Here, he said emphatically, reaching again into the closet for another ski jacket... put this on and come with me to the beach.

Why? Her green eyes peering out between the long frizzy blond hairs now hanging over her face, her lower lip falling ever so slightly as her head nodded from side to side indicating her utter confusion with his suggestion.

Go to the beach...now? Are your serious, honey? Her voice was cracking with anxiety.

It's a perfect night, he answered with an excitement in his - voice as he held out the jacket, his blue eyes softened from the light of the green lamp.

Look baby, all the conditions are right.

She pushed the hair behind her ears, her eyes opened very wide,

Sean...for God's sake...be sensible... you won't find anything, and besides I'm tired. All the bankers were down from New York today and I worked hard and tomorrow is Friday. You go with Wolf.

For a moment all he could think about was kissing her. He knew what she was saying but her lips were still wet from the wine and it crossed his mind to forget the beach.

There was silence. She starred down at the table, her eyes slightly fixed as when she had gone a little over with the wine.

The strong winds outside were sending the chimes into a frenzy reminding him of where he was going. When the dog heard the leash dangling from his hand he slid and scampered across the stone tile floors until he slammed into the front door a second before Sean turned it's handle.

Wolf, a barrel-chested Dalmatian with powerful shoulders and legs developed from running on beach sands and a soft golf course was anxious at the front door. In an instant he was in the back seat of the car with his head out the window, pitch-black nostrils sucking in the air, his jaw jutted toward the ocean. Wolf knew he was on a mission and as the car picked up speed on Tyler Street his black and white ears flapped with the wind, his eyes squinting toward the sea.

It makes no difference what she thinks, as he smiled to himself. She's about planning and I'm about spontaneity. Damn it, a woman always wants to know why...and we don't know why. Then he thought again... most often she is right, but sometimes a desperate decision may be the difference between destruction and success. Hindsight... pooh... it's always too late.

When he pulled up to the beach even, he was surprised to see the December ocean as rough as it might be prior to a summer hurricane. There were no lights on the sea for the fishing and pleasure boats were in harbor and with fast-moving low-lying clouds covering what little moonlight there was he could not see very far beyond the waves relentlessly banging onto the beach.

His eyes began to tear from the wind and sand as he zipped up the thick down jacket for it was a chill that had driven animals, birds, lovers, and bums from the beach. The dark forms scattered across the beach looked very unnatural, like heads sticking out of the sand as far as he could see. To the south hotel lights were visible as far as Miami Beach whenever the moon's flashes peeked through the gigantic black and white clouds. To the north the beach disappeared into darkness beyond Hollywood Beach with barely a few lights at the end of Dania pier near the notorious Whiskey Creek that runs through old mangroves in serpent like trails whose dark waters hosted many mysterious murders in old South Florida.

Wolf, who usually burst into a gallop when first on the beach at night had all four paws dug into the sand as he pressed his pulsating ribs against Sean's leg, his eyes darting here and there reflecting his confusion with the strange dark lumps sticking up all over his beach.

You pussy... Sean yelled and roared with laughter.

AAAAAAaaaggggggghhh grabbing wolf by the back of the neck in a fit of hysterical laughter as he wrestled the dog and flipped him over, both rolling on the sand for a split second before Wolf squirmed from his hands like a live fish running across the beach so fast it looked as if his paws were not touching the sand.

Chicken shit bastard, ARWFFfff.... ARFfffff.... on all fours barking like a dog. You're afraid... you spotted pussy, laughing so hard he could barely rise to a standing position.

It was a maddening night. The surging seas had deposited thousands upon thousands of piles of seaweed with hundreds upon hundreds often resembling shapes the size of bales. A glance down the darkened beach was not sufficient, for that one pile larger than the others, may just have been the jackpot that could buy the bankers, lawyers, ex-wife, woman he was living with, and most importantly supply a little security for his children now living up north.

Semineaux and Wolf became like one. One mad magnetic rover moving from pile to pile in a surrealistic dance through the piles of dark mass, two creatures obsessed. The one pile missed would be the one. The line between the animal and the man became a very thin one and at times Wolf looked at him in confusion, especially when he howled like a wolf and laughed like a hyena. The word of description for the night, was obsession.

Within a nine-hour period the two of them covered nearly the entire coastline from Port Everglades cut in Dania to the Haulover cut in Miami. He was glad to see the rising sun beginning to peak through the darkness for the night had not yielded any contraband from the sea.

By the time he returned to the house Ashley was up and putting pieces of silks and cottons around her body that immediately took his mind off everything accept how to entice her to undress what she had already covered.

No, none of that. I have to get to work. Did you boys have a good time at the beach last night?

I'll tell you about it later, and he went on down into the kitchen to make her some coffee.

Chapter 2

The mystic sea spits up forbidden treasure

After Ashley left the house he slept four hours before the afternoon sun moving west sent thin rays of white through the pinhole openings of the closed blinds where the strings held the slates together, reflecting off glass picture frames on the far wall transforming their power into laser beams penetrating both closed eyes in an otherwise darkened cool room, sufficient to rouse him from his deep sleep.

He stretched and rolled out of bed before parting one slat to look into the pool below, noting how bright the sun seemed for this time of year. The door to the master bathroom adjoining the bedroom was closed and when he pulled it open he drew a deep breath to take in Ashley's fragrances that still lingered, snapping him awake along with the total sunlight coming through the two uncovered narrow windows facing north reflecting off the old l930 tiles covering the floor, walls, and ceiling.

He took a very hot shower for a very long time as was his custom during winter months to allow the heat to penetrate before the emersion into the cold pool water below, wrapped himself in a hooded terry cloth robe and ran down to the glass door pool entrance.

The downstairs was warm from the low burning gas log in the fireplace and the second he opened the glass doors a cold blast greeted him. Within seconds he discarded the robe and his ability to ever reproduce. The trick was to swim before the muscles lost the heat gained from the upstairs shower.

The laps began slowly with only the use of the arms as he pulled his body through the water with the silence and the sleekness of an alligator. Each hand cutting through the crystal-clear water before disappearing beneath him in complete harmony with the other hand slicing through the surface above. Every twenty laps the tempo automatically increased, back and shoulders swelling, as smooth grace gave way to an animal pounding of the water. After fifty laps he shortened the reach of his stroke and glided his body with six more until he stopped.

What a way to wake up. I'll never live up north again, and when he saw the image of himself in the glass door with the white hood and robe, he shadowed boxed for about three minutes, jabbing, and laughing the entire time. Maybe I should have been a fighter. All this education just gets you hooked up with all these women who think too much... which he pondered until being distracted by four heads peering out beside his own reflection, the heads of two cats and two dogs.

SCAT, he yelled waving his arms and breaking into hysterical laughter as all four ran for cover in different directions, the cats way ahead of the dogs.

He entered the house, made a pot of coffee, and spent the rest of the day in his upstairs studio writing about why the Soviet Union was not the threat the Reagan administration was claiming.

Ashley returned home, and expected as always, it being Friday, they would try and have some fun; if only to have a few friends over to eat a good meal, smoke some green, drink a little wine and listen to music.

But there was a different mood in the air this evening for Sean was very quiet.

What's going on in that mind of yours chap; I can hear you thinking, she said very softly.

There was no immediate response until he rose from the table a minute later and reached into the closet for his jacket.

Do you hear that? ... nodding his head in the direction of the glass doors to the pool now covered with a heavy wall to floor curtain. The wind, the wind; listen, it is up again, his eyes wide and head shaking.

Not again, her words ringing with a pleading quality... this is ridiculous, her mouth agape, her expression confused. Sean, let's

go to a movie or go visit someone.
  You don't have to go, but I must. He said as if a fait accompli.
  OK... I'll go. Her head thrust in the air, he looking impressed. But you must promise me we won't stay too long. It's been a long week and I'm tired.
  He reached back into the closet for a second ski jacket. So nice to be a woman and change one's mind just like that, knowing if he voiced that particular thought aloud it would likely provoke her into changing her mind again, and not go to the beach.
  Outside the front door the umbrella palms were bending West from the strong winds coming off the ocean and two large palm branches had fallen from the tall royal palm trees and were draped over the front wall which ran the length of the property, both still green rather than brown indicating premature severing from high velocity pressures.
  Darkness had not taken hold and there was still light in the evening sky as he backed the car onto a deserted Tyler Street, the threatening weather keeping enough people indoors so one had the feeling it was a Sunday rather than a Friday.
  The beach was as deserted as the streets, the winds having driven everyone away. He parked the car halfway between the notorious McGowan's bar and the Bible College, the massive complex sitting on the beach that had one time been an exclusive beach front hotel built in the 1920s called the Hollywood Beach Hotel complete with tennis courts, swimming pools, exclusive bars and restaurants with the sophistication of a touch of European elegance; recently converted into a militaristic looking bible school.
The new owners tried their best to actually de-construct the old atmosphere and give the complex the look of a fortress, blocking off the entire access to the ocean front beach by replacing every door and window looking seaward with concrete block and stucco, keeping the students on the bible rather than sun, fun, and pleasures of the flesh. The minister who started the whole thing prayed to God for a million dollars and received it from an "anonymous donor," but within a few years took a sizeable cut of the money and ran off with an eighteen-year-old female bible student. But the complex had yet to be converted back toward its old splendor.
  They walked the forty or fifty yards to the water's edge in

front of the bible school with the wind blowing small specks of sand into their faces, but by the water's edge the sand was replaced by moisture and salt spray. There was only a hint of light remaining in the sky.

As Ashley looked east to participate in the search for the phantom bale, he was distracted by the concentration she was exhibiting, thinking how pretty she looked profiled against the clouds blowing in from the Bahamas to the east, momentarily completely forgetting why the two of them were on the beach.

Then, a strange feeling came over him. One he could not have anticipated. As she intensely starred into the misty twilight, he was falling in love with her all over again, in such a place, at such a time.

She was standing directly in front of him partially blocking the wind as her hair blew around and past his face. His eyes focused first on the back of her ears which he always felt so sexy and then east toward the Bahamas at the huge clouds blowing in like trucks on a sky highway; blue, red, purple, white, gray, some high in the sky others riding the tops of the ever surging waves speeding toward them. The ears, then East, back and forth he looked from the ears to the East as his thoughts became quite separate from hers.

She had no idea where his mind was. She was looking into the sea and thought he was doing the same. But flashes of memory were taking over inside him.

His eyes strained to look east beyond all in his vision for he knew over there, far over there, was Nassau town. Nassau, where years before, he had raised more hell and consumed enough gin and 151 rum to kill an elephant in attempting to kill his pain. A constant pain he could not shake, the pain that kept him awake nights and rendered all daylight reality nothing more than an illusion. His only son, the most beautiful little boy he could ever invent had died at five, leaving his father with a pain he could not shake.

The booze did not kill pain, but it brought out his pre-marital wildness as he fought with his fists, challenged men at the end of their gun barrels and laughed in their faces at being cowards, speared fish in shark infested waters as hangover therapy, and seduced enough beautiful women to fill a Sultan's harem.

These remembrances flashed through his mind at the speed of a computer transaction and then he was thinking of this woman whose body was leaning against his. This beautiful

English girl who left her husband to live with him and who had come to love his two daughters, who sometimes shyly teased him about getting married and having a baby of their own.

It was a very strange time for a moment of truth, a very strange time to decide to put his entire past behind him. But he became completely oblivious to why they were even on the beach at that moment.

He pressed forward and put his arms around her waist and squeezed tight around the thick ski jacket and spoke into her right ear.

"Ashley, let's get married and have that kid, I love you."

It was so hard for him to even get it out of his mouth, for they had lived together for seven years and both were now divorced from their former mates.

She did not seem to hear what he said so he repeated it,

"Ashley, let's get married and have that kid, I love you."

She had been straining her eyes to see something off in the water and was mesmerized in trying to identify whatever it was, the noise of the wind leaving her with only the feeling of his body without clarity of his words.

Then she screamed.

"Sean... Sean... what's that???? What is that thing????"

With the wind blowing so hard he did not quite hear her but was somehow slightly annoyed that she was not responding to his proposal.

She screamed again, "SEAN LOOK," this time louder while tilting her head back toward his ear, "for God's sake Sean, what is it???"

Her excitement broke his trance. He looked around her head and out into the surf, and there it was.

Perhaps fifteen or twenty yards off the beach, a wet, shiny, black leviathan rose out of the water as powerful waves thrust it toward land, the dim light ever so slightly exposing the thing's dark glistening underside.

Sean, what is it? Her voice shuddering as her head nodded in the thing's direction, her hands and arms remaining tucked close to the body as if she were afraid to extend a hand in its direction.

He did not answer. The light was not sufficient for identifying this thing the shape of a small coffin. The day not completely ended nor the night yet descended; but he had already discarded his jacket and sweater and was five yards out into the waist deep surf charging at the mysterious looking form as she yelled, but did not even step in its direction.

Don't touch it... don't touch it... it may be a body. Oh God, it's a bloody body.

"Body hell," he yelled back, to him no mystery. He knew what it was and was trying to grasp what appeared to be a string or rope floating slightly in front of it.

"Goddamn it's big... fucking huge..." he yelled.

Are you sure it's not a body? Her voice louder, her hand partially covering her eyes. "Are you sure it's not a body?"

When he finally seized what was a rope, he expected to quickly jerk the thing toward his body and the beach but was taken back by the dead weight of this bulk that seemed to be anchored to the shallow bottom beneath the waves. Again... he pulled at it. It humbled his sense of physical strength, the contents inside were saturated with seawater, and its weight impossible to estimate.

He glanced over his right shoulder to see how far he was from the water's edge, not expecting he was a long twenty yards away; the intensity of the rush into the sea diminishing his sense of measurement.

He set his mind hard on this one. Squeezing the rope with vice locked hands whose veins pulsated up into strained forearms, his back muscles spreading like wings from his armpits to the waist, he leaned toward the water's edge screaming and moving it but inches at a time, a few inches closer with each thrust.

Fucking thing feels like an aircraft carrier...

Move...move you bastard...

He screamed into the fierce wind, his lungs sucking and yelling. Will power and body, now a foot at a time... now a yard at a time... MOVE YOU BASTARD...

Her quietly cheering him on from the beach, but at the same time she was a little afraid. She had never before seen any man in such a rage.

He finally beached it...and could tell since the seawater returning from the waves on the beach ran alongside the bulk rather than pushing it back into the sea as it did those last five lunges from the water. It did not move. It stayed in one spot. Down on one knee with an elbow leaning on it as he sought to catch his breath. She stood speechless, and a strange sexual passion running through her body as she starred at him, kneeling. His eyes fixed on the thing as if he had conquered something from another world.

By now most of the light had faded from the sky and the bright outdoor security lights on the rear of the buildings were beginning to reflect in the changing colors of the twilight. The sky to the east was dark purple and foreboding, while the tips of the waves somehow captured the last fading light to the west.

He quickly caught his breath and after a few seconds managed to drag and push the waterlogged bulk a few more feet onto the damp sand at the high-water mark; its form appearing larger now on land than in the sea. He stood and dropped his arms by his side as sea water and sweat poured from his thick curly hair over his neck and body, actually dripping into the sand from his fingertips.

Let me drag this thing onto the dry sand, he said without looking at her. Keep your eye on the beach road for any cop cars...and even look over there, now pointing toward the large parking lot. Keep your eyes open while my back is to the road. There's always a cop driving on that beach road looking for broads.

What should I do if I see one, her voice losing its normal composure, her green eyes opened wide anticipating an immediate answer, her hand trembling ever so slightly as she pushed her hair behind her ears?

He said nothing.

Tell me please, her voice pleading as if she may be overheard.

Don't worry baby, a lighthearted tone in his voice and a smile on his face for the first time... just keep cool, like be English.

Well I'm scared; I've never done anything like this, her eyes glancing to both sides as if expecting someone to approach.

Christ... neither have I.

Yes, but I'm not like you... then she hesitated... then her mouth opened wide as in fright.

Sean, my God... people.... coming right at us.

From where, he said without even lifting his head.

Toward us... two chaps, right there, two of them.

He looked in the direction she tilted her head and less than seventy-five yards away two people were walking along the water's edge coming directly at them, a man and a woman.

How the hell do you hide a fucking hulk like this, he thought to himself, for even the not curious want to know what it is the sea spits up that is this large.

Here baby quickly, sit right on top of the bale. She was wearing her ankle length full pleaded French skirt and when spread it covered the entire front from top to bottom.

Good...nice to have such a long legged broad.

I'm not amused. Oh God, the chaps are coming right at us.

He pulled off his shirt stripping to the waist, grabbed the choke chain around Wolf's neck, quietly ordered him to sit and whispered sounds he had trained the dog with to create growling that intensified as the people approached, the chain wrapped tightly around his fist, his arm muscles still enlarged from the exercise, and a nasty look on his face. Two nice middle-aged people just continued talking, walking, and looking at their feet and avoiding any eye contact with whatever the strange strangers were doing.

The psychology worked and they passed quickly discussing something about a movie, any temptation to peek diminished by the sounds coming from the beast now showing his teeth and fangs.

He could hear her sigh of relief. His mind now flashed back to the beach road, remembering sometimes several cops would stop in their cars to bullshit behind the buildings.

Their car was parked in the lot between McGowan's and the hotel; but it would be impossible for him alone to drag all that dead weight so far away.

What will we do now? She was whispering.

Very loud he said, KEEP YOU EYES ON THE ROAD FOR COPS.

Ssshhhhhh she begged, bending over as to hide, looking as if she were going to have a stroke.

He was now on one knee laughing very hard. When he was able to get his breath... The wind baby... we can just about hear each other, don't worry nobody can hear us down here. Starting to laugh uncontrollably again as she tried to punch his back with her little clutched fist. Oh, I could kill you sometimes.

Gaining his composure. Now look. I have to get this thing up to the road and we'll bring the car over to get it, and throw it in the car and get the hell out of here.

Could I help pull the bloody thing?

No, it's too damn heavy and with my back to the beach I can't see behind me. If a cop comes around that corner we are done. You have got to keep your eyes sharp.

He started to pull the monster but it dug into the sand so

much he was only able to move it a few inches at a tiedown, I thought I was stronger than this. His muscles bulged and the veins in his arms, neck, and legs looked as if they were going to burst from the strain. He stopped pulling and jumped to the other side with his back to the sea, dropped down into a blocking position with his head up and shoulder dug into the plastic cover and began driving the hulk through the sand pumping his thick thighs and seventeen inch calves, moving it up the incline from the water line and upward yet as the beach became a hill in itself.

He was moving it but every five yards he had to stop out of exhaustion. Breathing hard with sweat pouring from his body as if in a shower he would begin again, only to have to stop five yards later.

Goddamn this is killing me, am I a wimp?

Don't hurt yourself, can I help?

Help? Of course, he was now coughing... just keep looking. Any cars? Any cops? Then he pointed off to his left beneath a palm tree, "See that bush... up there... that's where.

I want this fucking thing... that bush."

He continued... you walk toward that bush. I can see your feet... I'll just follow your feet.

He was now on a straight path toward the bush and drove his feet deep into the sand and pushed with all his strength until he fell in love with the weight and the pain and even managed to laugh with his eyes following her feet, for her toes were elegantly pointed outward as a dancer's, so sexy to him... until the last ten yards which he did by nearly rupturing his body... until it was actually beneath the bush itself. The bush was just barely large enough to conceal the huge shiny black plastic hulk.

They now both sat. Him still puffing, her starring, the dog sensing the tension also sat. No cops, no cars, but his car was about eighty yards away... a long eighty yards.

He decided she would sit across the road with her back to the building wall facing the little bush with the dog by her side. He would walk a direct line to the car in anticipation of returning quickly and scooping the bale from beneath the bush and leaving the beach. Once inside the car they would be safe.

When he walked away it was not long before she could not see him and immediately became tense. Wolf's head was pressed against her breasts with both her arms around it as if it were a life raft, whimpering sounds emanating from the dog.

"Oh Daddy... please hurry," her heart pounding as she looked down the thin road running next to the continuous wall along which he would return, sand and sea weeds blowing across it's black surface. She would look to her right and then to her left, over and over, but could not look directly ahead to the bush hiding the thing, its shiny black plastic reflecting up enough light from the spotlights above to peek out at her like an evil eye. Her still believing perhaps a body concealed within, and felt as if she would die on the spot if a police car rounded either corner, north or south. From her sitting position she could not see Sean's car, nor hear anything but the wind, fear building up quicker than she felt capable of controlling.

The car failed to start, not even a sputter. The tension most likely slipped beyond his control for a split second causing him to flood the engine with too much foot action on the gas pedal. It was too dark for Sean to see the two of them sitting against the building, but he had slept with her enough years to feel her anxiety even from this distance... waiting the two minutes before attempting to start the car again, the seconds like an eternity. What if a cop came around the corner? Knowing what fools some of these cops can become when they see a pretty girl.

Probably make a wholesale investigation out of it... get out of his fucking car... bother her... ask questions... Christ, I should have brought them with me... why the hell... no, don't second guess... you were going for broke... they are guarding the stuff... that was my motive...maybe Wolf will bite the cop's dick off...Start you mother, or I'll take a sledgehammer to you....

The car must have gotten the message for a mere tap of the ignition switch and boom, no more flooded carburetor. A wonderful sound as all big eight cylinders roared, even heard by Ashley who at that moment was doing her best to fight back tears, now lifted her head and giggled in glee, her lungs opening to the sea air as tension evaporate from her body.

Within a few seconds he had the car parked in front of the bush, all four doors open, grabbed the huge hulk at one side and rolled it the few feet off the sand onto the macadam, and with a great heave-ho was able to flop it into the back seat of the large car where it just about fit after the front seats were moved forward six inches. But "in" it was, and in a split second the doors were closed and they were moving, safe for now.

He circled the old hotel and ran up the ramp over the inland waterway canal bridge turning north off the first side avenue at the base of the bridge to Tyler Street before turning west again rather than drive along police infested Hollywood Boulevard.

She turned the radio on, Jimmy Buffet was singing "Made enough money to buy Miami, and pissed it away," and the two of them began to laugh hysterically.

Come here baby, I love you... as she reached for him, he was pulling her across his chest as they laughed and hugged.

Chapter 3

A gift or a curse?

They were both relieved when seeing the outlines of the Spanish roof, then the palm trees, then and the house with the wall.

With the car backed into the drive way he managed to drag and roll the bulk from the car into the vestibule of the front entrance, pulling it over the stone floor until it settled in the middle of the living room floor just a few yards from the fireplace.

He went directly into the kitchen for a carving knife and by the time he walked back a large puddle of sea water had formed beneath the bale and a small runoff of water had formed at the front door. There was no smell other than seashells. He had no doubt about its contents, but she still contended it must be something else, like a dead body.

When he inserted the knife into the black plastic seawater gushed out over the knife right up to his wrist. The cut exposed the tightly bound contents looking like a wet bale of hay in a farmyard. At first sight he knew it was not just tightly bound but so compacted, which made its weight three times heavier than a bale this size.

When he tried to grab a fistful of the stuff only a small piece broke off from the tightly compacted contents, but he knew it was marihuana and quickly calculated it could be worth over one hundred thousand dollars, unless it contained a package of cocaine at its core as bales often did in those years before the demand for grass was supplanted by a demand for the synthetic, deadly, white power. Cocaine he did not like, but was curious if there were any at the core.

Christ, I told you we'd find one of these. Just look at it. I predicted it, his hands on his hips and a wide smile on his face.

Is it really bloody marihuana, her tone indicating she still did not fully believe it, her eyes staring at it and her hand to her mouth?

It was so wet and saturated with seawater that it fell apart once it began to unravel, revealing one mystery, that it was actually two bales of ganja not one as originally thought. No white mystery was hidden at the core; it would be no Trojan horse.

As the bales broke up they began to spread the contents across the stone tile living room until the entire floor was covered with about three to four inches of the darkened grass, about four hundred and fifty square feet of floor space now looking like an unkempt lawn, and just now beginning to given off any odor.

He grabbed a handful and held it up, I can't believe there is so much of this shit...smell that resin, pushing his hand in the direction of her face.

She turned her head very quickly, nearly chocking, now stepping away from his outstretched hand. Phew, we should open a window, her voice retaining some anxiety.

They quickly opened the windows and a breeze blew through the room and brought some relief, for even in this wet condition its soporiferous odor was beginning to gag them. At this point they decided to shower, eat, and just relax a little.

As soon as they finished eating he ran to the second floor and retrieved a pile of old sheets from a closet, laid them out around the large pool deck, rolled a wheel barrel in from the garden, with a flat head shovel began to scrape the piles of grass from the living room floor into the wheel barrel, and dumped each load onto the sheets surrounding the pool. When he finished the with a fortress like concrete deck with nearly six hundred square entire pool, deck was covered. The pool was larger than most feet of flat surface.

In the daylight the pool area would not be visible to a passer-by from any direction. The large aluminum screened in frame was lined with eight-foot-high bamboo and on both sides of the pool were two fifty foot wide lawns that ran into a five hundred and fifty foot long concrete wall that surrounded the entire estate along with dozens of varieties of tropical trees, palms, bushes, vines, and flowers that in some places grew in jungle proportions enclosing everything beneath the second story of both houses in the compound, not allowing peeking eyes to penetrate this little secret of privacy. The wind had by now calmed down to a gentle ocean breeze and the air still held it's chill.

The pool area looked like an unkempt lawn for the thick layers of hemp contrasted sharply with the white concrete deck barely visible now in the foreboding darkness of the night; for the clouds were impacted overhead blocking any light from moon or stars making it feel even colder.

He walked inside. The fireplace was glowing and Ashley was stretched out on the sofa next to the fireplace sound asleep. She was wearing his white linen robe with the blue Chinese lettering. He began climbing the stairs but stopped and glanced at the scene beneath him. The track lights between the exposed beams in the ceiling were dimmed to a dull yellow glow and the light directly above the sofa shone on the leaves of a small palm tree imprinting the shape of the leaves onto her shapely breasts and rounded rear end that protruded from beneath the soft fabric of the robe. Her long thighs were wrapped tightly with the cloth. Her hair fell across her face and down her back.

From his small perch on the landing he viewed the scene beneath and mumbled, this is art itself, as he watched the track lights casting the shapes of all the plants onto the white walls as they seemed to be making love with shadows and flashes of light intermingled with the tips of the fireplace lights that slow danced along the floor, dropping off at the far end of the room into the library with its dim lights revealing the hundreds of volumes of books packed from the floor to the margins of the white cathedral ceiling that seemed to rotate with shadows from the large white circulating ceiling fan suspended three feet from the roof.

This is mine. Somehow, I created this. Oh, if life could only stop right now at this moment. Is this beauty an illusion? Is this simplicity or is it greed? Will I always be here? Will this woman but a few feet from my hands and my heart always be with me and love me? Why can't I just be...this, her, those books...it will go, like everything I love.

Then he heard a noise out in the pool area. He descended the stairs and walked back to open the glass doors. There was still not much light. The moon was nearly hidden behind layers of purple, black, and dark blue clouds with some reflection from the water. There, something high to the left distracted him. Something was up there on the aluminum pool frame. No? Perhaps it was his imagination.

He walked between a few piles on the deck and moved halfway down the outside of the pool, keeping his eye on the spot where he thought he had seen something, but the layers of rolling purple clouds were too dark to reveal anything.

And then it happened. There, perched on the beam, and barely revealing itself, as years before, sat the cute little square headed owl but six inches tall.

Hi... how are you, cutie...? I haven't seen you in a long time.

He could not believe this little bird that he had seen several times years before. One, the night his son died. Later, a night years ago when he was down from New York to repair some damage tenants had caused. The later sighting was significant for it was on the same date as his son's birthday, which he had completely forgotten that particular day until the sighting of the bird at night.

Can I get a little closer, he thought now frozen in his tracks for fear the owl would fly away so fast as he did on previous occasions...for it seems as if it disappears?

The little owl sat motionless and kept fading in and out of Sean's focus against the faint light behind him in the sky. He rubbed his eyes as if to enhance his vision and get a better look at the little bird as the fast-moving darkened clouds blocked the intermittent flashes of the moon's light outlining its size and shape.

He walked slowly around the piles of contraband balancing on one foot and then the other with knees bent and arms extended as if holding onto a support, his head up with eyes fixed on the top of the metal beams, straining his vision to get a better look at that small little flat face.

Speak to me little guy... please... so I don't think I'm nuts. Who are you? Do you remember me? My son? Please talk to me... please fly on my shoulder... please don't fly away. God, where the fuck are you, little guy. I'm not going to hurt you. Where are you?

He frantically moved between and around the piles of ganja searching the metal beams, straining his eyes, imagining he saw him one second and gone the next. No bird, it had gone as before. He spent the next few minutes hopelessly looking up to where it had been. But this time, he got a good look at it and ran into the house and up to his study where he surveyed the floor to ceiling bookshelves until he found the large book with the title "Birds of North America," flicked on the desk light and within a few seconds found the section on owls.

Then he found him and at the bottom the caption read that the owl's southern habitat extended as far south as Georgia and sighting below Jacksonville, Florida were rare, end of information.

He returned to the pool area looking up and around but the sky was even darker and within a few minutes decided to call it a night. He carried Ashley up to the bedroom. She never woke. He stripped down, climbed into bed, and pressed up against her kissing her lightly on her neck, "love you baby," and inhaled the smell of her body until he fell off into seeing blue and green images of elongated bodies floating and flying as in a Chagall painting, then her smell, and faces of little owls, was it sleep or daydreaming.

The sun was streaking in from the blinds. It was morning. He climbed out of bed and was trying to remember what it was he had to do this day as he ritually glanced out the window, and there it was surrounding the pool. He thought he had dreamed it. But the brown stuff surrounding the blue crystal pool was not a dream, and he was still trying to sort it all out in his memory when he cracked open the glass slatted windows ever so slightly when the strong smell of cannabis snapped him awake. The stuff was baking under a sun that felt as hot as an August Jamaican afternoon; which was not normal weather this late in the fall. Last night was the storm, and now this extreme.

Christ, I now own over a hundred pounds of this shit, and began to think of how he got involved in marijuana a long time ago.
Semineaux had always been an athlete and never got into the drug culture, even during its heyday in the sixties and seventies when people were experimenting with everything.

But he remembered how marijuana once changed pain, horror, and nightmare into something bearable. And as he looked down into the pool area, he recalled seeing his son sitting in a chair at the far end.

They had just returned from the hospital after the first operation had failed to remove the entire cancerous tumor from his brain. Repeated sessions of chemotherapy left the boy looking like a cross between Casper the Ghost and a starving child in Africa. At worse, the effects of chemotherapy made the boy so ill that vomit would sometimes spew from his mouth without any warning, leaving him too weak to even cry for help or for sympathy. Semineaux would hold his little boy in his arms with a cloth beneath his mouth praying to God to stop the sickness and pain as he spoke soft kind words of hope and confidence into his son's ears. The heaving sometimes was so intense that after the convulsions he would fall dead asleep in his dad's arms, unable to feel the wet tears falling on him from above.

Semineaux prayed and prayed, to mainly Mary, to please help his son. During the previous year he had gone to mass and communion every day after his son had survived his first brain tumor operation, having bargained with God that in exchange for his survival he would attend mass every single day for the remainder of his life. He prayed to God and all the saints and angels in heaven, and would repeat prayers in Latin he had learned as a young altar boy.

But this violent sickness following the last operation left the child sick and vomiting for weeks and weeks. One night seemed to mark a turning point in Semineaux's faith. After one of the boy's most violent attacks he fell to his knees in the next room and cried,

Devil... Satan... Lucifer... where are you. If you exist speak to me. Speak to me. Make a bargain with me. What do you want? I will disembowel myself if you give him health and life. I will get a butcher knife and do hara-kiri. Speak to me you fucking devil... devil bastard... what do you want me to do??

With no God helping the boy and no devil appearing with a bargain, he settled for the numbing ritual of shots of Old Bushmill Irish whiskey, his Irish Grandfather's choice of drink. First it was shots, and then it was fifths, and then the quarts.

Up to that point he had been able to hide his pain with forced smiles and handshakes with friends and those with whom he worked, except for the obvious new patches of white streaks appearing in his full head of youthful hair. He had even continued a grueling work schedule, working three jobs, one teaching at the local university until one day the Old Bushmill began to take its toll. One of his many admiring students, actually walked up to the front of the room where he normally starred as a lecturer, and with a great deal of loving sympathy, led him away from the class room and to his car.

After waking sober the next morning, he decided to take the day off and drive up the coast to old Port St. Lucia to visit an old Bahamian brother from Nassau town. They had met years before after Semineaux had been discharged from the military and the two were employed as divers to find Spanish shipwrecks and gold treasure in Key West and the islands. Once a year Semineaux had visited his old friend in Port Saint Lucie, spending a day fishing, drinking a little beer and telling old stories of when Semineaux was twenty-two and he was forty-two; times they referred to as "151 times," named after the potent rum they had drunk in the islands.

His friend MacDonald was called Mac for he had no first name. For the last eight years the old diver had lived rather well off with a white woman, a widowed American lady, on an isolated piece of land in Port Saint Lucie where he fished the inland waters and still managed to dive for a little lobster on the reefs off shore.

In the old days Semineaux had been the youngest of the group and they nicknamed him "kid," now only used for serious talk every few years, setting Sean's ears up whenever he heard,

"Kid... you know Mon..."

"Ut ooo... something serious... when you call me kid."

On this day they were outside a small shack by the Port St. Lucie River on Mac's property sitting under an old hanging ficus tree whose branches dipped into the stream. A simple card table between them as they spoke and drank.

Mac's demeanor changed instantly that day. He stopped smiling. The lines in his long black face disappeared. He looked very intense. The yellowed eyes run through with red veins locked into Sean's.

Yes... it is serious kid. Even now you do not fool me. Your eyes show sadness and pain. You look hallow. When you call me from Miami late at night you are really in the tank Mon... And you don't even remember talking with me a few nights before.

He then pointed a long, dark finger at Sean's eyes. You used to be so good in the water Mon. the best swimmer and diver I knew. But you didn't drink heavy then, his head bobbing as he looked at the half empty bottle of gin, he had placed on the table only a short while ago. That shit is the curse of the Irish, he said in a low, deep voice.

I am worried about you. You tell me a lot of shit on the phone. His eyes became wider and more intense.

Look at me brother. You are drinking yourself to death, the yellow in his eyes seemingly ablaze. You are not helping your son by destroying yourself.

They both sat in silence for a long time, only the sound of a train far away.

Then Mac raised his voice in an uncharacteristic way, for he was one of the gentlest of men Sean had ever know.

Again, pointing his finger at Sean's eyes. Listen to me brother. I will tell you a way to help your son and save your own self at the same time.

He reached across the table and placed his hand on Semineaux's, looked out at the water as he drew deep on a cigarette rolled a few minutes before, smoke rising into the thick foliage of the tree as he blew smoke between his gold capped teeth.

Then he lowered his voice and released his grip. In the islands only the white folk could afford doctors. My mother and her sisters and both my fathers worked in the homes of the whites. They always had medicine and sometimes even went to England for treatment. Sean noticed the far-off look of pain in Mac's eyes for the first time.

Us... we only had each other... no white doctors, little medicine, and a lot of pain. He now stood up and put one foot on the chair and looked out at the water as several fish leaped through the surface.

When our people were sick and dying the old folks smoked the sacred herb to ward off the sickness. When they would vomit and heave and cry out in pain... it was the only thing that brought relief. We had no drugs, no morphine, only the herb that God gave us to grow.

Wait here, he said as he abruptly left him alone under the tree, returning a few minutes later with a small tin in his hand. Here kid... smell this. In the can was green cannabis with yellow streaks running through it. Let me show you how to roll this stuff, as he rolled a few joints in a matter of seconds. I never showed you this in the old days. Those white guys would have fired me for corrupting you. Have you ever smoked this stuff since then kid?

Can't say I have Mac.

Now look... as he put fire to one and showed Semineaux how to smoke, then brought his face to within a few inches and gently blew the smoke into Sean's face.

This is how you blow it into your son's face. I guarantee it will stop the vomiting and much of the pain.

At first Sean was very skeptical, but after a few minutes he was laughing again. OK... Mac... I'll try it.

But promise me... no more of that heavy drinking. I love you brother, and I want you to outlive me. Now you go help your son.

When Sean left for Miami Mac gave him a small suitcase that was filled with about four varieties of the stuff as they walked to the car joking about the women they had known and the gold they never found.

The very next evening Semineaux was sitting next to his son's bed reading and sensed another attack... in a few seconds he quickly chose among the various brown and green samples in the bag, rolled a little into the paper as if he were experienced.

The boy's eyes were looking weak and sad and so helpless. The thin little hand that he would always place on Dad's leg or foot when he was reading slipped off onto the sheet, a sign that the nausea was taking its grip on him, taking him into a lonely tunnel of sickness and pain that even Dad's love could not overcome. His eyes looked about in confusion and withdrew from his father, his little body beginning to tremble so slightly.

Puff after puff he blew around the boy's head, beneath and across the nostrils. His hand placed ever so lightly on his tummy felling the convulsions coming, then blew a small amount into his little mouth as he kissed him on the lips, fearful that he would choke him.

But nothing seemed to happen. Until, he began blowing smoke rings toward the ceiling and the boy began to laugh... his eyes grasping for life... he managed to speak...Suuyyy... suuuyy...

Hey kid... you mean silly, don't you? Who taught you how to speak?

Laughter... more laughter... it was wonderful. He gently placed his arms around the skin and bones of a body and hugged him best he could, placing his head to one side to hide the tears streaming down his cheeks. The sickness and pain were gone and the little guy began to speak about things five-year old's find amusing.

And that was the way it was for weeks, then another strange thing occurred. When the room filled with the smoke and two of them laughed small tropical birds would gather outside the window through which the smoke was escaping. The birds came every day they smoked, and stared into the boy's eyes and his into theirs for long periods of time. And then one night it happened for the first time.

The sun had just set, the background sky was a dark purple with floating black mountains of clouds with small white clouds flashing here and there; and there it stood, where all the other birds stood in the afternoon. It was the tiny owl, its big eyes staring into both their eyes, the three of them in a silent communion for over five minutes before the little bird seemed to disappear.

One day Sean stopped at a little store selling Halloween costumes and bought a full rubber mask of an owl. When he returned home, he popped his head into the bedroom to surprise the boy and make him laugh. It was too late, for he had already gotten sick over himself, tilting his head toward his father with a look of helplessness. This began the period when all that would kill the pain was morphine supplied by the doctor, which Semineaux would inject into the nearly hidden veins of his thin arms with those long sterile needles, his blue eyes crying out in pain and helplessness. On one of those occasions, after the boy had fallen asleep, Semineaux walked outside where he punched a palm tree so hard, he broke two knuckles on his right hand.

AAaaachhuuu... AAaachuuu... sneezing hard from the smell of the cannabis coming in through the slightly open window brought him back to reality, and the present.

Damn that stuff is strong. Even from up here. Christ... so many years ago... will I ever forget that. It's the past damn it. And just look down there. Shit... they are so afraid of that harmless herb.

Chapter 4

The hemp does smoke

He looked up at the spectacularly high perfectly clear blue sky against the backdrop of the tall gray majestic royal palm trees, the tops of their green canopy blowing in the soft ocean breeze. Beyond the green canopy of the trees were three or small aircraft streaking in various directions to and from the ocean to the east.

He took in a deep breath of air thinking, how wonderful it is to be alive; and began to chuckle to himself as the smell of drying ganja on the pool deck below the open bedroom window hit his nostrils... and then... like a flash of lighting out of the sky it came to him.

The planes... the airplanes... damn... aerial photos... surveillance planes... police planes... high altitude cameras...

Just them a small twin-engine plane passed low over North Lake just a few blocks to the east. He looked down again at the piles of brown cannabis surrounding the clear blue water of the swimming pool reflecting itself in the sky above; his mood changed quickly.

From ground level one could not see into the property, no less the pool. But from the air?

Yesterday's problems with judges, courthouses, lawyers, bankers, seemed impish against this awakening reality. Then he thought of his defiant tone in answering the judge's question as he was departing the courtroom,

Mr. Semineaux, the judge had said, where shall the court send your mail after today, her voice with more volume than ever before, her eyes fixed on Semineaux who by this time had his hand on the doorknob.

He spun around on the soles of his shoes and looked past all the others sitting along both sides of the table into the eyes of the woman judge, nearly laughing, for her face reminded him of an old boy from Kentucky who used to run a cesspool cleaning business not far from these very chambers,

Same address your honor, I have no intention of moving, his voice in low octave, slow and punctuated, "no intention" seeming to echo as he exited the door.

At that second his stomach dropped some, "Could that judge, would that judge... she looked pissed enough... bitch, a sheriff's eviction? What's the law on this? Could they be issued immediately? She did look like a fucking werewolf. I had to get a female. Never know what the hell they'll do.

Chuggggchuggggchugggg....A helicopter in the neighbor skies. Now alarms went off in his head. South Florida had become a war zone, where United States military pilots followed low flying "suspected" drug smugglers across bay and swamp waters and blew them from the sky during their landing approaches into clandestine Everglades landing strips. The U.S. military pilot who was drowning himself in booze at McGowan's, revealing to Semineaux his anguish with having shot down a plane carrying not only drugs but his brother in law. He had married a south Florida gal and the guy was his wife's twin brother, and his fishing buddy. Dangerous times in having anything to do with drugs, which he always vowed he never, would.

He went downstairs and found his woman cooking eggs. She didn't hear him entering the room for the windows were opened to the pool and her ears were filled with the sounds of leaves and chimes. She had remained in his linen robe and he pressed his body against her backside whispering love in her ear with the touch of his lips.

I can't believe it's out there, it's bunkers, her English accent so seemingly out of place.

Yes baby, it sure is bunkers.

Aren't you nervous, how can you think about that now, her feeling him?

Yes, I'm nervous... feel my heart pounding, as he pressed himself against her.

Now be a good boy. Get the knickers off your mind. I'm cooking breakfast, as she pulled her body away from his and walked to the refrigerator, tilting her head up,

Sean, how could you possible think about "that" with all that horrible stuff out there and all you have to do?

I'm not thinking baby. Remember... I'm not English... I'm an American man; we don't think first, we feel first, as he reached forward to pincher her as he walked out to the pool.

All those brains and all you think about is sex, she yelled in his wake. Daddy did say all you Americans were crazy.

He stepped out onto the pool deck and could not believe how hot it was for this time of year when another plane made a pass near the far end of the golf course but a quarter mile away. He decided to keep this latest fear of air surveillance to himself, for his lady was worried enough.

I feel blessed...he yelled into the house...could you believe this perfect weather? It'll dry this shit out in no time. I'm beginning to believe somebody up there likes me. That's it, baby, one of the first books that truly held my interest, "Somebody Up There Likes Me" ... about a tough fighter, Rocky Graziano... it made me laugh and made me cry.

Do you want to eat?

When they finally sat downs to eat both remained quiet for quite some time. Even the animals were quietly lying about stretching, yawning, rolling, and pecking in a lazy fashion for the tensions of the past several days had also affected their sleeping patterns. Big old wolf was fast asleep, but his loud breathing and snoring broke the silence... as they both began to laugh.

You wore the old boy out. His crazy daddy kept him up two nights running the beach...poor wolf... he likes it home and safe with mommy.

You should have seen him the first night when we combed the entire shoreline from Port Everglades to Government Cut. There were thousands of stacks of huge black sea weed blown in from the sea and he went nuts after somehow realizing what the game was all about.

How could he possibly know what you were looking for?

Easy, I brought a small amount of smoke with me and kept sticking it under his nose before I would send him running at the piles. Every so often I would give him a piece of biscuit, and then stick the smoke under his nose again. Believe me...he caught on fast. It was a great hunt. His tail was up and he was going nuts.

You really think he was looking for it?

Remember how nuts he was last night when we found it.

I've never seen him sleep like that; he looks dead.

Like a dog should sleep after the hunt, the ugly bastard.

Sean look, all the cats and dogs are asleep, ever the birds look sleepy... you tired us all out.

A lot of excitement around here and they were watching the whole show.

What are you going to do with it? Look at it, my God.

First, I have to find out what I have. The salt water might have killed it. I don't know.

Who are you going to tell? On first thought, no one. How long are you going to leave it out there? Until the sun goes down. With the sun this hot it should dry a lot of the top stuff. But it's so deep the bottom will still be wet. I'm going to cure it over there.

The "over there" was the smaller house at the far end of the pool area. A full apartment on the first floor and a complementary one on the second floor that originally, in the 1930s, had been the maid's quarters recently stripped of furnishing and the floors sanded in preparation for turning it into a writing studio and publishing business.

I'll turn on the oven in the downstairs apartment, close all the windows, roll all the grass up in the sheets they are lying on now, carry them up to the second floor, one by one, lay them out on the second story... the floors are so dry now that they are sanded... and set me up two electric heaters to blow hot air across the top. He had a faraway look in his eye. Damn, not the enterprise I anticipated for that room.

When the sun went down, that is exactly what Semineaux did. Transforming the room into a large oven, baking this cargo who's timing was, if not mystic as he believed, strange at the least.

That night he left the master bedroom windows in the main house open and about four in the morning was awakened by the strong smell coming from the back house. He dressed, went outside. The stars were bright in the high heavens with not a cloud in the sky to block the light of the nearly full moon. He opened the small gate at the rear of the property and walked onto the service road.

The odor of cannabis was overwhelming and he wondered how far the slight breeze coming in from the western Everglades would carry it. He walked fifty to seventy yards east toward the ocean hoping it would dissipate, but the smell remained.

His fears were backing up against each other. First it was the sheriff, then the planes, and now the smell. It was all too much for a guy that would have enjoyed a speaking tour with his new book on China, not this overwhelming experience. Quickly he returned to the house and bed and fell fast asleep.

The late morning sun was as hot as the day before, and he began raking the crop after laying out the bundles of sheets that had to be carefully carried from the upstairs, exposing as much of the moisture laden darker areas to the light of the sun.

It was Sunday and they had slept late, ate a long and late Breakfast, relaxed in the sun, read, listened to music, made love, and slept some more until the sun went down. This is where they felt alike, beyond the books, films, music, ideas, both feeling time as life's most precious gift. The trick being to control one's time as sacred, more rewarding than money, security, and material things, in this feeling for life they were soul mates. Make an hour into a day and a day into a week, slow down the time to fit your clock. Block out the world, so you may live in it.

Semineaux hadn't swam to avoid a run-off onto the pool deck but after again carrying the bundles to the second floor baking area he took advantage of the deck cleared of the crop and slipped into the water for a therapeutic swim vowing to do a hundred laps; a strong and steady freestyle until he began powering his way through the last twenty five laps, the invisible soundless wall between water and atmosphere hiding his screaming bubble curses and primitive emissions which drained the inner tensions and left his shoulders and neck swollen with pulsating veins and muscle. Then he floated about and watched his lady moving food from the kitchen to the table and enjoyed the beauty of her movements; lost in the simplicity of it all.

The pool water smelled and tasted natural for the afternoon sun had burned off the chlorine and the filters left it sparkling clear. He climbed from the pool into a robe rapping towels around his head as he ran to the second-floor master bathroom and stood in the green and white titled corner drying beneath an infrared light above, the sun was hot but December water penetrates it's cold to the marrow of the bones.

They soon sat to eat.

What will you do with it? She said so bluntly, looking him in the eyes. He said nothing at first. Her face toward his but she did not break the silence.

Smoke it all... with a wide smile... and then write a book of how I smoked a hundred pounds of ganja, all by myself. I'll call the book "Ganja Heaven."

Please, be serious, with such a beseeching tone.

Funny...when I first set eyes on that thing floating in the sea, I thought of how it would save our home. Not even as money, but as a facilitator in the process of saving the Fatherland. My little think tank from which to launch a thousand ideas to help somewhere in the world, and then amuse it some...then he went silent for a few seconds... hadn't much thought about much else, but I suppose I have to sell it first.

But sell it to whom?

Excellent question. I do know a lot of guys down here who deal but I don't want to get that close to them, even though I would trust them more than the majority of my academic colleagues. And, like I said, it may all be damaged by the seawater.

Well, perhaps... we try some, and see. Yes, bloody try some, she said in a rather audacious tone.

Right, he said before leaving then returning. Sean had taken a handful from a completely dry layer, rolled a small amount, began smoking as they continued their conversation until she interrupted him once, twice, three times, as they broke into continuous laughter. He could read her eyes and she his storytelling, they knew it was powerful weed.

During the next few days there was only one friend allowed to come onto the property. A young guy Semineaux had known for ten years with street smarts, knew a lot of people, a good head on his shoulders, and respected Sean's sense of privacy. He was Jack Budaux.

Jack was about six foot two with a powerful athletic build and an explosive agility that rendered him lethal in a street fight. He, like Semineaux, was French Indian Irish, feared nothing and moved fast. He had a wild animal streak that even Wolf picked up, for the dog seemed to follow Jack with some primitive radar whenever he visited, sensing that uncivilized core, making Jack slightly nervous. But Sean trusted his friend.

They spent hours discussing what to do with the cargo but it all came back to one problem... whom to sell it too. Semineaux did not want to sell it in his community. Jack would get exacerbated as his brownish/yellow eyes would widen in discussion.

"How the hell do you expect to get money to save this house if you don't sell it? I could sell the whole pile of shit to a guy who deals with stuff coming in from the islands and he sells it far away from here."

Who is he? He's got a boat yard in Fort Lauderdale and right now the Coast Guard and Navy have tightened up so much on the boats that what is coming in is only by air, unless they truck it from Mexico in through Texas.

Yea Jack, that's interesting... for if you think about it there a lot more pilots drinking at McGowan's these days than ship Captains. Funny, but your' right, Jack interrupted. The guy with the sexy broads who flew in from Oregon. And the guy from Nebraska last summer... remember with that fox from California, that girl we were all in love with.

You got it Jack... the ship Captains hit on the local broads that hang out in the joint, and the pilots bring their own chicks.

Yea, the guy with the boat yard doesn't have the control over supplies coming by air, he's mainly water connected. Used to be a fisherman. I've known him since he was just fishing, and I also know I've never seen his stash so low as in the last six months. I'll talk with him.

It's probably the same stuff that he was waiting for that I found, Sean laughing, then Jack joining. We won't tell him the ganja's history, tell him the shit was grown in Panama with seeds brought from Thailand. It's an exotic grass. Then they had a good laugh, for it did smoke well.

Remember Jack, Sean emphasized... the key, is "exotic."

In a few minutes Jack went out through the pool area and left the compound. Semineaux went up to his study and sat in his big old desk chair and took a deep breath of air, looked up at all the books on politics, history, Philosophy, psychology, civilizations past and present... and spoke, softly,

This is all about feeling. The feel I have for this place, like a man to a tribe and a tribe to place. I love this spot beneath the night heavens and in the path of the sea breezes. The laughter of children's voices still echoes in my head. Can I be forgiven if my survival instinct is now in control?

Chapter 5

The moral dilemma

The next day flowed uneventfully through time until the early December sundown brought on the dark, the shortest days of the year made six in the evening feeling like midnight. When Ashley returned from work and entered the house the lights were on and the smells coming from the kitchen told her Sean was cooking. Sitting at the dining room table, she kicked off her high heels, and poured herself a glass of wine. Soon they were eating and drinking, the conversation returning, as always as of late, "what are we going to do with it?" Do you think Jack can sell it for you?

Yea... he knows a lot of people. It's good, people will buy it...especially at the right price. How long do you think it will take to sell it all? Could go all at once. That would be nice, her reaching for a roll. But... I'm not going to sell it here, he said very quietly but deliberately. Pardon... what do you mean? A confused look came across her face as she tilted her head to one side, her hair falling over her square right shoulder beneath the white silk blouse. He did not answer. Her head now erect, shaking ever so slightly as if confused, Isn't Jack out there now trying to see this guy for you about selling it?

He took a sip of the red wine, placed the glass on the table and looked into the green lamp above the table. Today, I made up my mind not to sell it here. She pushed her hair back behind her left ear; her head back ever so slightly, and with a tricky voice, "being righteous"?

Whatever the hell you call it, and he rose and emptied more

food onto the serving plates, paced both hands on the table, leaned forward, I just will not sell it in the community. I've had so many opportunities over the years here in south Florida to make fast money, a lot of friends got rich fast. Guys I dove with in the islands, don't have to work and live like kings. Some own small islands, fast boats, and a lot of fast cars.

What will you do with it if you don't sell it here, where will you sell it, as she took notice of his well sculptured upper arms, thinking to herself how most other women like a man's strong arms, but not her? She found muscles repulsive.

He said nothing. But where? Her upper-class English accent sounding like "warrior,' as if it were a negative place, in a sarcastic shadow, matching her glance.

Where else? Where else could I sell it where no respectable American would care?

Where? Her expression alert.

To faggots in New York.

Faggots... she repeated, trembling ever so slightly. You sound so stupid... educated man of the world and you call them fagots. She rose from her chair and dashed into the kitchen and turned her back to him as she did when angry with him.

All the gay friends you have... you are such a hypocrite. Bullshit... you know I judge people as individuals... gay or straight... I know they are often more creative than straights.

Well why then do you call them fagots? I don't, just want to pull your chain. Yes, you do, you think something is wrong with a man who is not straight, her pushing it slightly. No, I just can't see what a man could like about a cock, except his own. The thought makes me sick. Your' disgusting, she said as she dashed into the small bathroom off the dining room, being gay is not just about sex, you think everything is about sex.

Semineaux's laughter nearly drowned out the sound of the soft tapping on the front door. It was Jack standing as rigid as a soldier, breathing hard as if he had just finished running with sweat rolling down his forehead and the sides of his long muscular neck, the veins pulsating as he gasped to catch his breath, his large eyes flashing like a wild animal.

You look as if you'd seen a ghost, Semineaux said as he grabbed his wrist as a gesture to enter, for Jack was always the gentleman never assuming he was automatically welcome. Come on in, what the hell is it?

I don't believe ... he blurted out walking into the light of the dining room. May I have a glass of water? What happened? Give him a chance to relax. He said he's thirsty. Hello Ashley. Hello Jack. Yes... get him some water... now what's going on?

I went to the boat yard to see bill, thank you Ashley, he drank it down quickly and placed the glass on the table. I always stand behind the fence and call him... he's got this damn dog.

I know what a pussy you are about dogs, Semineaux smiling ... and he won't let me teach him how to kill them. Be quiet, let the chap speak. Sit down, as Sean pulls a chair out from beneath the table. Jack takes another gulp from a fresh glass of water. Yes, go ahead Jack, her curiosity quite evident.

Bill lives in a trailer but his dog will sometimes lay in one of the dry-docked boats. He's attacked and tore up a couple of guys that tried to rob Bill. I never go inside that yard without calling bill. The dog is eerie. He doesn't always bark. So, I call Bill...no answer. I had just talked with him on the phone and he said to come over. So, I go over to a pay phone on Dixie Highway and call him again. The phone is busy. I wait. Then call again. It's still busy. I go back over to the yard. There is light in the trailer. When he goes out, he never leaves a light on. I call and call, no answer. The fucking dog. Where is it? Jack shifting his eyes from right to left to emphasize. So, I grab a three-foot-long two by four and slowly make my way into the yard. I'm waiting for that dog.

Ha ha, pussy. Be quiet.

Now I see the dog... lying at the bottom of the small stairs leading into the trailer... in a puddle of blood, with half his head blown away. I can barely see Jack through the screen door sitting at his desk, but I can see him... sitting straight up. I call him. He doesn't answer. I open the door, and there is Bill. His hand is over his heart...right there on his chest, as Jack places his hand over his own chest...like it's glued there. His blue eyes wide open and his mouth, as he was about to say something.

Yea, like don't shoot me... we know each other. Sean, don't interrupt him.

Then Jack, with the forefinger on his left hand points to the center of his right hand remaining on his chest, there is a hole right in the middle of his hand... a perfect hole... a bullet hole...behind him on the wall is some blood and pieces of Bill from a hallowed out shell that tore him up inside.

Christ... he knew it was coming. Yeah Sean, I think so. No

sign of a struggle in the room. Someone just plugged him. Yeah, and probably someone he knew.

A drug deal gone wrong or something like that. Shit... I touched nothing. Even took the club I brought in with me, slipped out of the yard as quickly as I could and threw it by the train tracks and ran all the way here. Ashley retrieves the glass from the table and goes off to refill it.

Christ, I'm glad your' ok Jack. You didn't leave any unusual footprints outside the door, did you? I don't think my feet even hit the ground until I got to Dixie highway. I ran down those railroad tracks without even thinking and it was pitch black for about five blocks. Thank you, as she places the cold water in front of him. Nothing was said as he was drinking the water.

Jack, Semineaux says very quietly, I sort of hate to tell you this right now, but in the meantime, I already decided not to sell it here in Miami.... I'm going to take it to New York.

Don't worry, I can find another buyer... right here.

No... You miss the point Jack. I've decided not to sell it anywhere in the community...and you may think me as Saint Ethics, but I did raise my little children here for some time... and... my boy is still buried here. Jack said nothing, just stared into Sean's eyes. But whatever... it's not phony... it's deep and I believe this to be honest.

Bullshit ethics... how about New York... it's a "community?" Sean knowing Jack had clicked on his debating brain, for his right lip curled up ever so slightly, a trait he noticed many times before with Jack not just in intellectual discourse but when he was on the verge of violence.

Yea Jack... but ethics are ordained by the society in which we live, and you know most Americans could give a shit about the gays in Greenwich Village... let the motherfuckers die... fagots all.

You mean that beastly...

Honey...of course not... please don't interrupt; Semineaux smiling knowing it was coming.

Yea, fuck the faggots, Jack said, go ahead.

Jack, I knew you would understand, She's English, what would she know about our America.

"The truck driver," she said disdainfully.

No, philosopher... English woman... ordained by a Medieval Scholarly Guild.

Come on... what about New York.

Well, no really cares about the gays in the Village. Especially with the AIDs outbreak this last couple of years, most Americans consider the gay community one big disease... like the Injuns, eliminate and eradicate; but this is the twentieth century. So, they are tolerated not wiped out, but there are millions who would turn their heads if some equivalent to the biological warfare used against American Indians were secretly let loose in gay communities. But on the whole, they take better care of themselves than most, exercise, eat good...actually real sissies about health.

No one knows Sean's gay.

First, I'm a beast who hates fagots, now I'm gay. Wish I were baby, and then I would not be so obsessed by your feline smells.

Pig, as she leaves the table and goes upstairs.

Well, the gays like to smoke. And so many make good money, like the good life, and have fun. They are arty fun bastards who drink hard and play hard.

But they are still faggots... I hate the fuckers, Jack blurts out.

Well, I don't exactly love 'em Jack, but I can identify with that part of them that wants to decide for themselves how they will live... not by anyone else who has no idea what drives them.

What does drive them? Sean... what makes a fagot a fagot, Jack asked in a childish way.

It's all chemistry... you know what you want to eat. You see it you want to eat it; you smell it and you want to eat it; you think of it and you want to eat it. Your taste buds don't lie to you. You know exactly what you like in a woman, for you feel it before you think of it. A chemistry that sets off sophisticated circuits, automatically and unconsciously, pure honesty. Fagots can't help it, that's how they feel.

Let's change the subject; the thought makes me want to vomit. How are you going to sell it to them? Whatta you gotta do, kiss 'im first, both laughing spontaneously, over and over again, until he said, cut it... now, there is a lady in the house and I can feel the dirty talk beginning.

Need me to come up with you? leaning forward. That's nice of you brother and I love you. But I have to do this myself. And don't worry, it'll be easy. A few will spread the word in the Village that I have this wild, exotic smoke. Then I'll go from customer to customer letting them try it. You know what a good bang you get out of this stuff. All up, no paranoia, no downtime. Just natural and fun. It's a great smoke.

How much? Jack said impatiently, now getting to his feet for he did not like sitting too long.

Whatever the market will bare... free enterprise... I'll lie and say it is the most exotic smoke I ever came across. The more demand, the higher the price, to a point.

It'll take you forever to sell it that way. So? I'll just stay in New York till I sell it... all, if it takes three months ... then I can save this home ... but right now I have to somehow get a car to move this shit north.

Chapter 6

Driving north and near death

The next morning over coffee the two sat quietly for quite some time. Without raising her head Ashley engaged the problem at hand, taking the lead.

"So you have decided not to sell the grass here in Miami, is that correct?" Now looking up, her face expressionless, but her eyes cold, as if she were looking at a stranger.

You got it, baby. I'm taking it north…a little distracted since he was trying to read an article about the confrontation in Europe over the placement of American nuclear missiles on German soil.

How do you expect to do that? Her tone anything but supportive.

One of those drive aways from Miami. But I don't have a driver's license. That disqualifies me from renting or driving a destination car, he smiled. Do you have a license?

No, I don't, her tone indicating she did not like the question. Wish I did -- I must get one.

A license is no problem. I have a good Arab buddy who knows his way through anything complicated. He'll know what to do and how to do it against any obstacles. I have complete confidence in his being able to lead me to a large power packed automobile that I am going to need.

The next few days were very hectic, for the auto traffic was coming south from the cold north. There were few autos being transported north. The choice of car you wished to contract for delivery was limited to a few boring choices of small cars and old big ones, take what one could get. Sean had completely forgotten about the time of year, all the activity in a short month and a half had shaken his equilibrium with nature and the smells of turning seasons.

He had known his Arab buddy Farouk for four years and a solid friendship had developed between them. Sean respected his opinions on very intricate subjects of politics, human nature, and women. It was thru Farouk that he began to understand the subtleness and mystery of the Arab mind, with its ability to make choices where no options appear available. Farouk's father was Lebanese and his mother was Syrian. His skin was white against a deep dark brown hair and eyes set within a warrior's face that resembled that of a young Jack Palance, the gunman of "Shane" renown and the fierce Mongol horseman of the Super screen age in American movie history. Lean, muscled, externally self-controlled, polite, and with a slight twitch of his eyes as a result of seeing his twin brother's face blow off before his very eyes at twelve years of age in the Middle East. His pain was as deep as his politeness and gracious manners, and his personality was strong even in silence. Semineaux and Farouk met two or three times during the next three days, but Farouk was unable to come up with a car. Christmas music was constantly on the radio by now. It did seem possible it was already that time of the year.

The difficulty was in finding a suitable car, for there were several models available but too small in body and engine size. None seemed to be the right one.

In the meantime, Ashley wasn't spending much time at home, for their seemed to be quite a few Christmas parties at Palm Isle Resorts with all the money guys flying in to Miami; reflective of all the secretary type presents she was bringing home. Things were getting complicated and tense. The uncertainty of the future was invading his dreams, beginning to turn them into nightmares. To add to this, he knew something was going on, for Ashley hardly spoke to him in the evenings at home.

One day, the wife of movie star Jimmy Goldstein had called about why her famous husband had Ashley's phone number in his phone book. And here Semineaux was at a very crucial moment of his life ... his scholarly study of China just published, the ex-wife and father in law with a team of lawyers trying to take his home, the frightening venture of taking all this illegal weed up to New York, and she was playing "English cold cunt with him."

Semineaux wanted to meet this movie actor who played leading tough guy roles in the movies, some roles as a gangster, and throw some knuckles his way, Philly style, and reduce the phony tough guy to the punk he is. For the science of man-to-man street combat was born in Philadelphia, as sure as was the United States Constitution. That art of the Philly boxer was legend in boxing circles long before the Californian Stallone stole the Rocky Balboa character from a Philly brother and immortalized the bare-knuckled street fighter.

And here he was not feeling loved by his woman, and wanting to fight ... kick the actor in the ass before knocking him out. Sean knew this tension was trouble at a time that demands self-control. At worse, he was feeling that the woman he slept with, and loved, was about to betray him. It was only a few days ago that he had asked her to marry him and have a baby, that she never did responded ... and now ... he wanted her to put her mouth, body, and wetness to him all night long. But her body never touched his, night after night.

Within a few days Farouk called, he had found a suitable car. It was a tank of a machine, a 1978 Lincoln Continental going from Miami directly into Elizabeth, New Jersey, across the river from Manhattan. It was perfect, he could run the stuff into the Village and then bring the car to its owner in New Jersey. They met to inspect the car, then Farouk used his license and pretended to be the one driving the car north. They got the keys to the car, and Farouk drove it out of the establishment's parking lot, and in a few minutes they were both driving the separate cars on Royal palm lined Hollywood Boulevard, laughing aloud, as the wind kicked up every flappable awning, flag, and palm leaf with a strong northeast wind coming off a choppy ocean but a few blocks away. They turned left a half block to Tyler street and pulled up outside his hacienda.

It took forty five minutes to put the one pound bags into a large traditional black storage locker suitcase Jack had supplied, putting the overflow bags into a handheld cloth bag, packed the car, drove it up onto the property driveway, locked it up, and left it sit till departure time was decided upon. They spent the next few hours talking, looking at maps, and considering the possible hazards the trip posed. The major concern was being stopped for any ordinary speeding violation or due to something unexpected like a burned-out turn signal or taillight, for having no license would trigger-off suspicions at any point along the interstate highways. And Farouk's words would echo in his head every moment of the trip... "If you get stopped for anything, you are going to jail." So, he had to at least look like he had a license, and decided to dress very conservatively in white shirt and tie, wearing his reading glasses whenever he was conscious of being within eyesight of any policemen. Unfortunately, he was thinking about "profile" at this early stage, but this crucial ingredient was recklessly abandoned the following morning, a flaw, that may have been the variable that changed his life forever.

By the time Farouk left it was dark and he anxiously awaited his woman's return from work, for this would be his last night home, and he somehow wanted to breach the distance and coldness between them. Ashley failed to call at her usual time, and then some more time elapsed as the early December night made him jittery. He waited like an anxious child for the phone to ring. Feeling foolish, he tried calling her, but there was no answer. Time moved and anxiety spiraled, and he thought..." She's been quiet, sexless, cold, and has been treating me like a piece of furniture. She's got to be thinking of another man. At a fucking time like this ... Christ ... all one puts out in the name of love... what bullshit. He found it difficult to sit.

Sean got his car keys, left the house, and within six minutes drove his car onto the parking lot adjacent to McGowan's bar on the beach. The bar was all lit up for Christmas, and he sat for a few moments thinking of all the wild characters that had passed through this place in the last two decades. They were the type of men who had to fight and struggle for every inch of life. Tough guys from Ohio and Pennsylvania steel towns, construction workers, merchant sailors, local red necks, bartenders, drug smugglers, soldiers of fortune, sailboat designers, murderers, hard drinking, chain smoking, lovers of women, street fighting wild men, that are nothing, if not original. He always felt comfortable with these men, and most liked him. He found a collective wisdom, about life.

Those ultimate questions we all eventually ask, if not to others for sure to ourselves, are questions about life and death, about doubts and fears. Experience is normally the only key to knowledge that opens to the creation of wisdom. And for these most important questions of our lives, these men have been there and returned, time and time again. It was no accident that he gravitated to this bar on the beach. He needed to talk to men that knew life's dangers, for he was so worried about doing something he did not want to do, his heart was not in it and consequently he could make a crucial mistake. The trouble would be hell. Hell on this earth just at a time all was to be just grand.

When he got near the door, he could see through the glass windows that wrapped all around the bar area facing the sea, and there were few patrons at this early hour of the evening. Once inside the door he recognized two friends he was always happy to see, two of the Kirklyn brothers. A family of five powerfully built, friendly sons who had a character of soul and spirit nurtured on pure determination to remain honest in dealing with others. A simple quality that could save the world from its killings. They could also be violent, all of whom were devastatingly deadly with their fist, knew how to use weapons, and were as tough as the steel mill towns from which they emigrated.

Derk, presently a commercial fisherman out of Fort Lauderdale, was well over six foot four inches tall, built like a young John Wayne, was essentially quiet and reserved, had large rough hands and wore glasses that somehow always fell upon the bridge of his noise, giving his a somewhat soft appearance.

Kevin, an iron worker, with a barrel chested six-foot two main frame, fore arms the thickness of a man's calf and fingers as thick as large toes, big blue eyes set in a happy smile with a healthy crop of blond hair, with a deep voice commensurate with his image. My man," Kevin shouted so loudly the windows shook, and Derk just smiled an approval as Kevin gave Sean a bear hug ...

"Where the fuck you been Professor, China or something?" "No, nothing so exciting, but I can't believe you guys are here because I came to the beach hoping, in the back of my mind, that you would be here. And how long has it been since we saw each other?"

For the next forty-five minutes Sean explained what had happened as both kept laughing about the whole thing, especially where Sean found it, so close to where they now sat. And they really had a good laugh when he related how the car would not start, in the very parking lot of the bar. When he told them his first idea of getting rid of it fast, they quickly offered to get it off his hands within three hours to a local broker, before they understood his determination to take it north, out of the community. At that moment Kevin startled him by interjecting that the two of them, without even asking Derk's approval, were going north with him ... "You could get hurt; we're going with you."

It was not a casual remark, for the two of them spent the next twenty minutes explaining why he needed help, or "more armor," as Kevin said, which was close to the truth. On his drive home he could not believe what they had just offered; to put everything in their lives aside to help him, and insist to the last minute, giving him their phone numbers to call them in a few hours or before sunrise. They were two guys who just loved adventure, like the men he met in Key West when he was twenty-two, before South Florida became commercial and was nearly as pristine as New Zealand. Before its natural beauty was raped and humiliated into concrete and plastic. Now with all his education and experience, he still, found kindred brotherhood in men like this, and trusted them more than any others.

When the lights hit the wall of his downstairs library, he noticed the complete darkness, when he had left lights on for his woman when she returned. "Could she have turned off all the lights and gone to bed?"

"If she's gone to bed ... that means...'don't touch me, I'm asleep, cold, or nasty, any, or all of the three...' Christ, not tonight. I'm leaving at sunrise." He should have known better, feeling such support from his buddies should have warned him to be aware of the opposite. But his guard was down, for he wanted and expected tonight to be comfortable enough to prepare him for the morning's departure. There were no lights at all in the downstairs, which was her way of saying "fuck you" since he always left low lit security lights everywhere in the house, so he switched on some lights, looked at what food he might take with him, decided to pack in the morning, climbed to the second floor to discover the total darkness again, not even the small night light in the master bathroom by which they often made love in its subdued warm yellow shadow.

Sean turned and went into his study, closed the door, and tried to think about what he had to bring with him of importance.

But his mind kept slipping into her, and he wished so badly not to desire her so, but he would feel whole again if she would lay on him and feel him. But she would take her English stubbornness to her grave. What could one expect of an English woman? It's in her genes, he thought, as his mind wandered.

English women are about power more than any other on earth. Only England could produce a Margaret Thatcher. Not being a gambler, but he would wage a large sum of money that Margaret's favorite position in sex, if she had any, was on top of the man.

That way, the man knows he is being used, to give pleasure, or perhaps to satisfy something else, that is more fulfilling then feminine physical pleasures. Pure speculation, but she was not the only English woman with whom he had intimacy, and there were patterns, as surely as with the patterns of southern Baptists girls from Texas, whose patterns are pure pleasure for a boy from the East.

He had to get this shit off his mind and at least get some sleep, so into the darkness of the covers he went. He rose shortly before sunrise, and turned on a few lights to pack and prepare to leave. He packed enough clothes to prepare him for any weather conditions he might encounter, ten copies of his China book, several copies of a proposal for a new book on nuclear, chemical, and biological politics in which the Rockefeller Foundation had shown some interest, his poetry, and hygiene supplies. In a small kit he placed a knife, flashlight, two types of tape, aspirin, vitamin c, and several Quaaludes, the later the best sleeping pill he knew in case he had to get a good crash sleep at some point. He was planning on taking a good hot shower, putting on a nice conservative suit, packing some food, perhaps to meditate, and leave peacefully.

At that very moment Ashley walked past him so quickly all he noticed was the sound of her silk robe slapping against the doorjamb.

Ashley somehow managed not to be in the same room with him, and maintained a distance, as she had in bed while they had slept. This drove him mad, as it has had ever since they first lived together in New York seven years before. "But, why now," he thought to himself. "A cold bitch all night, maybe a hot cup of coffee English woman. Where the fuck is that gaffers tape I want. wish I could spend the day in the upstairs back apartment preparing the room for the computer, printer, copy machine that will be used for the publishing house. I hate the thought of what I have to do. Not even a cup of coffee...stubborn, no wonder the Irish become so violent to get the English out of Ireland ... Oh shit ... she's part Irish, blows that ... the mixture probably makes her more dangerous."

He was shaking inside, trying to keep it in, for his anger and hurt were about to erupt. A mere hug from her, earlier, would have reduced him to a little boy, for he was basically scared about what he was doing. There was no adventurous motivation in his heart, only fear. "Christ, I want to write another book, not smuggle drugs.

Wish I was a faggot ... no man would turn on me like this." He completely forgot about dressing like a gentleman, and simple left with the baggy pants, sweatshirt, and running shoes worn upon getting out of bed in anticipation of eventually showering, a long, hot shower. Now he was out the door with his bags and winter ski jacket he remembered to grab in his confused state of mind. Days before he had planned to meditate before leaving. He had the powerful engines of the car running immediately, for there was a chill in the air requiring some heat inside the car, and the car radio, pathetic enough, was tuned into "Southern Cross," which went unnoticed by him until he got to Georgia. It was at this juncture she appeared in the door way, in her English father's robe. The engines roar distorted what he was hearing, and he could not read the expression on her face, so he heard nothing she said. But she could hear him quite clearly as his deep voice penetrated the engines noise and from a heart that wanted to cry out," I love you ... forever. I worship you," Instead, he blurted out, "Baby ... I'll see you in Eternity." And within seconds he was driving West on Tyler street with tears streaming behind his sun glasses, for he was determined, to never again, set eyes on her in this life.

The engine's carbonators momentarily dominated the radio's sounds as he speeds up the ramp onto I95, and if his old Pontiac flew like an F-16 fighter plane, this glunk was a long-range F-111. He immediately knew he was driving a fighter bomber, a vintage American powerhouse, whose metal content could now build nearly five compact cars, soon to be an obsolete species of motoring history. His stomach, heart, and lungs were screaming along with the engine's roar, till he consciously grabbed hold of the reality that he was speeding, and tears were blinding him and had somehow splashed onto the inside of his sunglasses, obscuring his vision. Within a split second he took his foot off the gas pedal, removed his glasses vowing to himself to forget her and take care of business, wiped the tears from his eyes, and as long as it takes to calculate how many humans, animals, insects, living things in the world at this moment, have just blinked ... in the blink of this eternal second ... a large white metal van whistled past him, directly across the front of his speeding car. The explosion to his rear he will never forget.

For the early rush hour North bound speeding traffic on 195, absorbed the head on meteorite of a van as its white metal and plastic splintered into a hundred pieces flying through the air, captured in his rear-view mirror, and now his mind. And the explosions of dozens of human driven autos colliding violently, like bombs going off.

And then the stillness, as if nothing happened. For it was now quiet inside the car, with the radio off, and the wind whistling through the partially opened window.

The quickness of it all, the sounds ... those crashing cars ... the sounds of exploding vehicles, dominated his entire consciousness for over two hundred and fifty miles of relentless driving to Orlando, not yet midway to the Georgia border. He kept thinking what could have happened if he had not slowed down, or wiped his eyes a split second longer. This near tragic event did not seem as though it even happened. The reality of it all was still echoing around in his senses. Yet, somehow the evasive aspects of the experience were perhaps the reality, which like life itself, may be an illusion. The next hundred miles were uneventful, as he daydreamed and thought about why he always felt that life was transient at best.

The transition from seeing reality in conventional terms began early in life, but after the death of his son took a dive into a Zorba-like spin Semineaux called Zorbanism, with its debauchery of booze, sex, and violence before the veils of realism fell, and the truths of nature were revealed. Zorba danced to kill the pain, but Semineaux learned one cannot run from this agonizing loss of a child, that which destroyed Zorba.

It was about this time something was disrupting his transfixed stare onto the long concrete line ahead. Something was stirring automatically in his subconsciousness. Then suddenly, state troopers flashed by like sharks driving in on a prey, first one, then two three and four police cars.

"Fucking cops all over the place, I'll get the fuck off 195, head west and pick up some parallel old road running North. Those bastards make me nervous."

This far north Florida becomes rural, so it was not too long driving west into the winter tropical sun with its cooled-down orangeness that he found an old concrete state road running north, alongside a watery canal serving the irrigated citrus groves. Now with the large orange sunset to his left, not a vehicle to be seen in either direction, he speeds on this narrow road with canals on both side of the highway. No cops but a little bumpy, demanding more concentration then on the Interstate. Having driven through Florida too many times over the years, he estimated he would drive longer on this stretch of road that it would take to drive from Madrid, Spain through parts of Portugal to the sea.

Determined to relax he turned off the music, checked his speed at sixty-five, enjoyed the clean air that whistled past his ear, completely forgot where he was or what was his mission.

The western sky was now a bright orange mountaintop sinking into the deepening blues and purple; cool, not warm, so why did he feel heat on his neck?

Now a bright light on the dash board, and a glance to his left, froze him in fear when reading the black lettering on the huge blue van passing him..." U.S. Government." The man in the passenger's seat with the little round face, black thinning hair, and thick black rimmed glasses was staring at him as he flashed this strange laser bright light now into the back seat. Time didn't stop, but without any obvious hesitation Semineaux raised his left hand in a sideway quasi saluting motion used by VIPs he had witnessed on numerous occasions, acting out, by keeping the head straight ahead, the behavior of important people. This time, he was lucky, for it did the trick and the little guy in the thick glasses, looking as bureaucratic as his blue uniform, nodded respectfully, as they drove off under the power of a very large engine.

He felt as if he weighed a ton, pressed into his seat. His speed had not dropped, but the bastards were soon out of sight.

But now, Semineaux was angry at himself that he had allowed them to sneak up on him. Somewhat motivated by defiance, or a damaged ego, he opened up the engines for the first time and cruised at 105 mph for about twenty miles like a drunk redneck on a rip. The road was not made for this speed and every so often a dip followed by a bump would make the huge vehicle airborne, creating a wild sensation in his stomach, normally, only felt on amusement park rides.

The road was getting worse, for in the years since 195 was completed the farmers were the main users and their heavy equipment had taken its toll, forcing him to reduce his speed to about seventy-five mph. Fortunately, for he would not have survived. The left front tire had been punctured in two places by some medal objects that most likely fell from some farmer's cart, and Bamb ... it blew out. He tried desperately to grab control of the car in tenths of seconds, hitting the brakes, gripping the steering wheel with strong hands and powerful arms, but nothing worked. The left front dug into the road as the rear end kept coming toward the front. When the rear end fishtailed, the left front tireless rim ripped through the last few inches of road as the macadam gave way to soft dirt, burying the left front rim in the soil causing the entire vehicle to roll.

It is strange how quickly the mind works, for as he could feel the car roll all he could think of were the birds that had been landing and taking off from the watery canals that had been glistening in the light of the sunset.

The central thought that dominated his senses at this point was that the car had automatic window controls, and he would dream of those silver switches for a year. Most everyone living in flood control areas with canals have heard some story of people being trapped in a car with electric windows. They are impossible to get down once the car is submerged under water and everything electrical is shorted out. The only way to normally survive this situation is to allow the car to fill up with water, and then crawl out the window and swim to the surface.

This he knew, and all this flashed across his consciousness in anticipation of the wet splash, hoping not to be knocked out in the fall. Fortunately, he had his seatbelt attached and was not thrown about, but was surprised when the car hit the bottom of the canal with such force. Even though the windows were shut tight, water would have entered the car through dozens of entrances almost immediately, slowly filling the car with water.

The major problem is that no one is strong enough to open a car door underwater, for the pressure of the water keeps it closed like a steel vault door. Only widows offer an escape from this slow submerged death. So ideally, the windows are closed when entering the water and when the car is nearly filled, one takes a deep breath of air, rolls down the window, and swims to the surface.

Lucky man, the canal was dry. The sun was down but it was not yet dark. Silence, all he could hear was his own breathing.

He felt pressure in his head, for the car was on its side and he could see the sky through the passenger window. The seat belt had held him tight. But his new fear was worse than old. The car catching fire. And with that thought he moved quickly, unlocking the seat belt, nearly standing and looking up at the passenger door, then fumbling for the switch that opened the window, just enough to crawl out onto the side of the car and take in a deep breath of air.

Chapter 7

The nightmare night

"Goddam ... Goddam...Yuawl ok partner." The voice startled Semineaux, for he never heard the large tractor trailer pull up behind him. He was standing in the overturned car looking up from the ditch at this redneck with a large belt buckle, a large insignia on his cowboy hat, dirty boots, dirty blue jeans, and it seemed that the man was attempting to say something, but his mouth was barely moving.

"What's that you say?"

"I said ... Goddam Sur ... yuawl ok??? I can't believe yuawl still alive or the car ain't blown up ... You rolled three times. I just came out of that side road when you started to go."

"Forget that shit for now my man. It's the cops that frighten me. Please ... please help me get this car out of here before the cops see me.

Our ya bleedin' anyplace partner... any broken bones? Wont' me to take yuawl to the hospital across county?

Semineaux climbed from the car and with a hand and a pull, or rather a yank, from the rather strong truck driver, he was out of the pit and onto the embankment.

"Thank you, brother, please listen ... I truly appreciate your concern... good guy you are partner. But I've somehow got to get this fucking car out of here, pronto."

The truck driver pushed his hat back slightly, scratched his head, squinted his eyes, and after a short pause, "Could get a backhoe, or one of those construction machines in here tomorrow. . . "

"Tomorrow???" interrupting, "no... no, this is life and death my man. Now-NOW"

"Umm ... Yuall a little upset maybe ... the cars is in ditch, and a deep ditch at that."

"Yes, but look up there, about forty yards, a dirt ramp that cuts into the canal. This ditch leads right into it.

"I do think I have a long chain."

"What's that "a chain?"

"Maybe could pull Yuall ... maybe not so crazy?"

I'm beginning to love you brother."

They first rapped the chain thru the windows and across the roof of the car, then tied the other end to the haul bar on the rear of the truck. The truck roared in low gear. At first a few tires spun, then took hold, and were able to bring the car upright ... at which time Semineaux let out a wolf cry "Ah hoooo .... Ahhh ooowwwooowo."

"You fuckin Yankees all crazy."

Next, they wrapped the chain around the front bumper of the big Continental, brought the truck as close to the canal bank as possible, as the truck slowly pulled until the chain was taunt, and the car tires began to move. The car rolled over the dirt bed of the canal, for it was fortunate no rains had come to this area for weeks and the riverbed was muddy but firm. Within seconds Semineaux jumped into the canal and was behind the wheel as the nearly dozen wheels of the truck dug in behind the powerful diesel engine which pulled the car up the dirt ramp like a boat being pulled from the water.

Semineaux could not believe his good luck. "Goddam ... The Confederacy should have won." "We did," without a smile on his weather-beaten face, deep lines and scars with traces.

Semineaux had long been out of orange grove country and well into cattle country so "partner's" truck was the heavy duty type needed for transporting live cattle, and fortunate for him "partner" was a kind hearted tough guy, a particular type which is only bred in the south, rural south that is; and "partner" pulled the huge heap of a car ten miles down the road to a Gulf station a quarter mile into the back country. That is called Southern hospitality. He would never forget "partner."

The station was in the "middle of nowhere" as they say, but he was so lucky, for he only had the Gulf credit card and a ten-dollar bill, nothing else. The car didn't look too good, but it could have looked worse considering it flipped over three times.

The roof was crushed slightly, resembling a saucer filled with mud. The driver's side was smashed inward. But the worse part was the trunk, which was not only crushed, but covered with inches of riverbed mud.

"If the owner could see this car not ... Oh Christ... what a thought ... with that name, he could be Mafia. Shit, I fought the Air Force, the Treasury Department, the IRS, the FBI, the CIA, the KGB, the ... but no, never the Mafia. Dam, just what I like about Italians ... you don't fuck with them. They have respect, and they won't fuck you, but if... Shit, I'll have everyone against me."

"Yuall got problems?" said an attendant he hadn't seen. Initially startled. "It's so bad, my problems are pregnant."

Immediately the attendant was howling and laughing ... and the both of them just stood and laughed. Sean immediately liked this guy, who looked like the old Fats Domino, a big black dude with a loving smile, a huge pair of hands, and movement, constant movement, as his big belly rolled around.

"Looks lock yuall' coming' out of a war sum plaace."

"No, just out for a little evening ride in the auto ... Chap ... the war is up the road.

Again, they just stood like too dumbos. laughing. "What's your name brother?"

"Horace-is my name," "Glad to meet you Horace. You have a tire I can buy with a Gulf credit card?"

"We ain't got no tarer to fit dis car. I'll got godown the roar. Be back, you looke out for station."

Within seconds Horace was walking out of the lighted area of the gas station which seemed surrounded by woods, for it was truly cracker country this far north, and this rural. Horace said nothing about anything, simple left. He was curious about where Horace would get a tire at this time, in this area, and leaving him with the cash register, a complete stranger, and if someone comes to get gas? It was quiet, and Horace did not return for an hour.

But return he did, with one of the best tires made, still in wraps. It would cost one hundred and thirty-six dollars, he could put it on the credit card, and while Horace mounted it on the car, he scraped off some of the large pieces of mud and grass that were attached to the car, making it look less hideous. When this business was taken care of, he started to thank Horace, when Horace pointed out to him that the one smashed tail light could cause him to stopped by the police. The tail light, something he had not thought about.

"Too many policemon from here to Joogia... they'll geet yuall for shur with dat ligdht."

And this he understood, since first crossing the border between Georgia and Florida years ago, always a lot of cops on both sides, for he had not thought about how close he was to the state border. But where could he ever get a tail light now?

Hmmm ... he thought..."Horace. you have any red paint."

"No. foo what?

"To paint the tail light bulb."

No, but I got sum oorannge paint."

"Orange is fine, that's close enough."

Horace brought him a can of orange spray paint which he instantly sprayed over the broken bulb, turned on the car lights, stood back and admired the effect, then went crazy spraying the entire back end of the car with the orange paint as Horace starred in utter amazement at this madman. But he was only concerned about this night. That long drive thru Georgia, South Carolina, and into North Carolina. Now the rear of the car at least looked uniform. Horace also produced some rope he used to tie the trunk closed, for it had been damaged to the point of not being able to lock or close, "With the Goddam stuff in the trunk," mumbling to himself. He managed to tie it shut without Horace looking inside.

He said goodbye to Horace and crossing the old state road was shortly alongside I-95. The damp cold winds were howling in from the north ending any connection with the tropical climate he left in the morning, for the cold rain sometimes hit the windshield as icy hail. He could feel he was in for snow, nasty visibility and a drastic drop in the temperature. He invested six of his ten dollars in six large cups of coffee, four cans of diet coke, and some mints at a restaurant immediately adjacent to the I-95 entrance, and a short time thereafter was crossing the state border into Georgia.

It was not obvious to him at once, but immediately disconcerting when he noticed so few vehicles traveling north, everything was coming south. It was a Monday night, partially explaining the empty highway, but then it was also the beginning of the migration of "snowbirds" from the north, a constant stream of people spending all or part of the winter in South Florida. But even the north to south traffic was light on this night. Which meant that he would have to be very careful about the 55-mph speed limit, no traffic to pace with, and he was all alone for the longest time until a Greyhound bus passed him at about 85 mph. He made a vow with himself not to go over the speed limit. But, a quick calculation told him that the driver of the Greyhound must know something he didn't, perhaps he had a radar detector or something. "Otherwise... why would the bus speed?" At this pace it would not be long before the bus would be too far ahead to catch, so he gunned the big engines and quickly caught up to the tail of the bus, which he followed from a distance of about a football field thru nearly the entire state of Georgia.

He felt proud of himself, which is always a mistake. If the bus did not stop, perhaps he could follow it thru South Carolina, for it was now only twelve miles from the border. And then he froze in his seat ... flashing blue lights ... the Georgia State Police behind him, it was all over.

In that instant he lost his future. Like the time the doctor said, "the boy could live six months or sixteen years." And then, like a miracle, which didn't happen back then, the flashing lights passed him and zoomed in on the bus. He couldn't believe his luck, for he had gambled on his experience that he had never seen a Greyhound bus pulled over for speeding. The probabilities were heavily stacked on his side, for he considered this decision a winner. And this "was" the first time, and to think the cop bypassed him. What luck ... he would now be much more careful ... never speed.

When he crossed the border into South Carolina the hail, snow, and coldness intensified. But within fifteen minutes the night was clear again, and by now the snow and ice had clung to the mud and dirt scattered about the roof and trunk. All the red and yellow lights around the car were uniform and working, legal looking, as he concentrated on keeping the speed down to the 55-mph speed limit. With only four dollars left it was fortunate there were Gulf stations available when he had to fill the large gas tank. On both occasions the wind was howling, first blowing sleet and then snow. He merely passed the credit card thru a six-inch window opening. He had not stepped from the car since Florida, conveniently using the Styrofoam coffee cups to dispose of the effects of the caffeine.

The break in the weather did not last long. The thick fog came out of nowhere and he found it difficult to even maintain 55 mph since the visibility was getting worse each moment. It would take forever to drive thru this long state, he thought. He was not to see another vehicle moving north or south on the interstate thru the entire state, excepting the Trailways bus that passed him in a fog bank doing about sixty, at a time when he was cautiously navigating thru the changing visibility at 45mph tops. He never dreamed of a scenario like this, the only vehicle within the jurisdiction of how many numbers of the infamous South Carolina state police units? Alone, with this cargo ... what a nightmare. And now, what a temptation.

In that instant, Semineaux again calculated the laws of probability and decided that if he had witnessed his first Greyhound speeding violation, the Trailways being the other major carrier, would be a good gamble. And besides, he prided himself on changing his mind like a woman. The vow was broken, and he locked onto the mesmerizing and often hypnotic vision of the multicolored rear end of the bus, which soon reached speeds of 85 and 90 mph as the visibility cleared. The hours flipped by, and when the bus slowed down it surprised him to find he had just crossed the border into Virginia.

A tinge of grey in the sky indicated the entrance of the morning was near. Even this faint light changed everything. In the snow, fog, and darkness the colored lights at the rear of the bus appeared as an optical illusion within a long tunnel, like carnival lights. This had been his entire reality, as if in some hypnotic trance. The morning's realities brought other vehicles, hills, trees, and houses. It felt as a communion was broken. He felt his speed change as quickly as it took the light to destroy the hypnotic vision which carried him thru nearly the entire state of South Carolina. A half hour at reduced speeds with increasing numbers of cars bored him, and he pulled into the first roadside restaurant, well into the state of Virginia.

When he parked the car, his body felt as if it were still traveling 85mph. He sat in the stillness for a few moments looking at the mud stained hood, then into the mirror at the face he had forgotten to shave. And he thought about her, for the first time since getting on the interstate four states ago. Of her softness in early morning hours, and to just smell her, which he would like to do the rest of his life ... every morning. He fell sound asleep in a motionless spiral of dreams, waking when the parking lot filled with patrons. First consciousness, then a realization of being refreshed, as if he had slept for hours.

All night he had fought the desire to stop, if only to glance at the curves of truck stop waitresses to temper the realities and tensions of the mind. Those visions that turn men to boys and boys to fools, the art of the female body. It felt good to even think about anything lighthearted. The image of the truck-stops he passed all night remained. He bounced into the restaurant expecting laughter from waitresses being teased by truck drivers, country music, bearded men with dungarees and boots. These environments had not changed since he was a strong bodied sixteen-year-old, employed as a laborer for all types of trucking firms. All the women were always flirtatious, and all the drivers would each have their time to open up with their little acts and remarks, some immediately, some during the meal, and some when leaving the tip. It depended on their styles and personalities. There was laughter, there were dirty jokes. Some jokes embarrassed the young boy, but the waitresses always laughed.

He wondered to himself what today's feminist positions would be on this one, which may have prompted him to give a rather devilish look at a waitress passing him with a firmly rounded ass, trying to be funny with a "good morning Mama." She instantly turned his way with a disgusted gesture, and if facial expressions could speak, she was saying... "low class idiot." It was only at that moment he realized the place was filled with alert, stern eyed men and women in conservative blue, grey, and brown suits, dresses, and topcoats eating breakfast and reading the Washington Post. Most all were on their way to an eight-hour day in the nation's capital, which was now Reagan country. And with his Irish cap, unshaved face, baggy pants and puffed-up ski jacket, he did not fit with the environment.

After five snotty waitresses flew past him like he was the garbage man coming in the wrong door, he felt lucky getting two cups of coffee to go. The only fun he would have would be back in the car, to which he returned immediately, through the body piercing cold of the morning. It was still warm in the car. The radio was playing "up" hip music, he rolled himself a nice joint that would snap him out of his drowsiness more efficiently than the coffee, and without hesitation pulled out of the parking lot and onto the short access road running parallel to I-95.

Once again on the interstate, but there had been a drastic change in the traffic pattern. The morning was in full swing with four or more lanes of cars near bumper to bumper, and this far from Washington. The big old mud-covered Lincoln with the orange rear end tied down with a rope, did not blend too well in this "man in the grey flannel suit" bureaucratic conveyor belt feeding into Washington. It was at this point that he wished he had stuck to his original plan of driving in a new, large, black conservative car and dressed in his dark suit touched off with his silver rimless eyeglasses. But there was something secure about the density of the cars moving in unison, giving the illusion of being escorted, like an air show on the ground with automatic pilot equalizing the distance between them. At least it was better than being the only vehicle on the highway.

He began to relax for the first time since getting into the car in Florida. and daydreamed ... perhaps it was Washington, for the Capital had always held his passionate interest with politics. Until those three short months a long time ago when Martin Luther King was shot, Bobby Kennedy was shot, his son died, and he ended any political ambition he may have had managing a Florida political campaign to help get Senator McCarthy elected President of the United States. The Spring of 1968 was to change his life in more profound ways than he ever imagined at that time or thereafter. He so greatly admired Doctor King, who taught a lesson so needed in America into the twenty first century ... to fight every day for what is yours, but without hate in your heart.

Semineaux thought of how many people wanted him to consider running for political office, and how he had considered a career as a campaign manager. He never considered running for public office because of the abundance of skeletons in his closet. Suddenly ... something in his mind was screaming, "full alert." Something was happening even before his eyes casually glanced into the rear-view mirror. His heart stopped for about two, three, perhaps six beats. It was an image of horror with the flashing blue lights of the police car and the intense eyes of the driver, right behind him. He pulled over into the lane to his right, he must be after someone else.

The cop was following erratically close, in hot pursuit. The full impact hit him. Out of all the thousands of cars going north, it was he who was being pulled over. The screaming siren was for him, and any further transgression of respect could turn this speeding violator into a criminal. He began to pull over and cross into one more lane of traffic with the cop following as he thought again of one thing, of what Jimmy said in Miami, that if he were to get pulled over for any violation, it was "right to jail." But he remained perfectly calm, and even took another drag on the joint, and thought to himself, "when an Arab is so certain, it's wise to ponder it as possibly immutable." If this were not so real, why was he laughing. But he would block out this "right to jail," this would not be the end, he determined.

He had come too far. The eyes of the trooper behind him allowed him to forget Jimmy's eyes warning him about being stopped. He pushed all the buttons on the left armrest lowering all four windows allowing fresh air to blow everything clean and cold, and quickly flicked the burning joint out into the still cascading lanes of traffic. And surprisingly, he was calm, and his heartbeat remained slow and steady.

Those pink eyes behind him never blinked. The light of the early morning was as grey as the frost that lay everywhere, blending the grey wool uniform of the trooper into the landscape, for he became the morning itself. The trooper became the only reality, and a big one at that, for upon stepping from the police car he gave an impression of a strong defensive end with wide powerful shoulders and long thick arms. But before the trooper had taken his third step he was met at the front left fender with a cascade of words, gestures, constant motion as this short, stocky man sort of dancing ... and trying to explain why he only had four dollars in his pocket and no driver license.

After politely listening to what amounted to a manifesto, the trooper suggested they sit in the police car while the registration and papers were checked. The very second the trooper got off the phone would be the moment of truth, but for now he had a chance to look closer at the trooper which he did little of during his speech. A side view of the red hair, long muscular neck, a mouth that looked as though it could take any punch thrown at it, presented the composite of the south's finest unshakable rebel. Quiet and polite, but damn tough.

Only the two men in the car will ever know what was said between them. But within a short time, he left the police car and returned to the battered Lincoln and drove off, free. He was extremely happy but did not laugh, for Semineaux did not feel like the slick talking dude described by others who later heard the story.

For it wasn't that way, for never did he feel any power over the cop. In fact, the twenty-minute ordeal was nothing short of terror as those pink eyes scanned the tied-down trunk dozens upon dozens of times in split-second intervals, with each glance stopping Sean's heartbeat. Farouk's warning had flashed across his mind, with fears of never returning to the fast-moving traffic, and here he was driving again, heading north.

It was very heaven to be driving again, and he felt safe in the midst of all those lanes of cars on the morning belt traffic around the Capital.

The sun was now up and bright, and the heavy traffic never thinned out much during the next several hours when the major concern was not police but just keeping awake for, he had now been on the road more than twenty-four hours. He had ruminated over being this far north ever since he first woke the previous morning, and the uneventful last several hours had taken him only miles from crossing the Delaware river into New Jersey, the last leg of the journey into New York. He felt the dangers were behind him as he pulled off to gas-up, take an eight-minute meditation, get more caffeine into his system, and get a little organized.

He was beginning to feel good and strong, and even felt a little glow of success emerging in his heart when easing the vehicle back into the steady movement of traffic moving quickly toward the Great Delaware Bridge. A magnificent bridge whose arc is so high the largest ships ever built can pass beneath them, such as U.S. aircraft carriers on their way into the Philadelphia navy yard for repairs, a hundred miles upriver from the Atlantic Ocean.

It was exhilarating climbing toward the bridge's main towers nearly two hundred feet over the river with the bright sunshine crystalizing the flashing reflections of blue sky and white puffed clouds into a prism like vision that would remain in his mind for the rest of his life. He felt like an invincible warrior piloting a space craft high above the slowly moving oil tankers so far below and in the distance they appeared like little toys in the river Delaware, provoking daydreams of a little wooden sailboat he used to sail in his pool years ago, before his son's cancer beaten body was too fragile to carry to the outdoor swimming pool; he would lay his little body on foam cushions at pool's edge, and push the little wooden sailboat from end to end and side to side, making so many silly sounds attempting to emulate the whispers and howling of the sea.

Sometimes the little game brought forth a painful smile on his son's little face, and once in desperation to make him happy he walked into the pool completely clothed in a three-piece suit and tie, grabbed the boat and blew water boat sounds with only his head out of the water, probably the last time in his short little life that he ever laughed. The tears streaming down his cheeks snapped his daydreaming into consciousness again.

"What the fuck am I crying about, goddam ... I just felt so fucking happy. Everything is going to be ok ... Shit ... I'll save my home ... his room ... will be where I write the books. I'll pay off the ex-wife, buy my daughters each a car ... yea, I'll just go and give my Dad about five grand cash," the thought of which made him laugh and happy. The water far beneath looked so beautiful with the thin white steam reaching to the red tanker ship heading to sea.

"That's it. I'll use my merchant seamen's papers and sail for a while ... After all this shit is over, I'll travel the world again. Find me a new woman. One that doesn't always cry all the time about how much she deserves from the world.

What the hell could I expect ... I love a woman who was abandoned and abused as a child. English mother dies from pneumonia and leaves twin girls who go to orphanage, then on to an abusive step-mother. Real mommy was probably run down from a little clandestine debauchery with American troops during WWII when "daddy" was away with the British air force. Always had the feeling from those pictures, had that same beautiful but naughty look as Ashley. But, very sophisticated ... polished ... upper class English broad." driving himself into laughter, "And I expect love from her, shit ... all my damn psychiatric training and education. She doesn't love herself; how could she love me. Goddam ... a man can't love a woman into love. Has any man in the world ever been told by more women than me that I was the greatest lover they ever had ... and what the fuck difference does it make. It must be more spiritual connection than physical to make it work that way ... Christ, it should be love. But it cannot heal the inside self-hatred of a beautiful woman's mind. Love does not conquer all."

The wind and fresh air at the top of the bridge freed his heart and mind from the painful concentration of the last twenty-four hours. He began to laugh as he caught the last glimpse of the long red tanker sailing toward the sea.

He attempted to visually capture that scene far beneath him of the ship with its tail of streaming white water as it headed out to sea, by quickly turning his head and taking glimpses as he came off the last span of the bridge, to ensure a memory of that image, a moment to recapture when all this was over and all was peaceful and secure.

Then the view changed to concrete before him and trees in the distance, but as he turned to again concentrate on the road something startling occurred. Two eyes ... a police hat ... a police car ... parked alongside a small side patch of pavement at the base of the bridge, and he turned his head twice, as quickly as he had in looking at the ship.

He felt the cop looking right into his eyes in that split second, he looked the second time. He was now in the middle of about four lanes of traffic. "Why the fuck is he looking at me, there are cars all around me."

Within seconds he viewed the signs designating north bound New York and points south. Perhaps the cop he could now see speeding into the traffic would pull off onto the south bound traffic. But he didn't. The lights again, the blue lights, and they were immediately behind him. Why? He had maintained even a slower speed than the lead cars coming off the bridge.

Why was he following him? To his right Semineaux viewed a small sign reading "Welcome to New Jersey," which meant absolutely nothing in these terrifying seconds as he now became fully aware, recognizing that it was he that was being pulled over.

At this point Semineaux somehow felt invincible, and was not the least bit nervous, nor was the heart pounding. Within a few moments the officer was next to his window asking the routine questions which Semineaux expected to deal with successfully, and in a short time be on his way to New York. He was surprised when the police officer asked him to step out of the car before even asking for a driver's license.

Something was wrong. Semineaux spoke, but much different than Virginia, and the explanations seemed to confuse, or perhaps disturb the officer. Semineaux looked deep into the young cop's dark eyes. A well-built man about three inches taller than himself who looked like one of those college students who work as summer cops in resort towns. But this guy was real, a New Jersey State Trooper, and he had known of their reputations for being hard asses since boyhood days when Philadelphia guys used to cross thru New Jersey in reaching the ocean or New York City. They never let you go.

What he did not know at that moment was that this area was

known as the notorious "cocaine alley" thru which drugs smuggled from Miami to New York were often interdicted by state troopers trained to spot profile types such as Latin couples with Florida tags. Millions of dollars' worth of drugs a year came over this bridge and more drug busts took place here than any other place in the entire country.

All the drug bust stories he had heard of, and somehow, never was anything said about the Great Delaware Bridge. If he had not been driving a car with Florida tags, if he had been wearing a suit and tie instead of the thuggish looking outfit with the Irish cap and ski jacket, if he had been wearing his reading glasses instead of the sunglasses, if the car was clean looking ... if ... if... Fortunately, the cop had not looked in the back seat with the overflow bagged-up pounds of the stuff, but he informed him that he wanted to look in the trunk. So here they were, the two of them talking softly beside the police car, the sun no longer shining, a chilly wind coming off the river, and the officer's mind was well beyond questioning anything about a driver's license, or any other routine things he would ask some accountant on his way to work. He wanted to look in the trunk. "Sir, you have two options. You can sign a form giving me permission to open your trunk. Or, you have the right to refuse, and then I will have to call a special team who will come and forcible open the trunk. Either way Sir, we will open your trunk."

Sean could not believe what he was hearing. He shook as a chill ran thru his body, his teeth began to chatter, and a stronger wind was making it difficult to even hear clearly, which was why he was standing so close to the officer. And he now looked into those eyes that could have been one of hundreds of nice young men he taught over the years.

"Sir, couldn't you kindly just let me go on my way. I didn't do anything wrong. I wasn't even speeding." Which was in fact the case.

"You were speeding Sir, that is why I stopped you." Which later Semineaux knew for sure was a lie.

"Sir, I won't speed again ... I promise Sir. Please, just let me go on my way, Sir."

By now he was mesmerized by the officer's eyes as he tried to read them like a riverboat gambler, and it was at this very split second that life could have changed in dangerously unpredictable ways. He was so close to cop. He knew all was lost, and they both seemed frozen in the chill of the wind's furry as he felt this deep, strong urge to drill the young officer between the eyes with the protruding middle finger joint like a steel chisel into his skull, a blow which could erase all sight, memory, and consciousness. "Only once before, in a strange foreign land, had he used this technique, learned from a Chinese martial arts expert specializing in killing rather than sport. It was just the two of them on this now isolated road ... he glanced about for a split second... no other cars ... "Take out this fucking cop... everything... my home, Michael's room ... my daughter ... God, now??? Like a king cobra ... strike ... on one will see it ... take the fucker out ... out..." Semineaux could have taken him out. He may have gotten away.

If unsuccessful, would probably still been in jail, if not dead. He would think of that second, and the choice made, for a long time. But his better sense prevailed. The professor won out over the savage beast. The moment he decided not to strike, the adrenalin in his bloodstream disappeared as fast as air from a punctured balloon. It was over.

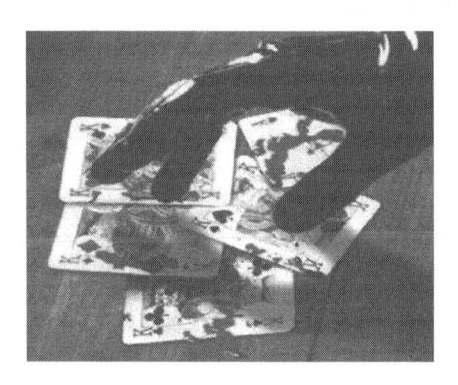

Chapter 8

The drug bust

The tree had fallen in the forest and no one else in the entire world heard it ... except him, and he felt so alone as he watched, first one. then two... three other State police cars swoop into the area.

First, they found the small bag with the ten to fifteen pounds of ganja on the floor of the back seat. and it seemed so unreal to be sitting alone in the police car watching four cops open the trunk. Then, the discovery, as if he were watching this story on television. without sound, for the air tight police car isolated him from the wind and the noise of the moment.

"Look at those fuckers ... must be so happy ... they caught someone. Fuck, this goddamn car is running... I ought to jump behind that wheel and escape these bastards ... God no ... I'd get fucking shot to death like Bonnie and Clyde. You've had it Jack. The fucking shit is going to hit the fan. Goddam Doctor, there goes your fucking freedom.

The worse part of the ride to the State Police barracks was the pain caused when the J. Edgar Hoover looking cop put the handcuffs so tightly around his wrists, for every time the cop car made a sharp turn the cuffs would tighten like a steel octopus causing his hands to go completely numb.

Once inside the beach house looking barracks, he was interrogated by four cops for an hour, but stuck to his story of having no idea what was in the car. Semineaux argued he was only delivering the car, he had the papers to prove it, and pleaded with them to let him go, that he was completely innocent. He was so persuasive that one of the cops thought his story might be feasible. Sean's main thought throughout the interrogation was observing the role like behaviors of the cops who watched too much television.

But aspects of the interrogation caused a little bewilderment with all the cops on duty at the time.

Here he was a suspected drug smuggler who lived in Florida and was on his way to New York City, now sitting in the midst of all these State cops in a little unknown hick town in South Jersey, a stranger refusing to even reveal his real name, he did not even own a wallet, or possess any identification, and he knew they would never have enough sense to identify him with the author of the book on Chinese politics of which he was carrying fifteen copies. To his surprise, he was getting to like these guys who were trying to intimidate him, for they reminded him of friends he knew. But they were shocked when he asked if they knew Bobby Marino. Their eyes widened and they were speechless. For even unknown to Semineaux at the time Bobby Marino was sort of a folk hero to these guys.

Suddenly there were five more cops in the room within a few minutes of his mentioning Bobby Marino, and the questioning changed completely, from the hundred ways he must have known the stuff was in the car to a much more intense level of inquiry, in an even more serious vain which he could not quite comprehend, even with anticipating their surprise at his knowing one of their fellow officers who had been killed in the line of duty. What he did not know at that moment, was that they had never apprehended the person who killed this officer Bobby Marino.

At this point Sean seriously questioned the desperate tactic of mentioning Bobby's name. Now at least five different cops were asking him cross firing questions, and it became obvious to him that he had opened a Pandora's box. If he were not careful it could possibly backfire into something mad, like being a suspect in this unsolved murder of a state cop, and a damn good one. Semineaux had known the slain officer over twenty years before when they both worked at the "Wildwood" summer resort town along the South Jersey coast where tough young men from Pittsburgh and Philadelphia worked summers as lifeguards, bartenders, and bouncers. He got to know Bobby pretty well since they had a powerful historical bond from having played football at the same famous catholic high school in West

Philadelphia, but Bobby played during the four years Sean was serving in the military, and they didn't meet until this shared summer experience.

After a few minutes he realized what they were trying to get at in their questioning, for unknown to Sean Bobby had been run over by a hit-and-run driver while giving a ticket on the New Jersey Turnpike. The driver of the car would not have any idea of the slain officer's identity.

Semineaux began to get a little nervous when all of a sudden, the questioning stopped, and he was led into the next room where his arms were placed behind him as he was handcuffed to a small iron bar, forcing him to stand, for the small iron bar was only waist high. Semineaux was unaware that an officer who was one of Bobby's many friends on the force had been called from off-duty to participate in this new interrogation, for they had never closed the file on who killed Bobby.

My mind ... my mind ... I got to keep it together, no matter what the fuck they do to me. I got to hang tough."

What he was concerned about was if his being chained to the wall was linked to their new suspicions of him as one who may know something about the unsolved murder of his old friend the cop, or was this chained to the wall treatment routine for drug smugglers.

He thought about those old movie scenes from his youth when the king's prisoners were chained to walls in the basement of the castle until they came to unchain him for a new round of interrogations. Now, there was an extra cop in the room and after each of the others asked question after question about his past knowledge of the slain officer, the new one stood squarely in front of him, looked him directly in the eye, and with a tone loaded with strains of confrontational psychology, asked "They tell me I look like I could be Bobby's brother. Do Bobby and I look alike?"

"Holy shit," Sean thought to himself, "this guy looks pissed." When I mentioned Bobby's name, I'd hoped it would help me, maybe even let me go. What is this guy trying to do?

"Do I look like Bobby?" His eyes now bulged.

If I tell this ball-headed fat ugly bastard that he only looked like Bobby when Bobby would pull down his pants, bent over, and mooned the young college girls at the beach parties, except the hair would be horizontal like his shitty-looking mustache.

But he knew diplomacy would get him more than honesty,

for Bobby had been the 1950's version of the blond Adonis, with bulging muscles, big white teethed smile, and a cockiness well earned on the West Philadelphia streets of his youth. He was handsome and charming, and this guy was ugly and nasty.

"Well, you look something like Bobby. You got good shoulders, but you know how powerful he was. I mean ... You stand like him ... cocky... but he was at least three inches taller." as tie took note of the St. Francis of Assisi hairstyle with the ring of remaining hair wrapped around his head like a sweat band, "And your hair ... same color... same color-blond hair."

With that the interrogator smiled, and looked pleased. as Sean thought..." Bobby was tough ... this pussy must have just admired him ... he wouldn't have hung out with such a wimp."

He sensed that his answers to Bobby's description satisfied the interrogators. No longer thinking he may know something about the hit-and-run, perhaps they would also believe he knew something about the stuff in the car he was contracted to drive to New York. Now that he had established his credibility as one of Bobby's old friends, perhaps they would release him?

No such luck, and again he was chained to the wall. But to his amusement, he now became a sort of celebrity. The same cops who just interrogated him, all somehow managed to pass through the room in which he was chained to the wall, but each of their personalities changed drastically, "from motherfucking inquisitors to friends," he laughed to himself. Instead of the serious cop face, they smiled. They said or asked nothing about Bobby, and all asked the same question in a variety of ways but it all came out to "How the hell did you get away from that State cop in Virginia?" And they all said, they themselves would not have been able to do that. And with each interview he conducted, he told them what to him was the simple truth...

"The cop could intuitively tell he was no criminal." And with each telling, the Virginia cop became more and more perceptive of just what a fine and decent guy was this old buddy of Bobby's. It was only a small stationhouse, and the cops could have walked around this little room as they had during his first two hours on the wall which at that time, he shared with a short Cuban man they had caught with a car load of cocaine. But each of them seemed to cut through often, smiling, always mumbling something about Virginia, and even laughing, like they somehow admired him, in this locker-room buddy communication. Sean was just beginning to feel that perhaps, maybe ... they would let him go, when two nasty looking punk types walked past him, and disdainfully glanced his way.

It wasn't long before he realized that the two new guys were some kind of special narcotics detectives called in to deal with this suspect who claimed to know nothing about the contraband he was charged with smuggling. He was released, but now in their custody. Maybe they would be taking him to public transportation in order to release him?

But their mood did not seem in a releasable mode, he soon discovered after the first five minutes in the backseat of their squad car with the wisecracking attitude of their remarks concerning his denials, with the new reality imprinted into his wrists by handcuffs so tight that his hands dangled like dead flesh behind his back as he flipped, flopped, and bounced helplessly as they raced across the darkened, snow-pocketed South Jersey flatlands like rednecks showing off their suped-up cars.

Chapter 9

The lie detector

By the time he was taken from the State Police barracks he felt a compulsion to say goodbye, for he had actually gotten to like them and never really felt threatened. They were gentleman. These two were pigs. Every society has them. Their personality types are ubiquitous in every corner of the globe. Men who are basically bullies, and if Semineaux ever hated any types, it was bullies. He had encountered bullies as a youth in Philadelphia; had seen them in China, Spain, former East Germany, even peaceful New Zealand. No matter what authority they represent, they love to beat on people. All degrees of sadism, which in ninety-nine percent of them stems from having been beaten as children, thus the rage and hatred. And in the deepest recesses of their hearts they are cowards, this he also knew from a lifelong experience of standing up to them, and fighting them when necessary.

"There should be a motherfucking International Law against child abuse and there wouldn't be creeps like you." Semineaux said matter of factly.

"What did he say?"

"Shut up back there."

At this point the driver pulled over to the side of the road, turned out the lights of the car, jumped out, and opened the back door against which Sean was leaning.

"What's going on back there?"

"Nothing, Sir."

It was a little stunt to unnerve him, for unbeknownst to Semineaux, the destination was the office of a "lie detector specialist." They were just trying to shake up a little fear that lies within most people's mind when they are held hostage. This would make it easier to get the "truth" out of him.

Sean was confused when they arrived at this very vacant municipal type office building and were met by this pudgy little guy with the Woolworth & Company tie and white shirt, a wedding ring, a plastic belt, and a nasty looking mouth. "If I ever saw a pussy-whipped man in my life, this is it," he thought to himself.

There were only three rooms with lights in entire building, and Semineaux was led into the smallest one where he sat for what seemed an inordinately long time. He still had no idea what was going to happen, or why they were there, and he nearly wished he were chained back to that wall rather than the terrible feeling of confinement in this small panel lined room, with the old ribbonless typewriter sitting on the desk in front of him. He starred at the typewriter and thought, "No matter what happens... remember ... you are a writer. A published author. You are a Ph.D. You are a poet. This is how you have defined yourself in this world. Not a fucking power on earth can take that away. I love what I have become. Fuck them. Whatever they throw at me during this catastrophe, I can take, for I have had more Goddam fun and adventures than any creeps like this could dream about.

Then he found himself banging away on the keys of the big old typewriter on the desk in front of him. The keys flew about as fast as one can type, as he felt a spark of glee for the first time since the bridge.

BANG ... The door behind Semineaux flew open and the taller of the three men was shouting, "Get you fucking hands off that thing ... Do you want the cuffs back on? This time, I guarantee you won't type with those fucking hands for a while when I get done."

"Sorry, Sir ... I won't touch it again."

Someone called from the other room into which Sean was taken. There sat the little machine he recognized immediately as the lie detector devise, as he laughed to himself, "I can beat these fucking machines on my worst day. These Assholes"

"Have you ever had a lie detector test before?"

"No sir, never..." he lied. And he knew exactly what they would do before they did it.

The administrator of the test explained to him in very soft and kind terms what the test was about, and emphasized that "I will even tell you beforehand what questions I am going to ask you. There is no secret to this procedure, and we put these little pads on your head, neck, and arms and wrap a belt around your chest. There is no pain or shock in this. These machines have never hurt anyone. Do you understand what I am saying?"

"Yes Sir, I do."

"These are the exact questions I am going to ask you. Let's practice. You give no answers at this time. Just listen to the questions.

What is your legal name? Where were you born? Where do you now live? Have you ever had a speeding ticket? Have you ever been married? Did you get in much trouble as a child? Why were you going to New York? Have you ever been arrested, for anything? What kind of work do you do? Have you ever smoked marihuana? Have you ever sold Marihuana? Have you ever been arrested for drugs? How old are you? How much do you weigh? Where were you taking the marihuana? Are you delivering this for someone? Who are the other people in this operation? Would you like to sign a confession?"

Now, should I repeat the questions? Do you understand?"

"Yes Sir."

"I'll go over them again if you like. No trick questions, very simple."

"No Sir, I understand."

"What dumb assholes ... all three of them, so smug and righteous."

The inquisitors had no idea of Semineaux's experiences dating back twenty years to his training in military intelligence as a cryptography, carrying the highest security clearance, for he often decoded and recoded messages to the President of the United States regarding those most vital secrets of the nation's existence.

There were times when only he, a few key spies, and the President of the United States, were aware of key information. The information the young Semineaux carried in his head was perhaps as important as the little black briefcase that is always within reach of the President, the codes to activate America's nuclear forces.

To protect this information in the event a cryptographic code center was overrun by Chinese or Russians the officer in charge was ordered to shoot all personnel in the code center, top secret bunkers with lead doors, vault thick walls, and piped in air. Often, when bored, a young Sean would detach one of the many automatic weapons placed around the premises and demonstrate to his fellow cryptographers how he and the Captain would shoot it out when the Russians came, for it was ok to die at the hands of the Russians, but never your own officers.

They were also trained for the possibility of being taken prisoner, and how to counter the psychological brainwashing techniques used by the Chinese and Russians, mind control techniques that he used ever since. Sean was bored with school most of his life, even up thru his college years, but when he decided to get a Ph.D. at twenty-five, this mind control training proved invaluable.

As the lie detector specialist walked toward him, he thought of how much he resembled a sized down dirty blond-haired version of the fat one of the Laurel and Hardy classic comic team. He knew this was the key to the rest of the session when the nice person behind the machine would begin to change the person's perception of himself and his environment. The voice would be slightly, almost undetectably changed, giving it more authority.

The administrator of the test would no longer be facing you, but would first stand behind you announcing that he was about to put a strap around your chest and back. Unnerving, for now you are being touched, and to have this strap wrapped around your body and tightened enough you can feel your heart beating inside your chest, as small electrode pads are glued to pulsation points on various parts of your body such as wrists and neck. If one is not prepared for this or experienced interrogation, it can be terrorizing.

At this point, the reality of how you see yourself, will change your perception of yourself and leave one completely vulnerable. You are more alone than in birth and death. And here come the same questions, but you are now a different person and are not even aware of it. Most feel under the control of some electronic monster or brain control mechanism administered by the enemy ... whomever may be interrogating.

The interrogator began with same questions he asked a few minutes earlier, and so it went. Semineaux still refused to give his real name. "Have you ever had a speeding ticket?"

"Yes Sir."

"Have you ever been married?"

"Yes Sir."
"Did you get in much trouble as a child?"
"No Sir."
"Why were you going to New York?"
"Just to see some friends."
"Have you ever been arrested for anything?"
"No Sir."
"What kind of work do you do?"
"Construction worker sir."
"Have you ever smoked marihuana?"
"Yes sir."
"How often, frequently?"
"No sir, only twice in my life. Once in the service and once in college. In fact, I hate the shit ... makes assholes out of people ... I like to drink, you know..."
"That's enough."
"Plus, I have asthma, and smoke would kill me..."
"I said, enough,"
"Sorry Sir."
"Have you ever sold marihuana?"
"Of course not, Sir. I lived in Miami for a long time and saw firsthand what drugs do to people, and I hate the shit, and I have had friends..."
"Enough..."
"You'd better not fuck with him," one of the cops shouted as he jumped to his feet.
"Sorry sir."
"Have you ever been arrested for drugs."
"Of course not," again and again no, no, no. The procedure was repeated three times and afterwards he was taken back to the room with the typewriter to sit for the time it took for the evaluation, which he knew, he won. "This time you won't touch the fucking typewriter," as his arms were handcuffed behind his back, but not quite as tight as earlier. He sat in amusement until they escorted him back where he was placed standing in front of the desk behind which sat the pudgy one with the machine while the cops each sat on either side of Semineaux, barely visible in his peripheral vision. Nothing was said, for a long time.
"Do you wish to sign a confession?"
"Pardon me sir?"
It went on like that for about five minutes, with two cops sometimes standing up in obviously angry outbursts about how

the test proved his guilt. He was caught, they argued.

"You have failed the test. Unless you cooperate, you'll go to jail for a long time."

Sir, may I ask a question?

"Shut up."

"No, let him, go ahead."

"Sir, how long did you go to school to learn to operate as a professional evaluator?"

"An intensive two-week course, and a follow up of hundreds of hours in an internship period."

"Sir, if you may, sir," Sean speaking quickly, "Psychiatrists are medical doctors who then spend three to four years studying the human mind and behavior. And after all that, they can't tell you shit about what a person thinks unless the person tells them. In two weeks, sir? And then you can read my mind. No sir, your inadequate education and this little machine cannot discover the truth. You are wrong in your assessment, and you know it. I have tried to never lie in my entire life. My mother raised me differently. To lie, would be to disgrace her, my mother. I am probably one of the most honest persons you have ever known ... and..."

"Shut up you bastard."

By now they were pissed, but also confused, and he could detect friction among them, and laughed so hard to himself when they hustled him out of the building and pushed him back into the rear of the police car, banging his head quite hard against the car roof from the rough treatment of these thugs with badges.

Chapter 10
The lock-up

It was now five in the morning and a damp clay cold rolled over frozen New Jersey flatlands like Fall's death and Winter's presence.

Again, they put the handcuffs on too tight, which was all that kept Semineaux from falling asleep as he wondered where they were taking him, and continued to hope they may let him go, a dream that evaporated when the car lights hit the old brick wall with steel bars on the windows that could be none other than a prison. He was so numb by this time he simple starred at the large medal door with the small light above it, like a backstage theater entrance, except on the other side of this door there would be no long-legged ballet ladies.

One of the cops pushed him up the steps nearly tripping him off balance for his arms were still handcuffed behind him. He now feared how they would treat him once inside the prison. His face was but inches from the large metal door as the two goons behind him rang the bell for the second time, one cussing about the delay when finally a small trap door about half way up opened to identify who was ringing the bell, thru which Sean could see two eyes staring at him, and finally the big door opened.

The man in the doorway was a huge black mass obstructing the view of anything behind him, for his uniform was as black as his skin, and the blackness was punctuated by only a silver badge, white eyes, and white teeth. Semineaux stood only about chest high to this man whose shoulders were as wide as the door and arms larger than most men's legs.

Perhaps it was madness, perhaps just a goofy sense of humor

which could have caused him trouble, or maybe the tension was getting to him, but Semineaux took a chance and spoke directly to the prison guard as the two goons were pressed behind him.

"Brother, did you ever do pushups?"

The two goons behind him were livid, downright pissed off. The huge black dude smiled, and looked Semineaux right in the eyes. Sean felt immediately this was not only a powerhouse of a physical man, but inside his heart was wrapped in security, and was kind and not mean. A man who most likely had a loving mother, not like the two assholes behind him.

"We have a prisoner for you."

"I can see," he said with a tone Sean desperately tried to read for there seemed to be some undertones of tension here, its source he could not figure out, and by now all three were inside the entrance by one step.

"First, take the cuffs off him."

"First, you book him."

Now his eyes changed, and Sean thanked God they were not staring at him as he repeated himself, "I said take the cuffs off him ... you are in my prison, my jurisdiction, you do as I say here. Now take the cuffs off the prisoner, and you can stay, or leave ... cause we don't really need you now."

Semineaux loved it. He could not believe what he was hearing, but being sandwiched between the three of them he could nearly hear the shrinking of the four testicles between the legs of the goons behind him, for the prison cop probably knew instinctively they were racist, and dealt with them appropriately.

The handcuffs came off, the goons left, and he quickly became very respectful of this gentleman in charge of him. Prison was his greatest fear in life, but now he was not afraid. As he sat, his mind again slipped back to his military experience. During four years of military service he had managed to get court-martialed four times, which may be some kind of record; and had seen the inside of a "solitary confinement" cell on more than one occasion. Back then he had vowed this would never happen again. After military service, education and respectability became important goals. He studied, married a girl from a "proper" family private country club homes at the seashore, and the rest of "it." Nothing had ever been important enough, that could get him to where he was now. He wanted to wake up from a dream and be relieved to be awake.

The black guard seated him at a small table and another

officer with paperwork in hand joined him. He knew he was lucky on this first contact in the prison and very cautiously reacted to the questions asked by this new guard, whom he could not read at all, but feared the worst. He knew he could remain silent. A power that was constitutionally his, demanding to see a lawyer before answering any questions.

"I want you to know that the questions I ask you do not have to be answered until you have a lawyer. But I am only asking simple questions that would have affect upon your case, for this is strictly an administrative procedure. You are in prison; you are a prisoner. We have to put you in a cell, but first we have to know your legal name, place of birth, social security number...you know, basic things about yourself...oh yeah, I see they think you gave them a phony name."

As the guard spoke, he tried to size him up and the only experience he had with the personality composite sitting before him were decades ago. Those lean tall blond teenage South Jersey redneck country boys he used to compete with high diving out of trees and underwater endurance races in coffee black streams that once ran through a South Jersey of earlier times that had more tomatoes than people, and was but a short ride from the summer heat of urban Philadelphia on the other side of the Delaware River.

But the prison was far south of this area adjacent to Philadelphia and retained those aspects of the rural culture of South Jersey he admired and learned through his cousin Joe, whom he deeply loved but had not seen in twenty years and probably would not for the rest of his life. Semineaux knew they could be pretty nasty with fast talking city boys, so he tried to be polite. But immediately, there arose some friction that he did not anticipate, for he had decided it would be in his best interest at this time to give his real name that he had been withholding but the guard remained suspicious since he carried no identification papers.

He was being so awfully careful with this guy, for he was afraid he may turn on him, but nevertheless, with tension and no sleep taking its toll, he lost control. "I'll let this dumb redneck know who the fuck I am," as he reached into his bag and fumbled through the books until he got to the stack of the beautiful white paperbacks with the red lettering, and his name printed on the front. He felt proud as he slapped the book onto the table, with "This, sir, is who I am . . . see . . . Semineaux. Sean Semineaux," while thinking to himself "Fuck you Jack, you're not going to take my dignity away."

Strange how pride is a foolish weakness in any human contact. The proud man slapping the book onto the desk was an asshole as all before him, since Plato first warned about the problem of pride centuries ago. Sean completely misread how the guard would react, as the guard slowly picked up the book, carefully studied its cover, let a few moments of silence pass as he fingered through the book, laid it down, turned his head, looked Semineaux in the eye and said "My wife is a librarian at the local library. She loves books" in a most respectful and shy manner.

Semineaux was shocked and embarrassed at himself for his behavior, for he had never expected the first two prison guards would turn out to be two men he will always love for treating him so kindly.

Chapter 11

Prison

He could not remember the last time he ate any food and failed to associated the pain in his stomach and the chill in his body with this abstinence, until the black guard, with a voice one would expect coming from some gentle Tibetan monk rather than this man whose body looked strong enough to stop a tank, asked,

"Pardon me, have you had anything to eat," a short minute or so after Semineaux had revealed his real name.

Semineaux nodded, the guard returned shortly with a plate of food he had not seen the likes of since his military days in the Arctic, but was humbly appreciative of this guy's sensitivity. The strange looking meat, lumpy pile of what most likely were potatoes, the grayish vegetables, the odor of which indicated they must have been leftovers from the evening meal at the prison, hopefully that night's, tasted as good as if they came from a five-star restaurant.

It took longer than normal for the completion of the forms for the white guard spoke of how much his wife loved to read, at which point Sean suggested his taking the book sitting between them home to his wife, offering to sign it, bringing a smile to the guard's face who expressed how much his wife would enjoy reading it.

He felt thankful at being treated so respectfully, and soon thereafter overheard a muted conversation between both guards concerning the cell in which they would assign him. They were concerned that the crowded cellblock conditions within the prison would be horrible for him and appeared vexed in finding a solution.

They actually contacted the inhabitants of what was considered the most desirable cell in the prison, but there appeared to be no room in this small cellblock that they were referring to as "The Penthouse." Semineaux was sitting alone, for both guards were taking turns talking on the phone at the central switchboard that controlled the communications network within the prison. In spite of having his back to the two guards he could faintly hear the conversation as the both of them took turns trying to persuade the inmates of this "Penthouse" cell to accept another person into their cell block.

He felt a strong surge of emotion swell up in his heart, for he could hear patches of arguments establishing the reasons why they should and could make room for this new prisoner, "whom they would like and find interesting," in their words.

It appeared they were unable to persuade them with confidences of his apparent character and background, and some deal was arrived at whereby the guards had to agree to something they resisted, the details of which Semineaux was never to discover.

It felt good that the handcuffs were off and he was following the guard thru the corridors onto the elevator with that ubiquitous high gloss, light green oil-based paint he'd seen at various times of his life in military prisons, FBI, CIA, KGB, Immigration, and Passport offices round the globe. He was in such a good mood he broke the silence with the guard now operating the elevator,

"Humpty Dumpty sat on the wall, Humpty Dumpty had a great fall, and how long will Humpty Dumpty be on his ass?"

"Pretty good brother."

"Wish I could sing," and then the elevator door opened on the second-floor ward, for the elevators automatically opened on every floor. The atmosphere on the wards were truly horrible conditions that were packed with men, cigarette smoke, a thousand radios and TVs all blaring at the same time, smells of sweat, and obnoxious odors coming from lavatories originally designed for ten prisoners, presently accommodating one hundred and fifty. He was relieved when the doors closed and up they went.

"You are a lucky Dude man, everybody in the joint would like to stay in the Penthouse. The first noise he heard stepping onto the corridor floor were female voices laughing, giggling, and talking since a few yards to the left of the elevator was the entrance to the woman's cellblocks; but unfortunately, or perhaps fortunately, depending on one's experience with females, he was led down to the end of the right corridor to the "Penthouse," to be introduced to his three hosts.

Three men who had given their approval, whom he would regard with respect and caution. The small cellblock was the only men's cellblock on the top floor set at one corner of the building giving the cell two windows, one facing West and one facing South.

The cellblock sat at the end of a short corridor and he was surprised when the jailer opened the large medal door for, there were actually three cells within this cell. It was truly a maximum security unit since there were three prisoners each sitting in a separate cell with thick jail bar doors, now opened, and a narrow corridor not much longer than fifteen feet which ran from the entrance of the main solid steel door with the small peephole that had just been unlocked by the guard.

The three prisoners came out of their separate cells as soon as the guard closed the solid steel door behind him and each put out their hand and introduced themselves. Paul, a young black man was in the first cell to the left. Magic, a thirty-year-old black man of Jamaican ancestry was in the second cell. Jamon, a Columbian citizen was in the last cell against the far wall. There was a cell with two separate toilets and a single sink with no mirror.

Magic was serving a ten-year sentence for bank robbery, and Jamon, a Columbian citizen, was serving life for cocaine trade and murder. Paul was serving five years for armed robbery. After polite introductions the three returned to their cells leaving Semineaux alone on the portable cot in the middle of the small corridor. At first Sean was slightly apprehensive for he felt vulnerable in the middle of the corridor.

The prison authorities had confiscated all his belongings, so he just sat there on the cot, wondering what would happen next. After a few moments of complete silence Magic stepped just outside his cell and handed Sean a clean sweatshirt and an old sweater. "You might like some fresh clothes," for it wasn't easy to see Semineaux was looking rather shabby, and smelled like he just came off the frontier. Next, Jamon came bouncing out of his cell with three pair of white sweat socks in his hands and a big Latin smile. Then, the tough young black kid presented Sean with two cotton short sleeve undershirts. When Semineaux

Miami 101

began to thank them they quickly backed away and told him to clean up quickly for it was about time to be called down for breakfast. Any prisoner not ready at the cellblock door missed that meal.

The prison cafeteria was plain institutional, again the pale green, and he followed his three cellmates through the line and remained quiet and observed the dozens of different patterns of communications and behaviors among the guards, prisoners, and inmates working in the kitchen and serving the food. The new guy was totally ignored and no one even made eye contact with him or spoke to him. Semineaux kept his mouth shut and felt all was going better than he had anticipated. The eggs were greasy, the grits starchy, the bread stale, but it all tasted great. Soon, they were back in their cells.

His first impression was that it was going to be a rest period, but quickly discovered they were going to the gym for this was the recreation period. In good weather they had outdoor recreation but never at this time of year. The indoor gym was rather small for such a large number of men. He was in no mood for exercise. and stepping inside the gym he immediately noticed that off to his left there appeared to be a prison library. It turned out to be a narrow room no more than seven feet wide and fifteen feet long with flimsy plywood walls and a front door resembling a screen door on a summer cottage. He was quite happy when Magic told him the library was normally an option to the gym, if one chooses it over exercise, darts, or ping-pong.

There were fewer books here than in either of his libraries in his Florida home. but he was pleasantly surprised to see Marcel Proust on the shelf. He slipped on his rimless reading glasses and quickly became lost in the nineteenth century prose about a beautiful woman that moved with the grace and eloquence of a swan, an exquisite piece of art written by Proust in a room specially designed to withstand exterior noise with its walls lined with cork for soundproofing.

This microcosm of a sanctuary rendered a momentary feeling of peace and he felt that is where he should be rather than out in the gum with the young bucks for, he had all the physical endurance tests any man needed since his sleepless departure from Miami close to forty-eight hours ago.

Proust's poetic verse simmering through the creation of images unfolding with each paragraph was nearly beginning to sooth his damaged self-image when Magic peeked his head into the room with eyes that pleaded and looked questioning, and in a most diplomatic fashion suggested that Semineaux "might consider some physical exercise."

After a brief interchange he understood that it was a plea for him to get off his ass and display some type of physical activity that could possibly justify his privileged living quarters in the most cherished cellblock in "the joint." He was later to discover each of his cellmates excelled either athletically or with pure primitive fighting abilities such as eye gouging, biting, and other fearsome techniques demanding respect in this primitive of environments.

They just wanted him to try doing something and hoped he would not embarrass them. He got the message and placed his glasses back into their case, returned the book to the shelf, and began meandering about the gym between those standing and jiving, some shadow boxing, some lifting weights. and some playing games.

He wasn't in the mood to lift weights but spotted a leather jump rope hanging on the shoulder of a sweaty guy who had jumped for about seven minutes and was trying to catch his breath. Sean politely asked if he were finished with the rope and found himself a vacant area in the middle of the floor where he started to jump and jump and jump.

The first few minutes were the most difficult for his body was cramped and tight from the ordeal but after ten minutes he was starting to sweat and to also attract some attention form the other inmates who all knew something about the physical demands of rope jumping.

Within a few more minutes he was beginning to feel cocky for he had been taught to jump years ago in the military when the boxing coach saw him punch a powerfully built six-foot four marine into unconsciousness in a bare-knuckled barroom fight, and insisted he join the base boxing team. The coach, .a black guy from Chicago, made the Philadelphia street fighter learn the art of boxing beginning with how to work a heavy bag, how to "rock the sky" with a noise that only comes from the rhythmical punching of a leather speed bag against a wooden platform, and how to make a rope sing beneath feet that dance to the songs in the mind and heart of a boxer. The young Semineaux did not really like boxing, for to him a fight meant one thing, knock the guy out with one punch, perhaps two; any more, something must be wrong. But he had always enjoyed the training, and continued it all his life.

His performance was beginning to spark a bit of pride in his heart. Then, his self-delusions were abruptly shattered when someone slapped the rope as it was flipping behind his head.

"You are in my space Dude."

He quickly spun around and looked up into the dark eyes of a young black man whose face had the telltale signs of street battles. His wide shoulders gave way to very long thick looking arms dangling alongside a ribcage and chest thicker than a man this tall and lean should have.

Semineaux reacted immediately and moved to one side never considering for a split second to do anything else, for this was not the kind of man you wanted as an enemy. He looked as if he could punch through a wall. Semineaux found a new "space" a few feet away and continued to jump as the guy and his sparring partner exchanged mock punches they were throwing at each other, breathing a sigh of relief as he jumped for not having done anything stupid, that would have bordered on suicide for this "dude" was bad.

For the next twenty minutes Semineaux found it difficult to concentrate as he jumped for, he was distracted by the snapping of the thick arms that were firing two huge fists through the air with the velocity and speed of a seasoned heavyweight fighter. It wasn't until after the two were finished that Sean was able to beat on the rope, which by this time was over a half-hour and beginning to attract some attention from men whom up till now had ignored him as if Semineaux were a piece of furniture.

One's body is a strange piece of work. As sweat dripped from his pours it also released the pent-up anguish, fears, and anger that had been strangling the vibrancy of his physical well-being. When he reached forty-five minutes he stopped for a few seconds, stripped to the waist, and continued as sweat poured down over his bare skin onto his belt saturating his pants.

He then went into a mad frenzy whipping the rope into a Zen consciousness as he flew back and forth across the floor space that had been recently vacated by the two sparring. The inmates just starred in wonder at this white man with graying hair who was pushing his body beyond limits they all somehow understood.

By the time he stopped an hour and ten minutes had elapsed, and everyone resumed their conversations, exercise, or game playing; and again, paid no attention to this new inmate. But

Semineaux was now "into it" with the adrenalin still surging through his body.

He made his way to the large heavy punching bag that had been punched and kicked during the entire exercise period which by now was vacated as it swung ever so slightly by its chain that dangled from the ceiling.

He was capable of hitting a heavy bag with the ferocity of a heavyweight fighter, but it had been at least a year and he knew his timing would be off and his power would be muffled.

The last thing he wanted to do was to discount his newly acquired image just earned with the rope. And this was an opportunity to deliver a message to all that he was a man who could defend himself against anyone attempting to violate his being in any way or fashion.

As a young high school boy he had played defensive noseguard and offensive running guard against mature upperclassmen twice his size with missing teeth and scars etched across faces that looked middle-aged, often beating young Semineaux into the ground as he learned to face fear, pain, and terror in the "blood pits" that lay within the shadows of the elevated trains running through Philadelphia. They wore helmets with no protective face masks and there was no mercy in the "blood pits," and for two years there seemed to be some plot by the upperclassmen to dislodge Semineaux of his two front teeth, for they were pretty teeth, allowing him to smile his way into a young girl's heart.

Then there came a time when the young Semineaux evolved powerful arms, eighteen inch calf muscles, a seventeen and a half inch neck set on thick shoulders and a warrior's chest, enabling him to deliver a blow with only six inches to a foot that could explode into the head or chest of a huge man with enough force to stop him dead in his tracks, or bounce his upper body into an upright position. This movement was the source of Semineaux's fabled bare knuckled fighting reputation. But he knew that at this moment he would be all too ordinary when punching the bag, but he also knew that no matter how clumsy his timing and coordination, the forearm delivery developed years ago would never let him down.

For ten long minutes he popped and slammed his forearms into that bag with enough power to break anything from heads to walls. In his mind he was hiding his atrophied skill with his fists, but all others watching knew by the clanging of the chain that strained with the weight of the bag as it snapped with every fall from the orbits of his slamming blows, that the new guy assigned to the Penthouse appeared to be earning his privileged space, somewhat. The exercise session ended and all the prisoners returned to their cells. Semineaux's cellmates said nothing about the performance, but shortly thereafter told him they could "use their influence" in retrieving any of his valuables that the prison authorities had confiscated. And it wasn't long before he had his leather briefcase with his two fountain pens and a few of his books, which he fondled like long lost friends. He knew his three cellmates were pleased.

They had secured his writing instruments for him although nothing was actually said, and left him to himself until the elevator door opened alerting all that it was already time for lunch. So far, prison life felt like a series of meals. Again, he sat with his cellmates. and somehow the atmosphere had changed for him since the breakfast meal. There was now eye contact with first one. then a few. increasing as curiosity about him seemed contagious. for Semineaux's image had sure changed since the morning.

The meal consisted of two sandwiches, plain white American cheese on the same white bread consumed at breakfast, a rice dish, and a piece of cake. It may have been the vigorous exercise but he was still hungry after eating everything.

When he indicated this to his cellmates, they motioned to the tall inmate who never seemed to sit down during the meal, who also happened to be the large black boxer, the guy who slapped his jump rope. Somehow, he got the cryptic finger language and walked over to the serving table, breaking all the rules by reaching with his exceptionally long arms over the serving trays to sandwiches stored at the rear of the counter set up to feed the lunch period for the women. He created an outcry not only from the kitchen personal but two guards who immediately swooped down on him.

Here was this big black man holding a cheese sandwich in each hand high above his head with three cooks and two security guards screaming at him. An act that could mean solitary, or perhaps even a small riot, for all the prisoners were yelling and seemed to be getting into what appeared to be the trouble of the moment.

"Put those back," a guard yelled with a loud command.

There was complete silence.

"My man's hungry."

He then placed the sandwiches in front of Semineaux without taking his intense stare from the guards now having encircled the eating area.

Wisely, one of the guards began to laugh, breaking the tension, followed by laughing and clapping by the inmates, then most of the other guards, except one whom Sean overheard say beneath his breathe, "I'll get your ass."

Just when Semineaux was thinking of this black brother he caught the not so friendly eyes of a middle aged black dude, the latter's glances reminding him he was in prison, and no one yet knew he was there.

Semineaux knew he was entitled to one phone call.

Sitting quietly on his cot an hour later, he came to the conclusion that he had no options. He had to forget his pride and call Ashley. After all, they had lived together for seven years. With a little effort she could contact his friends in the Miami area, for if she alerted Semineaux's brothers in Florida they would somehow collect enough to meet the bail and get him out. And Ashley had sources. Her boss wanted her knicker's so badly. One word from Ashley and her boss would kiss her English ass. Can't expect anything from that source! Semineaux thought to himself.

And then Jimmy Buffet was singing, "Son of a son, son of a son of a sailor, glad I don't live in a trailer..."

"Goddamn, she's not in a trailer ... She lives in my home. She is my woman. I need help. Christ. I'm in prison. I'll call her."

When Sean let it be known to Jamon that he finally decided to call his woman, Jamon put his mouth to the open talk space in the large cellblock door and called to the guard who soon took Sean down into one of the lower cellblocks that had a pay phone on the wall from which he could make a long distance collect call to Miami.

It was one of those cellblocks filled with some pretty cut-throat looking guys, noisy, smelly, and damp, but the phone was at one end of a hall and around a short corner allowing some privacy. He wondered if there was another phone some place in the prison for inmates where one could sit down and be comfortable, but was grateful just to be able to call and let someone know he's been locked up.

As the phone rang in his home, he felt a terrific sense of hope swell in his stomach for he felt some pride in the image of that phone sitting in his house with all its comforts and splendor, and could actually visualize her walking to answer it, which she did.

"I have a collect from Sean in New Jersey, will you accept the charge?"

"Yes, I will operator," he immediately felt secure and it was good to hear her voice, and to know she was in his home.

"Ashley?"

"Hello ... hello ... Hi honey."

"Where are you? What happened to you?"

"They got me."

"What do you mean?"

"I mean ... I'm in jail."

"Jail?? Oh my God ... When I didn't hear from you..."

"Look, I will not be able to talk long. They set a high bail ... Get me out of here before I go nuts ... I need a bail bondsman."

"A what'""

"Ah ... To you, he's called a Bailiff. Here it's a Bail Bondsman. Same thing. Just get me out of here."

"You bastard."

"What ... Please, no fighting now. I'm in deep shit."

"You ... you lying bastard ... all this time..."

"Honey," he screamed, "What are you doing, what are you talking about?"

"The ballerina, the Prima ballerina ... that dances with Rudolph Nureyev, you bastard."

"What," he screamed so loud you could almost hear him a block away, as they say.

"She misses you all the time. Where ever she is dancing in the world all she can think about is you. And she is worried about you because you lead such a strange life. And she loves you, and on the plane between dancing in Paris and London she could still feel your thing in her ... She can cut it off and have it ... you ... you bastard." "

He nearly went into shock, and then gained his composure. "Where did you hear this shit?"

"Kristeen ... Kristeen ..." she screamed. "Her letters, I read them all, you bastard."

He couldn't believe what he was hearing. This girl from the most "proper" English family violated his privacy by going into a closet in his study which he could have and should have kept locked, but trusting that her English manners would have translated into integrity.

For Ashley to find the letters she would have had to locate a package buried in the deepest recesses of information. Buried in a sealed envelope, in the midst of hundreds of U.N. documents contained in seven boxes, the coded marking on the outside allowing only him to distinguish, with all seven boxes partially open to look less important than the half dozen or so sealed boxes on top of them.

"How could you have gone into my privacy like that?" he said softly, thinking about was how she laid like a naked stone beside his naked body the night before he left, then recalled her drunken confessions of snooping through her English father's most personal letters from his concubine in Paris, when she was but a teenager. This was her. But then he loved her. "Trust me, trust me," she would say. Don't be so tough Sean."

"Now listen to me, please," Sean pleaded. I love you. You always said you would eventually leave me. I fucking adore you. Yes, I had an affair. You are such a bitch at times. Don't speak to me for two weeks when I want to love you all the time..."

"That's all you think about ... sex..." She screamed hysterically.

"You always said you would leave. What the fuck kind of man do you think I am. How fucking secure did that make me. One day you just pull up stakes and leave."

You dirty bastard. I don't care about you."

"Listen ... please. I love you. I dropped her because I love you and would not give up on you. She had money, houses, everything. But I dropped her and all her wealth because I love you..."

"Rot in Jail. Rot in jail." she screamed and screamed three times over before slamming down the phone.

The next split could have cost Sean Semineaux his life.

Unbeknownst to him, the telephone was the only link all the prisoners, in every cellblock, had to the outside world. There were no other telephones available to call wives, girlfriends, children, friends, lawyers, or anyone. And all Sean Semineaux's years of developing self-control thru meditation, martial arts, Zen, the Tao, Mo Tzu; suddenly he was reduced to a raging animal that perhaps should have been in a zoo rather than jail.

He punched the telephone box with a short-left hook before slamming the phone itself so hard, it spoke strongly of the strength of plastic and medal.

Instinctively his eyes scanned the room, for he knew he had

made a mistake losing control, and there, in the far corner of his peripheral vision, but a few feet away, came a man with a long, razor sharp piece of thick mirror shaped like an elongated arrowhead the length of a sword, about to plunge into Sean's vulnerable right side.

The eyes he had seen before. The eyes with the hatred that glanced at him during lunch, the fifty so year old black man who seemed to resent the respect the young dudes gave Semineaux, and the one who flashed that look as they vacated the cafeteria. The guy was serving thirty years to life for murder, what's a few more years.

He regretted banging the phone, but did not want to die for it. He had always disagreed with his teacher at the U.N. who taught to disarm one with a knife, for Sean's tactic was to move away. run from a knife, always get away from it.

But there was no time nor space to move, and Sean was much grateful that he had been an obedient student and learned the short inside disarmament moves his teacher displayed with the speed and decisiveness of a panther.

The lethal point of the shiny green glass weapon was but a flash of inches from Sean's side by the time he brought around his foot, and from a short arched swing, cut into the forearm so hard it cracked the main bone, stopping the forward thrust of the pointed glass, sending it sailing across the floor, rather than deep into Sean's stomach.

Now the eyes that flashed hate flashed pity. Charged with adrenalin like a wild animal he could have finished him off with a kick to the head ... walked. The man with the hating eyes withering in pain on his knees, holding his arm.

When the guard saw Sean's head at the cellblock door, he opened it and escorted him back to the Penthouse. His mind was in utter confusion, and his heart already leaking sadness into his soul, for he knew he and Ashley could never recover what was lost between them.

He wanted to sit quietly and think, but Jamon and Magic would not let him, for they sensed something wrong and wanted to help. When they learned what happened they said nothing about the woman. smiled about the fight, and each took their turn trying to push him into thinking of "who" was going to bail him out of there.

It was time to get out of the prison, Sean did not know where to turn. Ashley had the access to the money, but no mercy. But his cellmates had become brothers, they cared ... very much.

No, he said about a hundred times to their insistence he call his family. They were astonished he had family so close, and could not believe he would hesitate for a second to call them for help," after all, that is what family is about," as Magic and Jamon put it.

"Mon what's wrong with you, I worry at first, you so far from Miami. Your family. How will they help you?"

Now Jamon was standing in front of him as he sat, hands outstretched with palms up in front of his healthy belly, pressing close to Sean as Latins do, with his head bobbing ever so slightly back and forth, mannerisms Sean knew from over twenty years in Miami. When Latin brothers want to convince you of something, they not only tell you, but physically act out what they want you to know. If you do not appear to give your total attention, physical contact is imminent, as hands seem to touch ever so slightly, like a tap to that part of the brain responsible for "paying attention."

"Now you tell us you grew up not far from this fucking prison man. Your mother, father, brother, children ... Christ, gringos ... so nearby ... you so fucking lucky. Why you tell us you cannot call ... They are your family ... family ... Shit, now I need a cigarillo.

"This motherfucker cares." Sean was laughing so hard to himself, "I love this bastard," He watched as Jamon slid and weaved back into his cell to get a cigarette, lit it and blew away the smoke before assuming his position in front of the cot. Magic and Paul looking on from their beds.

Jamon s eyes dropped slightly, making him look like the old Jackie Gleason as he near pleaded and asked,

"Why ... not call?" as he switched his weight from one foot to another, Gringo ... do you want to spend my time with me ... I'm here for the rest of my life. Or Magic, just three more years if he doesn't fuck up. And Paul he'll probably be here with me, for he only had five to do, but you see how quiet he is, and not a very big dude. but he can punch the shit out of the biggest dude in the joint, and does when a new one fucks with him ... so he's bad, and now he's got twelve years to serve, he put two guys in the hospital for too long, twice. How long do you want to stay with us? huh?" again shifting weight from one leg to the other.

"Well, I have a real nice family. I love them all so much, but there is a conservative streak that runs through my family which

I respect and its painful when my life runs up against it, for I hurt them, and its painful. I am just me. I am of them, but my chemistry is different somehow, for I have always left home to explore, and I suppose they may have perceived me as a sort of renegade. Damn, sometimes I wished I were a woman or old."

Now the three laughed, but only Jamon spoke, "You wish you were a woman ... old?"

"Yeah, even when I was about ten. I was always in trouble. I thought back then, if I were a girl, or an old man, I would not be in trouble."

With a look of disgust on his face Jamon walks over to the cellblock door and yells for the guard,

"My man wants to make a phone call."

He shakes his head again from one side to another. and shakes his right hand into the air, "Gringos ... guard, hurry up, my man wants to call his brother."

Semineaux called his brother Joseph who lived less than an hour's drive from the prison and within two hours he was called from his cell to meet a visitor in the light green room with the small desk and two chairs, which turned out to be a local attorney who was a friend of a friend of Sean's brother. They spoke for an hour and a half. The lawyer seemed like a nice guy but looked too worried and unsure of himself, continually saying he had to look closer at the police report, and made Semineaux even more apprehensive when suggesting it might be better if Sean secured an attorney in Miami, which was not what he wanted to hear, for instinctively he knew his changes would be better here than in Miami.

He returned to an empty Penthouse without any confidence in this worried looking lawyer, and in a very short while was again called to the visitor's area. Waiting for him this time was his brother Joseph whom he had not seen in years.

Joseph was ten years younger than Sean but had assumed the role of the older brother in the family since Sean had been on the move since he was eighteen, and he did a good job.

Semineaux loved Joseph more than Joseph realized and was proud of his tall, handsome, brother with the Irish looks and big warm smile. Joseph had an engaging personality and a hilariously dry sense of humor with a quick-witted ability to point out what is not so obvious. He was so impressed with how Joseph had developed a sort of middle-class tribal existence with so many friends, and how important Joseph was to so many of his own friends and their families who loved this funny, gregarious, generous, sometimes foolhardy guy. At times he was bigger than life and made a lot of people happy. he had a natural gift.

Sean did not expect to see Joseph so upset, for when he first glanced through the small screen opening in the visitors box at the red mustache and curly thick reddish blond hair he expected a different look in those blue eyes, rather than the red road map lines produced by sleeplessness, stress, or crying. Joseph was definitely the Irish side of the family in looks and temperament. To see him in this emotional state heightened Sean's realization of how tragic and serious his arrest would be viewed by other members of the family, causing Sean to regret telling Joseph on the phone, "to please get me out of here. As quickly as you can."

It was quite obvious to Sean how truly concerned he was, and how hard he was trying to do just that, but something was drastically wrong.

"It will be OK Joseph, thanks for coming so soon, for the lawyer."

"I'm sorry, I can't get you out. The bail is so high. They have you on some stiff charges. The lawyer said ... He stopped, to catch his breath. Joseph's eyes filled, and they he continued, "He said you could get a lot of time for this. I'm sorry."

"Shit brother, I love you ... I'm sorry I got you so upset. Dam. You cold ass Irish bastard. Crying over me. What, you getting soft like our little sister?"

Now they both laughed.

"The lawyer said he'll handle it, but he wants a lot of money, and I don't have that kind of money. Maybe Ashley can raise some money?"

"Ashley ... shit Joe, she would like to see me hung. I'll tell you what. Maybe it's time to bring in the first string. You remember Tony Laconi?"

"Of course, I remember him. He's always in the papers."

"Fuck these Jersey lawyers. I need a brilliant Philly street fighter. Laconi is the best. Call him in Philly. He'll come across the river. He can walk on water."

"Do you think he'll take your case. You don't have any money."

"Tony ... Tony take my case. Are you kidding? He'll come across the river in a second. In fact, tell him I said to get his fat ass over here right away or I'll kick it all over Philly when I get out," but Sean's laughter could not change the etched worry on Joseph's face.

Look bro. Thanks so much for trying so hard. Just call Tony, and please don't tell anyone else in the family. I love you Joseph, and turned his head away from the scratched, thick, plastic window separating them and made his way back to his cell, laughing to himself as he began to recall his wild times with

Tony, for on too many occasions Tony nearly got Sean killed.

How ironic, he thought to himself on the walk back to the cell, that three of those near-death occasions took place in New Jersey. A guard getting out of his chair provoked the first memory when he rose from the shiny, red, canvas backed chair to open the outer cell block door. The color red.

It was a long time ago. Both Tony and Sean were in their early twenties. Sean had been recently discharged from the military and a college sophomore. Tony had graduated and was in his first year of law school. This was to be his first near death experience with Tony.

Tony always had big new fast flashy cars, and on this day, they were racing down to the Jersey shore in Tony's big red convertible with a red canvas canoe tied to the trunk. It was a gorgeous day with a strong off-shore wind blowing out to sea and they were in a festive mood pulling up to the sand dunes bordering the vacant beach; Tony and his girl, Sean with his, and Sean's kid sister with her boyfriend who had played football with Sean.

Before they had unpacked the car Laconi untied the canoe, carried it above his head toward the sea screaming like a wild man as he ran across the sand, nearly being carried off his feet as the strong wind filled the hollow canvas canoe creating a parachute like affect. Reaching the water's edge sixty yards from where the five others looked on, Tony threw the canoe from over his head into the choppy surf, and barely managed to jump into it in shallow water as the canoe shot out toward the breakers, driven hard by the off-shore winds.

As the others laughed Sean dropped whatever he was carrying, for he had worked the Jersey shore as a lifeguard and on several dangerous rescues was blown out to sea by similar winds, his own life being saved along with the victims he was rescuing by an alert U.S. Coast guard steaming out into a rough ocean.

Sean did not hesitate. He sprinted the sixty yards to the water's edge, and with a timing only gained thru experience, sprang out into the air from coiled thighs, hitting only the top of the choppy shallow waters as his upper body and arms pulled him through the twenty yards to the sand bar where he rose in the knee deep water and hurdled the waves across the ever increasing depth until it became too deep to run, forcing him to swim again.

He pulled and punched his way thru the now chopping waves, cutting directly toward Laconi in the canoe, never allowing any doubt, when in reality few athletes could have caught up with that canoe on that day.

The canoe was streaking out to sea not only driven by the winds. Laconi, oblivious to the danger, was in the front of the canoe frantically digging the paddle into the sea with his strong arms in order to gain speed, screaming like a maniac.

Forty yards of pounding thru the waves and Sean was barely able to grab hold of the canoe's stern, but with his right hand he locked onto it, and with little remaining strength pulled himself up out of the sea and flopped into the stern, gasping for breath.

Exhausted, he just lay there watching Laconi in the bow rowing Indian style, laughing and screaming. But when he finally regained his composure he screamed,

"You asshole ... How you getting back," and without turning his head Tony yelled, " Fuck you, you pussy," and continued pumping the paddle for another five minutes as Sean just laid back looking at the dark grey clouds that seemed to be racing them out to sea, skidding across the clear blue sunny sky until the sunlight disappeared. Still, Laconi did not stop.

Then the rain hit, and it hit hard. Lighting, thunder, and a cloudburst finally stopped Tony, for the canoe very quickly filled with buckets of rain. They were dead in the water and visibility was impossible.

Tony was still smiling at Sean when it abruptly changed into a look of shock as visibility suddenly improved enough for them to see an eight-hundred-foot-long oil tanker pass close enough to suck them under its draft. The lightweight canvas canoe had blown out into the South Jersey shipping lanes. The two of them froze in horror as the ship passed and the winds and rains came on harder than before.

"We are going to die. We are going to fucking die," Tony cried out, shaking with a fear Sean had never before seen -- for Tony was as strong as a bull and a good street fighter, but a swimmer he was not, and with so much thick muscle and heavy bone structure he would sink like a rock, and he knew that. Fear twisted Tony's face, eyes pleading humility, mouth agape like a woman in paralysis.

"Fuck you Tony ... we are not going to die," and from some subconscious, primordial, or ancestral source came a name out of Sean's mouth, a word neither Sean nor Tony had never heard, nor read, in their twenty-four years on this earth.

"TONKA WILL SAVE YOU. TONKA WILL SAVE YOU," as he handed Tony a child's sand bucket that luckily happened to be in the canoe, now nearly floating over the side.

"Take this fucking pale and bale. Bale, bale, bale," he screamed into Tony's helpless face, then Semineaux moved to the bow where he knelt, leaned forward into a wind that was blowing in five directions at once, driving the rain into his eyes in any direction he looked, and made the greatest navigational decision of his life having no idea which direction was land. Sean pointed the bow with pure instincts and pulled for over an hour until pulsating veins budged above his upper-body muscles and blood flowed from the open gashes on his knees and shins turning the water in the bow red as Tony baled.

Then, as if in a miracle, they broke through the storm, with visibility allowing them to see small objects on the beach, and finally safety. The blisters on his hands and wounds on his knees and shins would take over a month to heal, but the curiosity in his mind as to the origin of the word "Tonka" would remain for years.

Sean had not seen Tony in eleven years, but he did come across the river. Now Semineaux knew he would have one of the best lawyers.

Semineaux was brought down again, this time to a small, airless, windowless cell with a ceiling no higher than the roof of an Altoona coal mine, and Laconi's big smile and bearhug was more encouraging than the nice, but rather sad, morgue-like attitude of the Jersey lawyer.

First, Laconi put his finger to his lips and raised his eyes to indicate his suspicion that the place might be bugged pushing a pad of paper and a pencil across the small table to Semineaux who immediately scratched out an explanation about finding the bale of ganja in the sea. Tony laughed so hard tears ran down his cheeks.

Secondly, tony did not seem very upset about the hundred-thousand-dollar bail and was optimistic that he could get Sean out in a few days, and that "he would work a deal," beautiful words to a rather strung-out Semineaux.

Tony never mentioned their shared experience in the sea. But when he was leaving, he simply said, "I owe you one, and I will represent you. And this time, I will save 'Tonka.' "

When Tony left Sean was being escorted back to the

Penthouse when the elevator was delayed between floors because of some incident in cell block number four. The security lights flashed on and off, creating a rather claustrophobic atmosphere in the elevator, particularly since the guard was the non-talkative type, who not only failed to respond to Semineaux's attempt to communicate but appeared downright hostile. After five minutes the lights in the elevator went out except for the flashing red and yellow alarm system bulbs, whose image again conjured up another life and death experience Tony and Sean experienced years ago, which allowed Sean to take his mind off the very uncomfortable present reality in the air tight dark elevator.

It was the red and yellow lights which were similar to the lights on the control panel of Laconi's large cabin cruiser that brought a memory to the surface of Sean's consciousness of another time he and Tony almost died together, along with their wives. It was a long time ago; they were both young and they each had three children.

It was another crazy Laconi adventure. Tony wanted to go out of Cape May on his cabin cruiser on a very strange night with a full moon and unusually high tides due to days of heavy rains. The sea was dangerously rough and unpredictable. Perhaps only once in a decade that the waters off Cape May get this way, for the moon does strange things to the tides when combined with an off-shore storm. Even experienced mariners would opt to stay on dry land.

But out they went, and fast, for the high tide was driven by those off-shore winds creating huge waves that towered above when the boat slipped into the watery valleys. The two wives were at first laughing, unaware of the danger Sean sensed immediately. Sean watched Tony's eyes straining to see the stern of the boat as he adjusted the speed, for the roaring water was threatening to come over the stern, which would drown the engine's fire, damming the boat to being beaten into pieces by the huge pounding waves as it would helplessly bob in the darken valleys of water.

It didn't take Tony long to decide to turn the boat around towards shore and harbor, but as he attempted to turn into the starboard wind the bow lifted out of the water throwing the two women to the deck and Tony backward from the controls. Fortunately, Semineaux was directly behind Tony, and as he bounced off Sean, Tony was barely able to grab hold of the boat's wheel with his right hand and maintain a grip was those thick, unusually strong fingers, just in time to save the boat from rolling over as it more or less shot out the water.

Semineaux then pushed tony against the wheel, took the hands of the two women who by this time were on their knees looking up with a startled, frightened blank stare and pulled them toward the galley door, kicked it open with one foot, pushed the two struggling women down into the galley, and threw himself against Tony who was struggling to hold onto the ship's wheel.

You asshole ... You should have known better than to take this fucking boat out tonight," Sean shouted into Tony's ear as he held onto the forward bulkhead with two hands, pinning Tony securely against the wheel, for the boat was being thrown about as if it were a toy.

Tony said nothing, his face locked with terror, inimitable stare in his eyes.

At that moment the women opened the galley door, horrified at being down in the galley and feeling trapped. When Sean tried to stop them from coming up on deck, they struggled to get past him. But he knew they would certainly be washed overboard for water was surging across the deck beneath the small bridge, and he tried to push them back down the galley steps as they now fought to get on deck. In desperation, Sean kicked both women down the steps and latched closed the galley door as the pots, pans, coffee pot, plastic dishes flew around the room when cabinet doors opened and emptied their contents, bouncing off the two women being thrown about.

Semineaux turned just in time to catch Tony being thrown from the wheel, and with all the strength in his legs, again pushed Tony against the wheel and snapped both his hands onto the solid bulkhead on both sides of the wheel. When Sean leaned forward, he again saw the horror in Tony's eyes, which did not do much for Sean's confidence, for he knew Laconi to be a great sailor.

With both hands clasping the two handles on the bulkhead, Sean was able to hold Tony, and himself, from flipping out of the boat that Sean feared was about to flop over. Neither one of them could see the rudder, that at times was completely out of the water.

Sean could hear the dishes and kitchen things being thrown against the galley walls, knowing their wives must be terrified, for at one point he heard someone desperately trying to open the

118   E. Ted Gladue

galley door which he had secured from the outside. He could feel their panic at being trapped below deck, but it was better than the cabin being flooded with seawater, or the two of them being washed overboard.

Sean pressed up against Tony, "Get this damn boat into safe harbor or I'll break you in half."

"Motherfucker, don't you know I could kill you with my bare hands," the now smiling Tony replied.

"You'll be lucky if I don't kick your ass when we get this fucking thing docked."

Tony laughed, and they did get in safely, but Sean never forgot those little red and yellow lights on the cockpit panel that flashed on and off the entire time, the lights indicating the boat-maintained power. For without power, they would have been at the mercy of the sea, and not live to tell about it.

At that moment the main light in the elevator returned, and both Sean and the guard felt the power return to the elevator which took them to the Penthouse floor.

Only Paul was awake when Sean returned to the Penthouse, and he too fell fast asleep reading a book for only ten minutes. They had left the radio on and Sean laid there long after the lights went out listening to an hour of B.B. King and Otis Reading, fixing his eyes and daydreaming on the yellow lights visible in the window up and above. He too finally fell fast asleep after listening to Otis Reading's 1968 classic "Sitting On The Dock Of The Bay," which never failed to bring a tear to his eyes with his private memories of pain, alcohol, and Nassau, in the hot Bahamian summers, which most likely provoked a dream he was having of a summer years earlier when a clicking noise startled him from his sleep.

He rolled over onto his pillow glad to be dreaming and not in Jail, for he was not yet able to separate the dream from the reality until looking up at the yellow light from the lamp post outside that had earlier took him into the dream world from whence he just returned.

There was enough yellow light from that outside lamp post to illuminate the outlines of the cell block door that had been opened ever so slightly by the figure now quietly slipping into the Penthouse. Semineaux remained perfectly still and strained his eyes to see a grey-haired black guard carrying several small bags and tip-toeing into Magic's cell so as not to wake the others. In a few moments he left. closing the cell block door. The click of the lock reminding Sean of what woke him from his sleep in the first place, for normally there was too much noise in the area to even hear the click when the door was opened or closed.

Magic then left his cell to use the facility and returning noticed Sean was now awake, whereupon the two of them began a muted conversation so as not to wake the others. Semineaux had already developed a fondness for magic, and had always had a special place in his heart for Jamaicans who reminded Sean of the Irish in both sharing a great sense of humor. love of their music be it reggae or sad Irish folk, and a defiance of spirit nurtured each by their experiences with English brutality and hypocrisy. In Sean's experience when Jamaicans drink, they dance and laugh their way into a woman's heart, as the Irish too often miss opportunities and end up fighting each other. Jamaicans end up making love to the woman, and fighting less.

Magic turned up the radio which failed to even compete with Paul and Jamon's loud snoring and Sean began to learn more about this thirty two year old man who still played basketball six days a week when free, had the body of a nineteen year old, ten children with three different women, spoke about his family with more love and tenderness than any white man Sean had ever known. Most impressive, as all his children with the different wives considered each other as brothers and sisters in an extended family relationship.

To Magic family meant all, money little. But when his first wife's home was foreclosed upon, he became very upset and depressed because of his inability to help her and made the mistake of getting drunk one Friday afternoon after work. While walking home he got the crazy notion of just going into a half dozen banks and asking them for some money to help his family, and naturally they thought him nuts. Then, with the bottle of Bourbon empty, he walked into one bank and demanded the teller give him money.

The teller, relieved to see this bank robber pointing an empty bottle of whiskey at her rather than a pistol, turned over two hundred dollars to Magic who took the money, left the bank and walked directly to his first wife's home with the money. He was met by the police before he even got to the front door. He was convicted of bank robbery and gotten twenty years, serving only five with good behavior, now going into year two.

"I can't believe it Magic, no gun ... and all that time?"

"Well, you just do your time ... get through it. But the hell with that dude, I've told you enough about myself. You been married?"

"Of course, I've been married, doesn't every man get married at least once?"

"Oh mon, those women are powerful. They control us and we don't even know it."

"Tell me Magic. I have been trying all my life to prove how wrong my service buddies were about women."

"What's that mon," Magic with an inquisitive smile.

"In the military at eighteen I had two older buddies, my best friends, who were hardened combat veterans, one a marine the other army. Two things they tried to teach me. One, how the Chinese fight. How much they respected their fighting abilities. The other thing ... about women. They claimed women were all bitches; deceitful, every one of them. I was horrified, but they would laugh at me and claimed my views on women belonged to twelve-year-old boys. "A man should know better." They were now laughing so hard even Jamon rolled over from his dead sleep.

"Why do you think I play so much basketball. Now you take Jamon over there..." as Magic pointed toward his cell Jamon let out a fart louder than his snoring. "Jamon loves them ... he worships them. I wish I could. I've never really loved any of them. How about you? Have you loved a lot of 'em, like Jamon?"

"Wow ... a loaded question brother. Got to think about that one ... I thought I loved the only one I married ... She was a real nice girl. A good person. Then... well ... I had three kids ... It was then I knew love for the first-time what love was."

"Hey mon ... I'm with you on that one."

"Magic ... I do not believe there is such a thing as love between a man and a woman."

"What do you mean?"

"Just that. A human being does not experience love until they have children. Because love is everlasting. No matter what. And often it is unconditional. I will love my kids forever. You will love your kids forever."

"Well, what do you call what happens between a man and a woman when they are in love?"

"It's passion, It's addiction. It's companionship. it's friendship. It's habit. It's dependency. It starts off as greed, what one person wants and desires."

"It can become love. How many people are together for thirty years?"

"Yea ... but how after fifty years some just walk away. it's over. After two years, it's over. Not with children. You always love them, no matter what. It's everlasting. A woman can tell you she loves you a million times a year for ten years. then cut your heart out. Same with us men. We do the same thing."

"Again, mon people stay together all their lives."

"Yea ... out of habit. Mostly a bad habit." both laughed until they woke Jamon. Hey, you guys get some sleep."

"One more thing Magic. Look at the movie stars. They marry beautiful, gorgeous people. Then they make a movie with another beautiful, gorgeous person. Then they 'love' them ... for a while. I think most people would do the same thing if they had that temptation. We humans. We are animals. The only time we love is when we have children."

"Will you guys shut the fuck up."

"Magic," Sean now whispering... "One more thing. Who was that old guard who woke me up?"

"That's the father of my first wife. He had some things my present wife sent me."

Each day there were more and more intimate conversations with Magic and Jamon. Paul was the reserved and quiet one of the four, but he enjoyed listening as the other two would carry on. Jamon could always get everyone laughing when he would begin smiling and asking Sean, "why your lady so mad," and would follow- up with a belly rolling laugh. They were enjoyable conversations, for a joint was usually lit up, and they continually played Jimmy Buffet songs as they each took a few hits from the consistently excellent joint rolled always in yellow paper.

At first Sean was astonished they had any ganja in the place, and they soon trusted him enough to teach him the secrets of how they smuggled it in.

There were nights when he would dream, he was in bed with his woman, in his home, and awakened pressed against the thick, cold, prison wall that supported his narrow bed and was itself the main outside wall in that corner of the prison. He would press his forehead against the wall and try to free his spirit through the wall, or dream of actually taking blocks from the wall and escaping, for this was one man who would rather be dead than spend a long time in prison.

But then, there were times like this. when they smoked, and talked, and laughed, and he truly got to love these guys who were so much fun, particularly Jamon who loved life so much and felt so safe in prison. When they were high Paul just smiled more, Jamon would talk and sort of take command as he moved from his cell to stand directly in front of Sean. and back again, sometimes fast, sometimes dancing, always moving, always smiling or laughing. Magic, would just stand in his cell doorway, leaning against the bars, usually wearing a pair of sweat pants and short sleeve shirt, and usually smoking and playing with a cigarette. laughing at Jamon, and at times attempting to interrupt him from dominating the airways, which was not an easy task.

But when Magic decided it was time, he wanted to talk he had a way to shut Jamon down, for Magic was not only a gentleman. but the most respected guy in the prison, and the only one who could take the big young boxer in a fight. He would somehow speak, very low and look Jamon in the eye as he spoke and all of a sudden Jamon would be off doing something else, usually talking on the "telephone," which in itself was a hilarious surprise to Sean, for Jamon spent hours on the "telephone."

The "telephone" was actually a toilet. One narrow cell contained two sinks and two toilets serving the normally three prisoners in the cellblock.

One toilet was drained of all water, as was the toilet on the other side of the wall which happened to lead to the women's prison. They kept the toilet perfectly clean and one could put his head inside the toilet up to the shoulders and speak into that bottom part of the toilet usually serving to rid the toilet of discarded human waste and water.

Jamon's girlfriend on the other side would return his greetings, talk about what sort of day each had, and late at night make love to each other with graphic descriptions of sex and anatomy, which fortunately no one else could hear, for when one spoke into the "telephone" the sound coming into the cell was muffled beyond recognition, allowing privacy.

Arguments rarely occurred because only one person could speak at a time into the "telephone," so the relationships Paul, Magic and Jamon maintained with the women were extremely amicable, and the only physical contact they ever had was touching each other's hands and fingers through bars on those rare occasions when the prisoners were being transferred and the guard had a heart.

The image of those fingers making love to each other through those bars will always remain with Sean, to remind him how lucky it is to be free.

Magic had told Sean that Jamon spoke about his family, his wives, his mistresses, but little else about Columbia, for Jamon had been and remained a major player in the Medellin Cartel that controlled the drug trade and was worth millions, yet would probably spend the rest of his life in prison, by his own choice, since prison was safer for him than the outside.

Apparently, Jamon had become a little too independent for the kingpin of the cartel, Pablo Escobar Gaviria, and Jamon was as good as dead if he was released from prison, evidence by the three huge scars that ran from his right thigh up to his chest. One afternoon when Sean was alone with Jamon, they were talking about women and Jamon was saying how badly he felt for him being betrayed by his woman.

"I cannot believe it, your bonito senora, the greatest pain for a man is to be betrayed by his woman."

"So, you had an affair? She punched the shit out of you, scream ... oh how they can scream..." he laughed so loud. "Oooo, but they so hot. You know in that anger, they love you mon. You here in prison mon. She tell you to rot here."

Then Jamon got a serious look on his face. "Un cuchillo, With the blade, someone should cut her throat in my country. She's in Miami, just let me know, I can have someone cut this Ashley for you. She's as good as dead."

"Thanks anyhow Jamon, that is nice of you. You have friends in Miami?"

Friends? I have many friends in Miami. I love Fort Lauderdale, and when I got out of here once I lived in Miami, were I spent most of my time. Oh, with my bonito ... bonito wooman."

Jamon had already told him about his "woman," who apparently was somehow related to Jamon's wife and lived with his wife in some short of extended family arrangement in Columbia. He had begun to notice her beauty when she was twelve and by the time, she was sixteen, Jamon, the legend in his family, was idolized by her. Jamon was her hero and a mystery who spent most of his time in exciting Miami.

"When she was seventeen, I bring her here ... Oooo...I can tell you. The most beautiful Columbian woman you will ever see. I love her, kiss her.. lick her as my mother's milk for me. You see, I knew it was dangerous for me to leave here but a little money here and there and I am out. For a year I live in a secluded estate in Miami with my senorita.

"On her eighteenth birthday we go to Ft. Lauderdale. Such a wonderful night. The sky was beautiful. Everything was all alive on Oakland Park boulevard. I had taken her to buy this beautiful white silk dress imported from Paris, and no woman, could be as beautiful as my lady that night."

Jamon went on to say how he had made her learn to shoot, against her will, and had forced her to spend four days a week at a private shooting gallery in South Florida learning how to use a variety of weapons, but in particular a 9-millimeter revolver and a 9-millimeter semiautomatic pistol, known as "nines" on the street, firing a bullet the size of a .357 caliber which is devastating to human tissue when it hits, giving it the "stopping power" of larger weapons.

"The night of her birthday she does not want to bring a gun. She says, 'Please honey, not tonight, just tonight, no gun, for me, please."

"Wooman..." Jamon spoke so softly and slowly "...you know how they insist even when they are wrong?" his head tilted to one side, his long black hair waving with the slight shaking of his head from side to side, big brown eyes looking upward, both hands turned palms up.

"But," his head snapping up his eyes now locking into his, "I insisted she pack it." He took a few swaggering steps, the increased volume in his voice giving the statement authority, then again lowering his voice, dropping his eyes, the tone begging for acceptance "But amigo, I give in a leetle" as he pinched two fingers together and his mouth opened to expose all his big white teeth "She look so beautiful. That dress," becoming quite emotional. "Like a Goddess," he said, dropping his head and arms as if performing on a stage.

"So, I say 'Okay, don't take the big semi, but take the revolver' Oh...we have so much fun on Oakland Park Boulevard ... I love that place. We dance, eat."

"We come out of this place." Jamon is now walking slowly in front of Sean, his hands moving about and his chest swelled out.

"She is walking ahead of me, around the car to the passenger side and I am following her. Suddenly a car stops and a guy says "pardon me sir." Columbian accent, from the south. Jamon throws both arms out with his hands opened wide, as was his eyes.

"There are three of them in the car that I see," he points and stabs at the air three times with an expression on his face as if it were happening at that very second, a level of intensity in his stories that always brought smiles to the faces of Magic and Paul.

Jamon is now on his toes pointing. "The guy talking to me from the passenger seat while the driver is sneaking around the back of the car to cut me down. The lights so bright on Oakland Park Boulevard, I don't see him until he fires and hits me."

Jamon pulls up his shorts to the top of his thigh, displaying a huge ugly scar that ran halfway up his thigh. Then he pulls up his shirt displaying two large scars in his stomach, each with an indentation that was near being a hole, but healed.

"They get me right here, bang, three hits. I go down."

Jamon, to the surprise of all three of them, falls to the cement floor with a thud. "I am down on my back. About ready to be finished off by this thug." His hands flapping at the wrists "I am done. I am lying on my gun and cannot even reach it. Then..." He points to the ceiling as he raises one knee "My lady, my bonito ... I love her so much." He stops to pause.

"My little darling. She pulls her revolver. First, she shoots the guy who shot me, she shoots him right in the fucking head," as Jamon laughs very hard. "Pieces of him are still on Oakland Park Boulevard. She so beautiful, so courageous, she save me."

"What about the two other guys?"

"Bang, the guy in the passenger's seat just got out of the car and he gets hit in the chest, dead. The guy in the back seat is halfway out of the car, he gets hit in the neck, dead."

"My lady, she loves me so much." Then Jamon grows silent and walks slowly in circles in front of Sean. Then stops in front of him and places on hand on Sean's shoulder and looks intensely into Sean's eyes.

"Hombre, listen to me," nodding his head and looking very serious. "Hombre, that is a wooman who loves. She kills for you."

Jamon released his hand from Sean's shoulder, turned and walked a few paces away before continuing. "She cry, she cry, for days, weeks, months, my baby. She finally stopped crying. She saved me. Understand? That's how a woman should love her man. Understand hombre?" shaking his head, "not like this Ashley of yours. Gringo woman, puff" he blew and walked to the end of the cell block shaking his head.

The last day and a half in the prison was taken up with hearings before the judge. The obstacle of such a large cash bond was dealt with when brother Joey put his family home up for the bail bond. Semineaux was very anxious to leave despite the warmth of his cellmates who were as addicted to Jimmy Buffet as was Sean. The last night they talked well into the morning about their remaining years in the place and life itself.

"Where are you going to go as soon as you get out of here? You going back to Florida?" All three asked.

"No, I have a little mission up in New York. I am going to write a book about this nuclear, biological and chemical bullshit that is going to destroy this world. I have a proposal I am taking to the Rockefeller foundation to get a grant."

"Man, how can you still dream like that when you're lookin' at doing time brother." Magic said.

"Well brother, I just want to do my little part. And, I'm not thinking about coming back again. When I finish the book, I want to go teach military officers in Europe again, and see the waste of money on the military build-up. Sort of be my own spy, and learn what I can for myself.

"Don't forget me -- my name is Magic" he smiled.

"No brother, I will never forget you." And the lights went out.

The next day Semineaux did not see magic again for he was on prison detail as was Paul and Jamon, but as he packed his belongings he remembered how horrified he had been when Jamon had suggested that Sean give him his Monte Blanc German fountain pen, because Jamon said he wrote the most loving letters ever to his lady in Columbia whenever Sean loaned the pen to him. But Semineaux's ballerina had given that pen to Sean as a gift the last time he saw her in Berlin. He could not give it away.

But, before leaving the cell for the last time, Sean thought about all the kindness and fun, and placed the black and gold pen beneath Jamon's pillow.

Within ten minutes Sean Semineaux was escorted out of the prison, into the cold December air, a free man.

Many years later Semineaux's lawyer Tony wrote of his memory of going into the prison that first day.

"It was late Wednesday afternoon when I finally arranged bail for Sean. I knew his freedom was not only important, it was a necessity for, for you should never compromise a free spirit because you compromise a society. I was anxious to deliver the papers to the sheriff and free him from the confines of a prison. I walked into the dreary building and was greeted by a perplexed and concerned sheriff. He asked if I 'knew' by client. It was a strange question because police dehumanize their 'charges' rather than give them personalities. I said I did but why did he ask? His response was almost a reverent observation.

He said: 'Semineaux has been in the gym for hours, jumping rope without a break.' I personally, knowing Sean would have expected nothing less. I should not have laughed, but I did and the sheriff miss-perceived my humor.

The sheriff said 'all the black prisoners were walking around him at a distance, afraid to go near him because they said: 'He is one crazy motherfucker.' That was my Semineaux.''

Chapter 12

Freedom in New York City

Within a few short hours he was comfortably sitting in the first-class compartment of The Metro liner as it speeds across the bleak New Jersey countryside. He wanted to avoid all that was ordinary and spent the extra money on the first-class seat, since he knew not when or where he would be able to simply relax again. He had no place to stay in New York and was not sure if any of his friends would offer, a drastic change from the friendly accommodating social culture of the sixties and seventies when people traveled not just to other places. but to stay with friends as well.

The hospitality of his New York friends had diminished in direct proportion to the drastic rise in the price of apartment rentals in Manhattan. He knew it was risky going into the City with only a hundred and sixty-six dollars in his pocket, but there had been no vacillation about where he was going as soon as he had gotten into Joey's car outside the prison.

His first enjoyment had been the wonderful feeling of being able to open the car window ever so slightly in order to smell the clear, cold December air, which became invigorating while standing at the Princeton train station awaiting the Metro special from Washington to Boston.

He then experienced the second sensual enjoyment, the exhilarating felling of movement beneath him as the train clickety-clacked along the tracks, for he was beginning to feel free again from the numbness he developed in adapting to the confinement of the prison. He wanted to howl like a wolf, but discretion was in order.

After a while he settled down and started daydreaming as the little ordinary small towns began to give way to the pollution producing industrial monsters and concrete block businesses that seemed to have eaten up all the houses, stores, trees, bushes, and grass as far as the eye could see and nose could smell if he could have opened the window his head was leaning against; and then he thought of Ashley, and immediately decided not to think about her while in the city.

The City. No other like it in the entire world. It's ever moving and electric. All the ethnic types and races in the world under one flag, New York City. It pulsates twenty-four hours a day like the heart of the world. The closest thing to heaven on Earth for those who create and dream new things -- music, dance, theater, writers, poets, singers, actors. New York is freedom as much as a cool breeze blowing over island palms.

The closer the train got to New York the more Semineaux thought of life there, having spent the better part of seven to nine of the last twelve years, the best years of his life, in the heart and soul of all New York had to offer. The memories were pulling at his mind like a magnet, erasing thoughts of Miami and jail.

"New York was my town. I made it in New York. Everything I wanted to do in New York, I did. New York did not give me up, I gave up New York. Hey ... just like Billy Joel sings. 'I'm in a New York state of mind...'" as he laughed hard enough some people turned in their seats to look his way; with his excited state he was sitting high and straight, and now slouched down slowly into his seat to hide behind the seat in front.

"Ho ho ... he he... I'm sure I am. Damn, I forgot the place existed. Forgot I was going there" and laughed again, too loud, at this last thought. And for the first time since finding the bale he realized how obsessed he was with saving his home.

"The hell with that house. I left New York to write years ago. I don't need a home to write." And began to remember some of the powerful things that happened to him during those long years in the city, and as recently as within a year.

The last time Semineaux was in New York had been the three weeks attending the Metropolitan Opera House murder case, now nearly a year ago. A young female violinist had been murdered at the Met while Sean's girlfriend, the ballerina

Ashley just uncovered, and Rudolph Nureyev were dancing.

Sean attended the murder trial for he was writing a novel based on the murder since he was there in the Met the night of the murder. The trial, which was only supposed to last three days, went on for three weeks, and the suspect was found guilty. Even after the verdict Sean remained convinced that the real killer was still out there, for the police investigation had not been very good.

Semineaux was amazed that the police never questioned him for he had been in and out of the stage entrance dozens of time a day, and often brought guests backstage to meet his Prima Ballerina girlfriend. When the ballet company went on to perform at the Kennedy Center in Washington, D.C., the NYPD detectives came to D.C. to continue their investigation, but spent most of their time drinking and dating the young female dancers.

In researching this novel Semineaux had gone to Berlin before the trial where his investigations took him into East Berlin during some tense times of the Cold War. Back in New York he even turned up old West Side friend who lived in the same building as the murdered violinist.

"Damn," he thought to himself, "I'd love to finish that novel." But now there were more important matters than a murder trial bringing him to New York City. The irony of it all is that he would have been coming to the city this week to get support to write a book on the most sensitive political issues of human survival, and he had an appointment with the Rockefellers. Jail one week, the Rockefellers the next.

Semineaux had been carefully following President Reagan's appropriations for massive increases in military spending in preparing to fight the Russians which Semineaux, with ten years of experience dealing with Russians considered an overreaction, since the United States would not have to fight the Russians. And if we did, we already had superiority, for the Russians were basically defensive fighters.

Semineaux considered this expenditure a waste of America's vital economic resources, all because Reagan was feeding on America's false sense of inadequacy resulting from Vietnam and the Iran hostage crisis. The U.S. was the most powerful nation in World history, and yet, it felt inadequate. The standard cliché at the time was "are we just going to let Communists and Iranians take over the world?"

Many people were buying second houses, new cars, sending their children to fine universities, boating, sailing and skiing. But to Semineaux, America in 1982 was becoming top heavy with military industries and suppliers, fast becoming a war economy. But everybody seemed to be doing well, and Americans felt cocky again, like Jimmy Cagney in "Yankee Doodle Dandy." Anyone who whispered "beware" was exorcised from consciousness.

"What the hell am I going to do, try and save the world?" he laughed. He pushed these thoughts out of his mind as he did the Metropolitan murder story a few moments earlier and came to grips with the reality that he had no place in New York City to sleep that night. "Worry about number one for a second or you'll be on your ass for the night, and I'll bet that all night restaurant down by the river in Hell's Kitchen isn't even open these days with the vast increase of homelessness," he first recognized during a visit to the city in 1978, a time when few even thought much about homelessness as a sociological plague on American society. As the train settled into its scheduled stop at 34th Street, Penn Station he had eliminated nearly all his friends who may have lodged him, for when they saw him like this it frightened them and made them question whether Sean would survive, since they themselves had, by this Christmas season 1982, become witnesses to the growing numbers of people on the street who didn't seem to belong there.

The reality it could happen to anyone was becoming part of the public consciousness, and perhaps he brought the message home to them closer than they wished.

Semineaux had not even liked the term "homelessness" since it connotated a person losing some "thing." In essence, Sean believed having shelter was a basic human right we are born with, since we do not come into this world of our own free choice. No one came of their own choice. We come out of love, passion, lust, chemistry, alcohol, fucking, rape ... just a penis and a vagina and here we are ... nothing more, nothing less. We begin with sex then some of us get fucked again.

Shelter is not something to be acquired in a civilized setting, but a basic human right with no strings attached. It is not a thing to lose, but a human right more fundamental and important than freedom of speech, press and assembly. Who cares about speaking, writing, or socializing; when you don't have a secure place to sleep, bathe, a toilet and a place to cook?

Who else could he call than those friends who had been homeless in their lives? These were two dear friends who had been homeless refugees; the older, William, escaped Hitler and the younger friend, Joe, escaped the Communist in Bulgaria. They would feel Semineaux's plight, for the major experience shaping their lives was survival.

William was born in Vienna, Austria of Jewish parents persecuted after Hitler's invasion in which his father died and he escaped with his mother to Czechoslovakia until Hitler took that country, and then on to safety in The Soviet Union until Hitler invaded again, then on to Japan until the bombing of Pearl harbor, forcing them into a desperate existence in Shanghai, China until the end of World War II when a stroke of good luck brought William to Prindel College in Utah, and on to a Harvard Ph.D. along with his friend, fellow refugee, and classmate, Henry Kissinger. William was one of the two most important men in his Semineaux's life, for he was his intellectual Godfather.

Standing at a phone in 34th Street state with a handful of quarters, he decided to call Joe first, whom he had met years before while on a flight from Amsterdam to the island of Maorca in the Mediterranean. The plane had been forced to make an unscheduled landing in Nice, France with no explanation other than for everyone to remain in their seats until takeoff. The engines shut down for forty-five minutes making the air tight plane with no air conditioning unbearable under the intense heat of a Mediterranean August sun. Everyone obeyed the seating instructions except Semineaux and this Joe who were sitting in separate compartments of the plane.

The two strangers each make their separate way to the main door of the plane near the pilot's cabin when both were stopped in their tracks by four anxious looking stewardesses, one of whom was holding tight onto the handle of the door, not allowing any fresh air into the plane.

Sean and this stranger teamed up as though it were a game plan, with Joe charming the four women into his orbit for just the second it took Semineaux to force the door from the small hand of the stewardess allowing fresh clean air to pour into the cabin. But when they simultaneously looked closer into the eves of the four women, they suspected something other than their forcefulness, lack of self-control, or rudeness causing the tension.

The plane was being hijacked by an Arab terrorist who had forced the plane to land in Nice, rather than the sun filled Island of Maorca. One stewardess nervously whispered the message that there was a terrorist in the cockpit with a gun, as the two men who should have been in their seats moved instinctively past the bearer of the message just as the terrorist was attempting to open the door, that first slammed against the back of the stewardess leaning against it.

On the second attempt the terrorist succeeded in opening the door as the girl stepped aside and out, he came, pointing a small 9-millimeter automatic pistol, until a Semineaux special, the snapping knuckle punch, cracked the terrorist's arm just above the wrist of the hand holding the gun. sending the pistol skidding harmlessly across the floor of the plane.

So Sean and Joe met foiling a hijacking and forged an immediate friendship, baptized by the Captain's orders to allow the two of them all the free drinks they could consume on the remaining leg of the flight to Maorca; then Christened by the airline's gratuitous gift of a free round trip flight to Barcelona with accommodations and free tickets to a bullfight, which they took full advantage after only two days in Maorca.

Strangely enough, the two of them at the time actually resided not far from each other in New York City, and their friendship extended into uncharted ground over the next two years, particularly when Sean used numerous United Nation's connections to organize a mission to help Joe smuggle two of his younger brothers out of Bulgaria at a crucial point in the Cold War.

Within an hour both William and Joe were sitting in a West side restaurant trying to figure out what Sean should do to get himself out of this serious trouble, when all Sean wanted was a place to stay until his scheduled meeting with the Rockefeller foundation.

William was becoming somewhat frustrated with Sean for not wanting to discuss the "bust," and then appealed to Joe to talk some sense into him.

"How long have you known this guy Joe? Do you know how wild he can be? Maybe you can talk some sense into him?"

Joe skipped over the hijacking incident and brought William to tears laughing as he talked about,

"This character ... I tell you William. In my country, Bulgaria. When a man is truly free, we call him 'Seagull,.' And that's what this guy is, a 'seagull,' free.

"He's free all right ... but not for long. if ...

Joe interrupting William, "So free, sometimes He's crazy. We are at a bullfight in Barcelona. I am trying to explain him the bulls. Him, he's like this writer Hemmingway, and he should be interested in the bulls. No ... He ... seagull sees, way up behind us in a special booth, a very, very, beau..te ... full Spanish woman. Like no other I have ever seen."

"God, you remember her Joe? That long dark hair, the curves of that body beneath the white silk dress, those big, warm, feeling eyes."

"Shut up seagull, you were crazy. The woman is with two men. Seagull can't take his eyes off her. And crazy enough. She smiles back. He waves. She waves back. When the two men aren't looking. He blows her a kiss. She blows one back. At the end of the bull fight I can't talk any sense into this crazy American. He follows them home like a secret agent, except" As Joe begins to laugh uncontrollably.

"Shit, I'd hoped you forgot that."

"He's madly in love with this senorita now, and all he got for his effort is eight ... eight long knives at his throat in a little town ten miles from Barcelona. They almost killed him. He promises to leave Barcelona immediately and never return and they release him. I'm in a disco dancing with three crazy Danish chicks and he walks in smiling. and tells me what happens ... such a seagull."

"Yes ... we both know him. Do you know anything about New Jersey's drug law trends these days? This is quite serious, and I am glad you are concerned..."

And now his two dear friends were back to discussing his dilemma, for which he was grateful, but nevertheless wanted to forget and began to make his way back to the restroom which he bypassed.

A crisp December air blast was blowing through a slightly opened side door next to the men's room, and Sean made a spontaneous dash outside, as he had not yet rid his memory of the smoke-filled stench of prison air. With hands in his pockets, he slowly strode alongside the glass tavern window, but with darkness now set the patrons inside only saw reflections of themselves, allowing Sean to see both his dear friends huddled together over a small table discussing strategies to save him from prison, warming his heart as he glanced up Amsterdam Avenue, to thoughts of so much fun in all those years in the city.

"Where am I ... yea ... West Side," as his eyes took in the carnival atmosphere that is stock and trade of hundreds of neighborhoods. "Hell, I lived at 70th and West End," as he looked south. Thought another moment, looked west, "Yea ... 75th just off Central Park West ... what great times ... Central Park ... thousands of friends ... so exciting to live here," looking up Amsterdam again until the huge smile stopped and a worried look came to his face. "God, it wasn't all that good." A bad memory was stirring. It was the street on which he was standing.

Amsterdam Avenue ... then, a memory repressed, to this very night. An event that happened seven years earlier, four blocks from where he now stood, when Semineaux was pronounced dead.

He had been broadsided by a gypsy cab speeding through a red light doing about 70mph, wrapping the small Volkswagen Beetle Sean was driving around a poll at 78th and Amsterdam. crushing his body within the vehicle. The ambulance driver and medic who finally arrived at the scene of the 3pm accident, after the local hoods robbed many of his belongings, pronounced him dead right there, called a DOA (dead on arrival) report to Roosevelt Emergency Room, threw his dead body onto a stretcher and into the ambulance, and covered the corpse with a blanket.

But it hadn't been Semineaux's time, and as later told to Sean by the ambulance driver later contacted by his lawyer, he startled the hell out of both driver and medic when they heard him yelling, at the top of his lungs,

"What the fuck happened ... who the fuck hit me. Where the hell am I? ... and on and on... with a sailor's mouth, causing the driver and medic to nearly jump out of their seats, yelling. "The son of a bitch is alive. I can't believe it."

That memory of that story now had him in its grip, and he thought how dam lucky he had been. And then it dawned on him,

"Damn ... Ashley again ... I vowed not to think about her." And here he was in his old neighborhood, the upper West Side, where he had once lived with his wife and children, another time by himself and later with Ashley, before moving with Ashley and his children to Miami.

But it was Ashley's husband's car he was driving when he was pronounced dead.

Semineaux had attended a dinner party, against the advice of his close buddies at the time, that was given by Ashley's lawyer husband. Ashley had recently confessed her affair with Sean, and the husband was having all his friends from Harvard in for a dinner party, in addition to his own girlfriend. It was the seventies.

Sean charmed all her husband's friends, including the husband's girlfriend, drank about five bottles of wine, and found himself alone when the husband just about locked up the wife, not allowing Semineaux to see her. Bored, Semineaux demanded a car to drive to Manhattan. It was by this time about two in the morning. The husband, rather than suggest that the drunk Semineaux sleep it off, gave him one of his four cars, a little VW beetle rather than a safer car, which unfortunately, Semineaux proved to be a death trap vehicle.

Semineaux drove from Connecticut in record time, nearly rolling the little car over several times. Finally arriving in Manhattan he was cutting across 78th Street to get to Columbus Avenue and 72nd Street, one of his favorite hangouts in those days, O'Neil's Saloon, to have a glass of wine and a cigarette, and to be as bad as women themselves by calling an old girlfriend whom he knew would come out like a cat any time of day or night to see him. Somewhere in the daydream of her body, Semineaux was sent into eternity by the impact of another car, only to return again, perhaps for a chance to get it right and do some good.

For the two years prior to the court settlement he had insisted it was a gypsy cab driver speeding toward the Bronx who had gone through a light. No one believed him, even his lawyer. They did catch the hit and run driver, proving the truth of his story analyzed later by a psychiatrist as "Retrograde Amnesia." A condition resulting from the mind's ability to block out an experience that is so horrifying, for its split-second recognition of impending death. Something so potentially fatal that the mind deeply represses the impending doom, that which must occur to those facing imminent death, like those on a supersonic jet plunging to Earth in a hopeless spin. A week after Semineaux was discharged from the hospital he returned to the scene of the accident and the husband's car was still wrapped around the same pole at the northwest corner of 78th and Amsterdam, completely destroyed.

The sound of an ambulance siren snapped him out of his

daydream. He could now see Joe and William at the inside table in deep discussion. "And that was then, and this is now, and here I am back in New York City, and I ain't going back, to no fucking prison, anytime. I love them. Look at them. But I have to go. I don't want to face this reality. At least right now. Please forgive me brothers."

He went back into the restaurant, pulled his bags and jacket from the small cloakroom opposite the men's room, dressed, and slipped back outside into the night, mumbling something about hoping they would forgive him for not saying goodbye.

Now Semineaux was experiencing another rush of freedom, one that was very dangerous. New York had always given him such a feeling of good luck, like he always felt on the thirteenth of the month. He rushed away into the night without securing a place to sleep from either of his friends. He had not expected the talk about the seriousness of his plight to have such an effect on him. But he was now out there alone with a hundred and sixty bucks in his pocket, and just did not give a damn.

His mind's eye was beginning to open to the sounds and images of the New York that had exhilarated him for years. He danced. greeted strangers, yelled to cab drivers. To just get lost in the rolling crowd of the city that set no time nor pace; night lights and laughter. He passed O'Neil's Tavern on 72nd Street, that as late as the sixties was an Irish bar excluding women, later becoming a sort of saloon for artists, writers, actors, painters and original types before the change with the deadening discussions of Yuppies about brokerage firms and banks.

"This whole fucking West Side is so Goddamn fucking Yuppie, maybe that clandestine joint is functioning in some capacity?" as he made his way to the inconspicuous door looking like millions of small service doors on New York buildings, except this door led to a subterranean cavern build during the prohibition days as a speakeasy. The underground club so near the corner of 72nd & Columbus was so little known that lifetime residents of the neighborhood were unaware of its existence.

The entrance was a flat steel door flush with the surface of the building and painted the same color, so no one would guess it was a door, but when opened one descended down into a large bar with a dance floor and stage with other rooms opening up at the end of short and long corridors, each room with its own atmosphere.

The place still had a 1920s speakeasy feel to it, and a strange image flashed upon his mind of beautiful wispy flappers and strong young men, now in their eighties and nineties, sitting about the place, like a scene from an old age home. In the seventies it had always been a rock and roll joint with live music as bands from all around the world who were trying to get a foothold in the Big Apple. The place changed hands many times, but the entrance door remained the same.

Semineaux sat at the bar crowded with more young women than men most of whom were rather pretty but what was on his mind was what to drink.

He really wanted to get numb. He wanted to forget the whole past week. He sure was not happy, and could feel the depression rolling in.

"Well, let's roll the dice of life," out loud.

"What that sir?"

"Nothing my man. Would you kindly bring me a beer and a double shot of the best vodka you have? In fact, make that two orders, and where is the cigarette machine sir?"

"You mean you want two beers and double shots? You expecting someone?"

"You got it mate. One for me and one for the professor ... straight up, no ice."

The bar had begun to fill with people, mostly women, mostly very pretty young women, mostly smiling and the happy looking guy at the end of the bar, raising his glass to toast. The first double shot of vodka went down warm, followed by the cool refreshing bottle of beer which he drank until its contents was empty. Within a split second his head felt like lights and music went on for the first time, and he was truly enjoying being alone as he raised his second shot glass in a toast to his former cellmates. Thinking it was for them, the girls raised their glasses. Christ, if they could see these gals toasting them.

"It's a shame they could not be here to celebrate my freedom. Maybe I ought to organize a small army; damn, in Philly I could, and break those guys out of the fucking prison. Christ, I have enough friends trained to be assassins and saboteurs by the CIA, FBI and so many members of my Philly tribe. Shit, we could have those guys out of there in no time. I can just see my defense at my trial. Prosecutor: 'Why did you organize a small army to liberate the prisoners so soon after you were released?'"

"You see, I was in this bar in New York on a Monday night

soon after my release, and there happened to be an unusual consortium merging two polarized forms of the dancing arts, modern dancers and show girls meeting ballerinas from the various New York dance companies, all women. It drove me to insanity. I felt a moral obligation to repay these saintly men that comforted me in prison. I heard the voice of the saint who talked to birds, I forget his name, and he told me to do it. I'm sorry."

The jury, all male of course, finds me NOT GUILTY BY REASON OF TEMPORARY INSANITY."

Strange things happen to you after you drink six shots of vodka and three beers. The dual personalities of Norman No-good and Dudley Do-right become one ... Norman No-good.

"Bartender," he shouted in between songs "I just got out of prison, think any of the beaver here would dance with me?"

Needless to say, before the injection of the devil's piss he probably could have had mostly any woman at the bar, for charm he could do, but he was never again to look up and see the dozens of pairs of beautiful eyes smiling his way, at least in this bar.

He didn't get nasty, he was just in a silly mood like a jolly escaped ass, and really didn't even desire a woman for he was deeply worried and missed Ashley and wanted to be in her arms at that moment, whom he still considered to be the most beautiful woman in the world.

By now the jukebox had given way to the beat of a live band, but since there were only about five men and about sixty women only a few people were on the dance floor. One very strange and very ugly dark woman dressed in loose fitting third world colors danced by herself, apparently enjoying the beat of the music.

"Fuck all these good-looking broads. The ugly one, there, they always appreciate everything. I won't even have to tell a lot of tales; it'll be as easy as it should be. Yeah, I'll dance my ass off in honor of my brothers back there in the Penthouse, this is for you guys."

He proceeded to do just that, and simply began dancing with the ugly woman whose long black hair fortunately hid her rather masculine face, moles and black facial hair. But she could dance, with the grace and imagination that drew admiration from many of the professional dancers sitting at the bars and tables surrounding the large dance floor, sipping drinks, some making snide remarks about the fool now having someone with which to dance, for there was an underlying symbiotic consciousness among the females present that would have denied this chauvinist pig any dance partner.

And dance they did. A waitress kept a small table near the dance floor stocked with his beer, shots, her soda and their cigarettes. He danced and freely spent chunks of the only cash he had remaining in the entire world. Surprising to the ugly girl and the onlookers, this middle-aged guy could dance. He knew his talent, nurtured by female dancers in more cities, in more countries than he could ever remember. A unique style derived from generations of rock and rollers, black southern service buddies and primitive moves assimilated from years spent on islands around the globe.

It wasn't long before it got hot. He began to strip the layers of thin cotton and wool from his tanned, muscular torso, eventually displaying the full range of his powerful male body, laughing to himself in this celebration of freedom and Zorba-like madness. Every time they stopped for seconds between songs he would go to the table, take a puff from a cigarette, raise a drink to the air and toast:

"To my brothers in the Penthouse ... Magic, Jamon, Paul and to the motherfucking lie of property rights in America," which continued even after one of the waitresses warned him that the large man collecting the money at the door wished him to lower his voice and stop his profanity.

He knew he was showing off. He also understood enough about female psychology to know that some of these beautiful women could not help being entranced by the dance performance of this crazy male.

After an hour and a half, the lady suggested they go downtown to a couple of places "he would enjoy," and off they went into the night. By this time, he could have cared less where they went. They took a cab downtown to the village where the chick knew all the seedy places that could be found jumping on a Monday night. They went to places with no colorful canvas awnings, but were tunneled into basement level bars whose huge concrete support columns dominated much of the tomb like rooms with ceilings so low that the heavy sounds of music gave the illusion of being inside a speaker made of stone.

He watched her move and laugh as she danced her way through Joint after joint as they all looked the same, for the darkness and alcohol of the evening were the only recollections of where he spent the entire hundred and sixty bucks that left him penniless.

Semineaux tried to focus on his dream. Or, was he looking for a cab? But somehow, he was in a big comfortable bed piled with warm covers protecting him from the cold blast of air coming into the half-opened window. He was aware it was early morning and being in this soft warm bed, his senses registering before his mind was conscious enough to put the puzzling sensations together. The sun was not up yet and the room was totally black, but within seconds forms of furniture, heavy wooden enclosed bookcases and clothes thrown everywhere, became faintly real, or was it a dream, again. No, she was in the bed with him but he was not in Miami, and everything was different, and he had dreamt of Ashley, and he was here.

When he was able to activate his alcohol saturated brain, he remembered he was in deep trouble. He closed his eyes and the horrible events fell into place, but where was he? The lights coming into the wooden slats must be coming out of the East, that he calculated. and that he was somewhere in New York City, but where?

A tired female voice came through the covers asking if he were OK. and this too ignited perks of his memory. Then the light began to expose her physical ugliness as she reached beneath the covers and touched him, and mumbled something about him having a place to stay, as long as he wished, before she fell back to sleep.

He slipped out of the thick warm bed, took one long step to reach the wooden blinds, peaked between them to confirm the directional source of the light, discovering that he was looking at a river, "yes," the East River, between two institutional buildings across the street, and was surprised, "That building ... that's Rockefeller University. The Rockefeller Foundation. God! My reason for being in this mad city. The reason I came here. Or am I still asleep?" He was merely one block from where his New York Irish brothers, the Harts, had run the original "Friday's," and several blocks from Sloan-Kettering hospital where his pal Lodish had been in surgical residency, and a few blocks from his own little world at the United Nations where he had spent so many years.

The loud banging of metal against metal, against metal again, reminded him of New York's early morning penance inflicted by the garbage collectors unless one is fortunate to live high enough. But at least he would not have to panic at remembering where he parked his car or tow-away time. He looked in the bed and decided she was as ugly as his lady was beautiful. He slipped out of bed, dressed, stepped over a mattress in the middle of a book lined room upon which her fifteen-year-old daughter was sleeping, grabbed his bags and read the note with the telephone number. Before closing the door glanced back into the apartment thinking about her sense of humor, her kindness, and the beauty and grace of her inner self, wishing he had some spiritual power to sprinkle these two sleeping women with blessings, and a little good luck.

In his position he knew it was dumb of him to reject her offer, quickly confirmed by the blast of cold air that chilled his body the moment he bounced out onto the sidewalk, putting his hands into his pocket for warmth, discovered the last seven cents he owned. He would have to survive in the city for a week before his appointment at the Rockefeller Foundation. If he left, he had no way of getting back into the city for the interview. But somehow, he felt lucky, in an "up" sort of mood, with plenty of energy, so he headed cross-town to the old west side, again.

He had walked but a half block from the 1st Avenue apartment when he was overcome with a ridiculous idea. He had no money and really didn't want anyone to see him in this state, surely didn't want them knowing about his arrest, for as far as everyone knew, he was being published and all was going just wonderful. He walked for an hour to a bar across town and sat down.

"You're at it again," the bartender said.

"You always look 'bad' Jack, if I were as good looking as you, I wouldn't have to try so hard."

"Oh yea, my girl just cut my heart out. Took all the furniture and wiped out my bank account. I lived with her for two years. Hold on Sean," as he moved to wait on someone at the end of the bar. Semineaux went to the phone and called an old friend down in the East Village he had known for nearly twenty years. He hoped would feed him and put him up. As expected, he invited him to eat, and said he was placing a whole chicken in the oven immediately.

Semineaux borrowed twenty bucks from the bartender and took a subway downtown to 14th Street, from which he could walk over to 1st Avenue in the East Village. But when he changed trains at 59th and Columbus Circle the station was very crowded with holiday chaos, punctuated with little Christmas bells being rung by Salvation Army persons in the red uniforms, behind which, on a cold stone step sat a young woman crying her eyes out.

He stopped and bid her cheer up, "So pretty you are. And it's Christmas, why cry."

When she looked up and spoke, he was confused by the contrast. She dressed in conservative colors and silks befitting her delicate features, but her accent gave away her downtown origins. Remembering his friend's compassionate good Samaritan deeds during their long friendship, he decided it would be OK to bring this apparently brokenhearted girl to share the chicken dinner. especially since she was Italian like his friend.

But what he didn't count on was the extremely stiff demeanor of his friend when they arrived at his door smiling, and could smell the delicious dinner coming from the warmly lit apartment.

"As I said on the phone, you are perfectly welcome, but not her. Leave her outside, and you can come in and eat, "as he closed the door.

Sean was shocked, but tried to explain to the girl when they got onto the elevator that his friend was gay and therefore like a woman more than a man, and that every few years he, or she, would get so dam mad they would not talk to each other for two or three years. "Well, it will probably be another three years, for I am not going back without you. And now I have no place to stay tonight.

She offered to leave so he could eat, which he refused to do. Fortunately, she then asked him if he would like to stay in her apartment for the night. Without any hesitation they were soon on the subway and again on the upper west side that by now had become quite windy with sub-freezing temperatures.

She explained that it was essential he buy anything before they entered her building, for once in, no guest could leave and come back in again for the night, which left him slightly suspicious. until he saw the building as they turned the corner of 74th and Broadway.

It was his old neighborhood, and one of Sean's good friends had lived in this welfare type hotel with the solid plastic security door and twenty-four hour a day policeman on duty. His friend was a great Shakespearian actor from the streets of Brooklyn who had once roomed with Steve McQueen when they were young actors, before the stardom. His pal had told Sean that

McQueen was "a fucking prick," because when he made it big, he turned his back on his friends."

The last time he visited this actor friend Andy Biardi in this building he would never forget, for that day Andy made a dry remark about "that's the fucking way I'll go," as his next door neighbor's body was being hauled out of the room next door on a stretcher, covered over with a grey blanket. But it was a place to sleep on this very cold windy night.

As if the day had not been filled with enough surprises, about five yards from the front door out pops his old friend Andy Biardi, without his usual smile, good looks, and dry humor. His friend's head was down; he looked in pain, old, and walking with the aid of a walking stick.

"Andy, he shouted ... how are you?"

"Not so good," he said as he just kept moving. It happened so fast. He knew Andy long enough. Andy even knew his wife and kids; a level many intimate New York friends never experience. By this time, he and the girl were at the plastic door with the cop and the buzzer going off as he tried to get assurance that he could return to this girl's apartment after catching up to see his friend for a few moments.

The girl looked concerned. "They'll never let you back in here if you don't come now."

"I'll get back in," he said as he ran to turn the corner to catch up to his friend who said something about going to the Greek restaurant around the corner. Semineaux found the Greek restaurant and it was empty, and he even checked the men's room. He spends the next forty minutes checking all the restaurants within a short distance from the hotel, but no Andy. He returned to the hotel with that sweet girl on his mind, but there was no way short of a war or court order that could get him past the blockheaded guys at the plastic front door.

"Well asshole, now you are homeless in New York City."

It was freezing now, for an ice-cold wind was blowing off the Hudson River that somehow had not been so piercing on the lower East side of town. He knew he could not stay out in this bitter cold all night unless he kept moving, and since he had not eaten his energy level was dropping as fast as his body heat.

"Don't be stupid and make any mistakes, a person could die on a night like this," he thought. He didn't seem to have but a few options: all bad. He decided to walk down into hell's kitchen to the restaurant at 49th and eleventh hoping it would be open.

Within three blocks of the restaurant he could see it's lights were off, a causality of the plague of homelessness. It was so bitter cold at this point he quickly doubled back a few blocks to his Bulgarian friend's apartment in the heart of hell's kitchen, where he tried in vail to ring him up. Joe had told him the previous evening that he had been dating an East side girl and was perhaps not home, for Joe was always his survival safety net in New York City. Beyond this, he had no moves.

It suddenly became survival time. He knew midtown would be bad for everything would be locked up. Forget downtown, for he could not think of any area be it the Village, Soho, Wall Street or the East Side that would be a sure thing. He was lucky he had spent so many years moving about the city all night in the old days to have some feel for what he was up against. In eight years, he had been in more building that he could ever remember, and by instinct or repressed memory he knew to get up into the Upper West side above the expanding Yuppies who now lived where his Latino friends had once lived.

If he pushed far enough north, he would eventually find an apartment building with no doorman or security locks, for he knew he must get inside and away from the wind and the direct blast of cold air that was wearing him down.

He pushed his way through a dirty metal door on a block somewhere in the nineties that was going through major renovations, and climbed the wide stairwell up the dusty, dirty steps until he found a shadowy opening against one wall on the sixth floor. At first, he merely leaned his two heavy shoulder bags against the wall and stood catching his breath, as he slowly slid down the wall until his ass sat on the dusty floor.

The cold morning air coming through the window told him to put on his long winter underwear beneath the wool pants as he dressed the previous morning before leaving that comfortable East side apartment, and he had enough layers of cotton and wool on his back and head protecting him enough from the cold and dampness in the stairwell that he fell sound asleep for four hours, without moving.

First it was dogs barking. Then the sun coming from the east through a window that looked like it had not been cleaned since the 1940s. Then someone yelling at someone else. He managed to stand up, stagger down the stairs, and out into the sunlit morning. It was still very cold, but the wind had stopped, and he had managed to survive the night.

Now he had only five more days for his meeting at the Rockefeller Foundation, and he constantly checked to see that his white shirt, silk tie, slacks, sweater, blazer, and dress shoes were safely tucked into the bottom of his bag. He walked downtown and managed to slip into the YMCA on 64th Street where took a long steam bath and shower, and afterwards walked out into the sunshine feeling as though he had stayed at the Mayflower Hotel around the corner instead of the stairwell in southern Harlem.

Hungry but refreshed he spent the entire day traveling back and forth between the village and the west side, and by nightfall calculated four more days, yet, had no idea of his next move.

By early evening he passed a street corner art dealer that he had seen in two separate locations during the day, one directly across from the Met and now on Bleaker and 7th Avenue in the village. He had noticed the dealer, a stocky Jewish guy with a beard. He never seemed to be moving about enough to talk with the many potential customers that delayed at his exhibit long enough to be pitched for a sale. All in all, he must have passed this exhibit ten times, except this time there were no customers and his eyes met the eyes of the art dealer.

They first exchanged gestures, then words. The art dealer was so amused by this stranger's suggestion that he needed a sales assistant to push his art. He was losing sales and he hired him on the spot to sell on a commission basis. And that is what began a rather silly, carefree four days that could have been pure hell.

Within several hours the streets of the village were filled with more people than usual for a Wednesday evening but with a little more than a week until Christmas, everybody seemed to be outside. In the first forty minutes Semineaux sold two prints and one painting, and fifteen minutes later he heard the art dealer give an order for Chinese food to a young guy he later learned was the art dealer's "go-for." A short break came in the action so the three of them ate the Chinese food from the back end of the opened truck that warehoused the paintings and photography.

Semineaux's food was devoured quickly since he had not eaten a meal since leaving prison three days before, and remembered only eating a slice of pizza since. After the break he managed to sell five more paintings, bringing a smile to the bearded dealer's face, who seemed at times to follow a strange pattern.

On several occasions Semineaux nearly had a sale closed when the dealer would quietly interrupt him with his own pitch, always filled with interesting backgrounds of artists, art history, and the world of photography. Sean essentially did not like selling.

When there were no customers they would talk. He told Sean his last name. Sean understood more about the interruptions of his sales pitch. The dealer's name was Italian, Marino. Now he knew why, for every time he interrupted a sale it was always with a very pretty customer, which explained the behavior. He was Italian, and the good-looking women were more important than the sale.

"Marino, huh? I thought you were Jewish."

"Bullshit," he said, as they both had a good laugh. It happened again and again, and on each occasion, he was learning more and more about art and photography, for this art dealer with the beard was truly an oil painter and an award-winning photographer who lived in his studio in the Bronx. On one occasion a young lady had just bought a photograph with Marino closing in, when Semineaux recited one of his poems to her, which Marino overheard.

"So, you are a 'poet,' Marino said using the Spanish he knew from living in the Bronx all his life. After the girl left the two got to talking. He pulled his China book from his bag, bringing a huge smile to Marino's face. In between sales they talked about art, politics, writing, life, creativity and struggle; and he noticed more and more artistic looking friends stopping by to say hello to his new employee.

Marino told him to begin reciting his poetry out loud as he was selling to attract more customers, which it did, along with more sales. Toward the end of the evening it got very cold, so they went into an old bar with green windows and Irish drunks to count out the money, drink a few beers. He actually got paid thirty-five dollars.

Man, I really like your poetry. I can really relate to it."

"Thanks ... You know that today was the first time I ever recited my poems except for some friends and family. You gave me the courage. For it's probably not such hot poetry. I was surprised you liked it.

"Come on now," Marino said with a big smile. You are a

cocky guy."

Yes, but this is art. I am just a baby against this creative God called art. It humbles me. You 'are' an artist. I don't even know if I have a beginning."

A fierceness appeared in Marino's eyes, normally as serene as his manner. "What bullshit," Marino nearly shouted, "You think an artist just waits around until someone says, 'Hey man, you are an artist?' Huh? I don't know. You got me all puffed-up out there on the street today."

"You're great Marino," as Sean caught Marino with a powerful jab to his beefy shoulder. It was nice to hear my words in the open. Maybe it was all that beaver around us. But you gave me strength, I never would have ever recited my stuff like that."

"Let me teach you something," Marino interjected. "I didn't go to school in the Bronx. My parents send me downtown here to a catholic school and then a creative art school. So, I lived in the Village since I was young. I've seen then all. An 'artist,' my friend, and listen ... an artist makes that decision to be an artist. You first. Like when you like a woman. Do you care about what anyone else thinks? You decide. I've seen people come to the Village from all over.

If they had said to their family or friends at home, I am an artist,' it would be tough to get encouragement, or they might laugh at them. That's why we suffer, because we allow things to be determined by others. They hire you and fire you, promote you or demote you. The artist is. You hire yourself. You must, above all, believe in yourself. for no one else will."

"Yea... and I have been so hesitant to take on anything that might distract me, like a full-time career."

"Your art must be your priority," said Marino, impatient with the interruption. It can't be part time. Shit man, you have to love it all the time, like a woman. You love your art, or you will lose her."

Don't get me started on that brother. They want more than love.

I can see you have been around. Remember this amigo ... You have a young heart ... that's you brother. Remember, everyone alive has an age that is quite independent of the age on your birth certificate. Don't forget that.

Marino ... I'm beginning to love you. Why couldn't you be a broad.

I don't know if you remember a friend of mine hanging

around. He got us coffee once. He wants you to go to this address here in the Village and read your poetry tonight. He's like the local talent scout and knows everyone, lived here all his life, and has seen them all come and go, from Ginsberg on.

I remember the guy. The big one.

He liked your poetry enough to invite you over to a reading at his house in the West Village. I'd go if I were you. Look, I have to go back to my studio. I have a chick coming over and I have to paint for two hours before I go to sleep. go over to the house. Just ask for Len."

"Thanks Marino. See you tomorrow."

It actually was a house in the Village. By the time he got there everything was in full session with dozens of people milling about on three floors, including an outdoor second floor porch that somehow did not seem too cold. The evening was strangely beautiful with a full moon and stars looking like the northern lights rather than Manhattan. The house was an old wooden structure with creaky wooden floors covered with old carpets thrown here and there, with paintings and plants.

Sean was suspect of the people. At first glance he saw new age type people who talked about how happy they were when they lived in Egypt two thousand years ago, in their second life. Upon closer observation, he began to hear and see every age, shape and sexual type. He found the kitchen, and was searching for a drink among all the cakes, fruit, tea and coffee. Then someone whispered his name and it was Marino's friend.

"I'm glad you came. I enjoyed your reading on the street. You'll be going on in around fifteen minutes. Just read, and if they like it ... just keep reading. You'll know when to stop. Just relax and enjoy yourself. All nice people here.

"Thank you for inviting me," and as the man turned to go into the reading, Sean went back through the kitchen to the back porch, and climbed down the stairs to the alley where he quickly walked a half block to procure three quarts of beer and a pack of cigarettes. He was going to have fun. He was now in tenth gear and the cookies and coffee would not do it.

He returned five minutes before his reading and drank one quart of beer, and along with the tobacco he was pretty buzzed when he sat in the midst of this very polite group and read a poem about Miami, then one written in San Francisco, and his heart swelled with delight for they were smiling and encouraging. Then he read a poem written in China, then one in

London, and on and on for nearly an hour, and closed with a poem called The Old West Side," with everyone clapping.

One guy came forward immediately telling him he could get him some readings around town immediately, and there would be some money for both of them. The guy had this black hat he had not seen since the likes of the "three musketeers" sword fighting movies, for the guy had long straight black hair, a mustache, long and lean, and weird black eyes.

The guy was fun and theatrical. Every night he got Sean a different bar in which to read his poetry; some fun places, and some with some hostile types. Every day Sean made ten to thirty bucks with Marino, and twenty-five dollars at night reading the poetry. This allowed him to eat good, buy the three quarts of beer he would drink during each night's reading, and blow most of it after the readings eating a wonderful meal with good wine with one of the young women he had met selling art during the day, with whom he would at sleep night, in the comfort of a perfumed, silky, bed.

When he first arrived in the city, time seemed to hang in the darkness of hopelessness. Now, the week went so quickly. It was soon Sunday night. He was booked into two small taverns to be followed by a reading at the famous White Horse Tavern were the renown poet Dillon Thomas drank himself to death.

That night it rained like a heavy tropical storm, all night. It was late by the time they got to the White Horse Tavern and he could not believe he was going to read in this place the great Thomas made famous. They were drenched, but he had a glow from the alcohol and smokes.

When they arrived, there seemed to be some confusion. The bartender that had arranged the reading was Out with a dying wife and this guy knew nothing, and cared even less, no less pay money for the performance. The negotiations did not seem to be going so well until a stocky old Irishman with meaty forearms told the equally beefy bartender.

"Bartender ... let me tell you something. You are just a fill-in here. We drink here. This is not just a bar ... Sir ... but a place where no poet would ever be turned away."

And then he stood up, leaned over the bar and said, "This poet reads, or I break this fucking bottle across your fucking ugly face," joined by even the few women yelling and jeering until the bartender capitulated and kept the drinks coming. And this is how Semineaux came to read his poems in the White Horse

Tavern.

The booze flowed, the laughter louder than the December rain slamming against the windows till the end of the evening. It was too late to call on the young lady he had stayed with the previous evening. He was concerned, for he had to look presentable in the morning. The Rockefeller foundation people.

In desperation he called an old friend from the seventies, a gay artist friend who lived in the West Village. Fortunately, he answered the phone and did not hesitate to invite Sean to stay, leaving the door unlocked since he had already crashed for the night. Semineaux felt so secure when he entered the apartment, for the rain was now surging into a storm. He found a short note and followed instructions into the living room at the end of a dimly lit hallway.

Within a few seconds he took off his shoes and wet clothes and crawled beneath the covers on the couch. Looking up he saw delicate silken Chinese butterfly mobiles floating with the undetectable movement of warm apartment air, throwing images onto the little hanging plants casting shadows onto bamboo curtains, themselves illuminated slightly by yellow streetlights peeking into the room's peace. The mobiles spun like a slow motion merry-go-around ... around and around. Soon, Semineaux was fast asleep.

Again, he was awakened by the banging of cans against metal trash jaws eating New York's waste, for he seemed to be following the sanitation department's schedule this week. He made his way to a bathroom with old fortress walls once dug and blasted from granite foundations deep within subterranean New York. His head began to clear watching the shower water running down the rough granite stone wall, like the surface of the waterfall.

Sean emerged from the bathroom conservatively attired from his soft leather shoes to the thin silk tie against a pure white collar off-set by the black "V" neck sweater covering a shirt that had somehow gotten soaked with water from the previous night's rain. Even the jacket was a little damp.

His friend had made a little coffee for him, and he thanked him before quickly departing into the early morning rush to get to the meeting with the hope of a financial grant from the Rockefellers.

Chapter 13

The Rockefellers

Just before entering the Rockefeller foundation he looked at his reflection in the large plate glass window and was pleased with the conservative he viewed.

The hot shower appeared to have erased the debauchery of the beer bloated face and red eyes. He emerged from the elevator onto the spacious reception room, encountering a professional looking secretary.

The receptionist escorted him into a conference room where he was seated on a couch before a knee-high glass table upon which sat a brand-new paperback copy of his China book, pure white with the red letters. The president of the foundation came into the room and introduced himself, sitting opposite Semineaux, with his own copy of the book, title facing him.

The president, Dr. Thurmond Cranford, III, was a very distinguished looking man with white hair, looking more like a bank president in an expensive Wall Street suit than the Ph.D. indicated in the literature given Sean by the secretary. He apologized for the rushed morning and suggested they get down to talking about the project. The secretary brought Semineaux a small white porcelain pot filled with a deep dark coffee. As the president spoke of how much he enjoyed his China book, Sean gulped down two cups of coffee, further clearing his head. Semineaux needn't have prepared for this meeting since he had written many pages in response to all the questions posed in the numerous correspondence between Miami and New York prior to this day; them wanting him to explain every contact he had ever had with any Russian, experiences even Sean thought almost nothing about, for so long a time.

The president held Semineaux's proposals for two books, one on nuclear, chemical, and biological politics to be written with a co-author and another on Soviet Perceptions of Global Politics which would be written alone.

"I must say Dr. Semineaux, I've never seen proposals like this. I think they are very good. Quite imaginative."

"Thank you."

"Well, they are to the point. And, if you excuse me, let me get to the point. On the proposal to write a book on the Soviets." He stopped and paused, as if to change an idea. "Well, you did write a very good book on Chinese politics, but you are not a Soviet specialist. You do not speak Russian, and there are so many Soviet specialists we could support to do the same thing."

For a moment they stopped talking and they both looked at each other in silence. The president again glanced at the proposals in his hand.

"You have only visited the Soviet Union several times, though I am impressed that you have been to Soviet Central Asia. Not many people can say that."

"I have always been interested in Central Asia."

As Sean said the words, he noticed the man breaking eye contact and looking down at the table. "Ah...ah..." as he seemed to stumble for the next words. Both remained quiet as he flicked through the papers in his hand, then himself reached for a coffee. "Excuse me," as he prepared his drink.

In the moment of stillness, Sean's eyes were fixed on his white hair. Who is this guy? Can you believe it? The President of the Rockefeller Foundation and last night I was with drunks. How does one get to hold such a position? A Ph.D.? Like me, yeah...shit, you can have ten Ph.D.'s, but if you are not in a club. Bet his old man never worked in a factory.

"You will have to forgive me for taking the time to go over this in front of you, but I just flew in from London this morning, and remember having many questions, from Soviets at the UN to that experience of yours up in the Arctic when you were in the military."

"Oh, up north."

"Yes, your experience on the early warning line. It's called the DEW line," Sean suggested.

"What is it ... what was your mission up there," as he learned forward for the first time.

"We set up early warning defenses to detect Soviet bombers that would have come across the Arctic ice caps in the event of war. We were parachuted into the snow way up there. I was the cryptographer who decoded and recorded the intercepted Russian messages. I always had a Russian language specialist on the outpost with me. The only English language broadcasts were Moscow Molly's broadcasts."

"Who was Moscow Molly?"

"Oh, she was this Russian gal with a sexy voice, like the WWII Tokyo Rose."

"Oh yes."

"Just to let us know that our air bases in Greenland and Labrador were infiltrated Moscow Molly would tell us to check a security door on some installation. It freaked people out when they discovered the door was unlocked. She informed us weekly about lights being out and flat tires on fighter planes sitting on tightly secured flight lines. Things like that to unnerve us. I was trained to not only decode what the language specialist monitored, but was given special training in arctic survival to protect and nursemaid these linguists."

"Were you armed?" his tone naive, as the academic he was.

"Of course, we were armed," Semineaux slightly laughing. "We were trained to maintain the efficiency of the small weapons arsenal we had with us such as automatic weapons, small rocket launchers, long range hunting rifles with great scopes, and grenades."

Why did you need such fire power up there?

There were Russians up there.

I never heard that before.

Our small war up there is one of the best kept secrets of the Cold War.

Semineaux dropped his head for a moment as if to gather his thoughts. Then he looked at the wall on the far corner of the room.

People have no idea what was going on between ourselves and the Russians up in the Arctic. Secret military operations where we fought Russians. Americans died. No one was ever told how. Hell, I lost two good buddies from military intelligence training schools who died in a little military spy thing in Siberia. Everyone was told they died someplace else.

Being a cryptographer, I could find out anything. I discovered the truth but couldn't tell anyone. Just like I couldn't tell anyone about my own horrible experiences in what we who fought called the "Ice War."

"You actually had a name for the war?" he quizzed, but before Semineaux could answer he leaned toward him. "You actually encountered Russians in the Arctic?"

"The Russians put their own guys there on the ice. Don't forget, even then they expected we could attack them over the polar ice caps. Subs had no firing beneath the ice capacity in those days, but long-range bombers carrying nuclear bombs could."

"What type of missions were executed'"

"They would parachute us above Thule, Greenland, to observe what the Soviets were up to. Most of the time it was routine. And quite boring. We'd monitor them, and they would monitor us. But one time..." Then he stopped and looked right into Dr. Cranford's eyes. "What does all this have to do with writing a book?" Dr. Cranford cleared his throat. "You have a point, but the foundation set these interview guidelines of investigation. I have to follow them. Sorry. Please go on."

"One time they were supposed to drop us a long distance from a Russian outpost, but some idiot dropped us right in the middle of their camp. There were two of us and ten of them. We could see these guys all huddled around a big outdoor fire stove. My first thoughts were how to negotiate a way out so there would be no fight." Sean stopped again. This time neither said nothing. Then he continued.

"It was late in the day when they dropped us and these guys were already drinking their vodka and were in a crazy mood. They didn't see us until we got our chutes off and only one of them turned to look. I smiled and waved a friendly wave, but it was useless for within seconds they began firing at us and running toward us. Fortunately for us they only had their small side arm pistols, having left their automatic weapons inside and we also had the advantage of firing down on them because we were at the top of a small rise." Semineaux stopped again. This time he reached for the glass of water.

"I was only twenty years old at the time and had never killed anyone . . . nor wanted to. We dropped down into a prone position at the top of that little knoll with bullets from their pistols flying around us like in a cowboy movie. From our position we took them all out. The last of the ten actually fell on my partner who broke down in tears, screaming for me to pull him off. We had killed all ten of these poor fellows all around our same age. And then, and then. . ." now talking quickly to move on" I immediately coded a message directly to headquarters and they sent up a squad to bury the Russians."

"I find this hard to believe."

"They pulled us back to Newfoundland and threatened us with Leavenworth prison if we ever spoke about it again, ever. And to tell you the truth ... I never have ... until just telling you. And six months later I had another firefight when I was all alone. I killed three Russians that time, and buried them myself, and said nothing." Then Sean became quiet, and almost choked. He found it hard to swallow and quickly took a swig of coffee.

"I can see this is upsetting you, let's change the subject."

"It's OK ... I'm fine."

"I am interested in your United Nations experience. You spent ten years at the UN, is that correct?"

"Yes, I was affiliated with the UN for ten years. Had my own office for six of those years. Traveled the world on UN missions for the Political and Security Affairs division."

"How did you get to know so many Russians?"

"I was studying the Chinese at the UN before the Communist came. I knew many of the ROC delegates. But when the PRC guys came to New York I got to know them and studied all their political positions. So, the Russians, or I should say the KGB, followed me. I even caught a high-ranking KGB officer assigned to follow me going through my research papers one day."

"Really, you caught him?"

"Yes, his name was Alexander Delgadin. Actually, the main drop off point for the KGB at the UN, we later discovered, was about twenty steps from my office in the Dag Hammarskjold library."

"What about the Russian you caught going through your papers?"

"He was stunned that I caught him, but particularly stunned when I got him on the elevator and told him. excuse my language Doctor ... but I said, 'You blockheaded Bolshevik ... I thought you were my friend. all this dumb bullshit you feed me about Communism. You are a fucking slave, a robot ...' "Sean began to laugh.

"Excuse me..." Then he stopped laughing. I said, "look in my eyes Alex. You have never seen a man as free as me. You say you are free, but you lie Alex. I know you are a KGB agent."

"'What do you mean KGB,' he said to me. 'I am a librarian.'

"'Sir,' I looked him right in the eye and said 'You fucking liar. And I am sick of your bullshit about politics.' And then I told him the FBI knew about him. He was shocked and in denial."

"How did you know the FBI knew about him?"

"Because they asked me to spy on him. But that's another story. So did the CIA."

Dr. Cranford began to ask a question, but Sean continued.

"After that day I never saw him again. He was eventually caught in California trying to bribe some technical information and sent back to the Soviet Union persona non grata. Actually, someday I would like to see him again. I personally liked the guy."

"Pardon me, your life has been exciting, but I don't see where you have something so special you learned that others haven't also experienced. I just don't see it."

"Well, to begin with, here it is 1982 and we think the
Russians are such a threat we are arming like mad. I think all this Marxist\Leninist ideology is going to fall apart."

"Communism, come apart? The Communists are getting stronger, not weaker." Dr. Cranford shot back.

"Yes, but I will explain that in my book. But what scares me is what I learned in military intelligence about how hair-triggered we have become with nuclear weapons. The Soviet Union is not going to be able to sustain this military buildup it began after the Cuban missile crisis so our pushing them is creating a dangerous environment"

"But they are making tremendous leaps in all levels of weapons development. They keep tight control on their people. They are strong enough to operate successfully in Angola, Afghanistan and Central America. While, I might add, building a powerful deep-water navy. They will create more Marxist revolutions.

"Sir, forget Marxist revolutions. The revolutions of today are Nationalists revolutions. Nation's want their freedom, just like we did in 1776. Most people don't want to revolt, they want to emulate. They just want to live better. They want a house, car, and good food."

"Ok, perhaps you are right. But why do you think you know

the Russians enough for us to give you money rather than a scholar who had studied them more than you? Fair enough question ... and it is getting late, I have another appointment." He was abrupt for the first time.

"As part of my Ph.D. program I studied clinical psychiatry at Mt. Sinai Medical Hospital, Department of Psychiatry. I took this experience to the UN. It did not help much with the Chinese, for they are closed people, reluctant to reveal personal things. That is the way of the Chinese, hold it in."

"Dr. Semineaux, I must interrupt. I know dozens of people who have had much more contact with the Russians than you."

"Perhaps so, but they did not ask the same questions I asked."

"What do you mean?"

"You know how the Russians drink. They brag about it. Well, I can also drink. I would drink with them, and do they love to brag. I always let them win the discussion on politics. I asked them questions about their mothers, fathers, brothers, sisters, girlfriends, loving, fighting, you name it. I learned how they really thought about life. The fundamental things that we must know when Marxism falls. The true nature of the Russian mind."

"There have been many studies of the Russian mind. Have you read Nathan Lites and..?"

"Pardon me sir ... but these studies talk about the aggressiveness of the Russians. I see it differently. I see the Russians as "B" personalities. They are passive as a culture. In fact, they are lazy, spoiled from childhood. The external world has always been tough in Russia. Totalitarianism, serfdom, dreadful conditions broke the individual's will. They became conformist, communal, greedy, xenophobic, and aggressive on the surface."

"You say they think differently because of this experience?"

"The psychology is not based on common sense. They don't think in logical and orderly terms as in western cultures with the emphasis on reason. It's OK to be emotional. Emotion is more important than reason. In fact, in Russia, to be smart, cleaver, intelligent, even rational, is inferior to being emotional, lovable, warm. Spirituality is important. This is the Russian soul.

"What about that spirituality? How does that tie into what you are saying? Marxists are atheists."

"Even their psychology is a collective misery. Even their salvation into heaven is a collective endeavor. Communism found a collective psychology. How can you translate that to mean anything?" the President said in a rather frustrated tone.

"A Russian once told me that it's OK to be a loser in Russia. You are suspect as a winner. He told me of an old Russian saying, 'The tallest blade of grass is the first to be cut down by the scythe, 'so it's best not to stand out. In fact, there is a tremendous sense of collective jealously. It's nasty, they are envious. This collective psychology goes back to the Tsars. The collective ethic of the commune of villages, the obshchina. They planted, harvested, worked together, shared a common fate. Perhaps we could call it equal poverty for all."

"You sure see them in different terms."

"Oh, they are also fun loving. To Russians, it is important to be human. As they say, not boring and dry like a bread crust ... it's called 'sukhar.' They indulged their children to a point of dependence. They spoil their children. The kids do nothing. Everything is done for them."

"We have spoiled children also."

"Yes, but American children are taught to be self-reliant. You know, make it on your own. The Russians I knew at the UN all thought I was nuts because I worked so many jobs when I needed money. I bartended, drove a cab, did carpentry, sold commodities on Wall Street. When in school, they don't work. They are not go-getters. In fact, they don't take risks. They are conservative and cautious."

"Well, how do you account for their global military expansion if they don't take risks. Look at the Cuban missile crisis and now Afghanistan."

"That's different, I'm talking about the culture. The Soviet threat in terms of expansion is not any different from all peoples on earth. Human beings, unlike animals, are not territorial."

"Pardon me Dr. Semineaux, human not territorial, how do you explain that?"

"If we were territorial animals, we would be more respectful of territory. Humans have so little respect for territory. That is why we invade each other, explore, intermarry, migrate. The Russians are no different than anyone else in that respect. What we have to do is understand the Russian psychology in a more fundamental way."

As he was talking Semineaux first noticed the gentleman touching his nose in a strange sort of way, the room was getting rather warm, and even though he drank all the coffee that was in pot, he couldn't completely shake the hangover.

"Don't you think Reagan understands the Russians?" Dr. Cranford asked.

"We have a President who is not intelligent enough to see anything but the surface, and doesn't even read, or think deeply for that matter. At a time when we have so much power. When we need a man like Lincoln. A man who has suffered, endured, read, thought, and worried. You see no grey hair or lines on his face. He worries about nothing more than how he looks."

"Well, the world seems to have a little more respect for us now that Reagan's president. And he wants to develop a sure defense system since the Russians are so unpredictable."

Missile defense shield, Semineaux's head raised. "You mean this 'Star Wars' idea. Bad idea."

"Why would you say that? It would give us some security if we can put the system in place."

"Let's say we could put such a system in place. It would just lead to more arms races. Other nations would build more weapons of mass destruction. "No, I think you are wrong on this," Cranford interrupted. "It would give us security without threatening other countries." "Dr. Cranford," Semineaux leaning forward, "It doesn't work that way. When a nation feels secure it is because they have powerful weapons. It creates insecurity in others by this very fact. It is the psychology that counts. My security creates your insecurity. Nations don't trust each other. 'Star Wars' is security to us, a threat to them. If we are not vulnerable, others will build enough weapons to make us feel vulnerable."

At that very moment a rather attractive secretary opened the door, "Pardon me sir, but you have an urgent phone call, perhaps I could bring more coffee."

As she moved to retrieve the little white coffee pot, Semineaux quickly moved toward the rest room, for he had finally detected what the hell smelled so badly in the room, him. His numbed sense of smell was returning as well as his memory. The clothes in the bag had not gotten wet from the heavy rains the previous evening, but from the several bottles of beer that were given to him at the White Horse Tavern. His clothes had been marinating among three broken beer bottles all night long, drenched, now dried, but smelling like a gin mill.

The rest room had all the amenities of a fine hotel and he splashed several different types of cologne on himself, and returned to the room seconds before Dr. Cranford.

"Sorry for the interruption, I had a call from Brussels."

"No problem, I was rather amused while you were gone."

"How's that?"

"One of your janitors came in here and found two broken bottles of beer in that trash bag. He said when he entered the room, though he was at the bar where he worked in the evenings," as they both laughed, the Doctor heartily, his forced.

"That's funny. My secretary just said something to me about the awful smell in the conference room. This room used to be our room, lately too many divisions are using this room, and who knows what has come in here?"

"Well, back to your proposals." As the doctor spoke, Semineaux listened. The bottom line was an offer to send him to the Rockefeller think tank high in the mountains of Bologna, Italy which housed an impressive library and provided comfortable quarters for a continuous flow of international bigshots from the world of politics, law, business, academia, to server as resource people to scholars like himself domiciled in Bologna to write a book. It all sounded so nice -- all the facilities were available to him free as a grant -- but all travel and personal expenses would have to be paid for out of his own pocket, or "from other sources."

It wasn't a place he needed, or access to resource people or research itself. He could write the book in Hollywood or Key West, could find his own resource people for interviewing as he had done for so long at the United Nations, and if he wanted research information he knew how to get into special think tanks for information faster than a spy, and surely faster than any professor he ever met. Money is what he wanted.

"How stupid," he thought to himself, "even a Miami gambler would take these odds," and who was to know what he might turn up, for any investment in finding solutions to these threats to life and civilization should be worth a few pennies to the Rockefellers. All he really wanted was a grant to support a modest existence while he wrote from his own head, books, research, and experience. The Rockefeller Foundation turned out to be full of wind, and within seconds after landing on the first floor he was out in the sunshine of a clear December day on sixth avenue, "If my Daddy went to Yale I probably would not be walking out of here with empty pockets."

It surely had not been a dull New York visit, despite the fact that instead of the one hundred and twenty thousand dollars he expected before leaving Florida two weeks ago, his pockets yielded four dollars and twenty cents. On the eve of the holidays the poetry readings were grinding to a slow halt, Calabro's street corner art establishment would be shut down until mid-week, so he set out to close up business in New York and get down to Philadelphia to see his lawyer, Laconi.

He went directly to the Mayflower Hotel on Central Park West where he had stored the rest of his belongings and rearranged everything, making sure to discard the broken green glass from the beer bottles, and started to move downtown and out of the city.

By time he reached 57th street and 7th avenue the midafternoon crowd was impacted on every corner and sidewalk of this wide intersection.

He had to walk into the street to make any headway. He was anxious to cut across to Eleventh Avenue and walk downtown through hell's kitchen to the Lincoln tunnel when a calling voice distracted him. He looked in the direction of this voice coming through the crowd to its source, a powerfully built black man in rear of a tunnel of newspapers and magazines in the newsstand on 57th street whom he had spoken with many times in the darkness of the night over many years. He stopped in his tracks, ducked over to the newsstand entrance from where he could get a better look at the man at the end of this tunnel like shed, and said.

"Hello and goodbye my friend, leaving town."

"Mon ... you always leaving and coming. Good to see you again."

"You too brother. God bless you. What's your name again?"

"Moses."

"Last time I said to you. Moses ... how could I forget. I'll never forget again," as Moses' huge white teeth nearly lit up the rear of the darkened shed, in which he had worked for nearly ten years. "Have a good day brother," he yelled over the noise of the passing crowd as he again was on his way.

By the time he walked the twenty blocks to the entrance to the Lincoln tunnel the sun had dropped behind cold, grey, December skies. He pulled a ski jacket from one of his shoulder bags to deal with the quick dropping of the temperature.

He felt sure he could thumb a ride from the New York side of the Lincoln Tunnel dressed as well as any gentleman could look. With a little luck he could speed across the ninety miles to the Pennsylvania border within striking distance of Public transportation into Philadelphia.

One gets an entirely different perspective walking into this vast expanse of roads that feeds into the Tunnel than from an automobile, for there were nearly a dozen lanes cascading with streams of cars leaving Manhattan for the Christmas holidays sounding like the pounding of a gigantic waterfall. There appeared not another person within the vicinity for two hours as the cars passed him in what seemed to be an urban infinity, as the tunnel swallowed millions of cars going West, and no one stopped to give him a ride.

It began to get dark as the lanes suddenly became empty, save for a few cars. He ululated like a wolf to hear his soul echo within this walled entrance deep below street level, on the ancient banks of the Hudson river, now sealed in concrete and steel. He would have to try his luck at the train station.

Darkness changed the environment from isolation to danger within a few short minutes with figures high up on the horizon peering down on him, so he hastily began to climb from the river level to the avenues above the tunnel entrance which never appeared so steep when driving. When he got to the first road he felt as if he had climbed a small mountain. He must have looked ripe for the pickings dressed so elegantly as a gentleman for he spied an angry looking scar faced guy who appeared to be in a full fighting dive toward him. He had watched the man stalk him from above for an hour, like a hawk sizing up his "dandy dan" victim. Now, not wanting to slow down a step as he projected an insane look into the eyes of this threatening scar faced stranger, who took the hint and peeled off to one side. "It's times like this I wished I carried a fucking gun," he thought to himself as the stranger now chocked and puffed just to get out of the way of this packhorse climbing the stairs two at a time with his back and shoulders weighed down, now screaming for the stranger "to get the fuck out of my way," as the would be mugger ran in freight.

Sean was trying to catch his breath and laughing about the thug, until he was distracted by two men who ran from a building between 10th and 9th Avenues, jumped into a large old battered car, and drove toward 9th Avenue as if they had just robbed a bank. Suddenly, they made a screeching "u" turn, ribbing the full power of the loud engines downhill, right at him, attempting to run him down on what was a very narrow 17th century street leading up to 9th Avenue. On their first pass they almost got him, and all he could think of was how many lousy TV series had scenes like this. He avoided the second attack, again, by merely crossing the street on a dead-run. But their last attack came as quickly as a shark, suddenly turning a complete 360 degrees, hoping to smash his body against the walls just to take whatever was in his nice-looking bags, which is why gentleman should not walk in certain parts of town at night.

The last attack nearly got him as he ducked behind a half dozen 18th century hardened steel pipes once used to tie horses, as the front bumper of the old Chrysler slammed into the pipes smashing the one working headlight, for he had just stepped behind the pipes leaving only about six inches of air space, saving his 20th century ass. Dirt covered the car windows behind which he faintly viewed two zombies looking, disappointed, dopes.

With only a dozen giant steps and leaps he landed like a parachutist from hell to heaven onto 9th Avenue with voices of two people discussing how a particular "green pottery would go well in the kitchen," with him sucking his pipe, her wrapped in a frumpy coat, both arm in arm looking into a store window. The flickering lights of 9th Avenue reflected off the few metal pieces on the rear of the Chrysler as the car moved slowly down toward the river as though nothing at all had just happened.

By the time he passed the third couple holding hands he felt out of the danger zone and slipped the Irish cap from his head and put the cigar stub into its small case, slipped his silk tie from beneath his shirt, took out his old leather briefcase, changing his image as he closed in on Pennsylvania station at 34th Street in his second attempt to cross into New Jersey.

By the time he descended into Penn Station a train was leaving for Philadelphia with a huge crowd anxiously awaiting to board in the. main departure hall. Somehow, he would get to Philadelphia to see the lawyer, and then back to Miami, but the concern at the moment was how, with no money.

Chapter 14

Going south

Without missing a step, he moved quickly among the thousands of people in Penn Station for the departure area was filled to capacity with people in movement for the holidays. The first thing he had to do was get on a train with no ticket.

He knew there would not be enough conductors to check all the boarding tickets and once on the train he would sit in an area populated by women rather than men, in case events became embarrassing, for he felt men would be less inclined to sympathize with his plight and might even help the conductor throw him off the train.

The first step of his "boarding theory" was correct for he was on the train without a ticket check and moved from car to car looking for that "right" seat, and upon entering the third car immediately dropped into the only vacant seat in a sea of grey-headed female passengers, hoping to sit next to a grandmother, creating a higher probability that the conductor be a gentleman.

As he slumbered into the soft train seat his body relaxed for the first time all day. Without looking left or right he feel dead asleep. Ten minutes out of New York his dreams were filtering in a voice that turned out to be the conductor about ten seats away. The timing was right. When the conductor was about five seats away Semineaux rose, walked up to the conductor looking very worried, leaning his head close to the conductor to whisper.

"Sir, my wife needs to take a pill," as he turned his eyes toward the seat he just vacated, nodding his head ever so slightly in the direction of the woman that was next to his vacant seat.

The conductor looked at the middle-aged woman who was by now completely absorbed in a book, then at Semineaux, still clothed in his Ivy league looking outfit from the morning's interview, looking every bit the husband of the woman.

"Two cars down there is water right past the lavatories," and went on to respond to a question a very irritated gentleman had asked before Semineaux interrupted.

Within seconds Semineaux was out of sight, but his bags remained next to the woman. After the conductor had passed through the car, he returned to the seat, pardoned himself without looking at the woman, took his bags and briefcase, and within a little over a minute was back in the car with the lavatory. He entered the men's section, took off his shirt, tie, and jacket, and put on his Australian sweater and baseball cap.

It was a long-crowed train. He waited between the cars for about ten minutes before spotting the conductor coming his way, ducked back into the men's room, locked the door until he felt the conductor had passed. When he opened the door, the conductor was just opening the glass and steel door at the south end of the train. Semineaux quickly opened the glass and steel door at the north end and walked from train to train, finally dropping down into a vacant seat next to a pretty young lady, having already slipped a conductor's stub from one of the seats he passed three or four trains earlier, putting it in the stub holder in back of his head.

The pretty young lady turned out to be very bright and within a few minutes the two of them were engaged in deep conversation. Sean never saw the first conductor again, and when the two other conductors came through, they completely ignored the young girl and the guy in the baseball cap who laughed and chatted, particularly since they both had stubs in the proper slot on the back of the seat.

He managed to get to Philadelphia and quickly took care of business with Laconi, the lawyer, and without calling anyone in Philadelphia, went to the airport. He was going to use an old return ticket to Miami. It was soon to be Christmas eve and Sean wanted to go south. Once airborne, he thought about all the dreamland until a few minutes over Ft. Lauderdale.

When the plane's tires touched the runway in Fort Lauderdale he felt like a man with no roots, of not belonging. Did the fat headed bank attorney send the sheriff to throw his books, plants, dogs, birds, and a cat or two into the street. Where was his woman? He was overwhelmed with insecurities and apprehension as he climbed into the cab outside Hollywood/Ft. Lauderdale international airport for the short ride to downtown Hollywood Lakes.

When the cab pulled up outside the big old Spanish house, he held his breath. It was not boarded-up and it appeared someone was inside. Perhaps, wishful thinking. A few lights were reflected in the downstairs windows. His heart was pounding. Glancing at a newspaper in back of the cab startled him into realizing how distorted his perception of time was, for it read December 24, 1982 ... it was Christmas Eve.

The same key still unlocked the door. It opened and the scene inside remained as ever. The air was filled with the aroma of a cooking turkey. No music was playing and the animals greeted him with strange apprehension, they seemed to know something he didn't. He wondered where she was, or even if it were, she that was cooking the turkey. The dining room table was set in preparation for serving, with little Christmas touches placed here and there. He felt good at that moment and turned toward the second story stairs, whereupon Ashley briskly floated down them into the living room, past him as though he didn't exist.

Ashley looked soft and feline with her hair falling around her neck and shoulders with the cotton skirt lying in the upper crack of her rear exposing the contour of her long legs, but it was the bare feet that aroused him in an ancient Chinese way. He came up behind her and gentle wrapped his arms around her body. Would all be peaceful?

Her body tightened and trembled in anger as she tore herself from him and flew up the stairs in split seconds. There had been no forgiveness in Ashley's upper-class English family. Borders were drawn in the air between people that lasted a lifetime, and grew as hedgerows of invisible hatred.

If there was one thing that he could not handle at that moment was anger, argument, or any disruption of the spirit. He quickly grabbed the extra set of keys in the kitchen, walked around the enclosed pool area to the smaller building and climbed the stone stairs to the second floor that had been the curing room for the bale of grass.

The room was just as he left it. There was one table in the small kitchen area and no other furniture, only a few empty plastic pound bags that remained scattered here and there. He could not believe how much grass remained lying on the floor between cracks and crevices that swept with a broom would measure nearly a half pound, reflecting the haste with which he had left that morning weeks before, presently feeling like years ago. Two near escapes with death, a tortuous trip the length of which in Europe would stretch from Cadiz, Spain, to Heidelberg, Germany, five days in prison, the conflict with his woman, the Rockefeller Foundation gamble, the Greenwich Village poetry readings, the homelessness, the heavy drinking, and now back in the studio apartment as if time never changed.

The worse part of it was that he wanted none of what happened. He sat down in the middle of the floor which still had the fresh smell of Dade County Pine this long after being sanded. The uncut strips of pine molding still lay against the walls to his right and left, pieces of sandpaper, small piles of sawdust remaining. He laid back and stretched out on the floor and thought of all the hope he had when he and his two young friends spent so many construction hours tearing, sanding, building, to give the elegant old apartment a facelift exposing its natural wood and whitened walls, preparing it to be used in the attempt to publish. This had been the dream, he would somehow publish his own books and those of his friends, even had a name for the publishing house tucked away in his mind.

"Guess ... it just wasn't meant to be. At least this time around," but he was frightened at what lay ahead. Some powerful forces were pulling him toward uncharted and dangerous adventures. "And all I want to do is fucking stay here and run, swim, write, and make love. Maybe she's cooled down some by now. First, I'll sweep the floor. Enough here to keep things mellow for about six months."

He could see the lights were on in nearly all the areas of the main house and the smells and coolness of a tropical Christmas season were in the air. He made a pledge to himself that he would not open his mouth, even in defense of her anger, which hopefully would be gone and she would take him into her arms for a moment, for he still loved her very deeply.

When he reentered the main house, the music was playing and the first glance at the kitchen and dining area revealed something was missing. She had taken the entire arrangement of dinner ware, a large cooked turkey and all the trimmings, the small pile of beautifully wrapped presents, and disappeared. Her car was missing.

By this time, he felt extremely tired. Ashley may have taken the food, presents, and everything else she could carry, but he was glad she didn't try and take their king-sized bed that he slipped into and slept well into Christmas morning.

Chapter 15

The "Beach" of Miami

Christmas morning was one of those rare winter days in Miami when the air felt like a fall day in the northeast, with a July like sun throwing tropical shadows all over the place. Having risen late he was quite compatible with the quietness and solitude that he needed to carry him through a day's therapy, Indian style, in which he would use the power of a South Florida sunset.

He would begin five hours before the sunset by following the sun's shadows from room to room, sitting and meditating on the sun's reflections from tree to tree, wall to wall, plant to plant as his mind flowed with the light of nature and color until he became one with the silence. He understood that he would not be able to think out his problems, but the majesty of nature could sooth and comfort the psychological pain that was now in his body.

When the last light of day no longer penetrated the house, he went out to the pool next to the waterfall topped with the Buddha, and sat in the lotus position for an hour after the last light disappeared from the Western sky. The thousands of flapping palm leaves and the falling water were the only sounds, as Christmas day ended.

A tapping disturbed the peace. Then a knock on the front door. Who was it, could it be Ashley? He moved quickly across the deck and through the house to the front door and opened it without checking the peep hole, praying it was Ashley.

"Sean ... my man. Merry Christmas. Am I disturbing you?"

"Hi, Bobby, come on in my man." It was an old friend he had

known for over twenty years, the notorious "Bobby Beach," a legend in his time.

"Disturbing me? Merry Christmas Bobby. What a nice surprise. You just caught me about to pull the plug out of the pool and go down the drain with the water. That way the mothers won't be able to get their fucking hands on me. I'll swim out the pipes to the sea, and escape...escape ... you fucker ..."

They laughed hysterically as they hugged. "Haven't changed, my man. You would escape like that my man," as Bobby's smile clipped the chains of pain around his heart. Sean couldn't believe he was standing in front of him, one of the most amazing men Sean had ever met in all his wanderings.

Bobby reached up and put his hand on Sean's shoulder, looked into his eyes and smiled, "I heard about your book. I am so proud of you. One of the guys actually writing a book. You understand? Do you understand brother?"

"Fuck ... writing a book Bobby? Easy ... just have to do it each day like digging a ditch. The tough thing is understanding those women. What are we going to do? Here I am in love with this bitch, and she dumps me Christmas eve. Christ, they always get us like "Pearl Harbor," bang, bang, your' dead bastard."

"Stop it," as he choked, and coughed, "You smoke too much Bobby ... I don't want to bury you."

"You are going to make me piss my pants, he laughed and coughed, "and I hear you are in some trouble, I'm worried about you, can I help you," Bobby said as he stood directly in front of him with his face up so close Sean could see that intensity in his old friend's eyes, enlarged behind the thick glasses that habitually rolled down a nose he feared sticking in no one's face, which he did often. That direct, forceful body language of a man so short in stature would not survive the reality of the circles in which he traveled, if it had not been backed up by a willingness to die rather than be humiliated, the culture of the streets.

Bobby had never visited Sean before at his home, for they sort of had an unspoken agreement that their relationship would not include Sean's home, for Bobby traveled in the fastest of Miami circles and Sean had family living with him. Bobby was always prudent about this, which Sean appreciated. Sean knew stories about Bobby attacking a friend's home with a hammer, surprise attacking by diving through the front plate glass window of the living room. And Bobby loved and respected that particular family more than any other. So, discretion was in order, for he was wild on booze and coke.

"Beach ... you are a life saver. I was feeling a little down and I hate to think lonely."

"I came by to take you to diner in celebration of your book, and introduce you to some guys who may be able to help you with your problem."

"Well, the diner sounds great, but forget the 'help,' I don't want to get fifty years with one of your schemes," bringing a smile to Bobby's face. For he knew how "dangerous" "the Beach" could be.

The Beach's real name, even though he looked Jewish, was Robert O'Callaghan, and he was originally from West Philadelphia. Sean first met "the Beach" years ago in Wildwood, New Jersey. Beach was bartending at the old Rainbow Club and one evening the large bully of a bouncer told Semineaux to leave for the wrong reasons, making the mistake of dropping a humiliating comment upon Sean as he left the establishment. Semineaux returned in the late-night hours as the bartenders were cleaning up their stations under the now bright lights. Bobby looked up just in time to see Sean's head streak by the bar on a bicycle that had picked up great momentum the instant he entered the stage door side entrance which was the highest point in the bar. The six-foot four bouncer froze like a sculptured wax statue on first glimpse of this speeding man sitting on a metal meteorite traveling at the speed of light, his eyes looking as helpless as an animal trapped in the glare of headlights. His overly muscled body hit the floor as if he had been hit by a rocket. The bouncer spent the rest of the summer working in the amusement park, pulling the lever on the roller coaster, round and round and round. But that was a long time ago.

Sean insisted on driving, that way he could have some control. Within minutes the two of them were in Sean's Pontiac picking up the tropical smells emanating from the Hollywood Beach Golf Course, a threatened pearl of nature's breath with many species of escaped tropical birds living high in the trees overlooking the ducks floating on the waterways doting the green; canals and waterways, which twenty years before teamed with large game fish and alligators, the later having feed on a few neighbors dogs.

"Smell that Bobby, some day they are going to fuck that up too. Never to be again. I love that golf course. When I bought my home, it was a little paradise of nature that resembled an Asian garden in the tropics."

"Yea, brother, what a sophisticated restaurant. I took twenty people to dinner their one night. Had my boy working as the matured, so he just ran the card through at the end. The bill was up near three thousand. We had a great time. Ended up with this dancer from the Castaways taking off all her clothes and walking into the pond nude, and came out covered with duck shit or something. Sean knowing without asking, the credit card was bad.

And then it started, Bobby telling stories and directing Sean where to go as they hit bar after bar from 79th Street causeway to Oakland Park Boulevard, places in which "the beach" was well known. Beach was greeted by everyone. Such celebration and brotherly good will. At a deep level many of these groups loved the Beach, for at some time in their past they were hurt, down and out, or a stranger, and this guy Beach gave them something no one else could; a helping hand, some money and most important, brotherly love.

Beach was bonded to more men than anyone else, Sean knew. They came from years in jail to find their way back into a new reality in which they were sometimes uneasy, and Bobby was their therapist. They came from Youngstown, Ohio and Pittsburgh, Pennsylvania; men with bodies of oak tree proportions who had landed in South Florida in desperation. The stories were nearly the same. Lost their job in a steel mill or factory. Men who are the heart bone and character of what American once worked to be. Men that bought the promise of security in exchange for the brutally hard work in American's industries as readily as they bought the god and religion of their families.

When things went bad in America, the white-collar executives took all the money and ran, leaving these tough men to hold empty bags, and no jobs. Increased drinking, upset wife, yelling at kids, out of the house to mother with the kids, painful restraining orders to prevent them from putting fists through doors, car windows, and the rest of the madness that flows from the outrage of hopelessness and turns a man against the very ones he loves so much, and wants to protect.

"I want you guys to meet my friend Sean, " Bobby would repeat in each place they visited, "he's an author, doctor, professor, and bad with his fists," at first causing Sean a little embarrassment, while being amused by how genuinely many of these men were asking about the books he wrote. And they always settled together at the tables, looking like a small army of men in rooms filled with music and dim lighting, all listening to what Beach was saying.

The performance was repeated every time they went into another bar, and at each place there was always one guy about forty, with gold chains, a huge smile, who embraced Bobby like a long lost relative. He usually owned the place. They all had a twinkle in their eyes when speaking to Bobby, which spoke of some wild knowledge only they and Bobby shared, always involving alcohol, drugs, and beautiful women. Men's history, but still felt.

The ride between bars was filled with fun packed stories about the guys Sean just met, a history of a Miami gone forever; the 50s, 60s, and 70s, when it went from a tropical frontier town to an overcrowded concrete inferno. And Bobby was Bat Masterson, Humphrey Bogart, Jimmy Buffett, and Willy Sutton all mixed into one guy, "The Beach."

Bobby kept to his promise to Lemieux of no afterhours clubs or gambling joints where cocaine usually popped up, driving Bobby nuts. To Sean's surprise Bobby even suggested going home before the normal clubs shut down at three or four in the morning; delighting Sean, for he had sufficient fun for the evening.

Sean drove south on US 1 with the radio blasting some Jimmy Buffet songs & Bobby telling one funny story after another.

"Sean... if you didn't know the area, you'd' think all those broads we passed were for real. Any broad walking the streets in this part of town has to be a hooker, a cop, or a guy in drag," as he leaned to put his cigarette in the ash tray, he noticed the gas tank was nearing the empty mark. "Sean, we need gas. Don't you check the gauge?"

Sean glanced at the gage and quickly pulled into the seedy looking gas station with the neon lights flashing the prices of six packs and cigarettes. Bobby was out of the car in a flash and insisted on pumping the gas. But they had never discussed how much they had left in their pockets, keeping in mind that Beach was a generous tipper, always leaving each establishment with the bartenders and waitress' smiling and happy looking. By the time the gas station attendant, who very much resembled Yassin

Arafat, got to the car Bobby had pumped $1.70 into the car, but their pockets yielded only $1.43. The Beach gave the attendant $1.43 and told him not to worry since his people already owned most of England and Southern France.

The now enraged attendant whirled and disappeared into the station. Sean was glad to see the Beach laughing with the other attendant, a young black man. Sean wanted no trouble tonight, as Bobby had promised. Bobby had also promised he had enough money for all expenses for the evening, why Sean had brought little money. So, it appeared the 27 cents was not going to be a problem and Sean slid into driver's seat.

The glare off the passenger side window distorted the vision of the stocky Arab, for the angry expression appeared to Sean as a smile, so he paid little attention as the attendant snuck around the rear of the car, and surprised Sean at his door with a pistol in his hand. Sean's immediate focus was on the hole in the barrel of the gun that was now inside the car window, for that hole became the only reality in this flash of the universe.

"The money ... the money..." he shouted out of the unshaven, dirty face of a man who worked seventeen-hour days in this war zone section of Ft. Lauderdale where the man had been robbed by everything from serial killers to drag queens. But in that instant, to Sean the gun meant nothing. This little bastard violated the privacy of his automobile. It mattered none what he had in his hand.

The adrenalin in Sean Semineaux was now fired. All rationality was now blocked out. He was incited to fight. In the split second it took Sean's feet to hit the pavement, the attendant, fortunately for Sean, had taken flight around the car after seeing the insane look in those blue eyes. The next split-second Bobby would talk about for a long time. Sean placed his left arm on the driver's side roof, flipped his legs and body over the car, smashed his right forearm into the steel roof of the passenger's side, landing with both feet on the other side of the car. The attendant, in full gallop, was about a step and a half from the station door, the steel roof of the passenger side was dented from the blow, and Sean froze in a crouched position with the look of a wild animal on his face.

It all happened so quickly. By this time the Beach was standing a few feet behind the car door laughing and saying over and over again, "nice job ... nice job, "as he flicked his ashes and slowly slipped into the car, closing the door, rolling down the window, and quietly speaking,

Let's go, my man ... he wants no part of Sean Semineaux." Semineaux was speechless.

He drove back out to US 1 heading South. "Beach, goddamn it, you almost got me killed, again. You promised, remember?"

"I've got one for you doctor," as he took a drag of his smoke, adjusted his glasses on his noise as all the gold on his wrists and neck were flashing in the night light. "Here is what we do my man. I got a question for you. You are a China specialist now, Bobbly speaking as if nothing just happened, Semineaux still preoccupied with images of a small dark metal tunnel into hell. "Tell me doctor, how can we make big money in China? Come on, think," flicking his cigarette out the window, Semineaux annoyed he was trying to change the subject.

"Bobby," a distraught Semineaux, his voice pleading, "before we left all I asked were a few ground rules," ... "I'll tell you my man," Bobby interrupting, "we can make a million dollars apiece in China. We manufacture gauze and bandages in China and sell them. Christ Bobby, there must be a million people trying to sell medical supplies in China. No, no, he said, we specialize and sell yellow gauze and bandages. Different shades of yellow. You and me in business, in China."

Sean looked at Bobby and said nothing, just pleased that the night was about ready to come to an end, but now had to continue driving slowly for fear of police. Another ten minutes and he would be in downtown Hollywood. But Bobby continued talking about how much money could be made selling yellow gauze to Chinese.

Bobby then became preoccupied with looking at the increasing numbers of hookers cruising the street looking for a trick. Sensing the motive behind the mischievous look on Bobby's face Sean increased the speed, for he could smell trouble in the air.

"Some good-looking broads on the street tonight."

"Might be, but I'd better keep my eyes on the road," as he again increased the speed.

"Wow, look at the ass on that bitch ... damn, and the legs on that ... Sean, slow down my man."

"Beach, you're fucking nuts."

"Slower ... slower," Beach insisted.

"Now were going so slow the cops will stop us for being too slow."

"Hey Baby what's your name." US 1 was right up against the sidewalk at this point and now Bobby was talking to a six-foot-tall, thin, black hooker with a tight fitting, long, red dress.

"What you won't," she answered defiantly.

"What you got. You be my female Santa. I got no presents. Make my Christmas baby."

This was really irritating Sean, he wanted no part of these hookers, frantically looked around for the police, and wanted to just get home. But somehow, he let Bobby command him to slow the car as the tall black girl was now leaning in the window touching Bobby and he touching her.

"Goddamn Bobby, get her the fuck out of the car window."

Now the Beach was kissing the hooker and her hands were all over him with the longest fingers Sean had ever seen. In desperation Sean started driving again hoping she would jump back, but by this time Bobby had pulled her entire upper torso into the car as he put his hand down across her backside, grabbed her by the crouch to pull her ass and long legs into the car on top of him, kissing her all the time.

"Pull into the driveway, quick, quick," Bobby pleaded with Sean, and like a fool, a dumb fool, cut a sharp right and stopped the car a few feet from the sidewalk to let old Beach indulge himself with the hooker whose red dress was now up over her head. Totally disgusted, Sean stared straight ahead, until he felt wet lips on his left cheek. It was another hooker who had walked around to the driver's side of the car, "Get away honey," Sean pleaded as he rolled the window up to about an inch from the top, just open enough to hear her say, "what the fuck wrong with you motherfucker."

At that second a commotion was stirring to Sean's right, for the six-foot hooker in the red dress was backing away from the car and Bobby was raving mad.

"My fucking wallet. My fucking money. My thirty-five bucks."

"Beach, what's happening?"

"The bitch took my money, let me out."

"No, forget it, were' going."

He was out in a flash before Sean could stop him, but the night was so dark she immediately disappeared into the shadows as Bobby jumped back into the car in mad frenzy.

"She got my thirty-five bucks, the bitch. We were going to have some breakfast. Quick, drive through that parking lot."

Sean made a quick U turn around the building to the other side of the parking lot and there stood the lone tall hooker in the red dress. Bobby was out of the car before Sean could say anything and within a few quick hops he was face to face with her, or at least facing each other, for Bobby was only about five foot six and was eyeball level at a point between her breasts and her belly-button.

"I want my fucking money, bitch."

"I ain't got no money of yours."

At that Bobby reached high enough to grab one of her shoulders, but was so drunk he was off balance, rocking backward on his heals prevented him from connecting with a wildly thrown punch aimed at her jaw.

"Bobby. Goddam. Let her go," Sean screamed as he leaped from the car. At that instant they both noticed a strange encirclement of shadows coming alive against the December darkness in the parking lot of rubble and dilapidated buildings. Small metal pistols and silver knives flashed against reflected light in the hands of a small band of wild looking hookers set to protect one of their own.

"Bobby. Please get into the car," for the doors of the car were open and Sean was now also exposed outside the car, and did not like the vulnerable feeling. Bobby would not stop raving about his $35, and in a few seconds, the small band of women became a small hoard, tripling in size, angry, and armed.

"What a way to go," Sean thought to himself. Shot and stabbed to death by hookers in a dirty parking lot on Christmas night. But Bobby heard nothing, and instead of making a strategic retreat into the safety of the big car, he ran at the crowd like a marine going up a beach. If there can be a flash of humor in madness? Sean could not help being overwhelmed by the choreography of the moment, with the Beach fainting attack, with no weapon; the hookers with the weapons retreating, then moved forward, they backward, like an allegorical battle in Plato's cave being dance by a Maurice Cunningham dance company.

But this was deadly. Sean's pleading had no effect on Bobby. Sean could not believe how lucky that so far, no shots rang out, even though he saw at least ten or fifteen knives flashing, slashing, stabbing into the air. Sean never once had the urge to jump into the car and save himself, for there was no way he could let Bobby go down like this. And the last thought he had at that very moment before leaving the security of standing on the driver's side of the car, was how was he going to explain Beach's death to so many guys, and his woman.

"Shit, here we go, you fucking madman beach," as Semineaux let out a primitive karate shockwave of a sound momentarily freezing everyone as he ran into the center of this assassination circle, grabbed Beach by the left wrist, who for the first time felt Sean's strength he so often bragged about in abstraction, and whipped him into the passenger's seat of the car, as Beach continued to shout obscenities to the girls.

"Close your fucking door," Sean screamed as he slammed his shut. In all the surprises in Sean Semineaux's life, nothing tops the helpless astonishment he suffered in that instance when Bobby caught the swinging door, he had pulled toward him with his foot before it closed, jumped out of the car, and into the middle of the circle, like Custard and the Indians again.

"Fuck him," Sean thought. "What the hell should I die like this?" It took all of his will power to get out of that car, by now surrounded by this small army of armed hookers.

Sean's voice boomed so loudly this time it could have broken glass windows, if there were any left in the boarded-up windows in the buildings which formed a U shape around the entire parking lot. Somehow, he got the crazy little Irishman's left foot inside the passenger's side, just long enough to yank him into the car, close his door, and then his own. The big old car was nearly soundproof

and it felt like a self-contained protective cocoon. Sean knew they were facing the open end of the U-shaped parking lot facing US 1, with South to the right.

But when he looked up, he could not believe their bad luck as a long, dirty, old, tank of a car just pulled across the exit blocking their escape. The chief pimp and heavyweight bodyguard had arrived. Sean jammed one foot on the brake pedal and the other on the gas pedal as the big engine let out a roar like a dragon about to pounce upon St. George as the front hood heaved upward, with the screeching tires sending up a smoke cloud of burning rubber.

The pimp got the message, and knew the big Pontiac was going to try and cut them in half even before the cloud of burning rubber could be smelled. When Sean popped the brake, they lunched, and the Pontiac just missed their rear end as it squealed onto US I and headed South. No blood was spilled, no steel was smashed, no bones were broken. The "Nude Girls" sign alerted him to how close to Ft. Lauderdale airport they were and the notorious no-man's strip on US 1 which had been a speed trap for thirty years.

"Home," Sean thought to himself, "sweet, safe, home."

"That fucking broad ... Sean my man, that $35 was big breakfast for us at that point on Route 84."

"Bob, forget it, I'm glad to be alive ... even though I am hungry it would be nice to end this night, now."

"You have to do me one favor, my man. Semineaux, I know you won't let me down."

"Fuck you Bob, I can smell it."

"Sean, one last favor," by this time Bobby had a big grin on his face as he flicked his cigarette and insisted that Sean listen, and when he heard what Bobby had to say he swore this would be the last night he would ever go out with "The Beach" alone, ever.

Beach claimed that the prostitute should be "taught a lesson" for stealing his $35. He wanted to get home fast, get his pistol, and have Sean drive Beach's car to avoid recognition. The plan was to park across US 1 from where the girls work, and Beach would teach them a lesson by "firing a few shots over their heads."

"You are fucking mad ... no doubt about it."

"No, no ... over their heads ... I wouldn't hit any of them broads. But someone has to teach 'em broads a lesson."

Sean was praying he was not serious, but as He looked into his flashing black eyes that appeared to be fed by those enlarged pumping veins running up both sides of his neck, he knew that the Beach was determined. But the strange part of it was that after all Sean had been through, Beach was actually able to make Sean feel slightly guilty for deciding not to go along with his plan, the Beach's powerful personality.

But now, Sean had a plan of his own. Knowing that Beach's ground floor Tyler Street apartment was smack up against the parking lot, the exterior wall of the living room and the bedroom in which Beach's lady was sleeping.

Sean hoped the parking space next to Beach's bedroom was open. A hundred yards away from the apartment Beach seemed convinced that he had talked Sean into waiting until he could secure his car keys and pistol from the apartment. When the car bounced over the small concrete parking barrier and hit Beach's outside bedroom wall as just a few miles an hour, that big old Pontiac hit harder than even Sean anticipated, and within seconds Bobby's lady was at the front door faster than a cat under attack.

Sean promised Bobby he would wait, three times he promised, but as soon as his back disappeared into the living room, Sean backed up and left.

Chapter 16

Like it all never happened

Sean was so glad to be alone, driving down Hollywood Boulevard all lit up with Christmas decorations, now only a few minutes from home. He vowed to never again go out on the town with Bobby Beach, unless others are present.

But, at this moment Sean had no idea that he would never see Bobby again. Sean's life was to change so drastically. He would live in many different countries and cultures, suffer much. and experience more than he wished. During these years, Bobby would have been shot dead, probably by someone he knew. He was shot through his left hand that had desperately covered his heart in attempting to stop the steel jacketed bullet from ripping through the flesh of his hand and the tender walls of his heart. Bobby did manage to lunge ten to twelve feet behind to grab the wall phone in his right hand, his last act in life, or perhaps beyond. Most likely a drug deal gone bad.

Only the receiver of that desperate phone call will ever know, for Bobby was able to communicate his cry of help from his mind to the black wires that drape through the trees with spoken messages, silently. They never found his killer. He traveled fast and everyone expected it, so they said.

Semineaux woke in his bed, tried to figure out if last night was a nightmare, or reality ... and the warm sun coming through the white blinds illuminated the images, causing Sean to pull the pillow over his head and moan. But he survived his woman's abandonment, Christmas, and The Beach; and today would be his, alone.

And the most alone thing he could do was to swim. After a ten-minute hot shower Sean slipped into his pool buck naked and began to swim lap after lap as the power slowly returned to his shoulders. The thrusting against the water healed the bodies pains, leaving his mind to rest.

Afterwards, Sean dried, dressed, drank a cold cup of espresso and wondered where Ashley had taken his dog -- for a dog is a man's pet, if given a choice, for animals can sense what is most dangerous.

Within minutes Sean had walked into the plush tropical garden of a golf course behind the old house and walked across the lawns called fairways to the small forested cluster of bamboo trees, knowing the mystical power of singing bamboo, this biological perfect little area cut through with a stream fed by the same water source containing game fish.

"My God," Sean thought to himself, this will all be gone. This he knew and it bothered him. It was the noises of nature, the splashing of the slow-moving water as diving birds and feeding fish meet upon a surface smooth, and bamboo leaves whispering music and nature's sexist melodies to make one feel alive.

Saved my ass, this little place, love from nature. Nature is truth like the animal who wants you to love it and the one that wants to kill you. I could live in the woods by myself forever. Nature is not about control, it's about life.

Sean lit up the herb of his ancestors that he had collected from the floor last night. He had hoped to smoke it with his woman. He laid back like Huck Finn on the soft Bermuda grass that felt like silk and took in the smell and sounds of nature. He began to fantasize that he was an invisible bird living high up in the giant trees that loomed skyward from the black earth and moisture of the golf course.

To you, it might be a fantasy, but I do live in a mystic garden, and am now expressing myself for the very first time. You must first understand, and you may not; I am an invisible Elf ... or don't you see? Of course not, for I can see your world, but you cannot see me. For example, I am presently within eyesight of perhaps five or seven people, but to them I am air, and you know air has no form, at least most of the time. It's rare when we see it like funnels in tornadoes, but fortunately I have never been part of one of those. I guess I am more like those invisible characters of TV comic strips like Casper and ... Oh, there is something I must tell you now. A small bird has just landed next to me. The bird can't see me either but for some odd reason the bird has an awareness of me, a feeling of me.

Somehow the trees, plants, and animals know I exist, feel me in some way -- and I might add with some pride, consider me non-hostile and even friendly. Now about that pretty little bird who flew in on a brisk wind out of nowhere. The little fellow is somewhat chubbier than a mockingbird, with a furry black and yellow body, a yellow head, and a black beak. He was so curious and excited about my presence that he almost lost his footing in the landing approach. Or it could have been a reaction to the two black birds that swaggered in on both sides of the little fellow, and they too seemed surprised by my presence in the middle of this wonderful garden that I visit so often because of its natural beauty and peacefulness.

Now there goes Eddy, he's one of the guys who keeps it all so green and quenches the thirst of all these trees and bushes and fairways with plenty of wet, clean, water. For a place as beautiful must be cared for. I see these nice men early in the morning tending to the garden.

Usually, I am up high in one of the tallest of the tropical fir trees that are scattered throughout the garden. It is so breezy in the trees and from the tallest trees I can see far out into the crystal blue shipping lanes of the South Florida Gulf Stream, for the garden is less than a mile from the Atlantic Ocean. I love the contrast. I see dozens of now wild escaped birds, some blue, some green and yellow, and one distinct pair of white parrots who make a lot of noise, and hundreds of smaller colorful creatures who sit above this rare habitat of nature's inner womb, enjoying its charm while it lasts.

Not even in the imagination of one's mind, could nature be as seductive as here. Its open, its wet, it smells, it changes each day as the tropical sun, water, and wind turn dirt into green, and oh those winds. We see it kicking up the waves far out at sea, or green, red, yellow night lights, the colors of my daytime friends, bobbing on the southern seas. Other things that we sometimes see, floating in on those driven seas, especially this time of year. Or is this a secret, which only I and the birds know, as the birds begin to chatter, squawk, sing, over the melodic tunes of Bamboo leaves and shoots whose melodies combined with splashing sounds of water over little rocks, interrupted by the splash of a large bird the size of a small Eagle. Sean stretched, and felt natural again.

He spent the next couple of days visiting the local universities and colleges with the aim of picking up a few courses to teach, running into the usual ones as he went from university to university, college to college.

At one Broward County community college there was a middle-aged alcoholic with a useless degree in education from some backwater Mississippi college who kept Semineaux from teaching. It is a non-competitive system based on tenure. Tenure allows professors to come to work each day and sit in front of students they often despise, read them old notes, and get paid with money from hard working parents, re-mortgaged homes, and savings.

At the universities the professors were arrogant, and at the community colleges they were insecure. So, he made the rounds of the shipping companies on the piers in Port Everglades and Miami, where men extended their hands and looked you right in the eye, knowing the importance of work in a man's life. Three small agencies hired him as a ship agent within days and he fell into that life again, when every other day a ship would sail at four in the morning or arrive between midnight and one in the morning. Paperwork and responsibilities for the ship in dock, no sleep; but weeks went by quickly, even in an empty house.

Then one day he received an unexpected phone call. It was from a Chinese girl he had met in China, calling from the Miami airport, who just happened to need a place to stay.

Semineaux, feeling rather lonely, was on his way to the airport immediately, remembering how he met her in China. He was first taken back by her beauty and approached her speaking Chinese.

"Pardon me Miss ... pardon me," he remembered saying five years before on a warm summer evening in Shanghai. "You are the tallest and most beautiful Chinese girl I have ever seen in all of China." She was stunning at nearly six feet tall with long black hair down to the small of her back, a face with a patrician forehead, high cheek bones, full lips, long and elegant arms and legs, and a seductive look in her black eyes.

"I am a German, asshole," she had said on that Shanghai street five years before. And half German she was, visiting her mother's Chinese birthplace, then, for the first time. Her father was German and she was raised in Hamburg, Germany. In China with her, Sean had one of the most torrid love affairs of his life.

Now twenty-two, Doris was more beautiful than he remembered when meeting her at the airport. It was a fun reunion. Sean taught her to swim in the pool. Then taught her to dive and spear fish on a stay in Key West. It was good therapy for Sean and a great vacation for Doris. For a month and a half, they had a wonderful time.

Then one night everything changed. It was actually Easter Sunday, and Doris was cooking one of the many dishes she learned from her Chinese mother. Sean was looking over some of the papers he had filled at the courthouse to challenge the legality of the eviction notice he had received.

There was a knock at the door. Who could this be on Easter Sunday evening? The outside light was burnt out making it impossible to see who was there by looking in the peep hole.

"Who's there?"

"Ashley..."

Sean could not believe his ears. What the hell does she want," he thought. He had not seen her since Christmas, but he opened the door and there she stood all smiling, dressed like he always wanted her to dress, but which she never did, except when he was out of town.

Ashley was wearing a white tee-shirt with little red art work that sort of hung on her large round breasts. Her hair lay down across her shoulders, and her black shorts accentuated the "V" gap between her legs that slopped into her long tight thighs.

He told her to wait in the foyer and went back into the kitchen to question if Doris could handle the situation. Doris just shrugged and laughed without stopping to cook.

"Won't bother me, I'd like to meet this Ashley I've heard so much about."

"Be careful, don't tell her anything about us meeting in China. We were living together at the time."

"Don't worry, I can handle her."

"Be careful, she's tricky." "We just met recently," Doris said looking innocent, "OK...?" "I like your confidence, but remember she is more experienced ... nearly old enough to be your mother."

"I love it," Doris said as she grabbed Sean by his balls.

Sean brought Ashley out to the kitchen and introduced them, went into the dining room to roll a smoke and got a pleasure looking back into the kitchen as Ashley and Doris chatted over the stove like two sisters, with Doris being taller in her bare feet than Ashley was in her heals, and tight ass protruding further than Ashley's.

Sean called the dog and walked out through the pool to the garden, lit the joint, and wondered as he looked up at the tropical sky.

"If you don't give a shit, they always come back. If you need them, you'll die in your own sorrow."

After Ashley left, they tried to figure out what she wanted. But all they could do was laugh, all the way to bed, and then some. But an hour later Sean woke, quietly left Doris' side, and went into his study. The visit had unnerved him. He still loved her. What shall I do? She'll fuck my head again.

Sean woke when Doris put her arms around him, slightly startled, for he had fallen asleep in the little lounge chair in his study. They kissed, and made love on the floor, neither knowing it was the last time.

Doris was swimming in the pool when Ashley called in late afternoon. When Sean answered the phone, the first thing out of Ashley's mouth was "Get that Chink out of my home."

He could not believe his ears. . . "my home," the phrase music to his heart, but he replied "I'm surprised at you. Miss Upper Class English Righteousness and Fair mindedness. 'A chink' ... How racist you English can be."

"I'm sorry..." Ashley actually broke down and cried.

In his heart he was laughing as he watched Doris swim, for he knew how difficult it was for Ashley to say "I'm sorry."

"When will she be out?"

"Soon," Semineaux replied

Chapter 17

The Foreclosure

Within twenty-four hours Ashley was back in the kitchen cooking a meal as if she had never left. Doris was on a train going to New Orleans to visit Sean's friend from his Atlantic City days. His old pal owned a bar on Bourbon street. He was a Louisiana boy, home bred, who would give a Doris a Job and a place to stay.

The first week of Ashley's return Sean was quite busy writing detailed notes for the beginning of his new book, the first chapter dealing with the major mistakes of President Reagan's strategic planning. He spent hours with close friends trying to help him arrange for an investor to buy the two garden lots on both sides of the houses and pool that were worth well over one hundred thousand dollars. All discussions were conducted with the stipulation Sean could buy them back when he was in a position to do so, for he did not want to break up the estate.

Each night that Ashley returned home he hoped she might discuss the new book with him, or the house itself, for Ashley was working with a lot of bankers and investors at Palm Isle Resorts -- but every time Sean would introduce the subject of "their" home, she would go off into her act, as she had done before their break-up, about "Daddy," and England, and Daddy ... while consuming a lot of good wine.

After a few glasses of wine, she would start with "I've never met a man more brilliant than Daddy, until you Sean." Then she would pause, mention her ex-husband, and then dismiss him from the running.

After a little more wine, she would shift gears into an avalanche of negativism fueled by confusion, malice, and self-hatred. She would drink herself into mental oblivion every night, as he would watch her beautiful face twist into a new form reflecting what was to come.

Daddy was an artist. These people at work have no ideas, no class, no taste ... "Did you fuck the chink more than you fucked the ballerina?"

He tried to stop this talk every night. "You promised, none of that talk if you were to come back. Did you forget that promise honey?" Sometimes this worked.

Sean swam and ran very hard every day, partially to be strong enough to absorb her mood changes. But one cannot escape the overflow of pain while living with someone you love.

One day they had a long talk and agreed to a truce. Ashley drank less and less, and they ate more and more. Their relationship was beginning to take a surprising turn for the better.

They began to agree that the world about them was in such turmoil, they would each do their best to have peace in their home. Sean began to love Ashley as he had in the past. Perhaps the legal petition being reviewed at the courthouse and one of the investors they were negotiating with would enable them to save their home. Perhaps, Sean would not go to jail. Perhaps, they would start that publishing house. Perhaps, they could learn to accept each other's cultural differences. They were beginning to live one day at a time. They were loving each other and beginning to heal the breaks. They slept more peacefully, and their dreams were happier.

Then, one morning it all changed.

"Sean, Sean . . . wake up. Someone's banging on our door."

Sean pushes up against her body and curled around her.

"Sean, please not now. There is someone making a lot of noise outside."

"Baby ... you feel so good. I want to smell you all over baby. To hell with the front door, they'll go away."

Ashley leapt out of bed, wrapped her robe around her body and opens the blinds ever so slightly allowing the white rays of the rising sun to bring Sean out of his semi-conscious sexual fantasies, now Sean is on his feet. "What the fuck is going on down there?"

"That's what I have been trying to tell you. The bloody chaps have been doing that for some time now."

Sean came down the stairs fast as a cat and leaped the last five steps with an agile fall onto the red tile floor as his toes grabbed the cold stone.

"Here it is again. A bully some place. Someone outside with enormous powers," Sean thought to himself.

"Who's there ... What do you want?"

"Mr. Sean Semineaux. Are you Sean Semineaux? Please open the door."

"I am Sean Semineaux. What do you want?"

"I am a Sheriff with your Eviction Notice and the powers vested in me to use force if you do not cooperate. Papers signed by Judge Rodger Butterfat and Broward County Prosecutor Cynthia Thatcher. Do you understand, Mr. Semineaux?"

Fear shot through Sean's heart, for this was not a property, but a Temple. he had filed a proper legal petition; an appeal for appellate jurisdiction, which court officials explained would necessitate a formal, registered, writ explaining the decision and reasons, ultimately giving one a final opportunity to wrap and secure a lifetime's personal treasures.

"Could you give me a few minutes to put on my pants and then I'll open the door immediately, Sir."

"I am not supposed to ... But ... I'll give you 5 minutes, no more ... understand?"

"Yes Sir, I heard, thank you sir ... 5 minutes."

Sean nearly knocked Ashley to the floor on the second story landing as he ran up the steps, both startled.

"I heard ... I heard" she sobbed.

Sean nearly wept, for no matter what anger had ever existed between them, he saw the look of fear in her eyes as never before, and knew he loved her as family and would die for her.

"Honey listens. I love you, and believe me all will be OK." Ashley's face now distorted in pain with tears falling over onto Sean's bear arms. "Listen Honey. Here are the car keys. I am going to let you out the door to the pool, you know how to get out a dozen ways. Go right to the car, talk to no one... NO ONE ... and drive to a restaurant and have some breakfast. Take your time and don't come back for an hour. Here is forty bucks."

"But ... but..."

"No but, but. You."

"No" ... Ashley nearly screams. "All my things in the bedroom. What ... what."

"I love you and promise you it will be ok," as Sean glanced into their bedroom now restored with all of Ashley's heirlooms in place as if they were husband and wife again. "I'll protect them baby, just go and be alone while I take care of these guys ok."

Sal is staying in the back-downstairs apartment, bang on his window and tell him the cops are breaking into the house and I need him. OK?"

With his arm tightly around Ashley's quivering body Sean led her out down and out to the glass pool door with the thick white drapes, slipped open the drapes, then the door, as Ashley slipped into the privacy which was not yet threatened. Sean bolted the door again, pulled the drapes so no light was coming in, calculated he had two and a half minutes left, went directly to his study closet and pulled his old lever action Winchester 30-30 rifle from its sheepskin case and slid seven shells into the storage chamber. He was losing it and he knew it.

"Fuck it. I'll take that fucking lawyer out. Cocksuckers." Unfortunately, Sean knew how to use that carbine which he hunted with in Labrador and Newfoundland whenever he got close in enough to hit a Moose, Caribou, or Bear. His whole life flashed before him. The violence and humiliation as a youth, beatings with fists, with sticks, until Sean said "no more." The degradation of his intellect in youth. The military, which Sean detested for its stupidity. His books, his family, his home. "There should have been a written response to my appeal" he screamed.

Everything was spinning around in his head. He thought of that huge bear he stood in front of way up on the ice. How proud he was then, to have stood in front of that angry bear, not afraid to be ripped apart, so far from civilization. No one would ever find the bones after the bear and snow did their job on his body. He could run at full speed, and fire the lever action rifle with deadly accuracy. He stood like a statue in front of the charging bear, placing the first shot through the center of the bear's shoulders, then one through the neck, and the perfect slug between the bears eyes. Semineaux was so ashamed of that now, for he often dreamed of that bear, and in those dreams the bear is human.

"I hate killing anything, anymore."

Another bang on the floor and Sean's body shakes violently. "OK Sean ... think clearly." Sometimes our chemistry brings us back to what we really are -- animals. Somehow, in his mind he knew, as no one else did, how many times he came close to death before guns. He never expected to live into middle age. So why not now.

"God ... I'd better get a grip on myself. It's only a fucking house. Christ ... on the front tabloids as a mad man killing authorities. But ... but... fuck this foreclosure shit. No one is coming through that door, alive." Sean had enough bullets to take on a small army. "Where the fuck is Sal?"

The Sheriff is delivering some pretty heavy blows to the door by now, pulling hard on the door handle. In an instant Sean was up against the door, rifle in hand, peering out the peep-hole to see the Sheriff. His hatred for the Sheriff was enraging his blood pitted soul. When he saw the black face, his hatred evaporated.

"Those bastards ... those white red-neck racist bastards. They sent a black dude." This man was the bear, he was not the enemy.

"Sir, please ... one second ... please..."

"I'm going to have to knock it down if you don't open it up."

"Sir, may I just ask you. Who is commanding your operation? Who gives you your direct orders?"

"Mr. Lubber. He read the papers to me before. And this is what I am supposed to do. Its hot out here, and if they knew I waited this long ... I'd be in trouble .... now."

"Lubber." Sean thought as his teeth clenched and his hands squeezed the rifle. Lubber, the nasty, gold toothed, bank lawyer who looked like the fascist dictator Mussolini, with constant beads of sweat on his fat face from overeating like a pig. Sean recalled the last meeting they had about two weeks before when Lubber delivered some papers to Sean on his way home, for Lubber lived only a few blocks away. It was on Sean's front steps and Lubber was already acting as if Sean was no longer living in the house -- very disrespectful, and threatening. On that recent occasion, Sean looked up and into his eyes and said.

"Mr. Lubber, you are now on my property. I know you think you are a bad ass. Let me tell you something. This is my home; I have a lady living with me ... my wife. You be gentle ... understand? You are a neighbor. Don't push me Lubber." At which point Lubber turned his barrel chested, lip snarled front, and as he walked away Sean thought of how he would like to put his foot up that big asshole in the brown suit. How many other Lubbers are there in America throwing peoples out of their homes?

"This is one bastard that going to get his." Semineaux was losing it completely, and was now out the back-glass pool door with one thing in mind. The bicycle at the back of the pool. He could ride the bike up the alley to US 1. He now had the rifle back into its sheepskin case concealing its form.

He stood for a second, envisioned his son, years before, lying on the chair across the pool, life draining from his frail little pale body, trying to smile. He decided to drive the bike to the attorney's office just across US 1. He knew how to slip in through the back from his knowledge of the building. Lubber's son, a thirty-three-year-old obnoxious geek, practiced with his father. The son was every much the elitist, racist, bigot as his father. For Sean had some pretty horrible phone conversations with the son. These two men became the enemy. Not the black sheriff, the Russians, or the poor bear.

"First I'll put a hole between the son's eyes. Then I'll make this mother fucker sit and feel the greatest pain a man can feel. To lose his only son. Then I'll kill that piece of pork called Mr. Lubber."

Semineaux decided to move fast, for he knew they would be in their office directing this whole thing. He would put a bullet through Lubber's belly like the first shot at the bear. Then one through the soft tissue of the neck. And while Lubber was still alive, he would put a hole between his eyes with a hot lead 30-30 slug.

He had the gun case slung over his shoulder and was about ready to walk the bike through the downstairs apartment to the side door in the alley, already planning his escape after killing the lawyer and his son. He knew some thick trees he could climb in the golf course, pull his bike up with him, and remain in silence until nightfall. He knew routes through which he could ride his bike all the way to the Port of Miami, undetected, and find his way onto any number of moored ships. The port of Miami would have more ships moored than Port Everglades, even though it was much further away from Hollywood. He had been on enough ships to know how to stowaway. And with his Seaman's papers in his pocket, he could be around the world in no time.

In a few seconds he would be riding up the alley. He would

spend the rest of his life on the run. But as he reached for one of the two doors that led into the downstairs apartment behind the pool the door opened, and out came a sleepy-eyed Sal Moriarty, whom Sean had completely forgotten about.

"Sean, what's going on. Ashley said something about the police at the front door? Where are you going? Is that your rifle?"

"Sal ... good, you're up. Look, Go to the front door now. They are about ready to break it down. Yell through the door and tell them I am in the bathroom and that you'll open the door immediately. Stall them as long as you can. Got it? OK."

"Where the hell are you going? That is your rifle in the case Sean."

"I warned that fat headed banker to let me make an orderly retreat if my appeal did not go through. I'm going to kill the bastard and his son. They are directing this thing from their office ... hear them banging. Please get to the front door fast."

Sal Moriarty, a Vietnam vet who had seen his share of horror in combat, was one of the few people who could understand Sean at this point.

"Are you going crazy Sean," Sal said in a low sophisticated voice as he got up close and looked in Sean's eyes with an intensity that momentarily froze Sean in his tracks. Sean respected Sal and listened to him. When he first met Sal, he did not believe his story that he was 100% Irish, for he had this waspish look about him from his fine boned physique to his wire glasses. Something didn't jive about Sal, he had a street sense no wasp could ever learn or cultivate, no matter how much they tried. Sean first met Sal when he was in Saigon in 1970, and later both worked as outpatient counselors for a state mental hospital in Florida. Sal lived on the family farm on the Canadian border at Plattsburg, New York. Sal's father had worked as a traveling bricklayer, returning home only between jobs that took him up and down the east coast. Sal's father was fifty and his mother a young girl when they married, and had six children. The mother raised the six children in the Bronx during the school year on the money received from the traveling old man, and they spent the summers on the New York upstate farm along the Canadian border owned jointly by the father and his two Irish brothers that had migrated from Ireland together. Of the three brothers, Sal's father was the only one who married. Sal had the demeanor and quiet grace of an upstate farmer, the passion and instincts of a city boy from the Bronx, and Irish blood on both sides.

"Take it easy, you can't just throw it away like this," his lean arm, years of farm work, a vice grip on Sean's forearm, and those soft blue eyes, intensely trying to read Sean's.

"They pushed me too far. They fucked with me. This is my home, this is my home, fuck their paperwork."

Sal's eyes are so close to Sean's they could see the heartbeats in each other's eyes. "Sean ... please... let's go back into the house. I'll answer the door. I can deal with these guys. Sean, please, come on man. You have kids. You have a family. You don't want to go to jail for murder."

"I'm not going into any jail. That I tell you. Fuck it, I'll leave the country."

"Not over this fucking house Sean," Sal, raising his voice for the first time. The banging on the door became pounding. Sal pleaded as his glasses began to steam up, "let it go Sean. Let it go," his hand tightening the vice grip on his arm holding the rifle. "Let's go back into the house."

Somehow, Sal succeeded, and the two of them went back into the house, Sean put the rifle into the back of a closet, and shouted.

"This is Sean Semineaux Sir ... I'm going to open the door now. Everyone be a gentleman. OK." He yelled, "OK."

"OK sir."

Sean cracked the door open ever so slightly as the bright eastern sun partially blinded his vision, but he could see the kind looking black face of the sheriff.

"Come on in." Sean said as Sal let loose a sigh of relief and Sean shook the sheriff's hand. "We can get out of here by tonight. My wife will be back in few minutes, and we will have a crew, as Sean spoke the ten men who followed the sheriff into the house began first picking up a few odd chairs and taking them out the front door and placing them on the sidewalk. Sean was in shock and suddenly felt overwhelmed.

"Sir, tell them to stop, now," Sean pleaded, as the goon squad of ten men just kept moving at the same pace, moving the furniture, and taking it outside.

The sheriff's face and eyes spoke of compassion. "But there is nothing I can do about its sir. The bank's attorney hired these men to evict you, and I am here to enforce the writ of eviction and keep order. That Mr. Lubber, he is actually directing things from his office."

At that moment Sean looked at the pairs of dirty hands that were now beginning to clear off the dining room table containing a half dozen books, some poetry, the empty wine glasses Sean and Ashley had drank out of the night before during dinner, Ashley's letter from her twin sister in Algeria, one of Sean's typewriter's, portions of his novel about the MET, a little personal love note he had written to Ashley, at which point Sean "snapped-out," as they say.

"FREEZE ... EVERYONE ... DON'T TOUCH ANOTHER THING ... HHIIIIIDDDDNT," the rooms seemed to shake from the sound emanating from Semineaux, a sound of battle, of anger, of a violence at the edge of human tolerance.

Sean's blue eyes strained with an outraged mad stare as he spread out his body and lowered himself slightly at the knees, with his arms and hands unquestionably resembling the movement of animals. His chest was huffed, his teeth were clenched, in his mind's eye that moment he was a big black panther. No one in the room that day doubted this man would not fight them all to the death.

Everyone did freeze, including his friend Sal who stood behind him, shocked, but intrigued, peering over Sean's shoulder into the eyes of the Sheriff, the first to move. The sheriff moved his right hand onto his holstered pistol, unsnapped the thin leather guard never losing contact with Sean's eyes that had just seconds before made contact with all ten of the men. This was the moment of truth.

The sheriff was standing but two long steps slightly off to Sean's left, having the advantage with his right hand on the pistol being the furthest point from Sean.

Sean could not make a mistake with his timing. Hesitancy would be death. It would have to be one step and a slapping foot to the sheriff's head, taking him out before he could draw and fire, for there was no way Sean could get to the gun hand fast enough.

Sal held his breath, for the second the sheriff snapped off his guard, Sean, pointed to the sheriff's right hand and bellowed, "NO, NO ... LET'S NOT BOTH DIE BECAUSE OF THOSE BASTARDS."

There was not a sound in the room. Everyone, just stood like wax figures.

"Please," Semineaux said respectfully, "Wait until my truck and crew arrive. Please." The sheriff snapped his guard back into place, and everyone breathed a sigh of relief.

When the Sheriff's body language relaxed, Sean stepped forward behind an outstretched friendly hand, and very humbly said, "Sir, thank you. God bless you."

"My God, look at him," Sal thought to himself, watching Sean. It is fortunate the sheriff was not some block headed redneck cop type."

At that moment two other official types showed up to break the tension, and the sheriff and Sean engaged them in a conversation. Apparently, they were not too happy with the marching orders Lubber had issued, particularly when one of the officials became immediately sympathetic to Sean after seeing his books, for his younger brother was a writer in Ohio. They confessed that they were confused as to why Lubber was so intent on a forced eviction, rather than giving Sean until sundown, or some reasonable period of time.

The first thing they did was to call Lubber about the possibility of giving Sean some time; but Lubber was adamant. He wanted everything and everyone "thrown" out of the house "immediately," whereupon, the official with the writer brother turned to the sheriff and said, "Fuck Lubber, let this man take his time and move out. Lubber doesn't have the balls to come down here and face this guy. So, we just say yes, and do no."

At that moment Ashley walked in the door. "What's going on chaps," she said, sounding just wonderful. Every man in the room smiled.

Sean knew by her eyes how frightened she remained, but Ashley was a very good actress, and carried it off with charm. The sheriff and officials bowed their heads and wished Ashley good morning, and each of them said something about how sorry they were for such an event.

At that point Sean felt everything was going to be all right. These were not Japanese or Germans, but Americans who had a mind of their own and would disobey orders if they thought them unjust.

"Christ, how lucky I am. Sean thought to himself, as Ashley asked if any of the "gentlemen" wished tea or coffee. The thirteen men just stood motionless, smiled, and said no thank you. Sal Moriarty witnessed it all.

"Think you'll need any of these boys to help you move out."

"No sir, I have friends coming over who will help us pack and move it .... thank you anyhow." As the ten men began to leave Sean took each one of them by the hand, looked them in the eyes, and said something nice to each of them. For the next thirty minutes Sal continued boxing books in the downstairs library, Ashley went into her kitchen, the sheriff left after a smile and a handshake, and Sean and the two other officials carried on an interesting conversation in Sean's upstairs library.

When everyone left, Sean said a prayer to himself, grabbed Sal Moriarty with one arm, Ashley with other, hugged them awfully tight, and allowed his crying to become nearly convulsive.

"Sorry you had to go through such horror honey," as he kissed her. "Brother, I love you. You saved me from myself. Thanks brother," he kissed him.

Many phone calls were made and for the remainder of the day friends came over to help pack everything from the books in the two libraries to hundreds of other items that really needed a week to organize. Sean made a phone call to a guy in Miami who owned four ships and a fleet of trucks. A large truck came over with about eight longshore men from the pier who loaded the dozen potted trees and dozens of hanging plants onto friends' cars and trucks to bring green to someone else's life. He gave away the appliances from the three kitchens on the property; neighbors took refrigerators, washing machines, dryers, stoves, ladders, tools, lawnmowers, a small runabout with engine. All but the books, paintings and personals.

After six hours friends, neighbors, trucks and laborers finally left. The house became silent with only the wind and trees to be heard.

"Sean, this will always be yours. No matter what. No one would believe the mystic things that have happened to you here, as I didn't when you first told me. But I know now since I experienced with you. The power here is with you. No one else will be able to live here. You know that. And you will have this back someday. I know you will Sean" as Ashley began to cry.

Sean stood starring at the emptiness. "Thanks honey."

"I'll go sit in the truck before I cry all over you. I know you want to be alone for a few minutes." Ashley went out to the truck. Sean had no feelings. He was numb. Like after a bruising fight. He walked out into the pool area, looked up at the tree tops, and simple said to himself "It's just a house. As the Buddha says, pain is a blessing." and laughed so hard that several birds up in the trees began to chirp, then others high up in the windless air, on trees nearby at first, then loud squawking voices of wild parrots hundreds of yards away, setting off the songs of countless birds as they swooped down from perches to the fresh cut fairways and shimmering ponds below.

And on a quiet night with no one in sight, Sean and Ashley left Tyler Street and drove toward the beach in North Miami where Ashley had made arrangements for them to stay.

Chapter 18

New world / new book

The next week was one of the most depressing time's in Semineaux's life. He, Ashley, and their dog Wolf were living in a small one room efficiency in an old motel on North Miami Beach.

Sean was crushed and mortified. This was where he used to hang out when he first came to Miami. Every morning after Ashley went to work, he would think of those days a long time ago. Miami in those days was a pristine tale of pure tropical nature with adventurous spirits.

Back then, Miami and Key West were the only tropical frontiers in America. To Sean then, it was like running off to a foreign country. It was a land of gold hunters, gun runners, and all the challenges of the Sea, which seemed far more exciting than going to college after military service.

When the young Semineaux came to Key West from Texas, it was a wild and rough trip since he had no cash and only a gas credit card. He landed in North Miami, sometime in the dead of winter. At that time there were only two bridges going into Miami Beach and he did not even have a dime to cross the small Biscayne Bridge and bartered his expensive official pro football and the shirt he was wearing, beautiful Hawaiian silk given to him by his good Air Force buddy from Hawaii, Leon Lum; and he was then allowed to cross. He was twenty-two years old then, and went down onto Miami beach to apply for a job after being warned against it since a mob from Chicago controlled the job market. After filling out the application forms, he had to fight his way out of the building when he was attacked by about six young thugs. For two weeks, he ate nothing but oranges and coconuts, but finally landed a job as a diver with a small group of men in their 30s and 40s who were obsessed with finding gold laden Spanish galleons, for which Sean thought them crazy. They thought young Semineaux was crazy for diving in any weather, into strange caves and wrecks in the Bahamas, and his love of fist fighting. But Sean loved these men who worked the hard Miami and Key West job market as lifeguards, swimming/diving instructors, milkmen, doormen -- all for their big dreams, the Spanish gold.

Each night they would pin maps to walls that they had received from the Universities of Salama and Madrid, who housed an archive of old maps, libraries or nautical museums and mailed maps all across the globe. Every night they would discuss the history of the old Spanish fleets, German submarines, water depths, women, women, women as they drank heavily and smoked continuously. But young Semineaux also saw something else in those days. Middle aged men whose health was broken by the hard life, who had that stare of a wounded animal, and could turn on you faster than you see the knife coming, or the pistol being pulled.

At twenty-two Semineaux vowed never to be like that. But he didn't want to do anything else in life, but dive. Just be a diver. Maybe dive all over the world -- for gold, for salvage, for anything, while knowing the fate that lay ahead for adventurous types, with no education. But in those days the washouts could fade into boat yards, camp along the ocean at Key West, Nassau, Fort Meyers; but as Florida developed they were quite visible at all the "motel rows" along the ocean, about the time non-wealthy old people discovered Florida, bringing another depressing image to light. Now the sick old retiree joined the burnt-out old sea-salt adventurer as Miami became paved, populated, and raped by developers and politicians.

That was a long time ago, but for some reason it felt like yesterday to him now. For the first two days after the forced eviction Sean was so horrified, he did not come out of his motel room all day, even though the front door opened to the beach and the ocean. When desperate for food or drink he would cross Alan to the store, always seeing a sun scared old drunk or a very ill looking old person that came to Miami too late.

Sean lost his protection from the world; his pool to swim in, his golf course to run on, his trees and isolation to meditate upon, and the sounds and smells of nature that were so fabulous in Hollywood Lakes. Every day before sundown he would take the dog for a walk on a beach that he remembered covered with thousands of palm and pine trees, now lined with old decaying motels built long ago, in need of repair and a beach that was mostly reclaimed by the sea.

One morning after Ashley left Sean picked up a legal pad, closed the fogged, non-transparent window in front of the small desk facing the ocean, the sun, and the international bikini contest that walked by, and wrote the first few sentences of what he considered to be the most important problem facing mankind ... nuclear politics. It would be an intellectual attack on the stupidity of the Reagan administration and all things nuclear, including industrial nuclear power. There were more important things than his private worries. Ashley's horror that he was going to write another book, his third, or fourth? She couldn't remember.

Each day Dr. Sean Semineaux wrote, like he never even had a trial coming up that could put him in prison. The Rockefeller grant would have made life a little easier, especially after they knocked down the motel which had been low rent. Life got tough as they moved from motel to motel in Miami, Hollywood and Dania, for each place had some drawback, and sometimes they moved just to save four or five dollars a night. Sean went to the warehouse and located the boxes filled with his research, every other day shuttling back and forth, and each day managed to write for a least five hours.

In the beginning Ashley would come home after work with a bottle of wine, and they would talk, eat, and walk on the beach with the dog after dark. The more disciplined Sean became in his work, the more he noticed the patterns of Ashley's behavior changing. She came home later and later, often glassy-eyed with hard liquor on her breathe. She always came home with flowers, perfumes, or candy, later and later.

Sean completed two chapters within four months, one dealing with all aspects of U.S. strategic policy that was becoming dangerously trigger happy and aggressive with the Reagan administration in charge. The chapter on the economy focused on the unnecessary American arms build-up for Semineaux believed we would never fight the Russians. A "war economy" was growing in America, America's industries becoming increasingly addicted to military contracts. Few people wanted to hear these arguments in 1983. He educated himself on the banking system and money supply, and wrote nearly thirty pages on the American banking system and its role in this developing "war economy," and the lack of interest in financing productive enterprises that could survive the Cold War and compete in the global economy.

He then moved onto the third chapter dealing with nuclear proliferation and the health effects of nuclear testing and the potential dangers from all industrial nuclear power reactors. Sean had collected enough data on nuclear proliferation from United Nation sources, think tanks, and extensive reading. He had scanned medical journals in addition to examining data from different time periods and different cultures; but there was one thing that was lacking, Sean wanted to know more about the physics of nuclear power reactors, or at least the engineering problems. To Sean, this was the most important chapter, for he had written in his first book "all reactors, worldwide, should be shut down, for they will all eventually leak." Sean believed this should be the most overriding environmental issue, one that even righteous environmentally conscious bottle/can/paper separators scoffed at.

Sometimes he would drive to Jensen beach where he used to spearfish twenty years ago, and sit watching the water pouring out of the vents and into the sea from nuclear power reactors at each end of this once tropical paradise.

Sean knew the University of Florida in Gainesville had the only nuclear power reactor in the state that could produce bomb producing plutonium, and decided to do some research and investigation in Gainesville.

The weekend before leaving South Florida Sean went diving with a close friend he had fished with for over twenty years, who had a Master's degree in marine biology, and was writing a very good book on the marine biology of South Florida, When the two old friends were about to cut through the outer reefs and islands of Biscayne Bay and out into the ocean to spearfish on Fowley Rock, he looked to his right and was disturbed by the view of the huge nuclear power reactor just south and west of them.

Sean would never forget that image, in these waters once ruled by local Indians. What overpowered him was how low in the water it looked. This powerful sea. The arrogance of all those who believed technology could survive nature's power, time, and entropy itself. Feeling a kindred spirit, Sean confided about his mission to Gainesville, and was shocked and embarrassed by the sharp critical reaction and stern glance of his friend whose voice was hardly audible with the huge outboard engine at full throttle.

"You're no scientists ... You are wrong about that."

This was a man Sean loved as a brother, so he kept his mouth shut. But he would never forget the image of his pal, standing there at the wheel of his boat, with that insidious nuclear tower sticking up out of the sea behind him off in the distance, and thought "how long before 'they' kill all life on earth, for they sit like king cobras on the rivers, lakes, bays, and oceans of the world with a poison more deadly than anything produced in nature."

Gainesville was about 250 miles north of Miami, and Sean felt that by going he would be putting a death kiss to his relationship with Ashley. But he had to go.

Chapter 19

Hello Gainesville, Goodbye Gainesville

Sean arrived in Gainesville with four dollars in his pocket. He first went to the university to see if there may be some lecturing or research job available, but as usual, academics are useless if you need them.

The first night he slept in his car in the back of a convenience store near the university, for he had seen a sign for a night manager and did not want to waste any gas driving back in the morning. He had been taught how to manage a convenience store by his good Arab pal who had rented the car in which he was busted.

His pal understood more about survival than anyone Sean had ever met. Caring for Sean's welfare like a brother, had him come to a store in Miami in which he worked; teaching Sean how to manage, how to add a dozen odd prices in his head, and a few survival tricks he should know before leaving Miami. Sean got the job as a night manager, and spent the first day sleeping in his car out by a lake.

The Rockefellers would not finance Sean's work, but now he had a corporate sponsor, one of the largest convenience store chains in America, "Super 39," who would unwittingly support this worthwhile research. By the second night Sean had only $1.39 in his pocket. The store had ten gas pumps, so by morning his car had a full tank of gas, its trunk stocked with toilet paper, food, soda, beer, wine, soap, and dozens of other minor needs; and with a job under belt was able to rent a little cottage in the "duckpond" part of the old town. The following day he went to the utility and phone companies, and soon felt like he had lived in Gainesville all his life.

He worked from 11 pm to 7 am, after which he would go to the university gym and jump rope for 45 minutes to an hour, shadow box, take a long shower, go home and sleep for five or six hours, and then spent five or six hours in the library. Once the basic survival necessities were taken care of Sean went to work on the global survival questions. His first weeks of research in the nuclear section of the library did not yield the information he wanted, though pleased he was to see a copy of his China book.

Each day he would read the New York Times and drink a lot of coffee in the university cafeteria before beginning his research. One day he went back into the kitchen and asked who had worked there the longest. The following day he asked the employee, a kind looking black gentleman where the secretaries from the nuclear physics department sat for lunch. Semineaux sat in the area the third day.

The ladies always had coffee after eating their meal, so the timing seemed quite natural when Sean refilled his cup, making his decision to start with the prettiest one, rather than the ugliest one. He worried that his judgment may have been impaired by his chemistry that was disturbed by a campus filled with more good-looking women than he had ever seen in all his travels. A gorgeous central Florida girl worked in the very area in which he needed information about the potential technical problems of the reactors.

She came to Sean's home for dinner one evening. Just after the first date, she began to smuggle copies of the documents he needed beneath the flimsy underwear pants and bras Sean bought for her in a Gainesville boutique. She had known only rough redneck types, and a few academics pretending to be adventurers.

Each week the documents became more and more interesting. They got along very well, even though Sean didn't see too much of her since she lived an hour's drive from Gainesville; and some other reason Sean never inquired about, guessing she may have been married.

The graveyard shift at the convenience store opened Sean's eyes to the underside of Gainesville's graciousness. It seemed so peaceful compared with the violent Miami to its south.

After he saved enough money, he sent Ashley a train ticket to come up from Miami, with a special compartment all to herself with a bed, toilet, and meals served. It was her birthday and he decorated his new house with ribbons and flowers and spread presents all around the place, including two beautiful black and white finches in a wooden cage. He missed her and enjoyed driving to the train station the day she came. In spite of the pending trial and other problems, he felt extremely happy that day cruising along the country roads listening to Jimmy Buffet's "Somewhere Over China" tape and thinking how much he loved Ashley. He thought maybe she would like his little two-story cottage with the screened in downstairs front porch and upstairs fireplace in a setting of weeping willow trees and old Victoria homes.

Maybe Ashley would move there with him and they would marry, have children, and this would be where he would write his books.

After he picked her up at the train station, they went home to her surprise party and then he took her to dinner. But something terrible happened. Somehow, they could never get it together. They passed a nice little French restaurant he had mentioned in his letters. He often read the NYT and drank espresso there, whereupon Ashley insisted they stop there. Sean had made reservations at another restaurant and they were late, but Ashley became adamant about stopping at where he read the newspaper. A terrible argument ensued, with Ashley accusing him of not wanting her to see the "waitress you are screwing." Ashley was now screaming at the top of her lungs "I want to see this girl you are fucking in that place."

"Here, takes the car -- the hell with the dinner and your birthday." He leaped out of the car and began to walk just to get away from her screaming.

An hour later he walked back to the house but she was inside with the keys and refused to answer the door, whereupon Sean began throwing huge stones at the sides of his wooden house and finally missing the side of the building and knocking out the back-bedroom window.

The next morning, early, he drove her back to the train station with neither of them talking, and no music. She broke down and cried when she got on the train and Sean cried for an hour in the woods before going to meet his only pal the "green machine" in a redneck bar, got drunk, and drove around the back roads drinking six packs of beer and singing Jimmy Buffet songs.

"He's somewhere over China ... it's a real live fairytale ... put a little distance between causes and effect ... what the hell did Marco Polo think when he ran into the wall, or the crazy flying tigers doing spins and loops and stalls ... just a taste for something different ... he's off somewhere over China, Shanghai, or old Peking ... on a plane or a boat. . feel adventure has its ring ... put a little distance between fact or fantasy ... I could buss the Himalayas, or roll above Hong Kong. We're off somewhere over China, taking time to live a little. so far from the nest ... to put a little distance between causes and effects ... like an ancient fortune cookie, telling what comes next."

That night Semineaux wanted to go to a few rock and roll bars but his pal the "green machine" liked the redneck bars. Sean and the "green machine" met the second day Sean was in Gainesville and got along great. He did not know his real name, but he appeared to be 22 or 25 years old, and had been an all-state linebacker in high school. Sean notice that his pal liked the middle-aged female bartenders at the redneck bars, and they liked him.

That night they sat by the lake for a while listening to Buffet and drinking the six packs. Sean related how much he wanted to swim in the lake but was told it was too dangerous with the twelve-foot alligators lurking in the dark waters. "Bullshit," the "green machine" said. He told of how he watched his grandfather jump from their fishing boats since green machine was five years old, and "showed" him how to wrestle the alligators, like the Seminole Indians. He said his grandfather taught him it was a psychology. Gators would not attack you if you showed no fear, like dogs. Sean understood this, for he had the same argument about sharks and dogs from his diving days. But he never did swim in the lake.

One day Semineaux read about the "green machine" in the newspaper. He was arrested for disturbing the peace. He was caught climbing up the side of the building where one of the fortyish year-old bartenders lived to party with her. He was going to surprise her by climbing in her bedroom window. She wasn't home. Someone saw "green machine" at two in the morning with a sack on his back. He was climbing the building with a case of beer slung in a sack over his back. The main charge against him was for public drunkenness and possession of alcohol; green machine was only seventeen. Sean never suspected, for these southern boys grow up real fast, as about five barmaids knew.

Sometimes when Sean was in the store by himself, he would think about Ashley and nearly cry. Then one day the most beautiful girl at the University of Florida walked into the store, and that is saying something special about her for Gainesville women looked like a vogue magazine in the south, with a little Paris thrown in. That first time she came into the store Sean recited a poem about Miami to her, and then she told him about working part-time in the library and he could visit her there, "if he wished."

She came in often after that first day, and always seemed to have little money. Sometimes she put candy back on the shelf rather than not buy a little can of cat food. One-night Sean gave her three bags he had prepared for her. One was filled to the brim with all types of cat food, cat nip, cat litter, cat everything. The second was filled with expensive frozen dinners, cans of white tuna, boxes of candy and cakes. The third had wine, beer, and champagne.

It was not long before she invited him to her apartment after his all-night shift. Semineaux gave up the morning jumping rope for the bath, back massage, breakfast, and fabulous love every morning for his last two months in Gainesville. The two of them laughed a lot as they drove around the country roads listening to Jimmy Buffet.

He maintained a six hour a day work schedule on the book, and read the technical writings of Szilard, Teller, Oppenheimer, Bohr, Meitner, Fermi, Lawrence von Neumann, and others to understand the documents smuggled out of the nuclear department. But he sure got tired of reading:

"Since U235 is responsible for slow-neutron fission, it is natural to conclude that only 1/140 of any quality of U can be considered as a possible source of atomic energy if slow neutrons are to be used ... but then ... the fission energy of most of the U238, if it could be used directly, might yet find indirect release." This whole process was dependent on the possibility that: "bombarding uranium with neutrons converted some of the uranium to transuranic that some thought might have been banished by the discovery of fission. When an atom of U238 captured a neutron, it became the isotope U239."

Just when he was beginning to understand that he read, The next element up the periodic table from uranium, element 19, which was selected as the likeliest candidate for fission not 93X239 which one physicist called eka-osmium ... and

94ekaOs240 changed from an odd to an even number of neutrons when it absorbed a neutron preparatory top fashioning ... 239 nucleons - 94 protons + 145 neutrons + 1 + 146, just as U235 changed to U236, ought to be even more fissionable than the lighter uranium isotope: in 94EaO 240, the excess energy would be even larger than in 92U236 and a large cross section for fission would be expected.

BINGO ... one day Sean decided he could not read another word, was beginning to miss the reggae music of South Florida, and ended it all reading Nietzsche's poem "Among Friends"

Fine to lie in quiet together
Finer still to join in laughing
Underneath a silken heaven
Lying back amid the grasses
Join with friends in cheerful laughing
Showing our white teeth together.
Am I right? Let's lie in quiet;
Am I wrong? Let's join in Laughing
And in being aggravating.
Aggravating, loudly laughing,
Till we reach the grave together and on.

Within twenty-four hours Sean was packed for a return to Miami to write the proliferation chapter and the concluding chapter on the psychology of the whole thing. He was getting bored with Gainesville after four months and had done mostly what he set out to do. He only had one regret, not meeting perhaps the most interesting person in Gainesville, Harry Cruz.

Chapter 20

love, chaos, publishers

Before Sean's Gainesville connection was coming to an end Ashley had surprised him by driving up to see him on two occasions. The first with two girlfriends, probably just to cushion her apprehension about his possible rejection of her. When he told her, he was returning to South Florida, she asked if they were going to live together again, and all he said was, "You know I love you."

They both agreed that they could not stand to live the gypsy life style along the motel rows of South Florida. Ashley said she was looking for an apartment. Sean decided to try and make a go of it again and found an apartment very close to Ashley 's work place, a huge place just east of US 1 in North Miami in a little wooded area next to a swamp which was a microcosm of what the entire area had been thirty years before, when it had been traditionally red neck territory.

Sean didn't particularly like the area, but chose it for its proximity to Ashley's job. He was hopeful it would enhance their relationship, for she was close enough to come home at lunch time allowing them to be lovers.

Sean soon got down to the hard work of re-writing everything he had written. He had been in Gainesville nearly four months and had more interesting research than he actually needed, but he somehow wanted the chapter on proliferation to be hard hitting in a way other literature on the subject avoided. Perhaps what drove him, even to the extent of going to Gainesville in the first place, was that perennial question deep in his gut about the relationship between his own son's brain tumor and the deadly nuclear fall-out of the pre-test ban treaty world of the 1960s. He had read enough scientific journals years before to see the relationship between things nuclear, children cancer rates, and high increases in cancer rates for adults of all ages; for people don't seem to remember the fact that some nuclear isotopes released in our environments remain deadly for up to 240 years. Millions of people losing family members to cancer somehow discount all things nuclear as a cause. He truly believed that unless the nations of the world stopped building industrial nuclear plants, the environmental health of the planet was doomed at some point in the future.

When he sat and looked at the piles of research brought back from Gainesville he felt as if he had entered foreign territory, sometimes hostile, and forced it to yield it's secrets. Not only had he translated enough of the foreign language of science to do a better job on the problems of nuclear power reactors, but had poured over enough medical journals at the University of Florida to get a good grasp of comparative cancer rates from nuclear fallout in areas as divergent as Utah and the islands of the South Pacific.

He now put this aside and went back to tighten up the first chapter on strategy, which he knew would cause a stir for some of its controversial positions such as arguing that Communism would fall apart because of economic imperatives and internal sociological problems; it's arguments for restructuring the military by bringing the U.S. Air Force back under Army command at a time when the expansion of air force programs were popular; cutting back large naval aircraft carriers and concentrating on rapid deployment built around small and more mobile aircraft carriers and looking at the Russians not as a threat but as a xenophobic nation with a defensive psychology, suggesting the Reagan administration was wasting our financial heritage for the wrong reasons.

Each day the small swamp across from their new apartment reminded him how much he missed his pool and the ocean breezes, but he tried to ignore this and concentrate on the continuation of some important reading he had been doing for the economics chapter which was not yet in a respectable form.

He had prepared himself for this economics chapter by immersing himself in everything from Adam Smith's two volume classic "The Wealth of Nations" that many quotes and few read, but believed it's analysis of "markets" still teach lessons for the contemporary world. Then on to Milton Friedman, Joseph Schumpeter, Karl Marx, and Joan Robinson. But most interesting were the works of a little-known economist, Thorstein Veblen. Semineaux found Veblen's books most interesting, since Veblen began his study of economics by first looking at the players rather than the economic activities. He argued that in order to understand the "business system" you had to understand the nature of economic man, his economic rituals and rites. He thought it important to understand customs and mores in any particular "business system." Sean believed that Veblen was really ahead of his own time and still timely in the 1980s and beyond, for American economist were just beginning to see the importance of understanding other cultures in order to compete with other western nations with more experience in these areas.

Semineaux was intrigued by Veblen's book, "Theory of The Leisure Class," which often brought him to laughing tears, but deep down inside he thought Veblen was describing a future American economy with two classes, a working class, and a leisure class.

Rough drafts of two chapters were already in the publisher's hands. They were handwritten, with pen and ink, as Sean preferred. This was the private arrangement he had worked out with Mr. White, the president of the company who had some sympathy for Sean's gypsy existence, and believed in Sean's work.

In one letter about the manuscript Mr. White had said "that Sean Semineaux's writing is so powerful, it may even change people's minds," giving him some confidence in these hard times. Sean knew that to change people's political perceptions was most difficult. For most people believe their perceptions grounded in rationality, when in essence the sources of their perceptions are emotional, irrational, religious, and addictively self-interested motives. Sean believed the greatest of all Western philosophers, Nietzsche, understood when he said that "Convictions are more dangerous enemies of truth than lies."

Life was uneventful but Sean was now writing feverishly and passionately. The concluding chapter was to examine the very pathology of the behaviors in international affairs, particularly between the two Superpowers now at dangerously intolerable levels of intolerance. Sean believed President Reagan so dangerous he wanted the publisher to make sure the book would be out in time for Sean to follow the President on the next campaign trail, in a truck loaded with copies of "Gamble For Survival: The politics of nuclear, chemical, and biological conflict," and lecture on the follies of the administration's unnecessary fear of the Russians.

He was truly not interested in fame or power at this point, just plain pissed-off that this great nation was run by the communist conspiracy wing of the Republican Party that had its origins in pre-WWII with the likes of ex-President Herbert Hoover and ace pilot Lindbergh, both of whom perpetuated the fear of Communism as the enemy at the same time they admired, supported, and praised Hitler's Germany. Hoover, probably the most well prepared of any man we have had for President, failed miserably but admired the efficiency of the Germany economy and believed that if America had given him, Herbert Hoover as President, the power to rule by order; America in 1937 and 1938 would be doing better than it was under Roosevelt, with his "socialist programs." Lindbergh admired Goering's Luftwaffe and its determination for air superiority in any future conflict, particularly against the "communist."

That wing of the Republican party supported fascists who were to send millions to the gas chambers, just as they supported fascist's dictators world-wide in the post WWII period who tortured and buried young university dissidents with torture tools supplied by the CIA and other clandestine and not so clandestine American groups. They finally captured the Party in 1964 with Barry Goldwater's nomination; unbeknownst to most Americans that this was the same un-American click that horrified the American consciousness during the un-American McCarthy witch-hunts of the 1950s, now in control of the Republican Party in the 1980s.

So here he was, the pretty face of the 1964 race for the presidency praising the glories of Barry Goldwater; it was the actor, Ronald Reagan campaigning for Goldwater who was warning about Communists.

The internal enemy that would cause America to lose its cockiness, its sense of security, its faith in the system to provide meaningful employment would in the end not be the "Communists" as warned by this Republican wing since the thirties, but American corporate and political leaders.

Generations of Americans were weaned on fears of Castro, Lenin, Stalin, Mao, Khrushchev, and those red ink blotches on the maps of Europe, Asia, South and Central America, depicting the spread of Communism. Traitors among us were dragged before our eyes so we could see for ourselves, the Alger Hiss and Rosenberg's and other baggy-eyed dangerous threats to our security and grand way of life.

We were warned it would be the Communists and it turned out to be our own politicians, bankers, arbitragers, junk bond specialists, corporate leaders, and lawyers; lawyers taking money made in America overseas to pile up even more profits while millions upon millions of Americans here lost their jobs to cheaper labor costs overseas. The Communist conspiracy was feared to be an internal one, but one we could at least fight; if an economy is considered the heart of a country, the American economy is slowly being reinvested beyond the reach of most Americans to fight back. Your livelihood is taken away by those who run the country, the corporations and the politicians they support. If the Communists were Satan, unchecked corporate power must be Lucifer.

And in the apartment by the swamp, he continued to write. And by himself he was most of the time, for though Ashley worked but a long walk away from their bunker, she never once came home for lunch, and she had access to all the Yuppies' fancy cars and villas. He has this dream that they would make wet, passionate love in the afternoon, and in the evening, he would read his work of the day, and they would eat, drink and discuss it.

At night he would drink too much, and she would drink too much. It was now no longer Eva the Ballerina but the imaginary girl that never existed in the French restaurant in Gainesville. When she got drunk enough, she would deride the shallowness, uncultured, and stupid people she worked with at the Palm Isle Resort, "for if they only knew where I came from," and back to the old story of Daddy, the large English home they had in Surrey, and the sophistication of all those family members with their leisure class symbols of fine cars, villas in France, silk dresses, expensive jewelry, charm, and intelligence.

The large apartment began to feel like a bunker. Very little light entered because of the lush tropical vegetation surrounding the property. Ashley did nothing to the apartment that women in love do, like put up curtains for evening privacy. Sean had stacked books on the windowsill ledges throughout the apartment, but in the afternoon, he was glad to get outside to the light. He particularly missed having a place nearby to swim and run. As his body softened, old fears began to make their way to the surface of his mind. Like the poor downtown ghostlike souls who inhabited the trailer park near Gulf Stream race track for the last thirty years in that sun-bleached tropical ghetto, with missing teeth, thinning grey hair, coughing spells, huge bellies, big old cars with bald tires, fading rusted paint, and illegal out of state license plates.

Or the other side of Gulf Steam race track, on Hallandale Beach Boulevard east of US 1, the greatest concentration of the ugliest people in the world could be found. Ones who had the money to fight time with hair dyes, wigs, false teeth, big flashy hats and umbrellas, white slacks with plastic green and blue belts, tasteless colorful clothes bought cheap looking cheap, standing motionless at sun burning treeless bus stops, or sitting lifeless in new shiny hermetically sealed air conditioned cars, on their way to buy more things for their tacky apartments or to eat large lunches, which would be the topic of conversation over a gluttonous, greasy sandwich, eaten at the late evening meal.

But he would soon be able to leave this place and these images, for any day now he would find out his publication date and be on his way again, into the shining world of hope.

And then, the terror struck. in the form of a letter from the publisher.

--

Dear Dr. Semineaux:
First, I would like to confirm our receipt of the final chapter of your book. As you may not be aware, the President of the company, Mr. White is no longer with us. I am the new President of the company. To be quite frank, Dr. Semineaux, I was shocked to find two secretaries taking turns typing a manuscript that is the responsibility of the author. I am returning, under separate cover, all four chapters, including half of your first chapter that has already been typed.

I would appreciate your having these chapters properly prepared for our editors to read so we can get your book into publication as soon as possible.

Thank you for your cooperation in this matter. If you have any further questions feel free to call me. You should be receiving your book shortly.

--

His body shook. The original agreement actually suggested

by the President, Mr. White, was for each handwritten chapter be sent immediately upon completion. He just stood there in the shade of a tree with the July humidity at an intolerable level and the temperature at 96 degrees, looking out across the dead looking swamp and the endlessly flat and boring afternoon horizon. He suddenly felt trapped in hopelessness, poverty, love lessness, and loneliness. He would end up in that trailer park; damned for his sins, his lifestyle, and his stupidity.

Then he went into a rage. "That fucking Hallahan ... that cowardly lying bastard owner of the House." It was happening again. His head was spinning. He knew who it was. The owner of the publishing house whom he did not trust, a little sleazy Irishman with a long nose who was never without a pipe hanging out of a thin-lipped mouth, who seemed uncomfortable looking directly into anyone's eyes. He fired that nice, gentle, literary type Mr. White and hired some hatchet man, a 1980s yuppie business type to do his dirty work. Sean knew that his writing was admired by Mr. White, but it was too radical for the owner, Hallahan, whose brother was Reagan's appointed ambassador to Grenada. Hallahan was one of those Republicans Sean was writing about.

"Freedom of the press, bullshit ... Only if you fucking own one," Sean screaming at a cat that was lazily strolling through the courtyard of the small apartment complex, for at this hour no one was home in the other three apartments to hear his anger. He rolled up the letter and threw it at the cat, who quickly made tracks.

"It's fucking happening again. His first contract on his China book had been canceled while Sean was traveling overseas, and it took him years to figure out the CIA connection with that publishing house owner, Fred Paget, whose New York publishing house was largely financed with CIA money to produce anti-totalitarian, anti-communist books.

He then signed a second contract on the China book. When calling to inquire about getting a rush copy of the first edition to send to his mother in Philadelphia, he was informed by the secretary that the owner and president of Caldecott Press had decided to cancel Sean's book. The book had already been edited and typeset. Even the cover had been designed and the advertisements were out on the book. It seemed like a matter of minutes, like a baby about to be born.

On that second occasion, Sean waited the weekend, and then

hopped on a plane from Miami to Kennedy airport arriving at daybreak, taking the shuttle into Penn Station, and a train to the publishers' office in the town of Port Washington, New York. He thought he had forgotten it all, but it was coming back to him.

At the Port Washington train station, he climbed into a cab and asked the driver if he knew of Caldecott Press, whereupon he shook his head yes and off they went on a dreary early Monday morning. When Semineaux noticed they passed the publishing house twice he leaned forward over the seat, told the driver to stop the cab, and said, "Buddy, you are fucking with the wrong guy now." The driver, embarrassed, drove him quickly to the company and said, "I won't charge You. and I'll wait out here for you for all long as it takes you to do business."

Sean said nothing, nodded his head and went into Caldecott Press. That morning, Sean could have gone to jail, for he wanted to knock the hell out of this liar and killer of books, and Sean's heart.

The secretary, although surprised to see him unannounced, was very polite and friendly. Semineaux spotted the boss in his office and immediately walked right in with the secretary following behind and softly saying "this is Dr. Semineaux, the author of the book on China."

The publisher, a bearded man, balding head, pot belly, and sagging chin just sat in his chair, astonished. He looked very frightened. Semineaux, surprisingly enough, remained calm and just looked at him with those piercing blue eyes, and said nothing. After a few nervous seconds the man called back out to his secretary to please get Dr. Semineaux a cup of coffee, asked what he wanted in it, and excused himself to go to the bathroom. By the time Sean had the coffee, the guy was back in the office with a tacky looking blue denim jacket matching his dungarees and mumbled something about having to just go pick up a few bank receipts and would be right back. "You enjoy your coffee, I'll be right back," and he put on a stupid looking matching blue denim hat shaped like an elephant hunter's hat Sean had once seen, and disappeared out the door, all six foot four of him dragging his flat ass behind.

After a few minutes Semineaux walked to the back looking for the men's room. He saw the numerous people moving boxes and similar duties in the rear warehouse, and immediately felt hostility to them also. They were part of this conspiracy. But yet, they all looked at him. Some smiled, some just nodded their heads. Evidently, the secretary had called back to them about his presence. One was so kind as to ask if he wanted a refill on the coffee. Sean was a little confused, but what he did not know at the time was that these people worked on his book, liked it, brought parts of it home to their families to read, and felt he was being screwed. They seemed to know everything.

The owner never came back to own office that day, and after a while Sean got the hint. The publisher had run away to hide. When Sean left an hour later, the cab driver was there to drive him back to the train station, and he was back in Florida by evening, thinking about another publisher, which he eventually found, but not after more heartache.

What particularly upset him was that he had not solicited the present publisher, Mr. Hallahan, nor had any agent. One day Sean had received a strange letter from this Mr. Hallahan explaining that he had just purchased Caldecott Press in Port Washington and found Sean's completely typeset, ready for publication, book on China. They would be interested in publishing the book immediately, signed by Mr. Hallahan. He received this letter shortly after the book was published in October.

Semineaux was having enough to think about at that time with the court date coming up for the hearing about the disposition of his property. He had no idea of what nightmares lay ahead for him at that time. But he did manage to send off a letter saying he was presently writing a book with a distinguished co-author, not on China, but on something they considered more important at this time in 1982, called Nuclear Politics. Enclosed, a copy of the proposal that they had already drafted for the Rockefeller foundation.

After the rejection of financial aid by the Rockefeller foundation, Semineaux secured the contract from Hallahan. Should he again fly up to New York and set this guy straight? For one thing, he had no money to fly anyplace. And after all, it was July 26th, Sean's birthday, and not a time to be upset. He spent the afternoon trying to meditate and attempting to forget about the nasty book business.

Ashley would be home in a few hours and they would celebrate his birthday, as they did last year in their home. Ashley didn't come home in two hours, or three hours. After three and a half hours Sean called her office and no one answered. She was probably planning a birthday dinner for him, or doing some last-minute shopping.

He was a little surprised when he had checked the mail and there was no card from her, but that would be with his gift. Five minutes after the light disappeared from the sky she came home. She said nothing and looked rather haggled. He asked why she was so late, and she replied that there was an enormous amount of work to do. She said she was very tired and wanted to rest a few minutes, but gave him a card and a gift before going into the bedroom. She kissed him on the cheek like a sister, gave one of her phonies

smiles, and said "happy birthday, I'll just lay down for a minute, as she quickly closed the door.

Sean wasn't sure if his heart was sucking up his stomach, or his stomach was eating his heart, but something hurt inside. He first opened the card. It was a silly card about birthdays coming and going, "but you will always be here," or something like that, signed, "Love Ashley." He opened the gift. It was a cheap little travel clock, the kind of thing she brought home so often, the dozens of trinkets and cheap things that all the men at work were always giving her. Nothing unusual.

He went out back and stood, looking at the stars and fast-moving white clouds coming in off the ocean not far away, trying to piece everything together. After an hour he went into the bedroom. Ashley was on top of the covers sleeping. Sean went over and kissed her gently on the cheek.

"I love you baby... let's celebrate my birthday now."

Ashley didn't move, except her arm, and opened a curled fist, "Here Honey, I am so exhausted, please ... here is the money I was going to take you out with," as the $50 bill rolled out of her hand, "You go out ... please ... I don't feel well."

"It's you, I want to be with baby. Please ... get up," at

which point Ashley snaps in an angry voice, "Just leave me alone, "as she put a pillow over her head and threw the $50 bill in the air, landing on Sean's lap. Sean put his arms around her and tried to cuddle her. She sprang loose onto the floor in a second, now on her feet shouting, "NOW I CAN'T SLEEP..." and walked over to her bag, took out thirty more dollars and threw them on the little stool, for they had no furniture in the room, only a mattress on the floor, and quietly said, "here, go out by yourself." And then she said: "Sean, I'm going away tomorrow to visit my mother in England, my sister is coming home from Algeria, and I am going to meet them. My family, you know. I wanted to wait until tomorrow to tell you, your birthday and all, and I don't bloody want to fight."

"What do you mean you're going away. You did say you would help me with some proofreading and copying of the book toward the end ... well, this is the end, and you have all those copy machines over there at Palm Isle Resorts."

"I knew you would not understand," as Ashley broke out into a fitful crying tantrum ... "I just want to be alone ... I'm sorry it's your birthday ... but I just want to be left alone," as she continued to cry hysterically.

He walked outside into the blackness of a now dark clouded low hung sky coming from the west this time, out of the everglades with the moisture and the bugs. Got into his car and thought, "You are on your knees you bastard ... don't stay there, or you'll be on your back next." In the good times, he would argue with himself that it was when you hit rock bottom, you knew you were paying a price for the unimaginable wonderful things that would eventually happen to you. But at this moment it was all "fucking philosophy," and around the corner he drove to the depressing convenience store and bought a six pack of beer, and drove down Hallandale Beach Boulevard toward the beach.

He was on his third beer by the time he took a right off US 1 onto Hallandale with all its tacky commercial buildings and remembered the first time he drove on that boulevard years before, a time when there had been nothing but forests of 100 foot pine trees fronted by thousands of coconut palms, the only interruptions before arriving at a beach also covered with pine and palm trees was an elegant old white wooden Crab House restaurant with a huge porch wrapping around the entire first floor, its red neon sign providing the only light in this forested setting. Before reaching the small Intercostal draw, bridge there was an outdoor movie theater which showed double features and comics every evening.

He crossed the new bridge muttering "Concrete ... concrete ... everywhere ... she didn't want to live in Gainesville, what the hell am I doing here," as he remembered she was leaving for England, knowing quite well that Ashley and her twin sister would eventually end up in France with her sister's in laws. Sean knew Ashley's preference for Parisian Frenchmen, particularly artist types. He had to beat one off when they first lived together.

Chapter 21

Happy Birthday in South Florida

When he parked his car on the beach he just sat and looked at a scene he loved. The tropical evening seas with the boats now bobbing from the wind carrying the increasingly mo-ist clouds. The red lights, the yellows, the ... after his fifth beer he knew how he was going to celebrate his birthday ... on the warpath.

Semineaux lectured on international politics and Chinese studies at the local state university now and then. There was a secretary who worked part time in the development office, a young artist who lived nearby the university in a trailer camp. She once told Sean he was the most interesting person in the entire university, and one day boldly gave him her phone number if he ever wished to see the paintings. Sean tried the three pay phones on the beach, but they were either destroyed by the salt or ripped apart by vandals. He was surprised when he called from a phone on Alan and she sounded quite happy to hear from him, and within a few minutes he was back on US 1 going south past the university.

When he arrived, he was horrified by the trailer camp, but quite impressed with the oil paintings hung from every available space within the trailer, creating an art gallery atmosphere with the dozens of small lights illuminating a sensational use of color. Sean could not paint, but his ex-wife had been an artist, so he knew something about technique and color, and having visited landmark art galleries all over the world, was able to appreciate what he as seeing. She got him a beer and started to change clothes by ducking behind a Chinese screen every so often as the two of them chattered non-stop about her painting and art and life.

He always knew they would get along fine if alone under one roof on some occasion, but never saw her get up from behind that desk at the university. As she moved about the apartment, he noticed the smooth skin on the exposed part of her thin ankle and long calf, her small waist and tight rear, and that. Beautiful-black hair hanging down her back which had always been up in a bun or pulled back at work. She suggested they go out to a local bar, hear some music and have a beer, but before leaving she rubbed against him in a way he could not read, and felt nice.

By the time they had ordered their second glass of beer at the bar she had already invited Sean to drive with her the next day to paint something in old Fort Meyers on the Gulf side, for it was her day off. They were eye ball to eye ball in conversation for forty-five minutes when he mentioned her name for the first time, which caused her to stop, and say how nice her name sounded coming from him.

"Lory, that's because you make me feel so good ... it's my birthday," at which point Lory looked into him with her dark eyes, put her hand behind his ear, "Happy Birthday Dr. Semineaux, as she placed her slightly opened mouth on his lips, and shivered slightly as Sean slowly moved his hand beneath her breasts, around her rip cage, as she pressed against him and took his tongue into her mouth for what seem like an eternity.

They smiled at each other, she kissed him on the neck, and said, "I've liked you for a long time." He couldn't believe what he was hearing. She was such a nice girl, and so feline. He wanted to know all about her, and began to push her on the source of her art. "Drew or painted since I was a little girl," she said, but Sean pressed on, "No, I mean it's usually in the genes ... I couldn't paint if you told me on my birthday, you'd make love to me," as they both laughed until she said, "I do want too.

There was this beautiful silence. Again, he pressed her about her source of talent, which she apparently did not want to discuss but divulged that her father was an artist and lived in Manhattan, and they both laughed. "I knew it," Sean said. Your father. But the smile slowly slides from his face as she said that her father was the art director for Vogue Magazine in New York for fifteen years before resigning and painting full time, at which point Sean asked her last name that he had never inquired about, hoping it was not Smith.

"Smith," she said. He gasped. "What's the matter," said Lory. He could not quite believe what he heard, for Smith had been his wife's boss in those days and the two of them became drinking buddies at a time when Smith, or Vincent Van Gogh as Sean used to call him jokingly, was going through a horrible child custody with his ex-wife that pained him so much, for he truly loved his little daughter, then six years old whom he named Lory after his mother.

This was her, now at twenty-one years old. He starred at her in shock as she released the affectionate grip around his wrists announcing she was going to the lady's room.

"My God," he thought... This is probably the nicest girl I have ever met in South Florida ... and she likes me ... a lot. Christ, what am I?? A lout, as Ashley says. Vincent was my friend, not all that close. But what a decent guy. In those days, he loved that little girl ... now she's twenty-one ... I just can't do it ... Christ, I could fall in love with her."

By the time Lory returned from the ladies room there were about six of her young friends who spotted her and came over to the table where they sat, including one obnoxious guy that talked bold and cute, and immediately annoyed Sean, particularly when he put his arm around Lorie's shoulder and began ordering beers, shouting to Semineaux. "Want a beer Dude"?

"I'm not drinking," he replied, and asked Lory the direction of the men's room. After getting past the now crowded bar he spotted the sign for the men's room as well as the exit light, and in a split second decided it was a good time "to split," and was surprised by the down pour of tropical rains outside. Once he got into his car it took a few minutes to get all the systems working to clear up the fogged wet windows. He drove around the building to the exit. A car parking forced him to stop, and out of the downpour came Lory as he opened the passenger's side to let her in, her hair dripping, her shirt wet to the bone.

"Why are you going?" she said with a pained look on her face. I knew something was wrong when you told Jordan you were not drinking. I saw you duck out the exit. What is it? I love being with you. Is it Jordan? I know he's an asshole."

"No, it's not that, "as he tried to explain knowing her father so well when she was only six years old, and the ethics of it all. After the shock of his disclosure, she waited a few minutes, and said, "I don't give a dam. I like you. It makes no difference. I never see my father. I wish you had not brought it up." And the rain poured so hard it hit the roof like a squall out at sea. "I have a life of my own down here. I'll get my pocketbook and come with you."

Sean leaned over, grabbed her around her entire body putting his hands on her rear with a finger pressed into the crack of her ass, kissed her with his other hand on her breast as she shook and placed her hand on his hardness, and they both squeezed, and then hugged. "You go back in ... I'll call you tomorrow ... OK ... let's just say... I love you Lory. The nicest thing that will happen to me on my birthday. Good night."

She looked empty. But smiled, and ran through the sheets of rain as Sean pulled out onto US 1, confused, and numb.

Sean headed north on US 1 ever so slowly for the visibility was down to a car length, giving him time to think, for the squall was coming off the ocean, dropping bucketsful of water on the road. Nearing old Fort Lauderdale airport on U.S. 1 he could read a red neon sign that he had seen for years and often scoffed at the thought that men would get that desperate to enter, "Girls ... massages."

"Damn ... what a great birthday present to myself. Two soft hands rubbing down my back, what could it cost? Happy Birthday Semineaux."

He opened the door to the semi-circle entrance of the once art deco front, now in need of a new paint job. The entire interior had been stripped of its heavy old Dade County Pine doors, panels, and exquisite wooden molding; and replaced with cheap plywood and flimsy hollow wooden doors. Behind a counter enclosed with wooden poles the shape of jail bars stood two men.

"What can I help you with"

"You ... nothing Sir," Sean said with a sarcastic look and tone.

Then another voice, from a shorter fellow, "Sir, what is it you wish?" "Just a rub-down," Semineaux replied.

"You want a woman?"

"I said ... a rub-down ... are you deaf? A simple rub-down ... She ... and it must be a 'she,' does not even have to go beneath my belt. Good hands... the head ... the back ... how much ... come on, what the hell takes so long to decide a price for a simple massage."

"OK ... Ten bucks ... said the taller one."

"Ten bucks you said?" "Yea ... that's what I said." I think I should have come here sooner. Ten bucks for a massage -- I'm in!" and followed a man down the hall, which itself pissed him off, for he had yet to see a woman, until they got halfway down the hallway with the outdoor brown smelly carpet, and then into the perfumed room where sat a pudgy little redhead about twenty five years old with a bright red and purple East Indian cape.

He could smell incense burning. She smiled. He thought she seemed nice, and was damn glad he had nothing else but a massage in mind, for she was one weird broad. If Semineaux was marooned on an island with her, he would live the rest of his life without sex.

"How nice," he thought as he looked around the room for the massage table.

"Here ... sit down," as she sat across from him, smiled as he sat, then opened her robe exposing her body to his eyes, and said "Here... you lick me."

He, thinking that perhaps she wanted him to sit on the thick pile of fake oriental rugs and crack his back before the massage or something like that.

"Close your robe. I don't want a whore. Just a rub-down. On the back ... only ... where is your table," as Sean was halfway up on his feet immediately.

"First, I want you to lick my pussy," she said in the sweetest voice. "That's the game. First you lick my pussy, then I give you a massage ..."

Without any hesitation Semineaux moved quickly toward the flimsy wooden door, as she yelled "The ten dollars is the entrance fee sir, and everything else you pay for. I offered you to lick my pussy ... that cost thirty-five dollars. And don't try anything ... the guys here have guns."

Wrong thing to say. He reached to open the door and it was locked. Wrong thing to do. He kicked it open with one blow from his heel, and loud enough so those at the counter at the end of the hall could hear quite clearly, "You fuck with me and I'll burn this place to the ground" he bellowed out, the threatening words echoing down the hallway and through all the thin walls, striking fear into the hearts of all the massage girls. "Just put the ten bucks on the counter" he repeated fast, over and over again. The ten bucks lay there. He grabbed it and left, and moving like a cat was in his car and driving north on U.S. 1 under a clear sky and well lighted part of the highway.

All I wanted was to be having a quiet dinner someplace with Ashley, and look at this madness ... dam it's my birthday ... what the hell will I do now? I don't want to be with strangers." Then Sean remembered his pal's bar out in Davie as he passed the airport, took a sharp left onto route 84 heading West. It was a weekday night so his place would not be crowded and he would have a chance to talk with his friend Mike. It was a long straight drive out to Davie and he began thinking about Mike whom he had known from his New York days. Mike was one of a group of guys Sean called his "New York Irish Mafia" back in the 70s when they ran the original, pre-franchised, "T.G.I. Friday's" pub on 1st Avenue at 63rd Street.

The Hart brothers, two great guys, ran the place and Mike's father worked the door. Mike was a New York cop who worked the Bronx where he was born, saw so much violence in four years he decided there was more to life than police work, quit the department and moved to Florida.

About a year earlier Mike asked Sean to take a ride with him to Davie to see the bar he now owned, for he wanted Sean's opinion. Sean knew Davie a long time. One of his diving buddies from Key West and Nassau had his family roots in Davie that years before had been an amazing area of biological diversity on the edge of the Everglades with running streams of uncontaminated waters teeming with aquatic life, exotic trees and plants, game fish, alligators, snakes. Sean would take his son and two young daughters into the jungle like atmosphere and just watch his children's eye's boggle at the surprises of nature, one of the pearls in the fragile tropical garden of South Florida.

And then came development. By the early 80s it was another congested South Florida area that for thousands of years supported nothing but a few Indian tribes, and Seminoles now in a nearby reservation.

That night a year ago, Mike and Sean went into the bar he now owned. Then the bar catered to red-necks and bikers, with twelve pool tables, shuffle boards, and dart boards. Semineaux sized it up in a minute, for he also knew the under-side of Davie with its red-neck violence and high murder rate for such a small area. Mike told Sean his plans for the bar. He was going to gradually sell off all but two of the twelve pool tables, presently covered in red cloth with red lights above them. It was a huge bar. Mike would slowly get rid of the present crowd of red-necks and bikers as he sold the tables, gutted the place while keeping some of the present crowd drinking to keep the money coming in. He would strip it of its predominately red colors, rebuild the bar itself, throw out the remaining "bums," and turn the place into a restaurant/bar that the area's new Yuppies would welcome.

Mike's dream even included the color arrangement with Kelly Green predominant, down to the green and white checkered tablecloths. A place where a gentleman would bring a lady.

"You are fucking nuts" Semineaux laughed.

"What do you mean...nuts," Mike countered as he looked down at Sean. Mike was a big, strong, redheaded, Irish/German with a Bronx type background similar to Sean's West Philly environment, he wasn't afraid of anything.

"Brother ... You'll be the General Custer of the bar business. Instead of Indians, it'll be red-necks and bikers."

"What are you getting to be a pussy," as he smiled down over his red moustache, a cocky look that always made Sean laugh.

"I know what you want. You want to create a 'Friday's' in Davie, except that it will be in green and white instead of red and white."

"You got it brother, right on the head." And in record time Mike did exactly that. Just before the grand opening Mike came to Sean's house in Hollywood Lakes with a tall, good looking, and powerfully built Boston Irishman who had helped Mike clean the place out, bare-knuckled. Mike wanted Sean to work the front door, and argued that he knew of no one that was as good with "people."

Well, Sean was flattered that Mike thought that much of him. And Mike offered him a good deal of money.

"Mike ... thanks so much. But that job would be like a B29 WWII tail gunner. The door man is going to get shot." Mike laughed, but after the place was only open two months an enraged red-neck who was asked to leave because of rowdy, drunken behavior, returned fifteen minutes later and fired a rifle from a moving pick-up truck. The bullet did pass the doorman, but hit a twenty-one-year-old bouncer right in the neck, killing him instantly. The kid was the most popular employee in the place, everyone loved him. He was polite, funny, and intelligent, and happened to be a black belt who was one of the best karate fighters in South Florida. The boy's father also worked there; it was said.

Sean knew that business slumped after the shooting and worried about his friend Mike. And after three foiled attempts to celebrate his birthday with women, he would spend the rest of it with his old pal. Mike was glad to see him, and the place was nearly deserted. Mike was a tough guy and never allowed his concern to show on the surface, but not only was business bad, but Mike was no longer living in the nice house on the lake with his beautiful blond German lady. They had broken up and Mike was living in a little room in the back of the bar. They talked about life, New York, Florida, the old 'Friday's,' and the Hart brothers, until every patron left.

The evening was winding down when two young women from the Indian reservation nearby came into the bar and sat right next to Semineaux, for Mike was back in the kitchen putting out the lights at the moment. They were both of the Seminole tribe. One sister didn't look very Indian with her blond hair, but her sister was unmistakable Indian. By the time Mike returned from the kitchen the three of them were drinking the beers Sean had drawn from the tap, laughing and getting along just fine. Mike just shook his head as if he expected it, put a bottle of red and a bottle of white wine oil the bar, and said

"Sean, help yourself to anything. Just make sure you lock the door when you leave. Happy Birthday brother," gave Sean a big bear hug, smiled at the two girls and said something about "this is a nice guy," and went off to bed in the back room, leaving the music playing. "Have fun guys."

After about forty-five minutes the girls suggested that Sean come home to the reservation with him. He was fairly familiar with the reservation for he had a good Seminole pal who had lost one leg from the knee down in a motorcycle accident and knew part of the reservation through him, one of the best men Sean ever met. The girls lived in a modest family house on the reservation, and immediately turned on the lights and music as they continued his birthday celebration with the six packs and bottles of wine brought from the bar, topped off with some excellent smoke cultivated from generations of tribal seeds that predated the white man's poisoning of tribal culture with alcohol.

Both sisters insisted on showing Sean their bedrooms, and to his satisfaction, the one he was attracted to won out and took him into her room. She was about five seven with fine features and very sexy eyes. Her room was decorated on two walls with posters and photos of every sort, but the other two walls confused Sean, for they were entirely covered with smears of red paint from ceiling to floor. When he inquired, she told him that one wall was for daddy, and the other for mommy.

With her eyes still shining with happiness she explained that when Daddy got her upset, she did "this wall," after slashing her wrists; and when Mommy got her upset, she did "that wall." Sean froze as she turned over her- wrists exposing the now healed scars that were quite obvious, and quite relieved when the other sister came into the room demanding that Sean see her room, and pulled him out by grabbing him by the hand.

Her room, on the other side of the house was quite different. Her walls were all covered with pictures of horses. She had long black hair, a pretty face, and a strong and stocky build. She was only twenty years old, but as it turned out she was already one of the greatest horse busters in the whole country. She traveled most of the year to reservations across the country breaking wild horses and training them to jump. This took powerful legs and arms, and a special spirit enabling her to "talk" to horses, the latter accounting for her very sweet and tender inner self.

She showed Sean her scrapbook of horses, more photos than he wanted to see, and then without saying anything, kissed him, turned the light down very low, and began taking off her clothes displaying a very firm and beautiful body.

They made love. This sensuous girl whose legs were strong enough to break the spirit of a large powerful stallion or control jumping horses the width of a bull did not stop until the sun began to peek into the room after four hours and fell fast asleep, right after she said "happy birthday dude."

Sean woke to the sun reflecting off several photo frames on the table next to her bed. When she sensed him awake, she kissed him on the neck. He asked about the photos on the table, of two men who looked dam rough and ready. She told Sean it was her father and brother who drove over-the-road trucks. Evidently, they were both in jail for killing five men in a bar in New Mexico, stabbing two, and shooting three.

"Oh," said Sean, where are they now?"

"No one really knows, they escaped from prison last week." "Last week'" Sean said with a little apprehension in his voice. "We hope they don't try and come home because the 'states' have an alarm out for them, but we miss them so much ... that's their bedroom across the living room." "Oh," said Sean, as he remembered the blood-stained walls in the sister's room, declined her offer of breakfast, or even a cup of coffee, as he pretended to be worried about being late for work. The other sister never came out of her room, and the two of them hugged and kissed goodbye.

In a few minutes Sean was out on the main roads of West Hollywood heading East and then South, and could not help but shed a few tears as he passed the graveyard near Hollywood Boulevard where his son is buried, and thinking to himself, "what the hell is it all about?"

Chapter 22

hard work, hot sun, cheap labor

He didn't realize that Ashley's plans were so urgent. By the -evening of that day she was packed and ready to go to the airport. Not much was said between them when he drove her to the departure terminal, and she insisted he not come in to say goodbye. She kissed him goodbye and he wished her a good vacation. She wished him good luck with his book. On the way home he picked up a six pack of beer.

Once back at the "bunker" he sipped a few beers while sitting outback starring at the stars across the swamp, but the bugs drove him into the apartment after about twenty minutes.

The next day his manuscript arrived by a special delivery mail service with his four chapters to be "typed and returned as soon as possible." Sean put his typewriter on the kitchen table, the only table in the apartment with no furniture, and began to type after having several cups of coffee.

Each day he tried to type all day long, but each day he ran into the same problem. He could not just type the manuscript, he wanted to rewrite a few sentences, then paragraphs, then add something here, and something there, and before long he was driving to the outdoor storage bin, they had rented the day of the eviction. He had not supervised the packing of the bin which was the size of a garage, so finding the right books among his entire life's belonging was compounded by the tremendous heat and humidity in this low-lying area near Gulfstream racetrack that not even the Indians inhabited a long time ago.

Three or four times a week he would find what he needed

among the eighty boxes of books he had in storage. Before long he had books piled all over the apartment, with all the windows filled to capacity. The process became excruciatingly painful for he continually found something he wanted to add or rewrite. He missed having a nearby pool or ocean to swim in, or soft beach to run on for the tension was building up in his body. He had found a school track with a macadam surface nearby and each day walked over to run, but soon tore a muscle in his leg and could not run.

Some days he would walk over in the hot sun and just walk, until one day he was joined on the track by two fat housewives. By this time his body was fast losing the firmness that he had developed jumping rope and exercising in Gainesville. He was running very low on money and couldn't afford the six-pack he would sip outside each evening and had to resort to buying "Thunderbird," a strong wine, colorless like gin, and with ice cubes looked like gin.

As long as he wasn't training, he had cravings for a cigarette when he drank the thunderbird on ice each evening, so he started buying the only cigarettes he could afford, the cheap generic brand sold in the local convenience store. This went on for three weeks. He did not hear a thing from Ashley. She was only scheduled to stay two weeks, but a note from her co-worker stated Ashley called work to say she decided to stay another month. He would have called Ashley in Europe, but he had no phone number for her.

One morning he looked in the only mirror in the apartment and noticed his chest was beginning to look like tits. He had no diversions from this routine. He did not want to chance driving around Miami drinking, especially with no driver's license and out on bail. His trial was taking a long time due to the huge docket of cases before him. He didn't even visit his co-author, for he was embarrassed by the way the publisher was treating him. This man Sean loved and respected so much. He did not visit friends in his old neighborhood, for he did not want to go near his old home. At least once a day he wished he had shot the banker and his son.

The bottle of thunderbird on ice each night was not helping the situation, but it was the only fun he experienced while attempting to "retype" the entire manuscript, that he was now bringing up to date with the international events changing so quickly. One of the reasons he was pushing so hard was the hope the publisher could get the book out immediately, so he could follow Reagan around as planned. How, he didn't know at this time.

He was becoming very isolated, and then one day he received a letter from Ashley. It was postmarked from France. She said that she was very sad, but could not live with Sean when she returned, at least for a while. She just "wanted to get my own place and be alone." On this unbearable hot, humid, August day Sean wondered how much further he could fall. He looked in the mirror and his body were beginning to look like a fat woman. Then, came a knock on the door. His first visitor.

Sean peaked out between the books on the window sill. "Christ, there' coming to arrest me." His heart froze. He could not see who it was. Then he saw the face in the blazing August sun. It was Patrick Kelly, his good old pal. Sean was jubilant. Patrick was the president of a shipping company called Nordic Shipping, owned by a guy from New York named Antonio. Patrick ran four refrigerated cargo ships down into Central and South America. Sean had worked for Patrick as a ship agent, or wherever he was needed; sometimes sailing to Belize, Trinidad and other ports in one of the four ships.

Sean opened the door and there sat Patrick on his motorcycle with helmet, shades, no shirt, and looking like a movie star, the front tire but a few feet from the front door.

"Patrick, where the hell you been?"

"Just got back from Guyana taking that ship apart for salvage."

"Your amazing ... come on in."

Patrick got off his bike and took off his helmet. He stood about six two, with a strong athletic build, the handsome looks of a model that drove women wild, and a man's kind of man, an adventurer. Blond haired and tan he walked into the dark apartment and saw the books and papers scattered about.

"Sean ... what the hell is happening to you. Why don't you get the hell out of here? This is depressing. This is not you."

Sean quickly explained about the book being returned. "Who the hell is going to type it if I don't. It won't type itself."

"Ashley types."

Then he explained about Ashley. "Glad you came by. Just got a Dear John letter a half hour ago. What the fuck can you do? She's over in France fucking Frenchmen for the summer. Enough ... what are you up to pal?"

Patrick was the only person who visited Sean for a month and a half, while he completed most of the rewrite. Then, Sean decided to move from "The Bunker" and into an apartment in the old neighborhood. He would be near pools, the ocean, running beaches, and the old golf course. By now Sean was nearly out of money. Then one day after he moved from the "bunker," Patrick came by his new apartment on Hollywood Boulevard, unemployed. One day the FBI, just as Sean always kidded Patrick about, came into the office and sealed all the records. They were not after Patrick, he was "clean," but he was now out of a job, and was quite upset about it. Sean was concerned, for Patrick was another man he loved as a brother.

Before Sean became associated with Patrick in the shipping business, they used to work out together at a local gym, and the two of them would sit for hours in Sean's home trying to figure out a way to save Sean's property from the vultures. In those dark days before the eviction it was Patrick who pulled out a few business contacts to help put together a deal for the fifty thousand dollar lots on both sides of the house. They were good friends.

Pat, I'm just about out of money myself. I can just about afford the stationary supplies needed to keep this book going.

Sean, I don't like this being out of work.

Wait, I'll get the paper ... plenty of jobs in there.

"Any jobs for presidents of shipping companies or university professors or ship agents?"

"No, but look at all these 'mason tender's' jobs."

"What the hell is that?"

You know, construction work ... mix mortar, carry block, dig holes."

"Well, let's do it," Patrick said. The next morning, they drove up to a Pompano Beach construction office and walked in and filled out very simple applications, and within five minutes they were interviewed by the owner of the company. He brought them both into his office and the first question he asked was "Did you two just get out of prison?" for he was not used to white guys applying for these brutal jobs.

"No," Semineaux said. "We are mason tenders, and we will give you a good day's work. That I know."

The owner looked up at them and said, "I know you will," looked over at his supervisor and said, "Fire those four Haitians and put these guys to work."

The supervisor simply said "Be here tomorrow morning at 7 a.m."

The next morning Sean and Patrick were there at 7 a.m. sharp, decked out in work boots and hardhats expecting to be sent to a construction site giving them time to stop off to get something to eat and drink before beginning. Instead, they were to lock their car and climb into the back of an open truck with ten other men, two of whom were dropped off at each of the five construction sites with Patrick and Sean dropped off last at the furthest site West, far from the ocean, in what looked like a North African desert.

Their job was to help build the outer walls of a shopping mall on a flat sandy site the size of two football fields, with barely a blade of grass and no trees. Five huge piles of stacked concrete blocks sat in the sand like sphinx in an Egyptian no-man's land.

These were some of the blocks that would be used to construct the four forty-foot-high walls. Once the walls went up, then holes were to be dug in the sand for the plumbing system, then the huge concrete floor would be poured, the roofs put on, the inside structure, the electrical lines, and the remainder of the finishing work.

The first day on any new job is always the toughest. A new environment is disorienting. One can feel quite clumsy. It had been a long time since Patrick worked construction, and twenty years for Sean. They had no idea what to expect. Their first assignment was in the southeast quadrant of this rectangle encompassing twenty thousand square yards.

The major construction thus far on the site was the footing that ran around the entire compound two hundred yards in one direction and one hundred across. The twenty-four-inch-wide footing was a steel reinforced concrete slab that months before had been poured on top of steel reinforced concrete pilings that had been driven into the sand by pile drivers until they reached the coral rock deep into the earth.

The only wall already begun was a thirty-foot-high corner of this southeast quadrant with the section running north to south having been extended sixty feet along the footing going north, to which they were driven in a smaller vehicle. There were already four layers of scaffolding against this northern section of the wall, which they both assumed at the time was someone else's responsibility. On the ground, in front of the scaffolding, was a large pile of concrete blocks.

Sean and Patrick just stood looking at this scene and wondered what their first assignment would be, for they wanted to get started, particularly Patrick who was normally up and ready to go at dawn, like a rooster or a U.S. Marine. Sean was tired, for his owlish nature hated mornings. And then it started.

The foreman, a six-foot four-inch black dude with a pencil thin body and strong looking steely arms that were as long as arms can grow was introduced to them as "Tree." Tree asked Sean and Patrick their names, and then quietly said, "See em block," as he pointed to the pile of concrete blocks. "They go up there," as Tree pointed his long right arm up to the top tier of scaffolding, and walked away. They walked over and stood between this eight-foot pile of concrete blocks and the scaffolding both felling rather stupid, not quite sure what he meant, until Patrick figured out, he meant that all these blocks had to go up to build the wall to its destined height, forty or fifty feet.

Sean said, "Is he fucking crazy. For four dollars and sixty-seven cents an hour, or are we"' They both had a good laugh and then discussed who would do what. To begin with Sean would pass a block at a time to Patrick who would stand on the first tier of scaffolding until they got enough blocks on tier one, to repeat the process; but with Patrick now passing the blocks on tier one to Sean on tier two. The blocks each weighed about nineteen pounds, measuring sixteen inches long and eight inches high. As Sean passed each block up, Patrick would reach down and grab the nineteen-pound block with one hand, and then place it up on the second tier. After a short time, Sean learned to stay ahead of Patrick by placing the block on the scaffolding boards, and before long they had a nice pile of blocks on the second tier giving them some sense of confidence.

Then a voice screaming, "I'll be all day. Yu tenders? Were you work before, damn?" It was Tree, and in a second he was standing next to Sean, not looking at either one of them, but. simply reached out with both his unusually large calloused hands, snatched two blocks as if they were the weight of balsam wood, snapped them up to tier one, repeated the procedure in rapid fire succession until he had a dozen blocks on the first tier, bam, bam, bam.

"Dar," he said, and walked away.

Sean and Patrick got the message. Sean began to grab two blocks at a time and throw them upon the first tier, with Patrick also grabbing two blocks at a time and throwing them up to the second tier. They said nothing to each other but could hear each other's heavy breathing in the burning heat of the morning's sun. They had their first lesson, and learned it well, even though they could not understand at the time why so many blocks had to be put up so high, but a good stone mason can set two to three hundred blocks a day.

So up they went, both trying to prove to all those other guys in the yard how hard they could work. They were the new guys on the job, filling in for the four Haitians whom they replaced. They worked non-stop for forty-five minutes, Sean hoping his old back could take it, particularly since his body was fat and flabby from the effects of sitting with the book, the booze, and the depression.

The interruption at forty-five minutes came when a truck bringing supplies drove through the center of the site, looking rather indecisive, then heading directly at their wall. The driver with papers in his hand got out of the truck and yelled something to the two of them now standing on the third tier next to a large pile of blocks. Patrick climbed down immediately and went over to look at the papers, which he was doing, until a voice yelled, "Get the hell back up dire."

It was Tree nearly running from the other side of the site, furious that they had stopped working. When Sean and Patrick realized what happened they began to laugh hysterically, for when the driver pulled onto the site all he saw were two to three dozen black men and two white men.

Assuming the two white guys were the bosses, he drove over to their quadrant. Little did he know, they were not only the new guys, but also the least knowledgeable or capable of understanding what was to be done with the supply of steel roads being delivered. But they were the only white men on the site, for the carpenters were not yet on the job; carpenters usually had a few blond-haired boys or men in their crews. The block masons were now beginning to filter into the area and climb the scaffold, all non-union tradesmen, getting paid at non-union wages.

They worked three more hours at a brutal pace, with one fifteen-minute break when a canteen truck came with coffee, soda, cigs, and other goodies. When the lunch break finally came, they climbed into one of the other mason's cars and went to the Seven Eleven. Patrick bought a large Italian hoagie and a soda, and Sean bought a bottle of aspirins and a large bottle of diet coke, swallowing four- aspirins immediately, hoping his back would not stiffen. After the lunch break, they returned to the site of their agonizing first morning.

Men with mortar filled wheel barrels, entered the area and ran the wheel barrels up flimsily erected ramps to the first tier where they shoveled out the heavy mortar up to the second tier, a job they were both glad not to be doing. They were assigned to a new area up the line where only the footing stood, but the earth had been dug away from both sides to a depth of several feet, and they were told to stack blocks at the edge of the trenches and set up mortar boards. "Mortar boards?" This way the stone masons could stand down in the trenches, grab the blocks, and lay the most important part of the wall, the first course level. It had been so long since Sean worked with stone masons he forgot and Patrick never heard of "mortar boards." They figured out what the mortar boards where when Patrick walked confidently over to where one man was mixing the mortar, and seeing enough square pieces of plywood with dried mortar, brought four of them back to the trench, bringing a smile to Sean's face, and proud that Patrick had figured it out, saving them "face."

This job came to be painful since some of the masons wanted blocks piled in the trench itself which was not level at the bottom making it difficult to maintain one's footing while stacking the blocks two at a time down in the pit. In the afternoon they soon learned the variety of jobs necessary to support the work of the block masons. They wheeled barrels of mortar up and down the ramps when the masons were up on the scaffolds, struggled to push the rubber tire of the wheel barrel through the soft sand to the trenches and footings, carrying mortar when necessary. They soon learned the jargon in order to bring all the supplies needed by the masons, carrying the metal scaffolding and thick twelve foot long boards to different locations, erected and dismantled the scaffolding and, most importantly, to be on instant call of the stone masons who made the walls go up and up.

"Mud ... mud ... muddy...mudded...wire ... wire ... where ... where, shouted by masons which first they could not decode, but by watching the other tenders immediately responding and returning with mortar, block ties, shims, and paying particular attention to the changing consistency of the wet "mud" in the wheel barrels, as the constantly blazing sun and the intermittent winds dehydrated it. The "mud" had to be consistent enough to hold the blocks apart and wet enough to be "buttered" on the edges of the blocks.

By the end of the first day they felt like seasoned pros, and their muscles were bulging and aching as well. The following morning Sean was afraid his back was going to lock up, and was surprised to discover upon getting out of bed he only had a little soreness, no pain. The aspirins and vitamin C he later took may have helped; grateful he was to be able to return to work, for the rent had to be paid.

Sean didn't do much rewriting or typing in the evenings for a few days but it wasn't too long before his pudgy body began to take its old form and the excess fat on his stomach, thighs, and ass began to melt off, leaving him with more energy in the evening.

He didn't need to run or swim for exercise, so the entire evenings could be used to work on the manuscript which was now being advertised in the publisher's comprehensive catalog, worldwide.

The job became bearable once they learned the routines and many of the masons, most of whom were Jamaican and very pleasant guys that got a kick out of these two white dudes who not only polite and jumped to their every command, but were actually respectful. As the weeks went by a strange bond developed between Sean, Patrick, the half dozen to ten black tenders, and a few of the masons themselves.

Then there were funny episodes, as during one afternoon break when Sean and Patrick were sitting and lying in a shaded area with the other tenders. One of the main bosses began screaming something had not been done right and Patrick, leaping up even though they were on break, to assist. As Patrick walked fast and ramrod straight across the sandy yard Sean wondered, as he laughed to himself, if the other tenders would think Patrick an ass-kisser, volunteering, making them both look bad in the eyes of their fellow tenders. No one said anything, until Sean broke the silence.

"Don't worry guys ... my buddy isn't a pussy..." at which point they all laughed heatedly. "In fact, he never will kiss ass ... he's just so uses to being the boss. You know what I mean. . . "more laughter. "The bastard just got back from Guyana when he took an entire metal ship apart for salvage. He was the boss, but he works harder than any of us would. Guys that work for

Patrick always like the bastard because he pitches right in there and works. He'd do for you or me. Good guy. "Half of them shook their head agreeing. "Look at him now ... dam, up there with the boss -- doesn't he look like a boss up there." This time a couple of guys had to lay down they were laughing so hard.

The only friction came after they had been working two months. On a Monday morning one of the masons who never responded to Sean's polite attempts to say hello or just be recognized, suddenly burst into a loud tirade accusing Sean of not supplying a consistent enough mixture of mortar. The job site became very quiet with the only noise being the other masons buttering the blocks with their trowels. Sean, who for two months, had worked hard and was very respectful, countered, "Sir ... with that tone you can get your own mortar, "and began to walk away when the mason called again, loudly, "You are the tender ... I am the mason ... when I tell you to do something, YOU DO IT."

"Not for $4.67 an hour Jack."

"My name ain't Jack."

"It is now ... JACK."

"I'LL KICK YOU FUCKIN WHITE ASS."

Only the sound of the wind could he heard as Sean stopped in his tracks, walked back to the scaffold, looked up to the second tier on which the mason was standing, and simple said, "Come on down," The mason picked up a large sharped edged hammer and held it above his head. Sean took off his hardhat and sunglasses, looked him in the eye as he pushed closer to the scaffold's pipes and said, "Bring that down, JACK ... you'll need it."

The mason froze and said nothing. None of the other masons said anything" but for the rest of the day they seemed to be going out of their way to communicate with Semineaux.

The only other friction came on the last day, which was not supposed to be the last day. It was a day in mid-November that was as hot as any day had been in August, and everyone seemed to be tired because of the brutal pace of work the previous day with the owner of the company being there all day yelling at everyone in a way that could only be done in a non-union environment. He had even gotten everyone to work overtime for an hour and a half, and this was with no overtime pay, just straight time.

Everyone seemed a little edgy on that particular day, but

Sean's mind was preoccupied. He had finished retyping the book the first week of September, but the publisher reneged on his promise to "get it out immediately," therefore it would not be available before Regan's re-election in November. His attorney related to Sean that they wanted him to serve perhaps two years, which upset him to the point where he started making plans to escape to Bahia, Brazil where a former business associate of Patrick's was going to give him a job in the shipping business. On a day off he had gone to Miami and got his merchant seaman papers renewed, as well as his American passport. There was no way Sean was going back to jail.

On this particular day everyone was tired and irritable, and men who had never talked to Sean were mumbling curses about the boss all day long. In mid-afternoon the little concession truck pulled into the yard through the only remaining opening in the rectangular wall with its bell Jing-a-longing. The fifteen-minute break was due, and the men were ready for it, but the owner yelled, "NOT ENOUGH IS FUCKING GETTING DONE HERE," and sent the truck away.

You could cut the tension in the air. The men had mutiny in their hearts, but no one said anything and continued to work. By some quirk, five minutes later an unscheduled and unexpected concession Jing-a-lined into middle of the yard, the driver not hearing the owner yelling for him to "leave the fucking job."

No one moved. Sean who was high up on the fourth tier, for all the walls were in place by now even though they were built in a piecemeal fashion as had the "Great Wall of China," a nickname for the job that Patrick and Sean would laugh about in the evenings. But unlike the Great Wall where it took five years to build a mile of the wall, these four walls where near completion. All of the masons and tenders were up on some level of scaffolding, angry and pissed off. Then Sean climbed down from the fourth tier of the southern wall, walked north in a straight line down the middle of the hot, sandy yard to the truck while the owner screamed, "TREE ... TREE ... GET THAT BASTARD BACK UP ON THE JOB," as he himself yelled at Sean to get back. Sean just walked as though he heard nothing until he got to the truck where he asked for a diet coke. The attendant handed him a regular ice-cold coke! whereupon Sean politely said, "I want diet sir, "but by the time Sean had the diet coke in his hand Tree snatched him by the wrist of the hand with the can.

Sean never even looked up at Tree, simple said, "Tree, this is not between you and me. It's him and me. Stay out of it." The sad thing is that Sean had developed a liking for this non-union "pusher" whose main job was to drive the men harder, as in a work gang. And the feeling was mutual, for Tree had even asked Patrick and Sean to join him and the boys for a beer after work someday.

Tree, with his hand still on Sean's wrist said, "put it down and get back on the line, with a threatening voice."

Sean, again, without looking at him said, "Tree, if there was a time you could take me it was the first week when I was in pussy shape. Not now my man, don't try," as Sean was staring at Tree's crotch with his tight dungarees showing the outlines of his large balls which Sean would have punched into Tree's stomach before taking away his eyesight with an animal like hand thrust into the whites of his eyes.

"This is between him and me" as Sean just walked back to the South wall drinking his coke, and began to climb until he heard the bosses' bellowing voice, "YOU'RE FIRED ... HIT THE ROAD."

Without hesitating Sean climbed back down the few feet to the ground and began walking off the job, quietly. Then the owner made the mistake of using Sean as an example,

"And for the rest of you. If you don't work harder, you'll never get a break on this job again."

At which point Sean stopped in his tracks, walked back the forty yards to where the owner was standing, stood directly in front of him watching Tree to his right the whole time, grabbed the owner by the right arm, yanked him toward him with a jerk, and with a voice trained to lecture to large audiences, began

"Sir, when you have us working, you own us. But union or non-union, these men earn two breaks a day, and you have no right to take away these breaks ..."

There were men scattered along every wall but the north wall, and Sean's voice could be heard by everyone on that job as he continued, this five 5'9" guy covered with dirt and mortar from head to foot, with mud caked against the sun-screen he had applied to his dark, thickening skin, looking up into the shocked face of this tall owner,

"And when you give us a break SIR, THAT IS OUR FUCKING TIME, NOT YOURS, SIR," as he gave him one more threatening jerk before releasing him and walking off the job, slowly and defiantly.

Patrick climbed down from the West wall scaffold and walked to their vehicle behind Sean. They both had major car problems so they had been coming to work on Patrick's motorcycle.

"Meet me at that old bar on University Drive after work," Patrick said, for Patrick just assumed he should finish work himself.

"Fuck that ... when I walk you walk. And how the fuck am I supposed to get there, thumb it'"

Patrick said nothing. He just followed Sean off the job. Sean's adrenalin was still pumping so hard in his blood he could hardly hold the safety helmet as he put it on his head. He jumped on the back of the cycle as Patrick gunned the engine and drove up the rough patch of unpaved road, Semineaux letting out one of his loudest wolf howls, "AHAHAHAHAHAHAHOOOOOOOOOO AHAHAHAHAHAHAHAOOOOOOO." And over the noise of the motor cycle engine they cold both hear the dozens of whistles and rebel cries ricocheting off the interior walls, sounds of a brotherhood forged in the shared pain of brutal work, in the strength sapping sun, for as little pay as the law would allow.

"Hear that Sean?" as Patrick turned his head to talk.

"Well, they lost one grunt ... but management lost a supervisor, as they both laughed, for the architects, foremen, engineers had all gotten to like and respect Patrick's judgement which surprised them coming from a mere mason tender. "Let's go South on 95," Sean yelled.

For five minutes neither said anything, but Patrick was pushing the cycle at full throttle over slightly bumpy roads that had once only carried supplies into the Everglades. The whistling wind on I-95 felt great ... free ...

Patrick knew something was up remembering the pack they made when it was decided to use the motorcycle for transportation to work, since both their cars were broken down. "Never to use I-95," was the only way Sean would ride on the back of the cycle, for they had both witnessed a horrible automobile accident on I-95 during their first week driving in a car. So, the pack was made, for Sean felt so vulnerable on the back of that motorcycle on I-95.

For Sean to suggest riding on I-95 confused Patrick but more immediate concerns preoccupied his mind, as he turned his head slightly to speak, "Now what the hell are we going to do for a job? At least it was paying the rent."

"What do you mean," he said as Patrick ran up onto I-95, Look ... east and west ... the cranes, look at all those building cranes. That means Jobs."

"But remember that day we tested the waters and they needed no tenders."

"Tenders? Tenders?" what are you talking about my man. We are masons ... Stone Masons Jack. that's us." When Patrick turned his head Sean could see the wide smile of his face. "Yea Jack ... $12.50 an hour."

"I know I could lay block."

"Damn right you can. Look at what we learned in four months," as they both laughed hard. "We know tongue/groove block, bond block, corner block, about ties, wire, shims. Knowledge is power. We know how to run a mason's line, how to butter a block, about vertical rebars, pier walls, convex jointers ...

"That's us ... motherfucking stone masons," Patrick interrupting.

"We know troweling techniques ... six steps Jack... the motor must be stiff enough, the mortar to the head joint first, butter the edges with the inside head joints buttered down at an angle, lay the block on the mortar bed close to the line, tapping ... tapping baby, let it squeeze out, slip the excess off with trowel, swoosh..."

"Christ, I can lay a 'header' in place perfectly. I can lay the corners with three courses stringing the level line between the corners to get it perfect."

"Damn, are we the craftsmen ... look... the crane, looks like a big job, lets pull in."

Twenty-two minutes after being fired they had new jobs, and within thirty-seven minutes they were up on the fifteenth-floor scaffolding laying block at $12.50 an hour for "Kingly, Brannon, and Fisher Construction Co., Inc." And Sean thought of Ashley less and less.

Chapter 23

The Drug Trial

For the next four months Sean and Patrick worked on four different jobs sites for the construction company, each day becoming more respectful of the brutality of non-union work and the increasingly damaging rays of the sun; influencing Patrick to apply to law schools and Sean to pressure the publisher to live up to his commitment represented by a five hundred dollar advance on the royalties which Sean was able to negotiate, purely as a symbol of the publisher's intentions.

If Sean had not been waiting trial, he would have left the job one day with hard hat and all and flown to New York, gone to 36th Street, and held the sleazy Irishman in his office until he printed the book.

Sean was trying to save as much money as he could, for things were not looking good in Salem, and he was determined to go to Bahia, Brazil rather than go to jail. Patrick was aware of this plan, and the fact that Sean just renewed his merchant seaman papers and passport. It was Patrick, about a week before the trial, along with his pal Jack, who reasoned Sean into changing his mind, with the belief that "every little thing, is going to be all right," and he was not going to jail.

Nothing annoyed Sean more in these tense days than people he considered good friends telling Sean, "just do your time." "Fuck you," he would think to himself, "You do it for me," But as they worked side by side Patrick encouraged him to remember how lucky he was with so many good friends, or really brothers, actually a tribe. And they would save him. These conversations, while building the walls of a growing city, were what gave Sean the confidence to finally get on a plane when the time came for his trial, and not to escape.

A week before the trial Sean was informed of a plea bargain that offered him two a year sentence, and he could be out in six months with good behavior. Everyone was happy with this arrangement except Sean. Again, he wanted no "time," but he had to show for the sentencing and take his chances, for he had made too many promises.

Even if he had decided on going to Brazil as earlier, he would not have been able to go. The person who promised to pick up the twenty-five-thousand-dollar bail backed out on his support. There was no way he could jump bail now, for his younger brother, had put up his house in New Jersey and Sean would rather die than hurt his brother in this way. But it was hard to hold out hope that he would get no jail time.

Then came the day. Sean flew to Philadelphia, was picked up by Laconi, and was in the Salem County courthouse within an hour and a half. He was afraid.

And it all happened so fast. He was told to sit in the courtroom just as if it were a traffic court, and he sat there watching all the people before him go before the judge. The judge, this was the same judge that had released him on bail after his brother put his house up in lieu of the cash.

There was something very decent about this guy, the judge. Semineaux studied him with all his learning and experience, and stretched all his intellectual resources to understand him. Sean saw a very bright man. The kind of a guy who was a straight A student through school, but as a kid played sports, fished, was one of the guys. A profile was emerging. Intelligent, quick of mind, compassionate, could see through bullshit, had no pride blocking his judgements, was a good family man, liked to play baseball with his kids, was well liked and respected in the community. After watching the judge for twenty minutes Sean thought, "God, I have a chance. This is a good man."

Then his heart nearly stopped as the court officer called his name. "Sean Sanimax ... Sean Semineaux..." and Sean, dressed in his dark blue pin stripped, vested, Brooks Brother's suit, dark tie, black conservative shoes, walked up the isle and stood before the judge with his attorney at his side, breathless, but saying little prayers to himself.

Without hesitation, the judge, looked him in the eyes and said, Mr. Sean Semineaux, you are being sentenced for the crime of attempting to smuggle marijuana into the state of New Jersey, with the intent to distribute. The State of New Jersey charged you," as he outlined the charges Sean could feel sweat running down his spine, as the judge continued, these counts carrying a maximum sentence of two to ten years in a New Jersey prison. Sean froze. But never once took his eyes from the judges' eyes.

This man had an inner strength that was grounded not on what he was, but who he was. Sean felt safe with this man.

The judge began talking about it being Semineaux's first felony and seemed to be talking about leniency. The problem was that the prosecutor was objecting rather strongly, because it was becoming quite clear the Judge did not want to put Sean in jail, even for six months, prompting, the Prosecutor to object now rather vehemently.

"Your honor... we have a plea bargain working here. YOU CAN NOT PLEA BARGAIN A PLEA BARGAIN.

And the Prosecutor was correct, and he had been assigned the case by the District Attorney of Salem County because he was the best Prosecutor on his staff. A young, bright, Italian guy that was assigned the case because he was the best; for Tony Laconi's reputation was known far and wide as one of the best trial lawyers in Pennsylvania, and the Prosecutor was the quarterback of the first string. The Prosecutor knew he had a real battle on his hands with this brilliant street fighter from across the river.

Sean was now trying to read the Judge like his life depended on it, and his own attorney did not even seem like part of the show at this time; for Laconi was so quiet and smooth in his courtroom demeanor you often thought he was not paying attention. The young prosecutor was obviously upset and was pressing the judge; and the judge, standing firm, with a quiet inner strength that never showed any irritation with the young prosecutor.

The judge, looking exasperated, called a recess requesting the Prosecutor re-read the letters of reference written by people from all over the world on Sean's behalf.

"Please re-read these letters. Quite a few distinguished people think this man has contributed an awful lot of good to a lot of others. They talk so strongly about the difficulties Mr. Semineaux, or Dr. Semineaux, has overcome in his life. In all my years on the bench I have never seen letters like this. This man is not a criminal, he just made a desperate mistake. And I must say, it sure was a strange set of circumstances.

"But your Honor ... a plea bargain is a plea bargain ... it is the law. You cannot plea bargain a plea bargain ... Sir, what can I say."

"I am calling another recess ... Please re-read the letters."

Sean could not believe his ears. This Judge really cares," and the Judge left for his chambers, and Sean was escorted to sit down by one of the very polite court officers. Sean appreciated the very special culture and people of this small town with so much character. He was no longer afraid, just respectful of all that was going on before him in this courthouse, in this old sailing town on the Delaware River. He could take whatever was coming, but he would never forget this judge, no matter what the outcome.

Within ten minutes the Judge returned to the bench and the proceedings began again. But ... with the same arguments. Sean was beginning to feel sorry for this Judge who could destroy his life, for to put Sean in jail would be like putting a canary in a shoe box and wrapping tape around it. But the Judge kept repeating his argument about the letters from Sean's friends and professional associates. I have never seen letters like this."

Sean had never seen the letters, but he loved so many of these people who had written letters, and always thought he did not deserve such love in return.

Again, the Prosecutor, in exasperation, "Your Honor, you cannot plea bargain a plea bargain ... and the discussion between the Judge and the Prosecutor continued for five more minutes, with Laconi maintaining his usual confident profile.

Then the judge suggested another recess for the Prosecution and Laconi to meet in his chambers, after reading the letters again; at which point the Prosecutor looked more like a third baseman coach than an attorney, and said, "But your Honor, we did read them over and over. Why call a recess to read them again. This is supposed to be a sentencing procedure. Let's sentence Mr. Semineaux."

The Judge slammed his hammer, "I am calling a short recess, we will meet in my chambers."

By this time Sean was as calm as if he were with friends. Every few minutes the gravity of the situation crashed in on him, but he couldn't really believe it. And he was so grateful to the judge for stressing that Sean was "not a criminal," for there was nothing that important to Sean to have or possess. He knew at this moment just how simple he wanted life to be, and how simple he tried to make it.

Whatever happened in the Judge's chambers Sean will never know? But the only person to speak afterwards was the Judge, the Prosecutor never spoke again, except to accept the Judge's judgement.

"These letters, from the United Nations, from distinguished people in the business community, from people in the arts, Professors at distinguished universities, from Ambassadors, from China, the New York State legislature, ordinary people ... I could go on and on ... this is not the type of person who should be put in jail ... Therefore, Sean Semineaux ... I sentence you to do 600 hours of community service, and to pay the court a fine of $5,.000.00," as he slammed his gravel ...

Sean wanted to run up and kiss the judge, He wanted to kiss everybody. It was all happening so fast. He could have been led to jail at this point. "FREE, GOD, he thought to himself, and reached over and hugged Laconi... "

Many of the people in the courtroom were relieved it was over for their own cases had been held up. The Prosecutor quickly left the court, and Sean sort of just followed his attorney with the folder full of papers in his hand not knowing what to expect next.

Only a few steps outside the court and into the crowded hallway, Semineaux was stopped in his tracks by a tall distinguished looking guy who looked like Robert Redford except he had a more powerful build, with a few detectable fighting scars around his mouth.

"Sean ... what the hell are you doing here?" the six-foot four guys were saying.

"What do you mean, I have just been sentenced."

Unbeknownst to Semineaux, this was the District Attorney for the County. The chief Prosecutor. The guy who had appointed his top gun to get Sean. "You mean ... that was YOU??" He said in complete disbelief, as he put his arms around Sean, to the complete astonishment of Laconi. The two men hugged each other until about four sheriff's department officers ran up with their night sticks drawn thinking, he was wrestling with the DA.

"No ... NO ... shouted the DA ... THIS IS A FRIEND ... NO PROBLEM ... LEAVE HIM ALONE," as he escorted Sean to his office with Tony Laconi following, losing his normal composure, and quite confused by the two men in front of him.

Semineaux remembered the DA, even his name. It was Joe Dobbs. When Joe was seventeen, he worked as a lifeguard with Sean in North Wildwood, a tough beach to patrol with the strangest undertows on the East Coast.

All that Semineaux could remember was that he and his best friend Jim Sullivan, who were twenty-two-year-old veterans at the time, took Joe under their "wings." Joe, with his handsome looks, blond hair, and blue eyes was like a magnet with girls who just adored him; so, Sean and Jim did not have to go searching for women. And, perhaps, more importantly, Joe Dobbs could deliver a punch like a heavyweight champion, and loved to fight almost as much as make love to women.

Semineaux remembered ... this was an old buddy, for when men fight back to back enough times there is an inseparable bond between them for life, and Wildwood offered more opportunities for fighting than loving women, for the pretty one's didn't give it away easily.

Once inside the office The DA stopped and turned to Semineaux, leaving Tony standing behind him, totally confused, which was extremely rare.

"Look ... look around ... what do you see Sean ...???

Semineaux looked around and saw the framed prints of N.C. and Andrew Wyeth paintings.

"Look at these walls Sean ... You introduced me to the Wyeth's ... remember ... in college..."

"In college?" Semineaux asked, slightly confused.

"Don't you remember Sean??? Christ ... I couldn't get in college. You were teaching in Florida, and got me in college ... Remember I spent a few holidays at your home in Hollywood???"

"I'm sorry... you know I am still in a little state of shock at what just happened. Yea ... I remember... the recommendation and arm twisting I did with those priests to get you in."

By this time Laconi was just shaking his head in complete disbelief, and said, "Semineaux... I can't believe you, only this would happen to you," which was the last thing he said as the DA went on "You are God Dam right ... Sean Semineaux is unbelievable..."as he went on. "Sean ... don't you remember," as the DA's large crystal blue eyes sparkled with intensity, I couldn't get in law school, and you wrote me the greatest recommendation, and got me into law school. If it wasn't for you, I would not be here in this office, with these paintings ... and Oh my God ... prosecuting you... I had no idea." At which point Semineaux was beginning to remember. The DA stood, insisting ... that Sean stand also, put his hands on Semineaux's shoulders, looked him in the eyes in the most solemn fashion, and said, to Sean's complete astonishment.

"Don't you remember brother?"

"Remember what???" Sean said, for he was now standing about a foot from Joe, looking up, as Joe draped his arms on his shoulders and looked down into his eyes.

"Once a week I put my children to bed, usually on a Saturday night. I read to them, tuck them in... and think of how lucky I am ... and always think of you," as tears began to form in this his eyes, confusing Semineaux.

Then a few tears rolled down his cheeks. "I think of your boy, your son, he was so beautiful ... you were so hurt..."

Now Semineaux was straining to understand where Joe was going. "Sean, don't you remember ... I never left your fucking side brother ... the whole day ... at one time I wanted to punch the shit out of your mailman ... for accusing you of being so calloused for entertaining and laughing on the day your son died. I wanted to kill that bastard. You were being as tough as a man can be on an awful day."

"God ... Joe ... yes, I remember."

"Remember ... Christ, I was not just a pallbearer at your son's funeral, I was the CHIEF PALLBEARER SEAN ... I literally never left your side," as tears rolled down both their faces, two men just stood and cried, with Sean's attorney just sitting and looking, and repeating over and over.

"Semineaux ... Semineaux ... you are too much," for it was not just Laconi that saved him, it was mostly Sean's lifetime friends that saved him, Tony was coming to appreciate.

Sean began to remember, and tears rolled down his face as the two of them hugged. "Without you, I wouldn't be here," Joe said, at which point Sean broke the seriousness with... "Fuck you Jack, without you and your cops, I wouldn't be here." At which point the three of them burst into laughter, and after a few more minutes of conversation went off to a small restaurant for lunch.

At lunch Semineaux did not say much, for he was rather numb, and could not believe what had just happened, so he just kicked back and listened to these two great friends, talk lawyer talk, as his mind wandered, and began to take in the mystery of it all.

Chapter 24

The lying Publisher

After lunch Sean said goodbye to his former lifeguard buddy and student, friend, pallbearer and prosecutor, and was dropped off at the train station by Laconi. He looked in Tony's eyes and nothing had to be said between them, but as Sean climbed on the train Laconi said, "Take care Tonka," bringing a big smile to Sean's face as he waved goodbye to his old friend.

It was difficult to have his thoughts on anything else but the sentencing, but now that it was over his mind was beginning to clear somewhat and the first thing, he thought of was how close he was to New York City and the double talking, deceiving publisher, Mr. Hallahan. There was no question where Sean was going, and he was dressed appropriately.

Within an hour Sean was in Penn Station on 34th street, and he felt a new surge in his body as he ran up the steps to the street level, went into the huge post office to quickly send cards to Patrick, Al and Pat, and Jack ... which simple said... "Dr. Sean Semineaux is a free man, Thank you for your loving support, see you soon ... unless I kill this fucking publisher in a few minutes, yak all have a good day, Love, Sean."

He found the office on West 36th street, took the old freight elevator in this converted building to the fourth floor, brushed a few pieces of lint from his suit, and promised himself not to lose his temper, no matter what happened. He knew the President, Mr. White, with whom he originally negotiated the contract would not be there; he had been fired. When the door opened, he recognized the warehouse looking office on this fourth-floor loft, a recent trend in the publishing business because of Manhattan's high rents.

A woman came out of an office and asked who he was and what he wanted. "I am one of your authors, Sean Semineaux, I want to see Mr. Hallahan," and the woman gave a faint, sickly smile, excused herself without offering a seat, coffee, or anything. Just "I'll be right back," and disappeared in the very large, dimly lighted room to his right.

Images flashed into his head of the first meeting in this same publishing house, at another location, in a warm little office with smells of coffee and background classical music, the very pleasant secretary from Long Island, and the sensitive pipe smoking Mr. White, whose smile matched the sincerity in his eyes; the atmosphere punctuated with the pleasant glare of green and yellow lamps and the smell of half and half tobacco.

After too long a wait, he could see a man peeking around the corner of a partition, and then disappearing. A full minute later the man walked from behind the partition and toward Sean, and for a second Semineaux felt he was out on the street, for the demeanor and looks of this short, pudgy man with the suspicious, angry, ugly face was nothing that he expected in a publishing house, unless he was working on the loading dock of the company.

The only thing that distinguished the man somewhat was his suit and tie in which he looked very uncomfortable with his rounded shoulders. The tie appeared to be strangling a neck as fat as his pot belly. It was a long room, a former warehouse. As this man walked toward him Sean was surprised that his instincts were sizing this man to see how to take him, for his walk was aggressive with his arms hanging by his side like a dockworker, and he had this scowl on his face.

When he got in close to Semineaux he didn't even extend a hand to shake, and did not act respectful in any way.

"You want to see Mr. Hallahan?"

"That's right... I'm one of his authors, Dr. Semineaux."

"Wait here." As he walked away Semineaux felt the urge to put his foot up his big fat ass, for he sized him up already as a guy about forty five, whose fucked-up nose indicated he lost too many fights but somehow he learned to mimic the strut of a man much tougher, another dangerous creep.

While waiting Semineaux remembered a previous meeting

after Hallahan failed to meet a promised publication date. The time Mr. Hallahan did not seem to want to be alone with him. On that occasion Hallahan asked his secretary to be present and let her sit behind his desk while Hallahan sat across the room, far from Sean. Sean felt strange on that occasion, but they both guaranteed him the book would be published shortly.

Within a few moments Mr. Hallahan came out of a back office. "Hello Sean, good to see you," Hallahan said as he put out his hand, "What can I do for you?"

"First, send the goon away," Sean thought to himself, with this thug in a suit standing off to Hallahan's left, like a bodyguard. "Do you have the book bound yet?"

"Step into my office" as Hallahan pointed to an office off to his right, next to the elevator, which Sean knew was not 'his' office, and it was not even a working office for it only had a desk and a few chairs. Hallahan sat behind the desk this time, and the goon sat off to Semineaux's right, toward his blind side.

Hallahan looked at him with the pipe dangling from his mouth and spoke through his yellowed teeth. "We should have the book out soon. We had some delay with the binders." "Sir... You have had the book now for over a year now. You had given me your word on several other occasions, and it's not out."

"These things take time," the goon to his right interjected.

"Mr. Hallahan, I don't know who this man is. I deal with you. I want to talk with you, alone ... please," as the goon's eyes bulged and he squirmed in his chair.

"This is Mr. Swartz ... He works for me."

Semimean Sean never looked in Mr. Swartz's direction, but the reaction on his face must have been convincing enough, for Hallahan motioned to Swartz to leave the room, which he did, but not before giving Semineaux a nasty look.

"The bottom line is time, sir ... when will the book be out?"

"All I can say is soon."

"You have been saying that for a year and a half. You had promised to bring it out before the last election. My co-author is a very distinguished scholar and gentleman, and he has become very disillusioned. I love that man, and this I don't like."

"It wasn't much, but we did give you an advance on the book, just to show you we like the book."

"Mr. Hallahan, do you know what I say in that book?"

"I don't have time to read all our manuscripts, that's why I have editors."

"Well sir ... there are important issues we are confronting. Leo wrote important chapters on chemical and biological warfare problems, our nuclear escalation mistakes and the United Nation's role in arms control. I took on the entire panorama of American strategic thinking, tactical weaponry and strategic weaponry mistakes, the folly of SDI, nuclear proliferation and the proliferation of industrial nuclear reactors, the health effects of nuclear tests and industrial reactors, and the economics and psychology of the whole mess."

"Yes, the book covers a lot," he said without much enthusiasm, puffing his pipe.

"Cover a lot? Sir, it is a challenge to this administration's dumb attitude toward the Russians. Please read the book. I am saying that we should not fear Marxism. It won't last. Communism is stagnating and it is going to fall apart. This I predict in the book."

"Interesting ... but I have another appointment soon."

"Interesting? Mr. Hallahan. I consider myself a futurist. I wrote this two year ago now, in 1983. I am predicting the fall of Communism."

"I really have only a few more minutes."

"Look, Mr. Hallahan. I wrote this book because I thought these issues important to all of us. I should have written another book on China to beef up my academic potential, but I am an activist. We can break this deadly nuclear standoff between ourselves and the Russians ... the creation of more NUCLEAR FREE ZONES."

"I've heard of them. Rather impractical, aren't they?"

"If a couple of housewives in California can do it, the rest of the world can. By creating nuclear free zones, or nuclear weapons free zones, people can someday isolate the two superpowers and perhaps force us and the Russians to take the responsibility that great nations should accept, to keep the world from death.

"I really have to go," said Hallahan, again looking at his watch.

"Mr. Hallahan, one more thing. I am trying to go to the Pacific. I am interested in Japan's proliferation of industrial nuclear power on those volcanic islands. I did a case study on this. China is increasing its strategic nuclear capabilities in the area. Most fascinating to me, the Australians and New

Zealanders is debating the possibility of creating a nuclear free weapons zone in the Pacific, an NFZ. I don't know how I am going to get there. I may have to sail as a merchant seaman. But I am going to go. I want the book out. I didn't write it to get an academic position. I wrote it to help do my part to end this mad arms race."

"Can you call me in a week? I promise we will get the book out."

Sean looked him in the eye. "You have let us down before. Do you give me your word on that Mr. Hallahan?"

"Yes, you have my word."

Chapter 25

goodbye Miami, hello New Zealand

When Semineaux got back to Hollywood he had a surprise waiting for him. He could not believe how his luck was beginning to change, for there in the mail was a letter from the Prime Minister's Office in New Zealand inviting him to give a lecture on his new book. The following day he received another letter from the oldest university in New Zealand, the University of Dunedin, offering to pay all his expenses to give a lecture on China's nuclear strategy in the Pacific at a special foreign policy conference.

Someone from the Australian National Defense College had forwarded a copy of Sean's China book to New Zealand, for they were using it in the defense college program for Australian diplomats and military personal. He was to be a featured speaker in Dunedin, and an attached note explained that several think tanks and universities in the country and Australia wished to extend similar offers to him.

The big question was if the probation authorities would allow him to accept the invitations. The next day he mailed copies of his invitations to officials to ask permission to leave the country.

The next thing he did was to call Mr. Hallahan person to person, but it took two days and forty calls to get through to him. He was able to extract an agreement that Mr. Hallahan would send him one published copy of the book to take to New Zealand. Mr. Hallahan said that the book was "now being bound at our bindery." Semineaux was happy, and Hallahan promised he would express mail a published copy before he "got on the plane to New Zealand" and within a week would ship as many books as there were ordered for purchase. Despite his good feeling, Semineaux still did not trust the man.

The cold war was coming to the Pacific with a vengeance in these mid-1980s. The Russians were setting up submarine bases, the Chinese were expanding their coastal navy into a "blue water" navy, again bringing the USA, USSR, and PRC into competition. The French continued testing in the Pacific, but the Polynesians were finally taking toll of the number of children and healthy adults dying from cancer caused by French, America, and British testing.

The 1983 Law of The Sea created an environment for Pacific nations to enforce rights that conflicted with American, Russian, Chinese, and Japanese interests. When the Soviets acquired fishing rights and port facilities on Pacific islands, Washington responded by cutting off financial aid and increasing the number of intelligence operatives in the Pacific; an army of American spies running around the Pacific claiming to be businessmen, scholars, travelers, and diplomats. Right in the middle of all this political tension in the Pacific the New Zealand Prime Minister declared that his country would create its own Nuclear Free Zone, and invited other Pacific nations to join. New Zealand was a member of ANZUS, formed in 1951, which linked Australia and New Zealand to the United States, followed by the creation of SEATO in 1954, giving the U.S. complete military operations over the Pacific, as NATO had done for America in Europe. In fact, both ANZUS and SEATO were nothing more than an overextension and transplantation of the "containment" and "roll-back" strategies operating in Europe later applied to China as evidenced by the mistake of the Vietnam war, policies to stop and then shrink communism.

The Pacific was a good place to test dirty nuclear weapons after the signing of the 1963 Nuclear Test Ban Treaty banning atmospheric test. Pacific island people had little with which to resist America, France, and the British.

President Reagan was spending America's equity on trillions of dollars of weapons. NATO could not absorb all of it, so the excess was being deployed to the Pacific, particularity Reagan's development of a six hundred ship navy, the largest naval force the world has ever seen; along with the most awesome weapon system ever built by mankind, the U.S. Trident submarine fleet.

And New Zealand said no. American naval ships would not

be allowed in New Zealand ports unless President Reagan agreed to change the U.S. Navy policy of "neither confirming nor denying" the presence of nuclear weapons or nuclear-powered ships in the fleet before docking. Reagan said no, New Zealand said no.

And this was where Semineaux was headed, permission or no permission. Within a few days he received a letter from New Jersey authorities approving his trip to the Pacific; but he would have to contact the Miami probation authorities since they were administering that probation order.

Semineaux's exhilaration was dampened the moment he stepped into the sterile, jail like offices in Miami and had to deal with people dumb and nasty, who thought New Zealand was next to China. They said he could go, but must return in two weeks. Two weeks to travel to the other side of the globe. So far away it takes twenty-four hours just to fly there by supersonic jet. So far away that January is the hottest month. So far away storm winds spin clockwise rather than counterclockwise. So far away that water draining from a bathtub whirlpools and spins in the opposite direction. But close enough for him to be back in two weeks.

There wasn't much time. Two years of waiting and agony. He wasn't going to let this dampen his spirits, even though he found a thick, hard, lump deep under his armpit. that morning. Nothing was more important than trying to do his part to keep the world intact. He thought about all the political "activists" he had known, and laughed.

Once he received the two-week release papers from the Miami bureaucrats, he went about trying to put his life in order as best he could in a few days.

He stayed in his shorts and tee shirt and drove around the corner to his old home and parked outside. No one had lived in the house for two years. All the bushes and trees that he had planted over the years were so overgrown the entire first floor of the main house was hidden from sight. He got out of the car and walked between the two enormous bamboo bushes he had planted some time back that whistled in the winds, like someone laughing, joined by the flapping broken screens around the now coffee black stagnant swimming pool. Memories; he could not stay long, but before leaving he said a prayer.

He looked to the rear of this western side of the property at a fully-grown orange tree and thought about the day years earlier when he came to talk with the then owners about buying the property. His little three-year-old son picked a huge orange, the only and first orange, from a tiny tree that had been cultivated the owner (a tree no taller than his small son). He laughed to himself as he remembered, "Dad, here," for the little guy knew his dad loved oranges.

When gathering his things together the next morning, he found a copy of a book given to Ashley by her ex-husband, and thinking he may never see her again, decided to be nice and bring the book to her before leaving.

The sun was high in the sky and dozens of flags were flying in the breeze when Sean pulled into the area of the parking lot used by the lowliest workers at Palm Isle Resort. As he walked toward one of the towering buildings that seemed so out of place in such an ecologically temperamental place, he thought of how much he still loved Ashley.

He thought of six years before when she first worked there and would go to work with her hair still wet, with nothing but a tee-shirt and dungarees. He was proud of her then, for not buying into the glitter, gold, and bullshit of this shallow place. Sean and Ashley were kindred spirits, still bohemians in an age of consumption.

As he clutched the leather-bound volume, he had a crazy idea. She could so easily write herself a corporate airline ticket and come with him. They could start all over again, get married, have babies, write books, live in a nuclear free environment, survive any nuclear, chemical, or biological catastrophe of the future.

When he passed the security guards, he had to stop for a few moments to shake hands and say hello, for three out of the four of these powerful looking guys worked out at the same gym as Semineaux. They were his buddies.

When he began to walk through Palm Isle Resort's main building, he felt terribly nervous with the phonies and ugly people dripping with jewelry who never seemed to mind their own business. He took the elevator to Ashley's office. He had not seen her for five months. Perhaps he would not say a word, just throw her over his shoulders and carry her away with him to New Zealand.

When Ashley came around the corner, she was shocked to see him. He was surprised at what he saw. She was dressed exactly like all the other tacky women downstairs, gold and all.

Her hair was teased and she wore fake eyelashes covering her natural beauty. She looked gaudy.

"What are you doing here," she said in a surprised. but friendly voice.

"I'm leaving for New Zealand in a few hours and found your Shakespeare book that your ex had given you."

"That's bloody nice of you chap," she said sarcastically.

"Chap? You don't call me 'chap' baby. The first spark of tension.

"Why are you going to New Zealand, that silly nuclear stuff?" she asked, her tone quite unfriendly.

"That's right ... They don't want to ruin the country like Miami has been ruined."

"So silly Sean, you can't stop progress, and what ... what do you expect you can do all by yourself."

"I see you haven't changed," a little more tension brewing.

"Can't stop progress Sean."

"Where did you pick up that shit centered philosophy, in the Plastic Thinkers Almanac? What can I do by myself? I don't know baby. But remember ... I'm from West Philly."

"Still the macho." By this time, they were in Ashley's office and Sean was upset things were going so wrong. He wanted to tell her he loved her, but she had these razor-sharp defenses all around her, from head to toe, and was not going to allow him to say anything nice.

She had this awesome power to block anything kind or loving if she had predetermined a non-reconciliatory, unyielding attitude. There was never ... never ... a time when she yielded during the ten years they lived together. Which taught Sean something about the political stubbornness of the English culture, something that his Irish ancestors learned a long time ago.

He followed her to the window overlooking the Inland Waterway Canal that runs along the entire East coast, excepting for a short detour out into the ocean in the Carolinas. From this vantage point he could see a microcosm of what had been. Nothing but mangrove swamps along the entire canal; a little patch that for millenniums had been supporting the entire life chain, where the sea and the fresh water of the Everglades meet. It is natures intercourse of aquatic, plant. and bird life making evolutionary love. The exact area where Semineaux had taken his young daughter and son to fish, and experience the eerie sounds and sights of the primitiveness of nature not that long ago. Tree leaves and branch tips dangling into the canal's current, a symphony of white egrets, song birds, pelicans, flocks of them, flying in and out of thick green foliage teeming with sounds from hundreds of insects and aquatic species, all viewed by a flock of wild pink flamingos.

And there was Ashley standing in front of the large plate glass sterile window overlooking this womb of nature in her four-hundred-dollar suit. Sean could not help notice the rectangular, waist high table to his right covered with an overlay of blueprints, and asked Ashley what it was.

"These are the plans for the new building to be built just north of tower three."

"North of tower three? That's the only remaining mangrove ... How did anyone get permission to build there?"

"Well, you know how politicians can be bought off," she said with the defiance of a women who had been brought up in the Bronx or South Philly rather than Oxford, England.

"I brought you here to enjoy those things you are now participating in destroying."

"Sean ... that's progress ... You have to accept it."

Semineaux looked back down at the immaculately clean and orderly table holding the plans with its glass top. "Who takes care of this"

"I do ... it is my sole responsibility," and as she spoke the words, Sean was having a flashback, to Ashley's constant spilling of red wine over his day's writings that he would ask her to read back in the bunker, his writing about the environment and things nuclear, and Ashley's total disrespect ... and this neat attention she gave to this architectural death notice.

"What happened Ash?" Soft and in a pleading tone, he reached out and laid his hand on hers, touching her for the first time, calling her by a name never heard beyond their ears. Her demeanor changed; her eyes softened for the first time.

That silly girl I met in New York who nearly froze to death wearing a thin cloth coat rather than the warm fur one in her closet. He smiled slightly. She smiled slightly. You called those who shot the animals "beasts." The day in Central Park when we saw that young boy in the boat slamming an ore to kill a fish feeding just beneath the surface. You couldn't look at the fish being beaten to death. They both laughed. The girl who would stop on a New York street to pet a dirty stray cat or dog.

They both laughed hard. When we went camping you got so upset with people for not taking care of the woods. He looked at her beautiful white teeth and kissing lips as she laughed and began to speak. Ash...Ash... then squeezed her hand slightly, there in his mind and partly in his vocal cords were words of pleading for her to come with him to New Zealand. Start all over. Have a family. Make life an adventure again. The two of them, today.

She put her free hand to his mouth when hearing "Ash" and for a split second the green eyes softened like a cupid's belly. Love and understanding poured forth.

Then footsteps behind. Her head jerking up. Her mouth opening wide as if surprised. Her eyes fixating on the person whose footsteps startled them, never again to engage Sean directly. She pulled her hand free of his and sat up straight, for she had been leaning toward him, as if they would...

"Don't let me disturb you two" and in a split second he was standing next to Ashley, his arm around her, looking down at a disappointed Semineaux. "Oh, this is Warren" she said, never one to lose her composure. Neither Warren nor Semineaux extending their hands. "Come on chaps," as she stood and broke loose of Warren's arm which covered both of her shoulders. "Come have some beverage" as she walked into a small bar room off the office with the two men in tow.

At the bar Ashley busily gathered glasses and a bottle of water, with Warren seemingly telling her what to do, then him asking what he wanted to drink. The guy was over six-three, wearing a black silk shirt opened at the neck displaying layers of gold chains, complementing the gold watch and bracelets on his wrists. He was long and thin with wide shoulders, big hands and a large mouth, slightly twisted at one corner.

"Warren is a contractor." And as she began to speak, Warren again wrapped his arm around her shoulders while pouring white wine into the three glasses.

"Cheers chaps" raising her glass, "to a good trip Sean" she said tipping the glass and looking up at Warren as they all put the glasses to their mouths, Semineaux putting the glass to his lips but not drinking, studying the dark deep eyes of Warren. "This guy is all sleazy ... just like this place," thinking to himself.

He did not expect what came next. Warren reached down beneath the bar producing a small mirror upon which sat a bag of white powder, several glass straws and a single edged razor blade he used to lay out and separate thin lines of the powder upon the mirror. He then remembered Bobby Beach telling him on that memorable night about a guy he knew who sold pounds of cocaine on a weekly basis to the people who ran Palm Isle and their Hollywood friends.

"Be my guest," he nodded to Semineaux. This creep. My lady. Coke. Goddamn, coke. Miami. Thinking to himself but politely refusing while wanting so badly to bust this punk in the teeth. And nearly did so when Ashley took one of the straws, looked Sean in the eyes one last time with a stupid look, placed it inside the left side of her nose and snorted until a line on the mirror disappeared, along with ten years of their life together. Then they both laughed at Semineaux, Ashley looking up at Warren and blurting out "Sean is an athlete, he does not do drugs." At which time he noticed Warren's arm had dropped dow-n around her waist, and he was pulling him toward him.

"I think I'd better leave," Seminew said, embarrassed.

"What's the matter Sean? All righteous?" she said sarcastically without even looking at him. "Righteous? If that's what you call it. You know I never trusted anyone who does coke. This punk, this sleazy place you're in, this sleazy guy next to you. I thought you would at least be with a handsome tennis star or movie actor," and turned to walk away.

"Hey pal, get the fuck out of here before I throw you out." "Don't worry, I'm leaving ..." and at about the point where Semineaux had taken one step into the outer office, Warren was up behind him and made the mistake of grabbing the back of his neck with one of his huge hands.

Normally, Semineaux was not into lifting heavy things. But with agile speed he spun, snatching Warren between the legs until he had a handful of balls and ass; and with his left hand snatched his throat right between the large Adam's apple, lifting the big man off of his feet and sending him airborne until he crashed onto the glass table holding the blueprints.

In the next instant Semineaux saw a security guard look into the office and quickly disappear. Unbeknownst to him, the guard ducked back into the shadows of his office and picked up his "hot line" to his chief of security, who in turn alerted the various local police departments to whom the boss gave large amounts of bribes, a fact Ashley had divulged to Semineaux in their more intimate days.

Semineaux turned away from Ashley and walked toward the elevators. He was never to see her again. He got to the first floor and walked out the main entrance with the gait of a man much larger and by the time he walked by the security guards at the entrance gate they were all excited.

"Sean ... what the hell have you done? We just got orders to stop you."

Semineaux smiled and just kept moving fast. The plane to New Zealand was in his mind.

"Christ Sean, you'll get us fired for sure with this one," as they just let him walk. And these guys were tough enough to have probably stopped Semineaux. But they liked this crazy guy from the gym who had a theory on everything, and felt he was one of them.

Walking another fifty yards in the blazing sun and soon he was in his old red Buick, started the engine, looked in his rearview mirror and was horrified ... it was a cop on a motorcycle. This would kill his trip, and perhaps even worse, he was breaking all probation rules. He would definitely spend the night in the Dade County Stockade, like the image haunting him lately, Jake Lamott in the movie "Raging Bull," banging his head against the wall.

"Fuck it. I've a plane to catch" he said out loud before throwing the gear in reverse, gunning the engine to full throttle, and knocking the cop and his bike over into the dirt as the car hit him, pinning the cop beneath his cycle as Semineaux drove away, kicking up a cloud of the dry dirt in the parking lot beneath the causeway.

He pushed the peddle of the old Buick to the floor and all he could think about was getting back to his apartment, packing, going to the post office to claim his book, and getting on that plane at the airport. What he did not expect to see was the faint, mirage-like image of a motorcycle in the mirror, and pushed the peddle as though it could accelerate faster.

At this speed he could be off Palm Isle Resort property shortly. But he could not believe his eyes, and even tried to rub them before looking in the rearview mirror again. For the cop was surprisingly closing the gag very quickly, for he had one of those supped-up cycles that can tear like light, and a judgement had to be made ... real soon ... for the cop was now within fifty yards of him. There appeared to be no escape.

The animal within Semineaux took control as he just turned

the wheel hard to the right taking the vehicle off the road across the forty yards of grass without slowing down, then pushing into the taller grass, then the thirty yards of thin young trees and mature bushes cutting the speed of the vehicle from seventy mph to fifty, then slower, as it entered no-man's land with a forest of trees that could take the impact from the out of control vehicle as it crashed into the dense trees. Luckily, without a seat belt he missed the big trees as the car was stopped by the engulfment of ripped, strained, and entangling branches and bushes.

He leapt from the vehicle, leaving his keys and dozens of things people keep in their trunks and glove compartments, and took only his wallet before running into the forest of tropical growth ... and ran, and ran, coming out onto the Palm Isle Resort Country Club golf course, stretched his legs on open fairways until, startled by the noise of the helicopters above now scanning across the open skies of the fairways, quickly ducked beneath the cover of trees.

They were calling on the numerous layers of Miami's city, municipal, and county police that the boss had bribed over the years, and they were responding quickly with a coordinated effort of police helicopters making low passes across the expansive fairways. He immediately realized they would be looking for his white tee-shirt and white hat.

Now running beneath the trees as a copter made a pass he stripped to the waist, removed his hat, and continued beneath the tree canopy alongside the fairways dogging trees at full speed.

"Some of these guys must be ex-military pilots," he thought, for he had hadn't seen copters maneuver like this in a while. Off to his right was a hotel in the middle of the golf course that he never knew existed. He cut through some trees and bushes, replaced his shirt, put on his hat and walked into another world, where a uniformed doorman assisting wealthy people into their cars and limos, surrounded by sculptured landscapes, glass and stone reaching up about fifteen stories.

Bent over like an old man in pain, he walked up to the door man and said "Sir ... please help me ... the doctor, the doctor, please sir."

"Yes Sir ... what is wrong Sir?"

"My heart ... OH GOD -- MY HEART ... the doctor said I should not be out walking on such a hot day. I should have listened ... please ... please ... call a cab for me, tell them it's an emergency. Is there any place inside the building that I can lay down? I feel faint."

"I can call a Doctor sir, there is one on call at all times."

"NO ... my pills ... in my apartment ... I must get home to those pills. Please ... cab ... emergency ... where can I lay down?"

The doorman quickly escorted Semineaux through one of the large revolving glass doorways whose only sound was a wisp, taking him across the oriental carpets to a large sofa.

"You can lie here sir, when the cab comes, I will come and get you."

"God bless you."

Semineaux quickly sat up when the doorman disappeared through the glass revolving door for, he heard the copters making low passes over the building and the surrounding areas. Clack-kit clack-kit zoom ... kityzoom, and gone.

Within less than three minutes the doorman came back through the door and motioned for Sean to come, helped him to a cab, opened the rear door to assist him as he slipped him a ten-dollar bill before the door was closed. He slipped deep into the back seat, for the driver immediately threw the meter on and was speeding out of the driveway.

"Where you going?"

"Holly ... Hollywood, please, as quickly as possible," whereupon hearing his Brooklyn accent, made a quick decision to trust him, for Semineaux had spent enough time with Brooklyn guys in military brigs to appreciate the flexibility of their attitudes. By this time the noise of the helicopters was being drowned out by the screaming sirens of dozens of police cars. "Christ, you'd think I killed someone," he thought. "Would they have a roadblock at the

front entrance, or the side entrance?"

"Driver ... look, my man ... I had a little argument with my woman. You know how upset broads can get. "

"Tell me, that's why I'm not driving in New York anymore. We were together ten years. She had me arrested. arrested! Just because I called her the "C" word."

"I don't know what these cops are here for. But ... I don't want anyone to see me. OK...I'll pay you good. I'll lie down in your backseat. Say you are taking me to the hospital if they stop us, OK ... Hollywood Memorial ... OK?"

"Did yak kill her?" he asked, laughing.

"Of course not. How fast do you think you can get to Hollywood Boulevard between US 1 and the ocean?"

"Ten ... fifteen minutes. I should've killed mine."

"Do it in ten and I'll give you a twenty-dollar tip." With that he put the peddle to the metal as Semineaux lay in the back seat listening to sirens and helicopters, and was quite relieved when they got to the entrance on US 1 and there was no road block. The various police agencies and departments were converging on the golf course and the area in which the car remained embedded in a tangle of grass, branches, bushes, and small trees, like a small airplane that had crashed into the forest.

Speeding North on US 1 he sat up and began to evaluate his options. Would Ashley tell the authorities where he lived? They could be waiting for him outside his apartment on Hollywood Boulevard. He left all his keys with the car. How would he get into his second story apartment? The "X" in the equation was Ashley. Did she have enough left in her heart for this man who loved her so intensely for ten years? If she wanted Sean brought to his knees, she had a good shot at it now.

"They may even have patrol cars at the front and rear of the building? Driver ... please leave me off on Harrison Street at Sixteenth Street, ok?"

Scmineaux gave the driver forty dollars and walked quickly to Hollywood Boulevard, looked east toward the ocean with relief at not seeing any police cars outside his house or blocks away on this six-lane wide street. Then doubled back to the alley and was again relieved at not seeing any cop cars beneath all the fruit trees at the rear of his home.

He wished he had hidden a housekey somewhere outside, but was able to pull himself up onto the small back porch outside his kitchen on the second floor, picked up a seashell, smashed one of the six small windows in his kitchen door, reached inside and unlocked the door and sat breathless. After a few minutes he went into the refrigerator and poured himself a large glass of water, drank it, and began to take stock of the time and the condition of the apartment. It had the same lived in atmosphere as had his home on the morning of the eviction, for he had planned to return from the mission of love and remembrance at Palm Isle Resort and organize for his adventure.

He wasn't nervous, but the police could come to the front, back, or both doors any second. There would be no time for anything but essentials. He packed a small bag with clothes for a variety of weather conditions, put his three-piece pin-striped suit, a new white shirt, his blue and red tie, and a pair of black leather conservative shoes into a special little bag, all to its own. He then packed about seven copies of his China book, a prepublication copies of the Gamble book, and a little shaving kit bag with tooth brushes, solar cane, band aids, tape, and then the phone rang startling him enough that the jumped from the floor.

Should he answer it? Maybe it's the police. Or have they already notified his probation officer? God ... what to do????

He picked it up. "Sean ... Maria. It's Maria ... where have you been, with such excitement in her voice. A Spanish girlfriend with whom he had made arrangements to drive him to the airport, and even help him to pack and get ready. I've been calling you for two hours. I thought you left already. For God's sake Sean. I am a nervous wreck."

"Maria ... Maria ... I'm sorry. I had to return a book to a friend. Please come over now. Will you still take me to the airport?"

"Of course."

"Please listen closely. I am not going to be in my apartment. I think the police are after me."

"What" .... screaming.

No, not now…I'll explain later. OK, but where are you now? I'm just off Alan south of McGowan's."

"Good ... meet me at the corner of Harrison and Sixteenth Streets in five ... no ... four minutes."

As soon as Maria arrived Semineaux ducked into her little Honda as they sped to the post office. He went in, presented the registered slip, took his published Gamble book out to the car, and off they went to the Miami International Airport. The flight was to leave in an hour from the International terminal and Semineaux thought of the police stopping him before boarding.

"I've got to get on that fucking plane. Damn, Ashley knows my flight is leaving. She holds the key again."

"I hate what that woman does to you."

"I know you do Maria. Just drop me off at the departure terminal and say good bye," and after a passionate kiss and hug, he went through the terminal doors, leaving behind a very sad, but very nice girl.

Once through security he arrived just in time for first boarding call, and to his astonished relief, there were no uniformed cops. Just a very attractive stewardess asking to take his bags. "No thank you, I'm fine. Semineaux slumped into an aisle seat, tore opened the wrapping from the book, and just

Miami 271

looked and looked at the title on his new book, "Gamble for Survival," kissed it, slipped it into the security of the special little bag carrying his "dress-up" clothes, put the seat in take-off position, snapped on the seat belt and fell dead asleep, not even moving when the huge tires hit the underbelly carriage as the plane became airborne over Miami, and New Zealand bound.

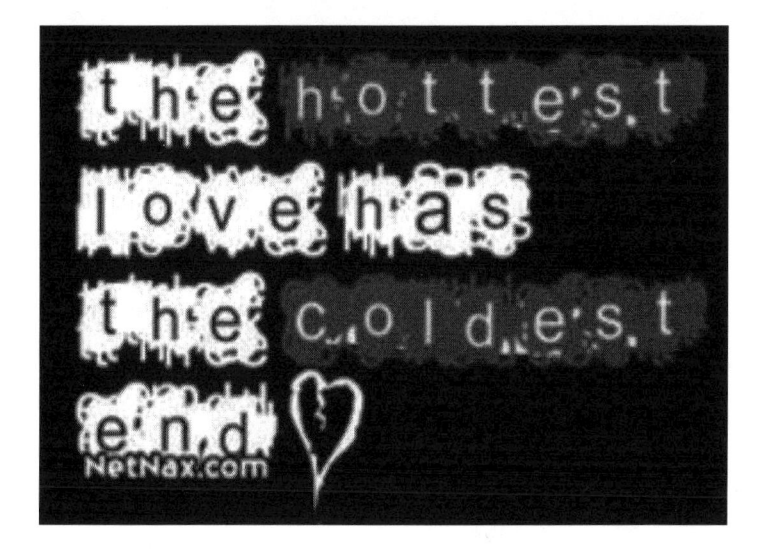

the hottest love has the coldest end

NetNax.com